# The Nine Realms

Emilee N.K. Robbins

ISBN: 979-8-9993436-0-4
BR Books
Illustrations by Grace Morris
Editor: Molly Spain

# Dedication

To everyone who pushed me to dream. To those who read every chapter. To those who listened as I gushed, cried, and worried. To those who are still standing by me.

My thanks could never be enough.

Trigger Warning: Dubious Sexual Consent

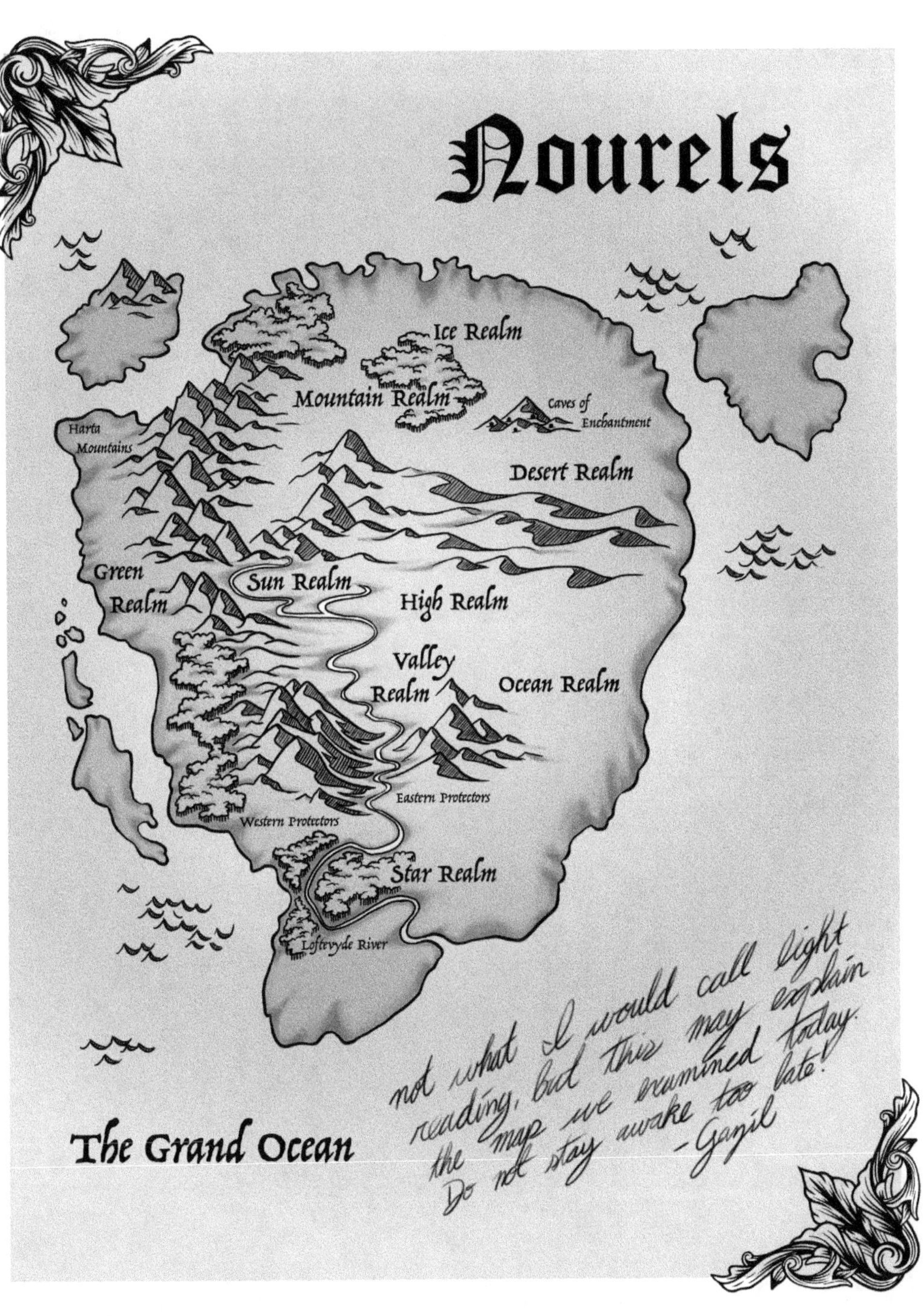

Nourels
Ice Realm
Mountain Realm
Caves of Enchantment
Harta Mountains
Desert Realm
Green Realm
Sun Realm
High Realm
Valley Realm
Ocean Realm
Eastern Protectors
Western Protectors
Star Realm
Loftvyde River
The Grand Ocean
not what I would call light reading, but this map may explain the map we examined today. Do not stay awake too late!
- Gazil

*Cold. Cold. Cold.* I try to move my hands, my toes. I'm not even sure if they respond, but I try over and over anyway. I can see only white, and I can hear only the constant whooshing of wind as snow whips through my hair. But nothing distracts me from the cold.

*Cold... Co... C...* The clattering of my teeth reverberates through my thoughts, and I start to lose track of time. *How long have I been here?* The wet frozen cloud of snow beneath me should feel like a pillow, but it feels like daggers in my soaking coat. The white begins to dim as darkness edges its way into my vision. *No, no, no. Stay awake. Try to move.* But my body is my worst traitor; it's frozen in place as the swirling blackness overcomes me.

# Part One

The Ice Realm boasts the most powerful Lords, the most breathtaking woods, and a mythology of magic that acts as an anchor for its people.

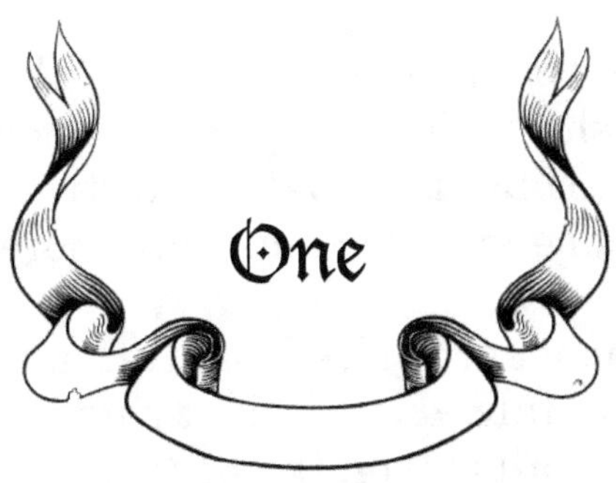

# One

The warm smell of pine and florals wakes me from a deep sleep. I shift, feeling the silk sheets caress my linen gown and keeping my eyes closed as my breathing settles.

"Finally awake, I see."

I shoot up in my spot on the large four-poster bed, eyes darting toward the gentle voice. It takes a moment for the blur of sleep to dissipate, leaving in its wake a breathtaking scene: a large suite with tiled floors and stone walls, a warm fireplace crackling to my left, and a man sitting in a red velvet lounger to my right. I scan him from his leather boots to the floral collar tied delicately around his neck. His grey eyes appear concerned as he reaches for my hand.

"You may be tired. And sore. We found you in the storm. We're not sure how long you were out there, but you've been asleep for four days."

His hand reaches mine and my cold hand warms briefly at the touch. A small smile graces his lips.

"I'll send for some food, but you may want to stay put until you're fully recovered."

With that, this stranger rises from his place, the pleats of his neat linen shirt crinkling slightly before he smooths the wrinkles. Clearing his throat as he strides toward the door, he turns his head toward me once more.

"I can't imagine what you've been through. Whenever… If you ever want to talk about it, just ring the bell." He nods toward the small bell on the bedside table before slipping out of the room; the heavy wooden door swings shut after he exits.

It takes a few minutes before I process the one-sided conversation. I shake my head to try to clear my confusion and then take a closer look at my surroundings. This place is remarkable. Across from the fireplace, one I notice never falters, a magnificent stained-glass window completely dominates the wall just behind my strange savior's red chair, casting a dim light of beautiful colors over the space. A deep sigh escapes my lips, and I feel the soreness he referenced—a dull yet consistent burning in my chest that radiates through my arms and legs. I move tentatively, swinging my legs slowly off the bed and resting my bare feet on the blue floral tiles. The movement increases the burning, but it is manageable. I take in a breath and hold it before pushing off the soft duvet with my hands. Another piercing burn in my thighs forces a wince. Again, I push through, and, seeing a large mirror angled in the corner, I set my sights on walking the expanse of the room. I step past a sitting area with a coffee table and two cushioned sofas.

Everything is lavish—the walls, the lights, the furniture. My eyes feast on the room's luxury while my mind registers the pain in the rest of my body. Each step is heavy, and it feels like an eternity before I finally reach my reflection. I'm not sure what I expected to see, but I gasp quietly anyway. I look weary, tired, ill. The dark circles under my eyes certainly don't reflect the forced sleep of four nights. The thin linen dress, embroidered with purple and icy-blue flowers, attempts to hug my body, but I'm clearly hollow. My cheeks, a bit sunken into my face, echo my frailty. I reach up my hands, which are riddled with small cuts and blisters, to trace the long red mark across my right cheek. I am unsure how such a mark is made, but its ruby shade contrasts my pallid face distinctly, making me look even more tired. My thick brown hair is plaited into a tight braid that reaches my shoulders, a few stray wisps curling along my forehead. After inspecting myself, I look forward, straight into eyes of glass. A tear drops from my lashes, leaving a trail under my lashes and over my hollow cheeks and the red mark as the realization sinks in:

I don't know who I am.

Nothing can shake the feeling of emptiness, although the warm bowl of potato stew and bath help. The Head Keeper, Mairette, quietly eases me into this world. She presents a wardrobe of clothing, offers various flavors of teas to find one I favor, and provides a general sense of comfort. Even during the first few hours since looking into the mirror, horrified by what I saw, I feel notably comfortable with Mairette. She is graceful and patient. Her red hair sits in bouncy curls that caress her round face and the pale pink of her skin beautifully highlights her bright purple eyes which are constantly beaming with optimism. She takes care of my every need as my mind returns to question after question.

*Where am I?*

*Do I have family?*

*Who are my friends?*

*What am I doing here?*

Mairette and I developed a sort of understanding during my first few days in the room: I needed to process what I did not know, and she seemed to enjoy the company. While it took me a few days to talk, she entered the large space every morning with sweet stories of sunshine and kingdoms, the drama of servants throughout the estate, and the recently happy temperament of the Lord of the home, Rostair. Though I am of average height, I stand nearly a half-foot taller than her. Oftentimes I find myself settled on one of the cozy couches while she stands behind the frame to braid my hair.

I've grown to love her visits; she has become a source of normalcy in the midst of such uncertainty. Her genuine transparency and kindness are a magnet to my empty soul. And, as my anxieties of the unknown often overtake me, it is a welcome reprieve to get lost in her tales.

I learned much in my week of solitude. I learned that this estate is massive, this being only one of forty guest chambers in this Wing. I learned a bit about the snow—that it is ordinary, only interrupted by a few months of flowers and green and warmth before returning to biting cold. Mairette speaks of this cold with fondness, an emotion I can only imagine comes from sentimentality rather than reality. It certainly is not the weather I would enjoy, not for my whole life at least.

I also learned more about my host himself. Rostair was known to be temperamental, but lately had been happy, jovial even. According to Mairette, "The arrival of a

mysterious and beautiful maiden only lightens his mood!"
I blushed profusely when she said this as I sipped on a
cup of orange and cardamom tea, reasoning away any
notion of his attention with the reality that such a
powerful and attractive man would not want for suitors.

"My brother once told me of creatures who could live on
both land and sea," Mairette says as she gently brushes
my hair one night. "He tells the most fantastical stories,
you know. He is much younger than me, nearly your age I
would guess, but he has always been more imaginative."
Her voice never sounds as strained as it does when she
describes her family, people she clearly adores with every
fiber of her being.

During our many talks throughout my days in the lone
room, she has painted a portrait of a fine Keeper's family,
with five children and two loving parents who are now
living amongst the elderly in a nearby town. Her siblings
all work on the grounds of Endoneth, Lord's Rostair's
estate. The eldest of her siblings delivers resources
between the various towns and estates in the realm,
allowing them the opportunity to check on their parents
every week or so. Mairette is the second born, followed by
a pair of identical twin women who both work in the
kitchen. The youngest, Jawar, is the storyteller Mairette
describes as the brightest of the bunch. The glow on her
face as she divulges tale after tale of their family lore,
from the most mundane to the most intense, reflects a
deep admiration. The kind of love and respect that I
imagine would propel her to do almost anything for their
well-being.

Mairette says as much: "I often wonder if the position of Head Keeper is more burdensome than an honor. It leaves me in a position of responsibility. For other Keepers, guests, and my family. If I falter, they are vulnerable."

I listen to the ringing of her words as she continues to soothe my mind with every stroke of the comb through the golden brown of my hair. Of course, I know not of my own family, if I have any. I know not whether they care as profoundly for me as Mairette cares for her siblings. I sip on the tea that she brought for me, losing myself in thoughts of my imaginary family, of their journey to find me, of their words of encouragement. The thoughts later ease me to sleep.

A week staring through stained glass was surprisingly healing; watching beads of snow fall gently to the forest floor and enjoying the silence between visits from Mairette. The window itself holds its own story, the glass molded in such a way to display a clear picture. In the center is a singular primrose of deep navy blue surrounded by a halo of red. The background on the left side displays an icy winter setting with falling snow and hills of white. To the right of the flower, there appears a clear spring day with a pale blue sky and small spots of flowers covering green grass. The window displays transformation, the primrose blooming at the end of one season to greet another. The days of looking at the window, then through the window, while calming my thoughts and emotions were essential, and it wasn't until today that I decided to venture out of the room. Like every other day, Mairette set out a dress for me to wear on the small ottoman near the fireplace and a cup of tea on the bedside table. Today, as always, the dress is stunning—a vibrant royal blue with golden laces along the front. Staring into the floor-length mirror, my hands run over the beaded embroidery, and I feel a smile crinkle the edges of my face for the first time since waking. A knock at the door jolts me from the moment, the smile vanishing. It isn't Mairette; I've become familiar with her short, gentle taps on the door.

A stifled cough precedes a sultry, "Hello?"

My heart beats against my ribs as I think of how to respond. It shouldn't be this difficult, and I settle on a simple, "Come in," before turning back to the mirror. In the reflection I see him. When I first woke a week ago, I didn't get a good look at Rostair. He stands a full head taller than me, with a broad build and a freshly trimmed beard. His hair is icy white with glimmers of silver and gold that shimmer as he strides into the room. Like our first meeting, he wears a fine woolen shirt with dark pants beneath a short, embroidered skirt. He flashes me a smile and my heart hastens once more. Still staring into the mirror, I realize I have yet to move, or talk, or breathe since he entered.

Embarrassment pushes me to action, and I spin on my leather boots to face Rostair. He makes himself comfortable in the red chair near the bed. I still feel the phantom warmth of his hand on mine and twist my fingers in the velvet fabric of my dress just thinking about it. He tears his eyes from me to briefly look toward the bedside table. I follow his gaze and see the small, golden bell still sitting untouched.

"You never rang." His voice sounds a bit disappointed, defeated even. My heart is now beating in my throat, and my breaths come in short bursts. I force myself to close my eyes, for only a moment, while I focus on my breathing. When I get control of my heartbeat, I lift my head to see Rostair staring at me, concern lacing his eyes. "It is alright, I knew that it would take a while for you to acclimate. I just hope I didn't visit too soon. I apologize." He lifts himself from the seat and quickly walks toward the door.

"No!" The word leaves my mouth louder than I intended. I clear my throat before explaining, "I'm sorry I never used the bell. Mairette has taken care of me so diligently and it's taken some time to fully feel... well, feel anything." I feel tears stinging my eyes and I briskly blink them away, turning my face toward the floor where the delicate tiles provide ample distraction. I may not know myself, but I certainly don't know this man enough to display such emotion.

"It must be difficult to not remember." Rostair steps away from the door and toward me. "We heard word that the daughter of a Lord in the Mountain Realm is missing."

His words ignite hope in me. I lift my eyes to my host, still brimming with tears. He smiles in return, almost giddy to see my reaction.

"I sent word to the Lord immediately; we will hopefully hear back soon."

I sigh and clear my throat once more. "I would enjoy a tour of the estate, if you have the time."

His eyes soften, the concern slightly dissipating. "Of course." Offering me a hand, he begins a rehearsed description of his familial home: "This is Endoneth, the Ice Estate. My family inherited this land and control of the surrounding woods and towns when my great-grandfather was a young man. The name reflects the magic inherent to this place, the northern Fairies still residing in the acres of forest that dominate the estate..."

He continues the monologue as we walk from room to room, each more extravagant than the last. The maze of doors becomes overwhelming almost immediately, and I can hardly imagine that I will make it one day without getting lost. Perhaps recognizing my growing anxieties, Rostair pauses a moment. "If you ever feel like you cannot find your way back to your suite, just look down." He gestures to the tiles below. I had not noticed, but as we walked, the colors of the tiles had gradually shifted. "It's called color mapping," he notes. "Each wing of this estate is designated its own color. Each room in that wing uses this color in its tiles. Your room is located in the Blue Wing. But as we grow closer to the Orange Wing," he gestures before us, "the tiles will tell."

I notice then. The tiles beneath my feet incorporate both blue and orange flowers in their delicate design. And, sure enough, as I look behind us, the blues are more evident while in front of us the oranges grow brighter.

"There are six wings in this entire estate," he continues, resuming our leisurely walk towards the Orange Wing. "The Blue and Green Wings contain only guest rooms, suites for the various travelers and friends who visit my court. The Orange Wing just ahead is mainly used for studies and the library. Now, the ballroom and other entertaining spaces are located in both the Gold Wing and the Silver Wing. The Red Wing is reserved for our Keepers, cooks, kitchens, and any other practical necessities. Anything needed to keep the estate running."

"Is this a common way to organize estates? Is this color mapping used in other spaces for other purposes? "A look of surprise sweeps over his face and his brows jump to his hairline. I can't blame him, as this is the first time I've presented a question and I'm honestly not even sure why I asked.

However, I won't show hesitation, and I stand straight as I wait for his explanation.

"Well," he starts with a glimmer of mischief in his piercing eyes, "it is indeed a common way of organizing groups—cities, maps, armies..." His thought trails off and his eyes glaze over, as if he remembers something. He snaps back as fast as he'd faded, a smile stinging his cheeks. "Let's continue our tour!" He beams.

The remaining wings take over three hours to walk through, but Rostair's company never loses its luster, even as he waxes poetic about the architectural geniuses of the winter estates and the impressive works of painters from centuries past. Endoneth itself is magnificent, to be sure, every window thoughtfully designed and every column carved by true artists. After my outburst of a question in the Orange Wing, I keep many others at bay. Rostair leads us to the Red Wing, one reserved specifically for those who manage the home itself and maintain its opulent charm.

"We cannot pass through into the Red Wing." He points down toward the tiles below at the gold filigree delicately intertwining with red thorns. I look at him inquisitively and he sighs. "I try to give my Keepers their space. This is their domain, and I won't disrespect that." I nod, impressed at the thoughtful gesture. Even in his home, Rostair seems to be a man who sets boundaries and holds true to his word. "While they are free to walk the halls, they also make use of passages throughout the estate. All lead back here, to their wing. This way they may transport food or goods to and fro without being bothered."

He takes my arm and ushers me back toward the Gold Wing, the filigree of the tiles sparkling brighter as we saunter away from the stains of red. He points to an archway and says, "Do you dance?" I crinkle my nose at the question, wracking my brain for any answer, but none emerges. After painful silence, Rostair offers a hand and a sympathetic smile, "Come, let me show you my favorite space." Just beyond the gilded archway lies the ballroom, a sight almost too dazzling to describe. The room itself had no walls and no ceiling, only the frame of a room, with decorative columns in place to keep the structure upright. Hanging from the columns, two lanterns glow in the far corners of the room—one tinted a delightful shade of blue and the other a powerful purple.

I gasp and reflexively take a step forward, then another, then another, until I am standing at the center of the room, head lifted to watch the snow fall above me. I expect to feel the cold but remain completely unbothered by the exposure to the outside. I consider that my understanding of snow itself may be another misremembering—that I don't even know simple characteristics of this world anymore. Anxiety creeps from my chest into my throat and my breathing becomes scattered. I really am lost.

"It is a work of magic." Rostair's words rip me from my thoughts. I turn to respond only to find him standing directly at my side. The surprise must appear on my face because he takes a quick step away before explaining, "The ballroom is preserved by a blessing, a spell. The magic allows us to see the beauty of nature and enjoy the snow without feeling cold or wet." I breathe a sigh of relief. At least I can identify the simple things, even if I cannot remember my name. The thought sends a new wave of sadness through me.

Rostair reaches for my arm once more, his touch sending waves of excitement through my body, and we wind through the maze of hallways until we reach a grand study. He leads me to a large leather chair, and I obligingly sit. His eyes meet mine for a moment before he rushes to a row of shelves behind a carved desk. I look around at the many stacks of books, wayward papers, and bottles of ink. While Rostair appears put together, his study offers another view. "There is a method to the chaos, I can assure you." He chuckles as he sits.

"Rostair," I begin gently. His eyes whip to mine, a look of endearment lacing the smile he offers. "Do you know how I came to be here in your estate?"

He slowly walks back to my seat, almost as if he is weighing his decision to share with me. When he finally stands before me, his figure shielding everything from my view, he lowers his head so it is level with mine. His hands barely graze the fine gold laces of my gown as he leans in closer and whispers, "I wish I could tell you how you arrived at my doorstep. Yet, I will never forget the look on your perfect face that night. The night that *I* found you."

I walk carefully back to my room, remembering the instructions Rostair provided before I left his study. A Keeper interrupted our discussion to inform Rostair of an important detail of a war ongoing in the realms. I admit, the hallways are confusing; however, wandering through elaborate halls filled with art and stained glass and beauty does not bother me, especially as my thoughts only make me either anxious or embarrassed or both. And, while I have established I have not forgotten everything, there is so much about myself that I cannot recover.

My embarrassment stems from another source entirely. My cheeks flush red thinking of how close Rostair's face appeared before my own, how gentle his whisper felt as he revealed a new layer of himself to me. He explained that one of his responsibilities requires him to ride the perimeter of his estate. He enjoys this weekly task and uses the time to catch his breath and clear his mind. A little over a week ago, dangerous storms that lasted the entire night postponed his perimeter scan. According to Rostair, these are common during the long winter months in the realm and may occur without warning. The following night, Rostair rode out to assess the damage. Near the border of his estate, he noticed a cloak buried in the snow. Curious, he stepped forward to investigate and quickly noticed a pale-blue hand resting in the snow. He spent nearly an hour unearthing me from an icy grave before riding home and sending for his personal medicine man immediately.

"Seeing you so close to death… it reminded me of another storm from long ago." His eyes grew distant, and it took everything within me to not reach out and cup his face in my hands.

Instead, I said, "Thank you for taking care of me, for saving me."

His grief was thick in the air. He curled a stray hair behind my ear and said, "I wish I could know you. And, even more… I wish *you* could know you." The shared sentiment hit me like a kick to the stomach.

The days following this discussion with Rostair were more blurry than usual. I woke every day and walked the perimeter of the Blue Wing, noting the hundreds of different tile designs and attempting to learn the paths from my room to other landmark spaces: the library, the gallery, and the ballroom, of course. I also noticed the Keepers in this realm, each seemed to be assigned to one wing where they complete a multitude of duties to keep the estate running. One of the lower Keepers of the

Orange Wing, Junsen, provided a notebook and inkpot for me to use as a way to record my days here, and perhaps attempt to recall my old life, my old self. I've written dozens of pages and each time I get close to remembering—when a scent or sound triggers a long-forgotten memory—my brain grows foggy and any link to the past becomes muddled.

Writing quickly becomes my escape. My refuge. At first, I attempt to scrub the ink stains from my fingertips before resigning myself to the perpetual darkness lining my nails.

I venture outside for the first time two weeks into my stay. Wrapped in bundles of fur, I walk into the sunny winter day, the winds quieter and the snow falling in gentle flakes rather than violent gusts. My eyes, sensitive to the sunshine, squint until they are nearly closed before they finally adjust to the brightness. Although I never fully feel comfortable with such light, the outdoors are a surprising reprieve from the extravagant halls of the estate home. The biting cold nipping at my cheeks helps me feel something, which is more than I can say for the many other moments that fill my days. My boots sink into the thick layer of snow as I make my way to a manicured garden. The flowers are beautiful—an array of silvers, whites, and blues that thrive in the cool winter air.

On this brisk walk, the gardens have become my favorite spot to lose myself in thought, the maze of winter plants and trees offering an escape from a world I didn't know, a world I may never know. I want their resilience to give me hope; perhaps not today, but maybe soon. As I continue my walk, I notice other guests of Rostair's estate wandering the grounds. A group of men practice archery, aiming at a pair of targets and whooping when one lands an arrow remotely close to the center. One woman dressed in an elegant green cloak sits on a carved, wooden bench reading a book. Another pair of men stroll down a carved path through the snow while other women stand beneath a small, iron gazebo whispering to one another as they survey the scene before them. According to Mairette, the guests of the estate are often wealthy and most members of this realm—accustomed to the cold and the social norms of this court. While I walk by each group at least once on my walk, none talk to me directly, despite the excited whispers and lingering glances. I often wonder who I am to these people.

"She is more beautiful than I imagined," a man dressed in a deep golden coat and pleated skirt attempts to whisper. "Those eyes are striking."

"No wonder she left them," retorts another lady in yellow. "Look what they did to that cheek." I hear enough and decide to retreat into the warmth of the house, blinking back tears.

Before I can take a step, I see a familiar figure in my peripheral vision, the red curls bobbing before Mairette's typically cheery voice takes on a more serious tone, "This inane gossip is tasteless! Do you not empathize with a woman so lost in herself? Take your conversation elsewhere. Truly, what do you mean to prove? That you are somehow better than her because you arrived here by horse and she rescued by the Lord himself?"

Silence follows her outburst, the guests embarrassed either by their unseemly behaviors or that such behaviors were highlighted, and by the Head Keeper of the estate no less. I hear the two mutter half-hearted apologies before I feel the warmth of Mairette's hand on my arm, her pink skin almost pearlescent in the sunshine of the snowy day. "Come, Miss. You should only associate with the kindest of people." The statement is made loud enough for the guests to hear.

"Thank you." The tears swell as an emotion of gratitude mingles with my sadness.

"We all need someone to support us, to voice what we cannot." She squeezes my arm as she whispers, "They are no better than you, dear one. Do not allow them to dim your shine, for it is a marvelous thing to see a strong woman flourish."

When the sun falls behind the horizon, Mairette enters my room again with tea and a smile, offering a few dress options. "What do you think we should do with your eyes tonight?" Mairette ponders, "Perhaps a flower design? I could emulate the flowers you saw today?" The suggestion makes me smile. I look into the mirror and admire my reflection, my image filling the height and width perfectly. Since my arrival two weeks ago, my face looks transformed, the hollow in my cheeks nearly gone and the circles under my eyes replaced with a brightness that reflects a renewed spirit. Despite the red mark, I could see myself as beautiful—my cheeks full and smile wide, eyes a startling blue surrounded by thick lashes.

"A flower sounds absolutely lovely." I grin softly before shifting the conversation. "Where are these guests from and how would they know me?"

The question causes Mairette to hesitate, holding the paintbrushes in one hand and a palette of face colors in the other. She slowly begins mixing the colors to create a stunning blue that mimics the winter flowers outside. Her brows knit together, clearly considering the way to approach her response.

"They know what I know," she began. "You are the woman from the wood." Her lips lift a bit as she continues, "Rostair has not shared much more, but there are stories circulating. The most persistent theory is that you are the missing daughter of a Lord in the Mountain Realm. That they banished you here and left you marked. Such a mark represents a sort of disrespect, either toward you or your kin. It's an ancient form of identification, one that is rarely seen now." She gently brushes her hands over the mark on my face. The gesture warms my heart, but the words build a new wall of sorrow within me. "You are special, though, I can feel it." The white of her teeth gleam as she smiles brightly in the mirror. "Now, let us prepare." She raises the brush to my face and creates her own magic.

I saunter into the ballroom in a striking silver skirt with a matching flowing top that reveals my shoulders. Dusty-blue flowers delicately frame my eyes and swoop into my temples. Mairette claimed she wanted to make a statement, and it certainly feels like she's succeeded. As I skate over the tiled floor, bobbing between groups of socializing guests, I sweep the room to find a safe place to land amongst the dozens of people when my eyes lock with his. Rostair looks every bit a prince; he is wearing a long blue skirt, gathered at the knee, and a silken blue tunic. His white hair is pulled into several braids that meet into a large braid down his back. The paint on his face glows silver with splashes of blue over his eyelids. When he sees me, he quickly ends a conversation and walks my way.

"Breathtaking. Mairette has truly outdone herself." Rostair's voice reverberates through me, and I can tell all eyes in the room are fixed on us.

I bend my knees in respect and allow my head to fall into a bow. "You also look grand, Rostair."

His smile grows wide, and he nods for me to rise from my position, offering a hand and leading me to the edge of the room. "This is a common event at my estate, a party for my people and the visitors of this realm." His eyes scan the space, lingering on every face in the crowd of people as if identifying each person and locking the information away. "This is just the first of many for you." He asserts, "I suppose this is also your official introduction to this group. Have you thought about what you would like to be called? I know you may not remember your true name..." He trails off, clearly upset he brought it up.

I set a hand on his arm as I turn to the trees outside. "I will ponder it...I have not thought it through." Mairette has only called me "Miss" and I truly have not considered being called or named anything. I watch as snow gathers on the branches of a large pine, thinking about what I have enjoyed about this estate, what brings me joy. "What is the name of this flower?" I point to the delicate flowers gracing my face.

Rostair grins once more. "Centrea. It's a beautiful name. Fitting, if I may say. The icy blue of your eyes reflects the natural glimmer of the petals." He flexes his hand at his side, as if intentionally working to maintain his distance in such a public locale.

"Centrea, I think that will be my name for now."

Rostair nods in approval. "Well, Centrea, let us share our first dance, shall we?"

The dance itself feels like a dream. I make a mental note to write down in my notebook later that I remember the steps to a common waltz as well as a group jaunt. Rostair and I share the first dance, the warmth of his hands easing the anxiety that plagued my mind all day. Although I recognize my limited knowledge of this man, it also feels like I've known him for my entire life. That concept provides such a peace that our closeness is most welcome. I share my next dance with the reading lady from this afternoon. Her rosy-pink dress swishes from side to side as we link arms and clap throughout the dance. The next few hours, I stay along the edge of the ballroom and merely observe the revelry. If this is my life, at least there is music and joy and dancing. And now I have a name, something to cling to, something that is now mine. *Centrea.* Here is the start of a new world.

# Three

Days become weeks. Weeks become months. Before I know it, the estate feels familiar to me—the only home I can conceptualize no matter how many hours I spend desperately trying to remember the past. But even desperation has its limits. I continue writing each night, thinking the practice can only assist me in my pursuit of knowledge and, at the very least, help me process the daily happenings at the estate. The lingering glances and whispers continue, people becoming bolder the longer I stay. A precious few of the characters haunting these halls do make a positive impression on me.

Gazil, a Lord of metal mines in the North, offers a safe place to escape during the expected social gatherings. While he attends the many dinners, teas, and the occasional party, he much prefers the peace of the studies near the main library. We often play cards together and he shares the gossip about this group of regular guests. He is an older man, perhaps sixty years of age, with a gruff grey beard in braids that reach his bulging stomach. A man of short stature, he typically goes unnoticed by the flashy groups of socialites which allows him to overhear the most scandalous of stories. I do enjoy a good tale and, even more, a good distraction as I wait to hear from my potential family in the Mountain Realm. Most importantly, I trust him.

Gazil is well-traveled, a fact that becomes thoroughly clear any time he speaks of his bizarre and variegated past. The man appears to have lived several lifetimes in his one, experiencing perilous adventures, embarking upon monthslong odysseys, and meeting innumerable dazzling figures. While he has mentioned many a romance, typically with dashing warriors in grand suits of armor or elegant dance attire, he has only made mention of one love of his life.

"Arin was the most amiable of men," he once described to me over glasses of red wine. "The man could charm anyone, despite hailing from the Mountain Realm, no offense dear." Gazil was one of many who believed me the missing daughter from the Mountains, though the war prevents any confirmation. "I thought to myself that I refused to be charmed. Ha! Isn't that how the tale goes? When he asked me for a dance at a ball one night, I could not resist. After ten glorious years together, I'd say setting my pride aside was truly worth it." He took another sip. "I miss him every day." Unlike Mairette, who attempts to mask any unhappy emotion with forced optimism or obvious dismissal, Gazil never shies away from his feelings, wearing his heart on his sleeve for all to witness. He tells the gamut of stories, from heart-wrenching losses to the most auspicious turns of fate.

Gazil can truly paint a picture in my mind with his stories; this magic impacts me far deeper than I would assume. He sighs as he recalls a past event. "Balls of the

Green Realm were much sweeter then, less squabbling and disagreements. It was about the fashion, the music, the food." He flicks his wrist to the side as he emphasizes each aspect of this other realm. "I do enjoy these Ice Realm events," he muses, almost to himself, "but they are, at times, rather… cold." He chuckles at the joke.

I smile and offer a soft laugh. "Tell me, friend, which realm has the most fashionable balls?" My eyes gleam as I try to imagine other places—realms with greenery and oceans and sand.

Gazil twists a braid of his beard between his fingers. "Hmmm, the balls of the Green Realm admittedly have the best cuisine, their crop harvests providing them with a variety of foods for their feasts. In the Ocean Realm guests often have the most exquisite clothes—the most current fashions and fabrics." He sighs at the thought, his baritone voice nearly whispering as he continues, "But, if I'm honest," he looks around us to ensure no one else can hear, but the study remains empty save a few Keepers sweeping the floor, "the Star Realm hosts the most glamorous parties. The sun rarely shines which allows events to go on for hours, dawn rarely forcing an end to the revelry." I cock my head to the side and meet his gaze, his eyes mischievous as he no doubt remembers never-ending nights of debauchery.

"When were you last there, in the Star Realm?" I question, my mind suddenly starving for information.

Gazil's smile dims for a mere moment before turning his gaze toward a nearby window. "We don't talk of such things anymore." His voice is now so low I can barely make out the words. "It is… complicated." He avoids the confused look in my eyes, desperately shifting his face toward the bookshelf behind me, a chandelier swaying above us, the glistening orange tiles below, anywhere but my eyes.

Gazil hardly spoke of politics, only in relation to star-crossed lovers. I reach my hand to grasp his arm, desperate to change topics. "Tell me about the best meal you've ever had."

He turns back to me and smiles. "Oh, I would have to choose between a plethora of options."

I place my hands under my chin and croon, "Tell me about them all!"

Gazil's words replay in my mind as I walk back to my room, tracing the stone walls with my fingertips. *It is… complicated.*" Could the Star Realm be the source of the violent war in the realms?

I push the heavy wooden door of my chambers and enter the space, where I'm met with the sweet smell of hibiscus. I smile and saunter to a small desk near the floor-length stained-glass window. A few months ago, I requested a place to use the writing supplies for my nightly notes, tired of clumsily sketching my thoughts while sitting on the edge of the ruby chair. Rostair gladly obliged, personally delivering a beautiful oaken desk inlaid with flakes of gold within its natural ridges. The desk perfectly fits the space and gives just enough room for stacks of paper, ink, and several brightly colored feathers in a cup. Tonight's visit with Gazil gives me much to write about. Realms, people, and a feeling of not all things being quite right. While the ideas swarm my mind, it's difficult to put thoughts into words on the page.

I shake my head, take a long sip of the tea Mairette prepared, and make note that this is my new favorite, a little sweeter and with less spice than the orange. I sit for a long while, the crackling of the fire the only noise breaking through the tortured silence. Soon the winds outside pick up, adding another layer of white noise in the room. The nightly snowstorms have progressively worsened in the last month, adding more tension to the dinners and social events. I suppose while guests enjoy the lavish halls of Endoneth, they want the satisfaction of knowing they may make a swift escape if they wish.

Such storms also mean word from the Mountain Realm will likely take much longer than I hope; already, it's been months since Rostair sent word. Mairette says the storms are a natural pattern during this month, although even her words are not always confident. Regardless, the noise of the wind and the ice and the crackling fire all coax me into a sense of relaxation, my mind swimming slightly from the effort of trying to remember again. I give up after almost an hour of holding the quill above paper, looking disappointingly at a page filled with the blots of ink that dripped off my feathered tool. The bed appears enticing, but I know myself enough to know I won't sleep in such a state; my mind is too restless despite revealing nothing to me. The influx of nightmares this past week also discourages such rest. I decide instead to wander the halls, something I've done for several nights now to quell insomnia or at least feign purpose.

Tonight leads me to the library, close to the study where Gazil shared a bit too much yet nothing at all. The floor tiles in the room picture small stories in their designs. My favorite is on the far wall lining windows that reach the floors. I pace along the wall, looking down at the intricate ceramic floor. It displays an archer who is on a hunt; he is searching for a fabled deer in a mystical orange wood. When he finally spies the beast, he is brought to his knees by its beauty. Rather than attack the deer, the hunter approaches it with humility, offering his bow and quiver full of arrows in exchange for a life in her forest. The beast glows and accepts his offering. In the final tiles, the hunter erupts into golden light and transforms into a noble stag. The two run into the woods together.

"A powerful tale, don't you agree?" Rostair's voice shakes me from my daydreams of the deer and their life together in an orange wood of a mystical world.

"It has become my favorite, truly," I answer sincerely, not tearing my eyes from the detailed tiles. I feel his cloak graze my side, the thin dress chosen by Mairette shifting as he slides by.

"Transformation is a powerful gift," he notes, his voice tender as he glances toward my downturned face. "Only some are lucky enough to have a chance at a second life." While the sentiment should make me happy, it only accentuates the hole in my chest.

"Can you tell me about the realms of this world?" I ask quietly. "I would love to hear you speak of them and perhaps see what I recognize." Of course, the notion is unlikely to yield any genuine memories from my past, but I would love to understand these matters all the same. If there are places Gazil is scared to mention, I need to know so I don't make any mistakes. I turn my head slightly toward Rostair, looking at him from my peripheral view and see him grinning.

"Well, we are in a library, the largest in this realm in fact." He gestures toward a large table in the middle of the room. "I believe we can find *something* to answer your questions." I feel a burning sensation rising in my chest and I attempt to push it down to avoid a blush rushing to my cheeks.

Instead of answering, I merely walk toward the table, my ink-laden fingers wringing the end of my tunic as I wait for him to follow. Atop the drafting table is a massive map with an intricate word stretching across the paper: "Nourels."

"It translates to 'the nine realms,'" Rostair explains as I begin scanning the map, taking in the lone continent surrounded by ocean and divided into nine neat segments. He points to each segment and explains each realm in turn, "Here we are in the Ice Realm where Endoneth towers above mountains of snow." His love for the realm shines in his eyes as he continues, "To the south is the Mountain Realm which borders both the Green Realm and the Desert Realm." He pauses as I take a sharp breath at the mention of the Mountain Realm, my likely home.

He continues, "There are three smaller realms that make up the center, here." He points to a cluster of three segments. "These are the Sun, High, and Valley Realms. To the east is the expansive Ocean Realm that extends beyond the land itself." He shifts slightly toward me as he leans over the map. "The final realm is that of the Stars. We know very little of this realm, although it has been the cause of much controversy." He places a hand on the small of my back, a gesture that awakens a longing deep within me.

"What are the issues in the Star Realm?" I whisper softly, enticing him closer to me as I trace the words "Star" with my finger. I see his free hand clench by his side.

"There is a Lord there, a mighty Lord of a grand estate much like mine. He believes that all realms should live in harmony, blinded by our many differences and past battles. To ensure peace, he thinks there should be one King, one man to rule all people, all realms." His face twitches with anger. "He just... he just does not want to understand us, our people, our traditions. He wishes to change us, and he will never hear reason." His breathing grows jagged as he squints his eyes shut. "The Star Realm has taken much from us in the past five years. So. Much. And the war he started, it just continues on and on and on." The hand on my back clutches my dress and pulls me flush to him.

"I am sorry, so sorry," I mutter softly, my cheek pressed against his chest. His heart pounds in my ear and it takes a few minutes before it settles. The embrace feels like a blanket, slowly melting away ice I didn't even know shielded my heart.

I cannot deny the thoughts that have crossed my mind these months. Rostair rarely speaks to me, but when we find each other in the same space it feels magnetic. This moment is no different and I can't help but give in. Just as I close my eyes and relish in the feeling of his arms around my waist, they disappear.

He steps away and clears his throat. "Apologies, Miss. That was an overly emotional response on my part." He stuffs his hands in the pockets of his coat and averts his gaze from me to the map. "Centrea." My name on his lips sends a jolt through my spine and my eyes search for his, though he continues to stare at the map. "There is a celebration for the green months of our realm after the long winter. If you wish, I would like to present you as a Guest of Honor." He moves his hand to brush his silver hair from his eyes and continues, "We still have a few weeks to prepare and Mairette can help you in any way you need—if you choose to accept, that is." I scan his features, desperately needing him to return my look, to permit me to see into his eyes and feel what he's feeling, even for a moment.

"That sounds exciting; of course I will attend." His eyes remain on the desk and the maps, and the space between us becomes suffocating, my body frantically seeking affirmation that I am not alone in this emotion swirling in my stomach.

"You will be a Guest of Honor?" he pushes, his words clipped and short.

I step an inch toward him. "Yes."

Only then does he return my stare, tears brimming his eyes and a soft grin lining his face, and says, "Grand."

The walk to my room that night feels almost as blurry as my memories. The tiles below me swirl into random colors and designs, making the map in my mind hard to follow and resulting in more than a few wrong turns. But it doesn't matter. It feels as if nothing matters. The look in Rostair's eyes, the sound of his voice saying my name, the name I chose, it breaks something within me. I've spent months attempting to piece together my past, and now I'm finally considering my future. When I enter the room, I notice Mairette has visited again to clear out the old tea saucer and clean up the soiled pages of ink. I sigh deeply and sink into the cozy covers of the bed. Sleep greets me quickly.

Mairette is a true gem. Walking through the estate day after day shows me a new side of her, my friend in her element. While her position as Head Keeper, I've learned, presents her with ultimate authority, she is overly gracious. Rather than using reprimands to assert control, she opts for loving guidance and understanding. The other workers in the estate clearly respect her, every cook, gardener, and Keeper pausing their various tasks to acknowledge when she enters a room or makes a small announcement. I note this when she greets me the morning after my library interaction with Rostair. The tea she prepared is a new flavor—a sweet peach and mint blend. While I slept through the night, I was constantly assaulted by night terrors that I could not seem to shake.

Mairette sets down the cup gently at my bedside table and flashes a soft smile. I wipe the sleep from my eyes enough to watch her glide toward the mirror, tidying the space a bit before leaving to retrieve the necessary tools for my hair and face. When she returns I say, "I can see that you are amazing at what you do at this estate. I would venture to guess the place could not run without you here."

Now it is Mairette who allows a bit of red to flush her cheeks. "That is kind of you, Miss," she states.

"I do not share what is untrue." I admit definitively, "I only wish that I knew more about myself so I could share those parts of my life with you. You are truly the only one I can fully trust." She nods at this, rummaging through a bag of paints, anything to avoid accepting a sincere compliment.

I then allow Mairette the pleasure of attempting the latest fashionable hairstyle—my hair woven into thick braids that are meant to create a sort of bow at the nape of my neck.

I spend the following days worrying more about the Greentime Ball, as I learned it is called. Rostair mentioned the importance of the event briefly, but I had not realized its significance until my first session with Mairette days later.

"We will spend each afternoon discussing the expectations of the ball," she exclaims over a cup of fresh tea. "The event is less than a month away!" We sit upon a velvet sofa in one of the communal gathering rooms and work through the details. Mairette shuffles through a stack of papers lined with notes on every aspect, pointing to a list of days each with a checklist of items to be completed. "We are but eighteen days away from the ball, including today, and, as the Guest of Honor, you inherit a wealth of responsibilities." I take a long sip of my tea, letting the sweet taste coat my tongue before facing these responsibilities she speaks of.

Mairette ignores any potential hesitation I display and continues, "The ball itself is the event of the year, an annual gathering for all lords and ladies of the realm and the hundreds of guests from nearby kingdoms."

She uses the paints to mark segments on the mirror before us, explaining the separation of weather in this realm. "The seasons of the Ice Realm are divided into four segments: two winter seasons interrupted by brief months of sunshine and spring. The long winter that precedes the Greentime Ball is where we are now—six long months of cold and ice before the reprieve of green grass and flowers. This is what makes the event so important; it is to celebrate the completion of another year, another long winter. Everyone in attendance must wear green and offer a plant to the Guest of Honor. The size or quality is less important, as long as it holds significance to the giver."

I nod and look down at my hands, the blisters now calloused over and rough. "We should of course commission a gown for you to wear. As the Guest of Honor, you need to dazzle." She smiles.

I sigh as our talk of balls comes to a close. "Mairette," I cautiously begin, smoothing the edges of my navy skirt before turning to face her, "have you ever attended such events? I mean, could you? I can't imagine facing the crowds without you." At the mention of others, I quickly sweep the perimeter of the gathering space and, unsurprisingly, the all-to-frequent looks and whispers permeate each conversation. I reflexively touch the red mark on my cheek before returning my attention to Mairette.

Her demeanor becomes serious. "There is a very particular order to things in this realm." She clears her throat slightly and twists her fingers in her lap, a habit I've noticed accompanies her displeasure. "I am a Keeper, and as such I know my position. I am only granted access to guest spaces due to my role as Head Keeper. Such a title affords me the privilege to speak to guests in public spaces, so long as the conversation is related to my role, as we are now." She gently gestures her hand between us. "However, Keepers and other lower-ranking workers are not permitted to speak to guests, not permitted to attend their functions, and are *never* permitted to pursue intimate relationships with those above their station." This statement shocks me. I think of young Junsen who offered me a welcome gift and an open ear. But I also think of my first tour of this estate and the Red Wing reserved for them, those like Junsen and Mairette.

"I apologize..." I twist the end of my braid in my hand with embarrassment.

"It is no worry, you could not have known." She places a gentle hand over my knee. "This is tradition, it is the way of the Ice Realm, and it is beautiful. Order is beautiful." I nod, although I'm unsure I share the sentiment. "Now, we should contemplate a dress. The fashion must be unlike anything the court has seen."

Mairette continues planning as if nothing happened, as if all of this was completely acceptable. There is a tight feeling in my chest that tells me it isn't.

After my meeting with Mairette, I decide to take a walk outside to clear my mind and let the wind numb my aching heart. I wear a set of furs, a colorful array of red and white pelts, and hasten toward the garden. Before I reach the first arch, I feel a tap on my shoulder. "You walk fast for someone unaccustomed to the snow." Rostair chuckles a bit as he meets my stride. Our last meeting in the library was a mere week ago, but it feels like so much longer and I enjoy seeing him.

"You were able to tear yourself away, how ever will the realm go on?" I lay a sarcastic hand upon my forehead, feigning concern. He bursts into heavy laughter, his head tipping back and silver-white hair swaying from side to side.

"There are few who would address me in such a way." My heart sinks a bit, worried I've irrevocably erred, finally meeting an end to this mysterious world. But he shakes his head and continues, "You are a mystery, sweet Centrea. May I join you on your stroll?" The delighted shock must be evident in my face as he quickly takes my arm in his and leads me toward the maze of plants. As usual, I am mesmerized by the beauty of the flowers, the trees, the birds. This place makes the things I cannot control a bit lighter to bear. I almost forget Rostair's presence until I feel a slight squeeze on my arm.

"How are preparations faring with Mairette?" The question is innocent enough, but I wish I could erase the memory of the conversation from my mind, an ironic desire that burns within me. I want to believe Mairette is pure, that this place is pure, but perhaps my ignorance has shielded me from more than I know.

The silence must have gone on too long. Rostair coughs a bit and changes the subject. "The weather is finally providing us a break from the hail. I suspect we will see green soon, two weeks perhaps." He has a way with words, something that eases me into a dull headspace where I feel free to relinquish my pessimism in exchange for hope.

"I am eager to see the ground in such a state!" I lean into his touch, our shoulders now forming an impenetrable wall. Maybe this is what pulls me to him, or at least the idea of him. The more I ponder the future, the more I want to share it with someone who can build me up and make me stronger. Formidable. "How often do you enjoy these gardens?" I ask genuinely, hoping to learn a bit more about my powerful host.

"I tend to work most days, spending leisure time at parties and other events. There aren't many moments where I find myself wandering the grounds." He pauses for a moment before saying, "But I would like to explore more. It's been years since I've truly appreciated my land, my estate. And I often think back to our tour of the house so fondly." He slips his hand around my waist and pulls me closer, nearly knocking me off my feet. "I would love to show you more." His last words are merely a whisper, one that makes my heart patter as I attempt to maintain a steady gait. The trees lining the worn path in the garden block us from the view of prying eyes and I wonder what would happen if we were completely alone once more. A flash of our moment in the library forces a burst of heat bolting through my chest, down to my stomach, and even lower.

I gather my composure as we continue our walk, turning with the winding path of flowers. "I would enjoy that very much."

Mairette pulls the curtains back to reveal beaming sunshine, which pulls me from my slumber. It is the first time I can remember having a full night's sleep and my body is almost bursting with energy.

"Good morning, Miss. Full day planned today?" Her singsong voice reverberates through the room. "The head cook suggested a flavor for your morning brew: a mix of jasmine and yellowblossom leaves—bitter with a bit of spice."

I leap from my bed towards a short table near the red chair. The kettle is carefully placed with a cup and saucer. I sip a bit, careful to feel the liquid on my lips to test the temperature before committing to a full swig. Of course, the temperature is perfect—Mairette would have nothing less.

"Here are a few options for today." She lays two dresses on my bed to examine before turning to face me. "I also have a few sketches of ballgowns for your consideration."

My brows shoot up. "So quickly?" I reply, clearly impressed.

"I spoke to a trusted artist directly after our afternoon discussion. I may have had them sooner, but I needed to request a few alterations to his first sketches."

She delicately tucks a stray curl behind her ear and gives a satisfied smile. "Thank you, friend," I say, returning back to my morning cup as I review the drawings. One is a dress that falls straight down the model, with a large bow draped along the back. The other dress catches my eye. It is simpler, tan fabric hugs the curves of the model before flaring out at the bottom. The back is left bare, the fabric sheer and draped low, exposing the lower back before curving just above the hip.

I point to the second. "This. I believe this would be wonderful."

Mairette takes the drawing from me with a grin. "I assumed you would choose this. It screams 'Centrea' to me." The words rush over me, a sense of identity building within me. I turned back to consider another set of dresses for today. While I usually make these decisions lightly, today feels more consequential. On one side lays a subtle orange shift dress that cinches at the waist. Next to it sits a golden lace dress with long sleeves and a slit up the thigh.

I turn from one to the other before settling on the gold, asking Mairette, "Do you have any fresh hairstyles you want to try?"

Her brows lift as she answers, "Of course, ma'am." I do love the intricate plaits she usually executes, however change sounds particularly welcome.

The gold flecks woven through my hair shine in the warm sun. Rostair stands in the archway where he surprised me just yesterday. While the cool weather remains, the sun provides enough warmth for me to keep my fur coat open, exposing the glimmering gold of my dress. As I approach him, Rostair's eyes grow wide, taking me in from the toes of my boots to my long, wavy hair.

"A new look?" He whistles, clearly impressed.

"Perhaps the sunshine brings new life." I look toward the gardens. "Would you like to take a walk through the gardens today?"

He shakes his head subtly. "I would love to show you another place." He grins and holds out a hand toward me. Smiling, I accept his hand, allowing him to pull me forward and place my hand on his forearm. "I sincerely believe you will enjoy it. I must warn you, the trek is a bit long, but the destination is truly worth the effort."

Rostair leads us down a few hills of packed snow. He did not overexaggerate the length of the walk; the path we follow has gone on for five miles before we finally see a stone building standing in the middle of a flat field at the edge of the woods. As we reach the doorway, I lean on the stone wall to catch my breath. Rostair opens the door in front of me and insists I rest inside. "It is warm inside."

He smiles affectionately and I nod slowly, my breath still coming in rapid gulps. As soon as I enter the foyer, I slide off the heavy fur, my sweat suctioning the sleeves of my gown to my arms. I think back to the orange slip from this morning and chuckle a bit to myself, realizing the error in my choice for the day. It takes me a moment to look around and notice where we've entered. The stone from the exterior continues through the entryway. Above me swings a beautiful glittering chandelier, shining a dewy glow on the walls. Just beyond us, the building extends to the left and right, like a large hallway. As I venture forward, I notice large swinging doors lining the hall, eight on each side. The air is slightly musky, with notes of strong pine and burning firewood.

I feel Rostair standing near me, the backs of our hands barely touching. A heat erupts in my stomach, and I quickly fold my hands in front of me. It is then that I realize we are seemingly alone, no Keepers sweeping the floors nor guests incessantly whispering about my apparent worth. The reality of our seclusion rushes me forward as my mind moves beyond appropriate thoughts and feelings toward my host, the Lord of this realm.

"This is a special place." Rostair's voice sounds more relaxed than normal, as if he has truly left behind the various stressors of running an estate while maintaining the realm. "I love to come here whenever I need respite. The Keepers of the stables only work at night, ensuring it remains relatively empty during the day. Sometimes I will see the occasional guest mount a steed and ride the property." He shrugs gracefully. "I prefer it like this though. It reminds me of times as a child, roaming these grounds and seeking excitement to rouse me from the tedious lessons and meetings with 'important' people."

The hollowness in his voice as he remembers his past pierces my heart. My expression betrays me as he stops in his tracks and turns to me. "I was raised to be a leader and that comes with expectations, even as a child. I'm certain my parents loved me, in their own way." It is not the statement that stuns me, an elite upbringing seems expected, but Rostair's reaction is heavy, as if he does not completely believe what he says.

My own childhood is, of course, a blur; however, I would hope I felt compassion from those who raised me. Though the continued silence from the Mountain Realm suggests perhaps not. "Did you have a cordial relationship with your family? Did you have any siblings? Any next of kin?" I look deeply in his eyes, hoping my sincerity shows through.

He smiles in turn, forcing my heart to beat hard against my ribs. "I had my parents, of course. Unfortunately, Mother passed away four years ago, my father along with her. She prepared me well for my position here and, as her only child, trained me well enough for a smooth transition of power. My father, however, did not necessarily care for me, seeing her overwhelming love and perhaps feeling jealous of it. I have only one uncle who rarely speaks to me. It is a lonely life to lead, but I love the people, I love the purpose." His fists clench a bit, but slowly release as he looks down, breaking the connection between us.

He leads me to the right, peering through the window of the sliding door while wearing a look of unbridled joy. "These are sky stallions," he notes gleefully as he places a hand on the door. "My family has spent centuries breeding the perfect beings, the most beautiful of animals." He slides the door open before us, revealing a massive, magnificent creature resting on a granite floor. The room is spotless save a few pieces of hay near a manger full of feed. The horse itself looks out into the snowy pasture through a blue stained-glass window and only turns to face us when Rostair takes a small step forward. My eyes are wide with surprise when the beast rises to its feet and stretches a pair of feathery white wings behind its back.

"Can they fly?" I look toward Rostair with delight.

He only smiles and says, "Would you like to find out?"

I am unsure if I have ever ridden a horse, let alone a pegasus, in my life, yet the feeling of pulling into a saddle feels natural. Rostair swiftly climbs behind me, pressing his chest close to my back and reaching forward to clutch the reins in front of my lap. "This is Storm," he whispers softly in my ear, each syllable pulsing through me. "She will lead us on a great adventure today. Are you prepared?"

He leaves me only a few moments to nod my approval before snatching the reins and leading Storm outside the great hall and into the snowy field. I feel a jolt in my stomach as Rostair suddenly kicks behind me and leads us skyward. A small scream leaves my lungs as we gain speed and altitude, climbing high above the trees and into the clouds. He pushes close to me, the tops of his thighs brushing me as I desperately squeeze my legs to keep me steady. If it were not for the terror of being dangerously near death, the proximity to this gorgeous man, one I've lusted after for months now, would be my undoing.

Perhaps the fear of falling is a blessing to us both, a distraction from the concept of a salacious affair with the Lord of Endoneth. Mairette has informed me on numerous occasions the expectations of a Lord in this realm: that he maintain his honor and only marry a woman of high breeding and, hopefully, wealth. Despite not knowing who I am, I know enough to realize a tryst with such a man of high social value would be a foolish endeavor, if he even wanted me at all.

I'm shaken from my thoughts as Rostair guides the steed to a large cavern of glowing stone. Clearly more at ease with the concept of flying, he barely slows down before swooping through an ominous entrance into a deep and dusky cave. Storm flaps her wings slowly and eases us onto a small shelf overlooking a pool of milky water. Still frozen from the jarring experience of flight, I remain glued to the saddle as Rostair kicks a leg around the steed to dismount. He pulls his linen shirt straight and runs his hands through his hair before turning to me and offering assistance. I look down at his stunning eyes and beaming smile.

"Come on!" he goads as he places a hand on the small of my back, guiding me off the saddle and into his arms. My breathing is heavy as we hold there for a moment before breaking apart and walking toward the edge of the platform.

"Where are we?" I muse, attempting to hide the longing in my voice.

"In these caves are pools of magic," Rostair explains, "The white swirls are said to have medicinal powers, or so the legends go. Most caves such as these are inhabited by the fairies of this realm; however, they gifted this cavern to me after I aided them in war." His eyes grow cold, distant, like that night in the library.

I place a steady hand on his arm. "It looks magnificent. Do you drink it?"

The look on his face dissipates and he chuckles softly, "I would not. The pools are meant for swimming. The water is sourced from somewhere deep beneath the ground, so deep that the water is naturally heated." He steps toward a set of stone stairs, and I quickly follow behind, becoming more curious by the minute. If the water truly is magic, could it help me remember who I am?

Nearing the water, I feel the steam emitting from the surface of the pool. The closer we walk, the more beautiful the glittering swirls become, the white water mixing with fluorescent blues and silvers. The water itself remains still, tantalizingly warm after our frigid ride through the air. I want more than anything to jump in. I turn to Rostair to see him taking off his tunic and boots and quickly turn back toward the pool.

He laughs again, the warmth of the sound again burning through me. "Do not fret, Centrea." I hear the unlacing of his trousers and feel my knees shake. "I often enjoy a swim after a long ride. The warmth of the pool, and perhaps the magic they speak of, helps ease the soreness of the body."

I hear his clothes fall to the floor and say, "Do you bring ladies to these caverns often?" A silly question, to be certain, but I can hold my tongue no longer. I need to know more about Rostair, about his intentions, and about why I feel this way toward a man I, in truth, barely know.

"I haven't… Not in a long while." Grief lines his words and the sound forces my head to turn toward him. It is a mistake. I knew Rostair stood tall, but laid bare, he towers. His silver locks brush his collarbone, just above a body that looks built to battle. His chest quickens as he notices my attention and I snap my head forward before I see anything unseemly.

"I am going to walk to the pool now," he says in a jesting tone, the smile on his cheeks evident in his voice. "Do not worry, if you would like to join I will look away as you disrobe."

A stinging red heats my cheeks at this suggestion. Mairette is going to murder me, but my body gives me little choice. When I see Rostair turn his head completely away, I begin to rip away the sleeves of the gown I so delicately chose just this morning. My fingers carefully unlace the bodice and it flutters down to my ankles with ease. I shiver a bit as my body stands exposed to the elements and clamor for the edge of the pool. Dipping my toes in first, I feel a rush of warmth and relief wash through me before fully submerging in the pool. Hearing me swimming closer, Rostair turns his head to see my head bob down then rip through the quiet surface. My hands wipe my face as I feel the paint wash away. I realize, looking forward, that the milky color of the water thankfully hides whatever lies underneath.

While the thought provides relief, I also begin to wonder what else could be here. "Does any being live in these waters?" The question comes out a bit frantically as I swing my hands to keep myself afloat.

Rostair looks at me gently and catches one of my hands in his. "There is nothing to fear here." The words force a gasp from my mouth as he pulls closer to me, our naked bodies only inches apart. The gravity of his words take on new meaning the longer he stares into my eyes. He reaches his other hand to push a stray hair behind my ear.

Even in the warmth of the water, my body shivers at this intimate touch. "I've observed you, you realize. I cannot say I have had the courage to engage you, but you are constantly in my thoughts, my dreams." His hand moves to sweep the round apples of my cheeks down to my pointed chin. "It is not customary for men like myself to find a match of compatibility, of love, if such a thing exists. But this," his hand nears my collarbone and moves to my shoulder, his other hand still clutching mine, "this could be different."

The words break down a fragile wall I built to hold back feelings of longing and lust. I pull his face close to mine with my free hand. Our breaths mingle and my lips quiver. Just as I gain the courage to lean in, a scream erupts throughout the cavern.

Rostair breaks away and swims quickly to the shore. "It is outside." He rushes out, grabbing his things before running to Storm. The abrupt retreat stuns me, and I don't move until I hear Rostair once more. "Centrea, we must make haste!"

I ease my body forward, attempting to swim to the surface as fast as he just did, and clumsily climb to grab my gown. I struggle to put the dress over my wet arms. "Come now!" The gentle whispers are gone, and I am snapped back into the reality that this is a lord, and I don't even know who I am, or who I could be to him. He throws a fur-lined blanket in my direction, and I struggle to keep up with his pace. Wrapping the blanket around my bare shoulders, I follow him outside.

The high-pitched screams grow louder and more desperate as we draw near the mouth of the cave. The sky appears darker than when we first arrived. How long had we been inside, an hour, maybe two? It's difficult to remember, a frustrating concept that riddles my mind completely until we see the source of the heart-wrenching sounds. A group of glowing lights huddles together at the edge of the tree line directly outside the cave. As we draw closer, I notice the lights have features: small arms, legs, and pointed wings. I also notice the sound is not merely one voice, but five voices in unison, using the number of beings to emit the loudest noise possible, an alarm in an assumed desolate wilderness. Rostair does not hesitate as I do, rushing to aid the frightened fairies.

"What has happened?" His voice is stern yet concerned, someone who understands his role as the Lord of this place. Bright sounds echo around us, like staccato flutes fluttering by our heads as the fairies turn toward us, revealing another dim light in the snow. A dark blanket of red coats the surrounding area, blood streaming from the small body of the fallen one. The fairies themselves are petite, as tall as infants and seemingly as fragile. As I step in close, I notice the beauty of their features. Their eyes are almond shaped and large enough to dominate their faces, their noses and mouths merely small lines against the pale blues, purples, and greens of their skin.

Rostair leans in, placing a reassuring hand on one of their shoulders as he examines the body. The bell sounds continue as a fairy in green explains the scene. I admittedly understand none of the sounds, a language far beyond my comprehension, yet Rostair nods at the sounds, his brows scrunched in a look of confusion and contemplation as he assesses the wounds of the fairies, their glow dimming swiftly as the time passes. It takes a few minutes before the ringing of the green's voice ceases and all that is left is the slight rustle of leaves and a delicate breeze.

"There is nothing to be done." A small tear barely leaves his eye before Rostair brushes it aside. "They have been slain yet their companions know not how."

I have never seen him so rattled. The picture-perfect mask has been pushed aside, and a look of fear and uncertainty replaces it. The faint blue glow that once surrounded the fairy lying on the ground disappears completely, leaving the body a pale-grey color. Rostair conveys something to the other fairies, his condolences no doubt, and we turn toward Storm who quietly stationed herself outside the cavern. The flight back to Endoneth was made in silence, Rostair's emotions seemingly shifting from confusion to anger to rage as we land near the stables. He stews on our walk back to the large home and mumbles indiscernible words under his breath, working through the event and how he should respond.

It is only when we reach the door to my room that he addresses me, "I apologize. That was unexpected. The fairies in the forests of my realm are under my protection and this is… this could be an issue that I must resolve. I just hope it isn't the work of another Lord, another realm…" His thoughts trail off. "No matter. I just hope you are not too shocked to join me again."

My heart is heavy at this display of honesty. "I will meet you again, if you wish it," I state with a small smile.

He nods with relief. "Good, good. Perhaps not tomorrow. I will need to explore this problem swiftly to protect the other fairy hordes. In a few days, yes?" With that he presses an earnest kiss to my hand and turns on his heels, still muttering to himself as he vanishes from sight.

We held my session with Mairette in my quarters that night where she explained how to enter the ballroom and when I, the Guest of Honor, would perform my first dance. My mind barely registers the information as it instead continuously wanders back to the events of the day. The ride. The pool. The Fairies. It was all so much to process and Mairette seems to notice my distance, cutting the session short and leaving me to sip my tea and eventually drift to sleep. The nightmares return, waking me several times throughout the night. I think of Rostair.

What is he doing at this moment? What is this thinking? What is he feeling?

The unanswered questions feel like torture in my broken mind.

I wake the following morning in a state of depressive panic. Pangs of sorrow fill my heart as I think about the fairies in the woods, their uncertainty and fear. I wonder how they mourn in their communities—if a funeral procession precedes a eulogy and burial; if they lay the dead with their belongings; if they cry. The thoughts are too much for such an early hour. However, other thoughts permeate my mind and increase my distress. I wish to make the events in the cavern disappear, but at the same time I want to hear Rostair tell me it was only the beginning of something wonderful. I have not felt this viscerally in years, not since Gallen.

I shoot up to a sitting position, my head banging against the headboard. The pain means nothing. Gallen, who... "I remember."

Mairette's knock at the door interrupts my thoughts. She barely waits for a response before barging in with a fresh kettle of tea. From my place in the bed, I recognize the sweet orange scent, and my anxieties shrink ever so slightly.

"Good morning, Miss." Mairette continues with her daily routine, unaware of the previous day's events and the life-altering realization I had just a moment ago.

"I think the hairstyle chosen yesterday would suit you today as well, if you like." She continues, "You may want a lighter skirt and tunic as the weather is warming more rapidly than expected."

She sets the tea set on my writing desk and flurries out into the corridor, no doubt fetching the aforementioned clothing. I slowly rise from my sheets and slide toward the tantalizing smell of tea. Mairette's tea always calms my mind, and I need such a tonic today. The first sip does just that, a smooth and sweet nectar quelling my concerns. I wonder if what Rostair said about the pool was indeed true, that such magic held healing properties.

Regardless, any memory is precious to me, and I quickly pull a sheet of paper and record the brief glimpse of my old life:

Gallen. A male from the water. With a voice of sunshine and hair of Light. I dip my quill into the ink and concentrate on the memory. I feel for him. And he has felt for me, before the world became difficult and cold...

My thoughts ramble as I try to recall the details of his face and our relationship to each other.

... His embrace is warmth, it is constant, it is safe.

"What are you working on?" I throw the page in a nearby drawer and spin to see Mairette gracefully placing a skirt on the bed.

"It is nothing. Well, nothing yet."

Her eyes grow mischievous. "Yet?" She mocks, "It wouldn't be poetry, Miss? I have heard whispers amongst the Keepers that you and the lord have been becoming more acquainted."

Heat floods my cheeks so deeply I'm sure the mark on my face is blurred.

"You do not need to share with me, just… be careful. I told you, tradition is everything in this realm and Rostair, he has a duty." Her words are laced with empathy and my shoulders lower slightly. She is right, I know, but these feelings aren't rational, and I know that as well.

"Let us ready for the day!" I say with my brightest smile, ignoring the pages in the drawer and the curiosity at what other memories may emerge.

"And notice how this map of the nine realms follows a similar color mapping technique as this beautiful estate," Gazil croons over a glass of white wine.

It may have been a mistake on my part to request an explanation of Nourels. I assumed Gazil would regale me with the intricate histories of the realms and their webbed dramas and interconnected stories. Instead, this is the second hour of him gleefully presenting the most intricate drawings and maps of the realms themselves and discussing the subtle differences between the spelling of words like "Valley" in different decades and some variances in borders depending on the source of the map.

"For example, a map of Nourels from the Ice Realm includes the south edges of the woods as their territory while the same land belongs to the Green Realm in their geographic depictions." The memory of his words bore me just as much as when he first spoke them. His current lecture is focused on the role of colors in Ice Realm maps. "Do you see the ways the colors gradually fade into one another and mix?" He points to where the realms of Ice and Mountain converge. "In this map, the cartographer attempts to capture our current political climate, who allies with whom."

My ears perk up at this statement; I'm eager to learn more about the realms and even piece together who threatens the fairies of this realm. Gazil notices the change in my posture, my sudden interest in the map and its contents.

"Based on this, you see that Ice, Desert, and Mountain are aligned, with Ice the strongest of the three." He points to the bright purple in the Ice Realm which fades into a pastel lavender as it reaches the Mountain and Desert regions. "The other two colors represent those who align with the Star Realm and those who remain neutral." Gazil lowers his voice as he continues, "Now as you will notice, the brightest red is located to the south with the Star Realm and bleeds into the surrounding areas in the center." He gestures to the High and Valley Realms.

"What of the other realms?" I ask, completely enthralled with this new information.

"Well, that is where this third color emerges, representing neutrality, or at least partial neutrality. The beauty of color mapping is the nuance in its application. You see, no realm is completely neutral. In fact the outliers—the Sun Realm and the Ocean Realm—are largely divided."

This concept manifests in the map; both "outlier" realms are made up of a green base and dotted with areas of both purple and red of varying shades. "There are of course areas in each realm that are more fanatical than others. In fact, there is a group in the Ocean Realm infamous for their allegiance to the Star Realm and their beliefs." He shakes his head gravely. "If you ask me, an old man at the end of a long and illustrious life," I roll my eyes a bit at this self-illustration, "none of us should be at odds. There is no time for such petty quarrels and disagreements. I am ready for more dancing, more music, more living."

He raises his voice slightly at this last point before quickly looking around and curving his shoulders inward. Rather than turn to see which guests are staring today— certainly a healthy amount considering the popularity of the library this afternoon—I focus on the map, the intricate colors blending into one another and swirling into a world of meaning.

"Why is the Mountain Realm where the most conflict occurs, if the Star Realm is most at odds with us here?" I feel my question is innocent enough.

Gazil clears his throat. "Centrea, why don't we discuss the Greentime Ball?" He sighs dreamily. "I have a few fashion concepts I would enjoy sharing, if Mairette is accepting outside assistance. I know Lord Rostair has his own designers, but you deserve to look absolutely ravishing!"

I smile at my friend, his finger twisting a braid in his usually fidgeting manner, a smile gracing his sweet face. "Of course, Gazil," I confirm. "What did you have in mind?"

Discussing new fashions triggers an even longer discussion with my friend than that of maps and colors. To his credit, Gazil's sketches are remarkable. As we discuss his references and design choices, he pulls various books from the stocked shelves to unearth historical images and fabrics. We spend hours collaborating on the smallest details: collars, sleeves, laces, hemlines. It is not until Mairette taps my shoulder that I return my attention to the present.

"Miss, I am here to remind you of dinner." She looks over to the sketches and gasps. "These are magnificent! And in time for the ball as well." She turns to Gazil and curtsies slightly, conveying both approval and respect. "With your permission, sir."

Gazil barely attempts to hide his excitement. "I would be honored to see my ideas come to life." I bid Gazil a good night and begin a brief walk to the room where Mairette has both a cup of mint tea and a dress waiting for me.

The dinner tonight is more of the same: discussions of the rapidly warming weather, the influx of new guests eagerly preparing for the upcoming ball, and the usual gossip. I learned long ago that my place in these spaces is one of spectacle, a marvel whose interesting and mysterious appearance always spurs whispers and conversation. Of course, as all drama, my presence has become less interesting to long-term guests; however, as more newcomers arrive (and would arrive in the weeks preceding the largest event in the realm) the more frequent the lingering looks and obvious gossiping becomes. I attempt to enjoy the plate before me, a mix of sprouted grains and meat, yet my ears are straining to hear any news of the fairy attacks from yesterday. It is possible such things will take time to discover, but this same group learns of even the most trivial details within hours. The lives of woodland creatures are not quite the same as a midnight tryst in the gardens or a misplaced gamble on cards.

By the final course, I lose hope of hearing a word on the matter until a quiet voice from across the table mentions something noteworthy: "Surely the value of these creatures will ensure their protection, eh?" the nasally voice asks her neighbor. "We all know the source, of course. It must be those from the Green, so easily manipulated to do their bidding." She clicks her tongue and turns her attention to dessert.

Her neighbor contributes a bit more. "Well, we all know why the grain this season was slim and the fish small.

That is why our armies struggle even more than we would assume. How long shall this last?" I tuck the information away to contemplate more later tonight but leave the dinner with a strange feeling. We are at war, that much is easily deduced, but what events would cause such a thing? And are we even safe here at Endoneth?

When I return to my room, my nightly tea sits atop a large tome.

A scribbled note explains, "Not what I would call light reading, but this may explain the map we examined today. Do not stay awake too late! -Gazil"

I cannot help but roll my eyes at his sincere concern, but I smile at this gift. I am certain there are political histories aplenty in the large library, but navigating what would be helpful to read is a thought too overwhelming to overcome. Gazil's consideration to provide me with his own suggestion prompts waves of appreciation to flow through me. I snatch the book into my hands and nearly drop it, underestimating its weight, but toss it on the bed before scooping my nightly herbal tea and settling down. I turn to the front page, *A Brief History of the Northern Realms and their subsidiaries.*

"Great..." I grumble. This is not my typical genre of literature, and the first few pages confirm my suspicion. It will take a while to finish the eighty-nine-chapter work, even with my curiosity brimming at any mention of the Mountain Realm's past. The taste of ink touches my tongue as I lick my fingers to quickly sift through the book. Each page is filled from top to bottom with tiny words that read as a dry lecture, a story with no soul. I sigh and close the book, a task for another time. I bring the heavy history back to my desk with a clunk and think of another important task. Sitting back in the warmth of my chair, I pull out the pages from just this morning and try to continue my train of thought:

Gallen. A male from the water. With a voice of sunshine and hair of Light. I feel for him. And he has felt for me, before the world became difficult and cold. My thoughts ramble as I try to recall the details of his face and our relationship to each other. His embrace is warmth, it is constant, it is safe.

I reread the old words over and over, tears brimming in my eyes and washing over my cheeks. These words mean nothing to me. It is all a blur once more.

Another sunrise comes and goes, the day filled with more lessons from Mairette and a quick picnic with Gazil in the warm sun. I refuse to return to my notes, disappointed with myself for my faulty memory. Perhaps my mind imagined the person Gallen. Every person desires warmth and safety from someone they care for, so perhaps my mind made that for myself. At least this male, if real at all, is from the Ocean Realm, a place of neutrality rather than an enemy. These thoughts plague my mind when a rough knock echoes through my chamber.

I pull my sheets to my chin and respond, "Yes, who is it?" I hear a stifled chuckle before the door opens just barely.

"Your adventure companion." Rostair's voice sounds far lighter than our last visit only days ago.

"Do come in!" I say, hoping to mask my excitement. He strolls into the room in a pair of black linen pants and a rose-colored tunic, lined with pink ruffles.

His white hair is braided into a top knot above his head and a grin lines his face. "A wise thinker once wrote, 'The most memorable adventures begin before dawn.'" His cheery demeanor is in stark contrast with the early morning hour. Rostair sets down a bundle of clothing on the edge of my bed, and my heart beats faster and faster with each step he takes toward me. "I will meet you by the gardens, as usual." He waves a hand toward the outfit before making his way toward the doorway. "Dress accordingly."

And, like a flash, I was alone once more, the crackling of the eternal fire filling the void of his voice. I sigh and roll to my side, working up the energy to move forward and face this day. However, one thought of the ride, the caves, and the pool, and I am up and dressed in the unusual attire Rostair left: brown linen trousers, a short, golden tunic with beads lining the sleeves, and a knit coat. I hurry to meet him at the garden's entrance, and he greets me with a smile.

"Good morning." The sentiment is laughable. While technically accurate—it *is* morning—the sun is far from gracing its presence in the sky.

"What do adventurers do at such an early hour?" I yawn and stretch my arms up for good measure.

"Well," he begins, "I wanted to present to you yet another side of myself." We begin walking away from the estate and toward the thick woods, the same trees I watch outside my window. "It's easiest to complete some tasks when the rest of the house sleeps. This way my social and political responsibilities take precedence in the day."

We wander into the trees, where the fresh smell of pine rushes through my senses. Although the weather has warmed, the early air is brisk, urging me to bundle in the oversized knitted layer. I wait for further explanation of our purpose here, but Rostair remains stoic, concentrated, and intent. The path we walk is worn, indicating frequent use. I look around at the greenery surrounding me, wet with a mixture of melted snow and morning dew. The trees themselves are magnificent, much larger up close and growing taller the deeper we venture through the dense wood.

After around forty minutes, he finally glimpses at me. "I apologize for the intensity of our past few walks. It is an unfortunate reality of my position; it requires a great deal of pacing to and fro." My performance is significantly better than our last hike, one filled with far more hills and sunshine. However, I have shed my coat long ago, clumsily passing it from one arm to the next as I stumble forward.

Unlike me, Rostair moves with the grace of a person who frequents nature, so comfortable in the wilderness of the woods. The trees must be miles above us at this point. He glances back every few minutes to ensure I am keeping pace before suddenly pausing.

"We are here," he states definitively. I look around, a bit confused. We are surrounded by more trees and bushes and melted snow. Clearly amused, he turns his eyes skyward.

"Not again..." I gasp.

He chuckles. "Well, not quite the same. Just follow me and promise you will not peer down." His words present little confidence as he rounds the corner of the nearest tree, one with a wide trunk. Once on the other side, a staircase emerges, carved into the deep brown wood of the pine. "You may lead, if you'd like," he offers, pointing up.

I hesitate a moment before walking slowly toward the steep stairs. My thighs scream in protest, still a bit sore from riding Storm a few days prior, but I push through, wanting to impress Rostair and satisfy my curiosity. The first few steps are easy, the grain of the wood providing ample grip to boost my confidence. Rostair joins not far behind, allowing me to set a steady pace. I lose count of the stairs by around fifty-two, my head growing light and my breath uneven.

I turn a few times to see Rostair nod his encouragement and begrudgingly continue, my legs now in open protest, quivering violently.

"A few more steps," he claims, placing a steady hand on my back. While I cannot be certain, there is no turning back. After taking a deep breath of air in, I push forward. A minute later, I feel his touch again.

"We are here." He points to our left and my jaw drops open.

In my pain and slight annoyance, I completely missed a large platform nestled in the canopy of trees. He jumps forward, landing on the wooden floor with a thud. I refuse the hand he extends toward me and leap on my own, my swollen feet unhappy with the decision but my pride beaming. The sun has barely started its ascent, and the sky begins shifting from a deep navy to a dark purple laced with oranges and pinks. Rostair smirks and tilts his head to the side before sending a bright whistle into the air.

In mere seconds, the platform is suddenly flooded with winged beasts of various sizes, squawking and chirping with reckless abandon. "I take my role as protector quite seriously." Rostair saunters toward a large bird with a bright pink beak and yellow feathers, passing a large hand over its back. The bird lets out a long, deep wail and, to my surprise, Rostair nods with empathy. He pats the yellow feathers gently and whispers near the bird's head. Whatever he said satisfied the winged creature as it spreads its wings wide, the brown feathers painting the underside peeking through, and rushes into the air. This ritual continues for nearly twenty minutes: Rostair approaching each bird, hearing their concerns before responding and letting them on their way. I watch in utter awe as each bird chirps their greeting, their request, then their thanks. And seeing the great Lord of the Ice Realm kneeling low and giving even the smallest of birds their due time warms my heart. Such a display hardly assists in my attempts to be grounded in reality, to remember Mairette's words of caution and how realistically I should heed them. But the gentleness in each interaction only encourages the imprudent thoughts and memories of us in the library and in the cavern.

When the last bird makes its unceremonious exit, Rostair closes his eyes and fills his lungs to capacity before blowing out a gust of air. He looks at me, where I'm standing, still stunned at the opposite end of the platform.

"I apologize, I should have asked you if you enjoy birds. I hear some people fear them, and I suppose they are quite loud..." He continues rambling, pacing toward me until he is at my side once more.

"That was incredible." I interrupt him mid-sentence. "I cannot fathom how you manage to understand them all. Are they speaking similar languages, singing the same songs?"

I have so many more questions, but the sun is now above the horizon, and I know Mairette will wonder if I am not in my bed.

"There are many languages amongst the beasts and birds of my woods," he grins and explains. "I have trained since boyhood to learn them all. Some I understand better than others, but all are beautiful in their own ways." He nods his head toward the stairs and says, "I can explain more on our way back."

My stomach hurts from the bursts of laughter that echo through the trees. "I do not find this amusing." Rostair can hardly hold back his own giggles as he adamantly defends his position. "I could not have known she would walk in! I feel a man should be permitted to recite his favored limerick in the comfort of his own home." He crosses his arms over his chest as I resume my incessant laughter.

I gasp for breath enough to point out, "The estate is constantly filled with guests, all seeking you to engage in conversation." I have noticed as much during the many dinners and dances, each aristocrat eager to prove their worth and perhaps win his favor. As he waves away the thought I press, "Additionally, perhaps the pitcher of spiced wine decreased your inhibitions."

He scoffs with a smile and concedes, "I suppose finding me in my bloomers was not her ideal end to the night..." His eyes shine, and I laugh once more.

"You must recite the limerick for me, please!"

This walk has been one of the few highlights since being at Endoneth. Rostair tells me the story of when he was caught in the main library with an empty glass in his hand and clothes on the floor; it is more salacious than anything Gazil has shared, although the affair between the Desert Realm's most prominent seamstress and a lord's daughter was quite the tale. I cannot imagine the reaction of the poor woman who followed Rostair into the public space, to be met by a raunchy poem and the Lord in such a vulnerable position. Rostair straightens a bit as we walk down a familiar path, quietly reciting:

"There was a young Lord from the Green,
Who often did nothing but dream.
When he drank too much rum
He shows off his bum
And now all the women are keen."

I explode in laughter, doubling over to clutch my aching stomach. "You said this is your favorite?" I ask.

He joins in my clear joy at this discussion, this walk, this story and says with a chuckle, "It was the first limerick I memorized, and it has stuck with me. Trust me, the poetry I enjoy is not typically so simple." He plays off the laughter, but I see a bit of blush on his cheeks.

I smile broadly. "I would like to hear the poetry you enjoy."

Rostair spends the remaining walk recalling poems of his past and present, those from trying times and moments of celebration. When we reach the entrance to the estate, I wish we could turn back and make the journey again if it meant more time to do just this. Instead, he leads me back and continues with his daily responsibilities, leaving me to daydream about what Rostair looked like that night in only his bloomers.

Mairette welcomes me back to my room with her characteristic joyous tone, yet I notice her slight concern at my morning away. I assure her that I was completely safe and am fine, yet immensely tired and intend to spend the afternoon in. She nods in approval and asks, "What flavor would you enjoy this morning? If you are sore from the morning's activities," the look of mischief in her eyes is palpable, "there are a few medicinal remedies I can mix in."

Smiling, I state, "I trust you implicitly, Mairette. Whatever you recommend."

With a bounce in her step, she rushes out to prepare my tea. In her absence I peel the clothing from my wobbling body; the fabric sticks to my skin after sweating through my journey. I have not truly looked at my body since my arrival in Endoneth. The memory of my frailty when I first arrived increases my aversion to my own reflection.

Today, the climb ignited something in me, a confidence I was unaware existed. I stand boldly in front of my mirror, taking a long look at the body that brought me here—beyond the traumatic first morning, the mental toll of the elite guests, the flight into the sky, and climb into the canopy. It is vastly different from the person I once was months ago, both physically and mentally. The fullness of my face is mirrored by the size of my breasts and width of my hips. I trace the slight hourglass of my side and smile at the fullness of my stomach and the strength of my thighs. I can confidently call myself beautiful. I stare into my eyes, the blue color not scared or weak but strong and confident. I touch the red mark down the center of my cheek and smile. I am proud of every part of me.

I appreciate my decision to avoid the outside world the rest of the day. While I feel restless, I would rather stay in my own space than feel the judgment of the visiting guests. I wonder briefly what appears so unlikable about me but remember Mairette warning me of what happens to Rostair's favored ones, the isolation that typically forces them away.

I turn to my desk and see the book Gazil procured. It would be nice to know more about where I am and who these people are. I take the tome from where I left it last, dragging it onto my bed. I run my fingers over the embossed words lining the front cover: *A Brief History of the Northern Realms and their subsidiaries*. I turn to the table of contents, divided into three main sections for each realm of the North: Ice, Desert, and Mountain. When I open the book to the first section, I see the same lecture-like explanations of the Ice Realm as I saw before. After taking a deep breath, I dive into the information, skimming the first sentence of each paragraph to discern which pages are most important. Page after page, I learn about the history of this realm beginning with a period of great suffering followed by decades of great prosperity.

The ages of each are marked by colors, unsurprisingly, beginning with the White Age, moving to the Silver Age, then the Black Age, the Green Age, the Brown Age, and finally the current age, the Gold Age. Each age is led by a noble family, one who helps manage the realm and its many estates. I flip through the other periods to focus on modern times. During the Gold Age, Rostair and his kin have held ultimate authority. It appears that before his great-grandfather gained this position, it was a family in the east who conceded this right to focus on oceanic exploration. While there are no monarchs, these lords oversee the realm as a whole while all other lords manage only what is necessary.

As I turn to learn more of Rostair and his family, I notice tiny annotations in the margins. The text outlines the relationship between Endoneth, the Ice Realm, and the natural world: *The worlds live in symbiosis; the lords of Endoneth provide protection and the woods provide resources for consumption.*

The nearly unreadable note in the margin accompanying this section says something like, "More fairies…yields…"

I scrunch my nose and squint my eyes to make out the rest to no avail. Another note is placed next to a pair of sentences: The Ice Realm has always found utility in even the most unlikely spaces. However, the Gold Age saw potential in the most unassuming places.

The bright green ink on the margin states, "check with Zeal." Yet another mystery. I jump off the bed to take my own notes of the book and its contents. At the bottom of the page, I write "check…Zeal?" and underline it twice.

A knock on the door rouses me from my work.

"Miss?" Mairette's shoes tap the tiles as she enters with a tray filled with food.

Swiftly, I place the paper inside the front cover of the tome before sliding it beneath the bed, assured that I will attend to it again in the near future.

"I thought I should bring you a bite." Her red curls waft backward as she briskly swings the tray atop the bed. I smile, my mind reeling at the knowledge that the afternoon slipped away from me, lost to pages of old notes and mysterious annotations.

"Many thanks, Mairette. I promise I will eat."

She merely nods before turning to leave.

I eat a few bites of bread before slinking into the soft sheets.

Once my head hits the pillow, I close my eyes and am drawn into a deep sleep. Sleep is such an unusual plane of consciousness, one where anything can happen, but it is all ultimately meaningless. This dream is no different. The earth parts beneath my feet and I am falling, falling so fast I can barely see, barely breathe. Then I'm suddenly in my four-poster bed, drinking tea, thinking in blurs with ink-stained papers strewn around me. I try my hardest to read the words on the page, but I cannot. The black letters swim through the air as I reach forward to snatch them. Thoughts are elusive. All I truly have is a feeling, a feeling that I am alone yet being watched at all times. Then suddenly I am in the snow, shivering in a thin night shift and sandals. I see a figure through heavy sheets of sleet, their legs trudging through inches of snow. Muffled screams pierce the wind, coming from the figure but also from behind me, around me, everywhere. The desperate pleas grow louder and louder until I shut my eyes and clap my hands over my ears to shut them out. When I open my eyes once more, I am standing in the library, looking down at the map of the nine realms, the colors warring with one another for supremacy, the red from the south growing larger, pressing toward purple with ferocity and intensity. In an instant, the map is engulfed in red, the paper itself bursting into a passionate fire that starts blazing in the room. Suddenly, the fire spreads to the books lining the walls, the air growing thin and smoke threatening to suffocate me. I gasp for clean air, clawing at my throat. I try to run, to move, to do anything, and my feet refuse to answer. Fear overwhelms me. I forget what air tastes like, what clear vision sees. I fall unconscious.

The nightmare jolts me awake. I gulp the air as if I were truly suffocating and pace my room to shake away this feeling. Outside my window the sun is low, painting the sky pink which fades into blue, revealing the stars barely peeking through for the night. Enough light reveals the melting snow and the blades of grass underneath. The sight of green on the grounds stirs hope within me. The vivid color against the last remaining clumps of snow reveals something alive and hopeful.

There is a small tap at the door before Mairette arrives with more food.

"I noticed you barely touched the soup," she explains, "I can also bring a few scones with your nightly tea if you would like." She smiles wide and holds her hands clasped in front of her.

I nod a bit absentmindedly. She notices my hesitation and worry shades her features. "Is everything alright, Miss?"

The sound of her care alone eases my still pounding heart. "I just, I've been having nightmares for the past..."

Her brows furrow and she gently leans on the edge of the bed, barely sitting but clearly wanting to appear comfortable and provide a listening ear. I sigh and slip into the velvet chair near the bed.

"I believe my memory lapses are starting to affect me." I consider telling her about my brief memory, about Gallen and the ocean.

Before I can, Mairette reaches for my hand. "You have experienced something immensely traumatic. Your body, your mind, your being has undergone immense change, and I cannot imagine how that must feel."

Tears well in my eyes, threatening to break free at the sound of her empathy. It is an interesting position to exist in, where almost all the people I see daily show such disdain that the most basic kindness stirs overwhelming emotion. If it were not for Mairette and Gazil, I am not sure I could survive in this place. Of course, Rostair's newfound interest in me provides ample distraction from feelings of isolation. But nothing can replace this:

Mairette holding my hand in hers, wiping tears from my cheeks, and hearing my greatest sorrows and deepest fears.

Mairette brings tea into my room after I have cleaned my face and changed from my sweat-stained clothes. The fresh nightgown is made of a green gossamer silk with tightly woven lace sleeves. I pick at the small embroidered pink flowers along the short hem. Tonight, the tea leaves smell like jasmine and rose, a relaxing blend to ease me into a calm stupor.

She asks once more about my dream. "There are those who believe dreams hold alternative meanings. Perhaps we can learn more about who you once were and who you are meant to be." This concept fills me with a bit of hope, although I cannot completely give myself to this reality.

But I trust Mairette, and I respect her traditions, the Ice Realm and their beliefs. "I want to know as much as I can." I admit, "What shall I do?"

Mairette's eyes brighten, and she walks out of the room so quickly a breeze follows behind her. I wait in my room a moment, the sun long fallen below the horizon and the sound of crickets awakening just outside. She takes her time gathering what she needs and enters the room with arms full of baskets and candles. She arranges the candles in a circle on the coffee table in the center of the suite. She places one basket on each corner—one filled with soil, one with gems, one with wood, and one completely empty.

I walk toward the table and lean over to observe the display as she carefully lights each of the nine candles. "There are beliefs, rituals known to the woods of the Ice Realm," she begins, staring into the flickering flames, transfixed by its erratic movements. "I learned them from my mother who lived amongst the fairies and wood nymphs. Their magic is like none other in the nine realms—tangible and pure. It is something worth protecting, worth harnessing and maintaining. We keep it alive through our own use. One of the most impressive aspects of this art is its clarity; you ask something of it, and it tells you." Her eyes turn to mine and a mischievous smile graces her lips. The joyous timbre of her voice shifts to something a bit darker and more powerful. Her bright purple eyes glaze over.

"Are you prepared to see your fate?" I reflexively hover backward, intimidated by this new being that has overtaken my friend.

"I-I believe so," I respond carefully, shifting my weight from one foot to the other in an attempt to relieve the anxiety pulsing through me.

She swings a hand out toward a nearby sitting area behind the table. "Please, sit, Miss." The raw power sends a shiver down my spine and, while slightly terrifying, the feeling is a bit exhilarating. Magic, real and tangible, just like she said.

The flames of the candles sparkle wildly in the growing darkness of the room. In the fireplace, the crackling of lumber continues, seemingly calling out to the flames themselves. I squirm in my seat, the soft embroidery of the sofa crunching delicately beneath my dress and the silk shift sliding in satisfying swishes. This is the only way to stay settled as Mairette, seated in the sofa across mine, continues arranging various objects on the table before me.

As she reaches for each element, she explains its significance. "The soil represents the land, a holy fortress that is meant to be protected." She grasps a handful of soil and allows the earthy grains to pass through her fingers as she hovers over the table, creating a twelve-pointed star with the soil at the center of the table. With her other hand she reaches for the basket of wood and uses the small twigs to frame the star of soil. "The trees in our woods represent life and strength. Wood fuels all: fire, home, work. Without wood, we are lost. The north cannot survive." The next element, gems, glimmers as she stretches a dirt-stained hand toward the pink and turquoise rocks. "The gems that line our caverns hold more than mere value; they also assist in health and meditation. They brighten the world that soil and wood create."

She kisses each raw stone and balances the jagged edges on the inside of each of the twelve corners of the star. She then grabs the final element, an empty wicker basket. She smiles warmly, almost maniacally, at the vessel, the deep brown tones of the dark wicker somehow gleaming in the darkness. "This is nothing." She places a hand inside to accentuate her point. "We must learn to accept that we cannot have everything; accept that the ice and grass and trees have given us all we need in this life; accept that anything more is simply a blessing and that, more often than not, the blessings may not appear."

Mairette sighs deeply and closes her eyes, tipping the basket forward, as if pouring liquid on the makeshift star. She continues, her voice growing more stern and coarse. "We must accept nothing, embrace nothing, become nothing. That is when we truly see... we truly see who we are and why we are here." Her eyes flash open on the final word, the basket falling into the center of the star, somehow leaving the elements themselves unscathed.

But her eyes are no longer her own, not the violet, kind eyes of my confidante. No, these eyes are completely black and cold, no trace of color or emotion. "What do you seek, child?" The words sound almost painful as the being before me, whatever is possessing Mairette, cocks her head violently to the side and bares her teeth. I am struck by the situation, reaching for the embroidered flowers on my nightgown once more to offer my hands something to ease the tension, to help clear my mind and calm my increasing uncertainty. "I will not ask again." This next statement startles me, and I jump back a bit.

There are so many questions that plague my mind; however, there is one that I've pushed aside for far too long. "I want to know who I am." My voice quivers a bit, yet I'm sure. I so badly wish to know so much more.

A spiteful laughter fills the room as Mairette's head tips backwards to fully release the sound into the dark air. "You foolish child! I am not here to answer petty questions. I am here to deliver a message of your destiny." My face surely echoes the pain radiating through my chest.

"Now, you are dreaming, I assume." Her tongue swipes over the front of her teeth, creating a sickening slurping noise.

"How did you know about my dreams?" My surprise lifts my voice an octave.

She smiles and cracks Mairette's neck, turning her head to look the other way. "I know all, see all, but reveal little. Now, what elements of your dreams most trouble you?" She places her long fingers on the table, gripping the edge as she waits for my response.

"I... uh... I suppose the figure. The figure in the storm. Who was it? Why could I not hear them?" Now my hands are twisted into each other, crossing my fingers over themselves and watching the beast's reaction.

"An intriguing figure, masked in sleet. And he says little, sees little, knows little." Mairette pauses for a moment and closes her wild eyes. "There is someone coming for you. An enemy, someone meant to destroy you and those you have grown to care for, to love."

My stomach turns as I pinch the silk fabric between my fingers. "Who is it?" I demand. "Who is coming for me?"

Her face turns solemn, black eyes glaring into mine as she grumbles, "Red is on the horizon."

The candle's flames whoosh out and we are left in near pitch-black. Even the fireplace is quelled to only embers, quietly crackling for dear life. The dim blue light left by the remaining logs forms a halo around Mairette's silhouette as her shoulders lift and fall with her slowing breaths. I fear looking into her eyes, unsure if I will find the joyful purple or the soulless black.

"What... what did you learn?" The whisper is almost indiscernible, her voice certainly back to normal yet more sheepish than usual. I almost fall back into our typical routine where I tell her my experience, but I don't even know what I would say.

"How often do you hold these rituals?" My voice comes out slowly and the words cause jabs of pain through my throat. I suddenly notice the dryness of my mouth, the need for water or wine or something overcoming my other senses. I then also notice the slightest orange glow through the stained glass. "How long did we speak?" It felt like mere minutes. But, as I stand to investigate the window more thoroughly, I see the sun barely surfacing above a horizon of both white and green. Can magic hasten time? I rub my eyes with the palms of my hands and turn back to Mairette who sits motionless in front of her tools.

Finally, after what feels like hours, her eyes meet mine. "What did you learn?"

When Mairette finally leaves, unable to answer my questions and unable to squeeze answers out of me, I spend a few hours staring at the ceiling, another element of this home that exudes luxury. It is painted the color of the night sky, a breathtaking navy blue accented by golden crown molding. The longer I stare, the more details I discern: small specks of shining silver in curious designs; natural paint strokes of the navy base color; the delicate filigree of the crown molding filled with flowers, swirls, and leaves. My eyes ached to close, to ignore the look in Mairette's eyes, the sound of her voice, the crackling candles.

I think over and over about the details of the nightmare, hearing Mairette's voice:

*An enemy...*

*Someone meant to destroy you...*

*Red is on the horizon...*

The voice lulls me to sleep.

While I wish I could spend the following day resting once more, Rostair planned another of his "adventures" around the estate. Fortunately, he visits me in the late morning, which gives me a few hours of restless sleep after a night of terror and confusion. Despite my aching head and tired body, I can't help but feel excited, even if I cannot show just how much.

He notices my demeanor straight away and assures me, "The day's plans will not require an arduous journey."

His smile offers little comfort, the sparkle of mischief still glimmering in his eyes. He did not bring a set of clothing, which does give me solace. The skirt and soft tunic Mairette brought me today is a light peach color lined by a pale blue thread; she slipped in during my brief nap to set a fresh cup of blackberry tea on my bedside table and lay the clothes on the ottoman near the renewed warmth of the fireplace. I am thankful she allowed me to sleep, although I am eager to face her once more and debrief the events of last night. I have grown so fond of Mairette, and I would hate for this to come between our friendship, especially when there are few friends for me here.

Rostair sits on the sofa as I finish my tea. "What tea is your favorite so far? You know, the Ice Realm is known for our warm beverages." He grins.

This is the best side of Rostair, the lighthearted, stress-free side I only see when we are alone, away from the judgmental eyes of his many guests and Keepers. "I still feel the orange is the most comforting to me." Even thinking about the tea brings a bit of citrus to my senses. "Although, all the teas Mairette prepares are wonderful."

He leans back. "Come now, there must be a few you have not favored? Don't fret, I will not be offended." He places a hand dramatically on his chest, feigning heartache.

My eyes roll and a smile teases my lips. "I do prefer sweeter blends." I take a long sip and flick my gaze toward him as he rests his arms along the back of the cushions and sinks down. The visual is a bit jarring. I have never seen him so relaxed and unguarded. Rostair is typically careful and precise, understandably so as the ruler of a great estate and, as I understand it, essentially the Ice Realm itself. Here he is comfortable and at ease, his face soft, a few stray hairs gently falling over his eyes.

"I love learning about what you enjoy." A bit of sadness laces his voice. "I can't deny, I think of you often." I feel heat searing my cheeks, and he stumbles over his next words, one of his hands leaving the comfort of the couch to rub the back of his neck. "I mean... I think about your predicament. How lonely and suffocating it must feel, to be in a land you don't know and also not know yourself. I promise news from the Mountains must be arriving any day now. The battles continue which prevents much communication..."

He shakes his head, his eyes downcast for a moment before he raises them to mine. "Regardless, I was thinking of you last night." He coughs, his own cheeks gaining a bit of a pink glow to them. "And I thought that perhaps we could investigate who you were... who you *are*." I place my cup onto the table carefully, leaning in close to hear this proposition, water brimming my eyes as I contemplate what Rostair says. "I know it may be overwhelming—"

"Yes," I gasp, the word slipping out before he can finish his thought. "I would like to learn more, about who I am now. Maybe it will help me learn more about who I was before I got here." I consider asking to return to the cavern, but I dismiss the thought, my cheeks growing a deeper shade of red remembering our swim. If Rostair's new plan yields nothing, then I may consider returning to the pools of magic. I cannot deny I haven't thought back to that night, the feel of the water, the warmth of Rostair's body near my own, the view as he walked briskly toward the cave's entrance...

I notice his inquisitive look as I return back to the present. To my relief he continues to detail his idea, either ignorant of my thoughts or politely avoiding the conversation. "I have researched memory between meetings and strategy sessions and the library has much to say. There are tactics to elicit sensory responses, ways to restore certain memories from even decades ago—not that you appear decades old... I mean, maybe two decades, but certainly no more, I would think, although even so it would not alter my view of you as a beautiful individual... not that it matters what I think of you... "

I allow his nervous rambling to continue far longer than is generous, his posture shifting from comfortably sunken into the cushions, to leaning forward with his forearms resting on his knees, then sitting upright with his hands nervously combing through his glistening, silver hair.

"I completely understand." I giggle, and Rostair breathes a sigh of relief as I allow him a moment to compose himself.

I haven't given much thought to my age. My face holds a few creases along my cheeks, but not nearly as many as some women at court. I am certainly half the age of Gazil, the wisdom of his many years reflected in the deep lines along his face and the calm speed of his gait. I make a mental note to question him about this at our next library meeting, ignoring the fact that he expressed the social impropriety of asking such things.

Returning to Rostair, who is settling back into a restful position, wiping a bead of sweat from his forehead, I grow more excited about the prospect of knowing myself. "What shall we try first?"

Of course, when Rostair leaves, all I want is to tell Mairette of my newest strategy to learn my past. My heart aches as I sip my tea and hover over the half-filled page in front of me. I have developed nearly a book's worth of notes, mainly scribblings of thoughts and poems as I sort through my feelings. An embarrassing number of pages describe Rostair, his piercing eyes, his wicked grin, his braided hair, and his various fashions. Other notes include my many conversations with Mairette and Gazil, both sources of immense entertainment and knowledge. Rudimentary doodles and sketches of small animals or flowers join the words on the pages. I grimace at the many attempts to remember myself, who I once was.

Despite Rostair's efforts and his memory tasks, I find the end goal impossible to attain. I organize the pages chronologically, placing ideas about my past first, followed by my first months in the estate, and ending with the last few weeks. I am more resolute than ever to focus more on the future, of balls and my place in the realm. I pull an empty page and smooth it out in front of me. Dipping a feather quill into the fresh blue ink, I begin penning a letter to Mairette. I wish I could say writing it is simple, however the words are just as difficult to find on paper than in person:

*Mairette,*
*I apologize if I disrespected the rituals close to your heart. I was just scared...*

Shaking my head, I crush the paper in my fist and throw it on the floor. I repeat this process a couple more times, smoothing the paper, writing a few words, then throwing the paper away. I take a breath and hold it for a brief moment before slowly releasing the air into the room. After sipping a gulp of tea, I attempt writing once more:

*Mairette,*
*I can only guess what you are feeling. I know we both wanted your idea to yield a memory of my past, but I want you to know I am not disappointed or frustrated. Thank you for helping me understand myself despite what is still unknown. You are a bright light in my life here, my most trusted companion. I hope we may remain close as we were. Please, when you feel comfortable, talk to me.*
*Yours,*
*Centrea.*

The letter could likely be better, but I'm not sure if my eyes will allow me to stay awake much longer. My lids are heavy and eager for sleep. I place the feather down on the desk and rub my eyes closed, thinking I can take a moment to rest before attempting another draft of the letter.

The nightmare presents another combination of mysterious figures and imminent danger. This time, I find myself in a field of green picking at the petals of a small flower. The lilac petals feel like soft silk in my hands, each drifting to and fro before landing gently in the grass. The sun feels warm on my back, and I tilt my head behind my shoulders to soak in the rays. Gone is any trace of winter. There aren't any trees in sight for miles, just rolling hills of green grass, swaying gently with short gusts of wind. I reach the final petal of my flower, tossing the stem behind me and reaching out for another. The gentle breezes around me begin gaining speed strong enough to push my loose hair behind me. As my hand lands on the blue petals of the new flower, I hear a whoosh of wind that knocks me onto my back. The shock temporarily stuns me. I struggle against the moving air, attempting to lift my head but failing against its power. I scream out in frustration but can't hear my cries over the sound of the wind, gushing in waves over and over me. The sun remains shining as if pleasantly unaware of my turmoil below. I wriggle against the onslaught of wind. My body struggles with contradicting senses: The grass and soil below offer a comforting bed that caresses the curves of my body while my chest and limbs are pinned down by the harsh gale. Frantically, I shift my arms to break free of the prison. I try to lift my arm once again before a new gust presses it into the ground. Soon I am unable to even twist my arms or shift my body, completely glued to the ground. Out of the corner of my eyes I see a dark shadow growing closer, unfazed by the cyclone keeping me captive. Its eyes blaze with the color of fire before leaving my field of vision. My head is pinned in place, incapable of moving to face the creature. Before long, the shadow is at my feet in my line of sight. I smell wafts of honey and vanilla as a hand grasps my ankles. Suddenly, the wind halts, leaving my ears ringing from the constant rush of noise that preceded the silence. The stranger's voice pierces the stillness: "I will find you." Regaining feeling in my hands, I place my palms on the ground and shoot into a sitting position, the movement forcing my mind into a daze that shocks me awake.

The early morning is quiet as I regain consciousness. I look at the note written only hours ago and sigh at the smudged words. Grunting in frustration, I crunch the letter into a ball and throw it down along with the others. Standing slowly from my writing desk, I move to the mirror to see stains of ink along my cheek. Luckily, my dress remains unscathed. Turning briskly toward the water closet, I pour water into a bowl and dab my face with a small cloth. When I return to the mirror, I still see slight traces of ink, but the majority is gone. I also notice the poor state of my hair. A few days without Mairette's assistance is taking its toll on my appearance as well as my mentality. I clench my fists and walk toward the door, defiant and determined. I need to speak with her. This cannot go on for another day, and if she would like to keep avoiding me, I suppose I must go and find her myself.

I pace in the hallway near the Red Wing for nearly five minutes contemplating what to do. I could wait here all morning until Mairette leaves or I could disrupt the boundaries of this estate and enter the wing myself. While tempting, I am certain that exploring the wing myself is not the answer. And even if I followed the tiles of ruby red, I would not know where she is or where she stays. My fingers pinch the ridge of my nose as I think. As I stand there, lost in my own thoughts, I hear the tiniest footsteps pinging on the tiled floor. My head turns toward the sound to see a mousey young lady popping her head out from behind a nearby column. Her bright hazel eyes are curiously following my movements.

I turn to face her directly, offering a slight wave of my hand before saying, "Hello? I'm sorry, I know it is early, and you must be merely accomplishing your morning tasks. But could I possibly trouble you for a moment, just to answer a question?" Her head turns to the side, and she pauses, thinking through my words and considering the risk of speaking to me directly. I look behind me for a moment to the entrance of the Red Wing and nod my head in understanding. "We can move away from this wing if you would feel more comfortable elsewhere. I promise I won't tell a soul if we talk." Memories of Mairette explaining the strict hierarchy resurface only briefly before I swat them away. Station should not determine a person's worth.

The young Keeper steps out from behind the column carefully, moving as though chained to a heavy rock. She gestures behind her, and I nod in understanding. "Yes, that way, of course." I swiftly follow her directions, moving into a hidden hallway in the Gold Wing. The hall's bare walls are painted a pale blue and glass of various shapes and sizes hangs from the ceilings. The golden tiles contain a swirling design that mimics the artistry above.

When we are halfway down the hall, the girl looks around us to ensure our privacy before whispering, "I cannot believe you are here. I cannot believe I am speaking to you. The real woman of the wood."

I am taken aback by the glee in her voice, as if I am a celebrated patron rather than a lost misfit. She must have noticed my confusion as she explains, "The Keepers of the Red Wing are rooting for you. I know your kindness toward Junsen made an immense impression on us all."

"My kindness?" The confusion lives on my face. Junsen and I shared only a few words, mainly related to him helping me find supplies to write.

Her small smile widens. "Apologies, Miss. But the honored guests of Endoneth are indifferent at best and vile at most. It is refreshing to meet someone who *sees* us."

The final words touch me to the point of tears, but I blink them away before inquiring, "What is your name?"

She giggles gleefully. "Piré, but you mustn't say my name in public. It would mean social punishment for you and perhaps menial punishment for me." Her smile fades slightly, but her demeanor of excitement seems unfazed as she sways side to side.

"What can you tell me about Mairette? I haven't seen her in a few days."

This question halts her. "Miss Mairette is a very busy person," Piré begins, twirling a loose curl of her blonde locks in her pale hand. "I know she has been extraordinarily busy with the Greentime Ball. The week of the event is always the most stressful, everything having to be just so." She nods her head, almost as if to convince herself of her words.

"I would very much like to see her," I state plainly, hoping this young Keeper has enough sway to find Mairette and bring her to me.

Instead, the girl shakes her head slightly. "I am not sure I can…There are hundreds of Keepers, and I am but a lowly one. I have never spoken to Mairette, only heard her address our grouping." Her eyes turn to the floor as she anxiously shifts her weight from one foot to the other. "I am sorry, Miss." The defeat in her voice threatens the tears to return.

I reach out a hand to pat her shoulder. "It is perfectly alright, Piré," I whisper. "If you ever need a listening ear, merely convince your superior to provide me with my nightly tea. Better yet, I will request you by name."

The young woman's hazel eyes fill with wonder at my suggestion. "I can lead you back to the Red Wing once more if you would like to wait for Miss Mairette," she offers.

I shake my head. "I will return to my quarters, but thank you."

She nods in understanding. "I'm afraid I must return to my work!"

And with a brief bow of her head, she skips toward the end of the hall. I sigh as I watch her depart, a bit of sorrow for her position and the restrictions that accompany this life. But, as I turn to leave the hall of glass, I smile to myself as I remember my promise and hope to see her again soon.

The sun has barely begun its ascent as I make it to my room once more. When I pry open the wooden door, I'm startled by a kneeling figure hunched over my pile of incomplete letters. The curly red hair lifts slightly as the door shuts behind me.

With a page in her hand, Mairette turns to face me, two stray trails of water lining the edges of her cheeks. "It was my fault." She softly crunches the edges of the note. "I should not have encouraged it. I could not control it. I thought I could... could help." The more she speaks, the more tears stain her beautiful pink skin.

I rush to her side, kneeling to meet her level as her stray tears morph into sobs. My arm rests on her shoulders as they rise and fall in a sporadic rhythm. "Mairette, it is alright. You are not at fault! You were attempting to help, and I know that. It is alright."

I offer calming shh-ing along with continued assurances that she is completely blameless. We hold each other like this for a few minutes as she finds her breath.

When she is able to speak clearly, her words emerge in only a whisper, her voice exhausted, "Thank you, Miss. I promise… I promise I thought it would work."

I turn her shoulders to face me. "I know, my friend. I know."

I sternly request that Mairette remain in my suite to rest a bit as we leisurely—very, very leisurely—ready for the day. I offer her my morning tea, which she prepared and brought in the room before rummaging through my discarded notes, but she instead suggests making a fresh kettle for the two of us to share, since, in her words, "Cold tea is not true tea."

The trip to the kitchen and back takes around half an hour, enough time for me to tidy the balls of paper and put on a soft linen shift. The tea is gloriously warm and perfect for a cozy morning in. Notes of honey and dandelion wafting through the room. Rather than place the tray down and return to the Red Wing, Mairette sits in the red armchair while I curl up on my bed. I would offer to share the large space atop the duvet, but I know the disruption to her daily routine alongside the added rebellion of sharing my morning tea is enough of a stretch for her. Either way, the smile she offers as she sips from her cup is infectious and it soon feels like normal, as if the ritual had never occurred and we are simply taking a long morning to enjoy each other's company.

"Have you thought at all of the Greentime Ball?" She sips loudly after the intentional reminder of the important event. "It is a little over a week away and we must finalize the fabric for the dress you chose!"

While I barely thought about the ball during my time with Rostair, I know Mairette has spent hours stressing over every last detail. Piré's conversation confirmed to me that this ball is a reflection of not only the Ice Realm and Rostair, but also of her and the other Keepers. In that moment, as Mairette sets the cup on the petit saucer, her eyes gain the sparkling that accompanies a good idea.

"I know how much you have grown to appreciate the flowers of this realm. Perhaps we can incorporate them into the design." I see the wheels turning as she describes the gown. The conversation lingers on the topic of fashion for a moment before turning to cuisine then music. After a few hours it becomes clear that Mairette has a hand in almost every aspect of the ball itself, and that she revels in the planning process. It does follow her character as a routine-oriented and organized woman. I must admit, watching her glimmer with excitement lightens my heart, something that is needed after days of disappointment.

"Miss, what do you truly think?" She places a hand on my arm, jolting me from my thoughts.

"I am so sorry, please restate your question." I cough a bit before sipping the last of my cup.

Mairette does the same before smiling, "Is there anything you wish to include in the ball? A particular dance or food? A song or banner?"

I am honored by this question, and more than a bit taken aback. Mairette considering the opinions of an apparent outsider to this realm lightens my heart even more.

"I, uhh…" Nothing initially comes to my mind, but I hate to disrespect her after such a generous request. "May I think on it? This is gracious of you, to include a part of me in this momentous occasion. I want my choice to be more than meaningful."

She moves her hand to meet mine, her eyes shine with moisture. "That is a thoughtful decision, Miss."

"Nothing is working!" I slam my fist on the table in frustration. Rostair and I have been attempting this newest tactic for hours now. We've spent the past three days oscillating between the different memory exercises he found during his research.

The first day we listened to a variety of music, Rostair calling upon his best rotation of musicians to play different compositions, most from the Mountain Realm. We spent the entire day together, eating breakfast while listening to a lively waltz on violin; taking a stroll through the gardens followed by the court flautist; enjoying afternoon tea listening to a somber piano medley; and joining estate guests for dinner accompanied by a calming harp composition. I felt a spark of joy during tea, but nothing out of the ordinary.

The following day Rostair needed to tend to matters of the estate, which allowed me the opportunity to see Gazil and hear about the latest drama amongst the many guests visiting for the warmer season.

"The Southern crowd typically visits with the grass and leaves when the first flake falls." He sipped his black tea. "Most come to enjoy illicit affairs far from their homes, thinking the gossip won't reach beyond the walls of the realm. Most are right, which means we are always in for a show come Greentime Ball."

His laugh warmed my heart as he continued on, discussing the fashion trends and what he would look for at the ball. When Rostair finished his work later that second day, he insisted we return to the task of reclaiming my memories.

The next activity included paints and canvas. "The book claims that art encourages cognitive recovery," he explained, a look of confidence dispelling any doubts in my mind. While painting sparked no concrete memories, seeing Rostair struggle at something for the first time was well worth it. Smudges of pink and green paint stained his fine linen suit and orange streaks colored his hair as he feverishly developed his piece. My smile never wavered that day, my face grinning so wide it was sore as I lay in bed that night.

Yesterday's attempt to restore my memory involved learning several sporting games. Rostair claimed that playing familiar games could reveal a long-forgotten memory. We spent the morning on the large lawn, now bright green with grass and dotted with a few small flowers, playing a number of games involving throwing, kicking, and running. Rostair needed to take a break to visit the forest and stables, so I rested in my room. When he returned, we spent time in his personal study, learning a number of card games. My favorite involved matching pairs of cards and betting chocolate coins. Although I could not pinpoint a specific memory after those three days, I did learn that I have no talent in paint, an unusual knack for accuracy in field games, and a deep love for chocolate.

This brings us to the present attempt to recall my past. Goblets filled with various colored liquids line Rostair's wooden desk. I stand near the desk, a silken scarf covering my eyes and gobs of candle wax stuffed in my ears. We spent the hours together smelling each and every liquid Rostair's Keepers could find, after speaking with the head cook to prepare an array of options. He claims the scents may force me into a memory, one where I experienced similar smells, and isolating my other senses will increase the possibility of success. However, hours have passed, and with every new smell, I only become more frustrated with my lack of knowledge, the blurry memories flooding my mind and keeping me from any sort of clarity. The other activities were at least amusing. Spending more time with Rostair is never a chore to be certain. This is different. I can only hear muffled grumbles and see vague brightness.

"This is not working," I say again quietly, no fists involved, and I slowly pull the wax from my ears. "I feel no better now than I did when I first arrived." The words may sound harsh, but hopefully he understands the sentiment. My emotions frazzle as the wax breaks apart in my ears.

I feel Rostair shifting toward me, the rustling of his pale green skirt growing louder as I claw out clumps. As he nears, I smell a medley of sweet florals and calming eucalyptus, stronger than I've noticed before. The last ball of wax falls into my hands and I reach for the blindfold, eager to move on and possibly find more chocolate coins. Before I reach the knot centered behind my head, I feel the gentle touch of a hand, gliding over my fingers and holding them in place. "Perhaps there are other ways to help you remember…"

His words trail off as I feel his hand drift from my hands to my cheek, his thumb grazing the outline of my face and following the line down my neck. My heart pounds in my chest, thundering loud enough that I'm sure he senses my nerves. This brings up memories, memories of us. Flashbacks from the past few months, from laughing and strolling and feeling surprised and safe. Thoughts of Rostair flood my mind, taking over my senses. How can I feel so close to someone, yet know so little of them? I know his title, his responsibilities, his family. Yet who *is* he? Has he loved another before? Does he want to love again? The questions swarm my mind in seconds as one hand leaves my face and instead traces a finger along my arm, leaving goose bumps in its wake. The other hand holds my own near the knot of the fabric.

The blindfold feels like both a blessing and a curse. I want to see Rostair as he looks at me, see his eyes and what they express; but the unknown, the lack of control is thrilling. With each stroke of my arm, my excitement grows. I nearly jump back when I feel Rostair's lips whisper softly in my ear, "Does this remind you of anything? A person? A place? A moment?" The words are both calming and urgent, grasping at the possibility that I could remember. I hold my breath as his hands shift to my neck, tilting my head upward. My chest hurts from how fast my heart is beating and I cannot imagine the blush dusting my cheeks. Rostair traces the red mark I've grown to love despite its meaning or the unknown enemy it represents. The air in the room has grown thick with lust. I only hear our careful breaths mingling between us, as if we are both walking on precarious ice, hoping to savor one another in this moment without facing dangerous consequences. His grip tightens as I feel his nose nuzzle mine. Warmth spreads between my legs and I bring them together to relieve some of the tension.

Then, as the soft touch of his lips meet my own, a knock at the door disrupts the fantasy. I wish he would ignore it; I wish he would push me on his wooden desk and press his lips into mine more deeply. But, as soon as the Keeper knocks a second time, Rostair is already pulling the silken blindfold from my face and retreating behind the desk, concealing anything noteworthy from view. I retreat to a nearby armchair, a deep brown leather seat that smells of mahogany, and attempt to appear innocent.

"Come in," Rostair's voice booms through the study, sounding no longer like the sensual male from mere seconds before and instead commanding respect.

The lower Keeper trips through the doorway and lowers his head before announcing the arrival of a message from a realm commander. As the young lad recites the request, I can't help but admire the effect our closeness has on Rostair. His icy-white hair accentuates a flush of pink over his skin, and it takes his chest a moment to return to a normal pace. The bulge beneath his skirt is unmistakable, which explains why he hid behind his desk. When the Keeper finishes, offering Rostair a roll of parchment, presumably with the commander's letter, he bows his head once more before turning on his heel to leave.

As the door closes with a satisfying click, Rostair turns his attention to me. "I apologize, I must deal with this." He raises the scroll in his hand with a defeated grimace. "More work, I'm afraid. Men dying on the front."

I nod absentmindedly, avoiding eye contact as I imagine the fearful soldiers fighting for the realm. "Would you like to meet again tomorrow? We can take a break from brain teasers if you would rather visit the gardens or the stables?"

I wonder if Rostair processes intimacy more quickly than normal or if I merely take longer. "I would love to join you tomorrow," I say pitifully, giving a half-smile. "Wherever you would like to go."

Rostair rises and adjusts his skirt to mask any lingering evidence of our time together. "Stay here as long as you wish. I must meet my generals." He smiles, "Tomorrow?"

"Tomorrow," I confirm.

I linger after he leaves. Rostair's study is a curious space filled with objects strewn in piles across the floor. Chaotic. Cluttered. Utterly antithetical to his character.

I look through stacks of books behind his desk, curiously, until something catches my attention. While most objects are strewn here and there, a brown, leather bag is neatly settled beneath his desk, partially hidden by stacks of papers and books. While a violation of Rostair's privacy, the satchel calls to me; it seems so familiar. I duck my head under the wooden desk, though it's an unsuitable act to take from one's host, I'm sure. But, once the cool leather reaches my fingertips, my heart lifts.

I pull the strap of the bag over my head, clutching it near my chest as I rush to leave. My heart is racing, as if stealing something valuable, something precious. Sweat beads on my temples as I stalk the hallways, weaving my way through crowds of guests until I finally arrive at my room.

In the solitude of my chambers, the satchel almost glows with promise, looking more like a beacon of hope than that of uncertainty. Seated on one of the two couches, I trace the threads that hold together the tough leather. A gold pin clips the loose flap of the front clipped closed. The bag itself is small, only three of my handwidths wide and almost two tall. However, it is stuffed to the brim with something light. I unclasp the golden pin and patiently lift the flap to expose the contents. I turn the bag upside down and gently shake. A scarf falls to the ground with a satisfying plop followed by a small knife. My fingers reach for the smooth satin scarf, and the smell of cinnamon and citrus wafts toward me as I examine the piece more closely. The color fades beautifully from grey to onyx; the cotton strands sewn on the frayed edges are a shining silver. I graze my fingertips along the embroidery on the end of the scarf: an exquisite moth woven into the cloth with purple and blue thread. As I pull the scarf closer, it unravels and I hear a clanking of metal on the tile floor. I set the satin on my lap and peer over the side of the sofa. A small dagger rests on the ground, its marble hilt gleaming in the setting sunlight. My hand hovers over the weapon, as if holding it might sting, until I calmly swoop the handle into my palm, the black marble cooler than I anticipated. The steel of the blade is sharp, lethal, and feels natural in my fingers, an extension of my hand, of myself. The feeling of the blade brings me a sense of pure power and anticipation, like the knife itself breathes new life into me as I hold it close to my side. Before I get a detailed look at the delicate patterns shaped into its blade, a hurried knock disrupts my examination.

I rush to the chest of drawers on the far side of the room, open the lowest drawer and stuff the satchel and its contents inside.

"Centrea, may I come in? I convinced Mairette to let me bring you your tea, and she said I am allowed a few hours before she readies your hair for dinner." I am caught off guard by the sound of Rostair's voice. He sounds distraught and tired.

I look back at the chest of drawers to ensure the satchel is safely inside. "Come in!" Rostair looks as distraught as he sounds and certainly as tired. His hair is mussed and his clothes are abnormally wrinkled. He glides over to the sofa and places his head into his hands, rubbing his eyes and letting out a deep groan.

"Long day?" I ask casually as I join him, placing my hand on his knee.

He jolts back at the touch before looking up at me. "I am sorry, I haven't told you the full circumstances of the war, but it can be daunting at times." His voice catches a bit as he details the warfare erupting just beyond the borders of the Mountain Realm. "Our warriors have gathered in pockets throughout our allied realms, but we are struggling to face their numbers." His hand reaches to grasp mine, his eyes glued to the table in front of us. His entire body is tense, as if the world has fallen onto his shoulders and he—despite his best efforts—is struggling to hold the weight.

"There is one silver lining." Rostair pulls parchment from the inside pocket of his suede vest. "News from your family, Centrea."

A rush of joy seizes my chest. I grasp at the paper that holds the truth of my past, the truth that put me here in this place. Or, more accurately, the truth that left me in the cold wilderness of the Ice Realm.

My eyes feast upon the ink on the page, the words written in an interesting pattern of wide loops and sweeping punctuations. It details the story of a daughter who left her family—a family who wanted her, loved her—to fight in the war. The words from my father are sweet, apologetic.

"It seems you wanted to contribute in some way. Went against your parents' wishes. And they miss you, Yara," Rostair says softly.

The foreign name unsettles me. "Please, call me Centrea." That is who I am now, of that I am sure.

Rostair smiles weakly. "This news is wonderful. Yet, it makes me feel even more at fault for your position here. I know it has not been easy for you. The guests are perilous. And the war, you could have—"

"You can talk to me about anything you need." I feel his hand squeeze mine and I continue, "Even if it is not about the war or the court or any of it. I am merely here."

Rostair raises his other hand to touch my cheek, a look of desire shading his eyes. "Or we don't have to talk at all." I feel his fingers tangle into the knots in my hair, and he pulls my face forward to meet his.

The moment our lips meet feels like glorious wildfire, my entire body tingling as I press deeper into him. I stop the kiss just for a second to consent. "No, we certainly don't have to talk."

Rostair's kiss is different from our first admittedly brief experience. This is less deliberate and more impassioned. His hand leaves mine to trace the seam of my skirt until he reaches my shirt, slipping it up a bit to touch my bare back. The feeling of his coarse fingertips on my skin clouds my mind, every one of Mairette's warnings chased away until all that is left is my longing for this, for him. I throw my arms around his neck and pull him closer, and his knee shifts a bit to face me completely, leaning into my grasp. The hand on my back rubs circles while he pushes his tongue into my mouth. I moan as his tongue swipes along my bottom lip, and I welcome it. My hands furiously work to feel his body, untying the ribbon holding his tunic closed and running my fingers over his chest.

A knock halts our movements. "Miss, we should start preparing for dinner if you would like to make it on time tonight." I immediately pull back, running my hands through my hair and attempting to cool my blushing cheeks. Rostair looks equally frantic, lacing his tunic closed and pacing toward the opposite corner of the room. Mairette pops in without hearing a reply to her initial request and bows her head when she notices Rostair cowering in the corner like a reprimanded child. Clearly, he believed she would allow the allotted few hours she promised before seeing to my hair and face for the night.

Clearly, he was incorrect. "Good evening, Mairette. I will leave you to work your magic for the night's festivities."

He hurries toward the exit offering a brief, "I will see you at dinner, Centrea," before slamming the door.

I avoid Mairette's judgmental look as she sets down her tools. Nothing could bring me down from the high I feel. She brings a few brushes for the palettes of eye and lip paints as well as some gold to thread through my hair, as I have started to favor the style. For the evening, I change into an emerald spring dress that flares outward and cuts short at my knees. The top is gilded with pearls of various sizes, individually sewn to create a masterful pattern. The colors on my face echo that of the dress. Mairette creates a deep green with the paints that covers my eyelids and spreads toward my temples. She even manages to place delicate pearls along the swooshes of green.

"It is beautiful, as always," I gasp. Although I should be heaping praise upon Mairette to shift her attention away from what she saw between me and Rostair earlier, I truly mean the compliment.

I suppose I am glad to not indulge in too much praise as she ignores the statement and instead approaches the topic I've been trying to avoid with no hesitation. "What were you thinking?" She sighs, wiping the brushes on a cleaning cloth and peering into my eyes, concern and frustration mixing together in seas of violet.

"It… it just happened. I could not tell you how, or why, truly. I just, it feels natural and safe."

Mairette sighs again, a bit more sympathetic this time. "It is like I have said before, I am only interested in your well-being." I begin to suspect her early arrival was not a mistake as she continues, "While I am sure he is interested in the mysterious and breathtaking woman from the wood," I wince at the nickname on her lips, "I feel his intentions are not to be with you completely. And I do not want to see you hurt."

"I am a mystery no more," I whisper under my breath.

Mairette's eyes grow wide. "Are you not?"

My smile grows. "Yara, apparently." I curtsy slightly. "Though I do not feel connected to such a name."

She nods in return, her eyes scanning the tiles on the floor, as if piecing together the information that leads to this truth. "I am happy for you," she whispers.

I look again in the mirror before me as Mairette makes final adjustments to the gold flakes settled in my hair. "I appreciate your friendship a great deal, you know that right, Mairette?"

Her hands stop their work, folding on her chest as she responds, "Yours is a friendship I will forever treasure, Miss."

I twist on my heel and face her. "Please, call me Centrea." I wait for her to shake her head or provide a lecture on the proper ways to address a guest of Endoneth.

Instead, she takes my hands and smiles, "Centrea, my dear friend." A tear rolls down her cheek before she hastily releases my hand to wipe it away. I feel there are more words unsaid, yet Mairette merely continues her work.

The dinner that night was uneventful. More guests arrive daily, and thus an overflow dining hall opened to account for the increase. I often wonder how much food it takes the kitchen to prepare for such a large household of people. In the height of winter, when I arrived at Endoneth, there were around forty socialites staying at the estate. Now the number is more than double that original estimation. Mairette claims most Greentime Balls boast more than five hundred attendants. The additional guest wing, the Green Wing, opens the week before the ball, providing ample space for the abundance of visitors. According to Gazil, some leave directly following the event, merely showing face at an elite ball for clout before making their way to a warmer climate.

However, many stay for the majority of the Greentime season and leave before the second winter arrives.

Gazil asks me to join him for dessert and drinks in the library after dinner, to which I happily oblige. "You know, the longer I live in this estate, the more I see patterns of behavior. Look at this one." He nods to a lady clad in red walking alongside a tall man dressed in a silver gown as we round the corner toward the main staircase. "She purposefully sat near this lad to gain his attention, and drew him aside to isolate him from the other guests." He chuckles a bit as we ascend the stairs, the tiles shifting from a pleasant gold to a bright orange, the designs filled with winged creatures similar to those Rostair spoke to on the platform. "No doubt she will ask for his favor at the Greentime Ball, and he will have no other option but agree."

The mindless gossip is such a pleasant reprieve from my thoughts of Rostair and the dagger in my bedroom drawer. "What would that imply?" I look inquisitively down at Gazil as we step onto the second floor.

"A favor implies that you agree to save your affections for only one during the entire season of first spring." Gazil reaches for one of the braids of his beard. "This is an important promise, a bond that is honor bound. And to refuse a proposal comes with its own implications: dishonor upon the proponent, disrespect for their house or realm, even an intentional jab at their position in the realm. All relationships are ultimately about power, remember that." He squeezes my arm as we enter the main library, settling onto our usual couch and shuffling a deck of cards to ready a new match.

Gazil consistently chooses to drink during our meetings, typically hard liquor and typically more than one glass. Though I do not believe I have seen the man in a drunken stupor—he holds his alcohol well—there have been a few times where I notice a bit of a slurring of his words. Whether nervous about the newcomers who arrived just this morning or worried about the completion of his outfit, Gazil finishes his fourth drink and calls Junsen to bring him one more.

"Just a glass of wine to finish." He clumsily waves his hand toward the pale boy, and Junsen's deep brown eyes plead for me to care for my friend in his growing vulnerable state. I could already feel the eyes of others judging his heavy-handed pours tonight, and I would hate for him to be the topic of gossip for the nights to follow.

"Gazil, would you want to join me for a night stroll?" I grasp his clammy hand in my own. "You know how I do enjoy the gardens and, with spring upon us, it is finally warm enough to see them in the moonlight."

Gazil's milky eyes peer at me with sudden amusement. "My dear, that sounds like a fantastic idea!" He bolts to his feet so suddenly, dragging my hand along with him as he reaches the door in an instant. I look back to Junsen, a bit surprised at the spryness of my old friend, and nod my appreciation. He returns the gesture, a look of relief on his face as he turns to serve the remaining patrons in the room.

When we arrive outside, I realize I severely underestimated the chill that thrives without the sunshine. Goose bumps cover my as I run after my friend, and the short sleeves of the dress provide no warmth from the breezes of cold air. Gazil, however, appears utterly unfazed as he saunters in a zigzag pattern along the paved walkway toward the archway of the gardens. His thin tunic is unbuttoned at the top and his silken pants are certainly unsuited to brave the cold.

"Gazil," I call after him, stepping quickly to keep pace. "Gazil, do be careful. I feel as if your mind might be working faster than your feet."

Perhaps not the truest statement, at least not in his present state, but I needed to say something to bridge the gap between us so I could at least assist him in navigating the maze of florals. He pauses to consider my statement enough for me to grasp his arm and link it with my own, inadvertently working as a crutch for his quickly tiring body.

"My liver cannot hold liquor as it once could, when I was a mere boy traveling the realms with not a care in the world." Gazil sweeps his hands toward the sky as I slow his pace to a natural stride. "You know, leaders, warriors, they all believe they truly understand what the world needs, what real people need. But it is the observers that know… that know exactly what is going on and who should get what and when."

His words are definitely slurring now, and his feet are becoming like cinder blocks dragging along the ground. I think through a map of the gardens in my head to contemplate the quickest exit and turn his body to make our way there.

"You see, I did everything, and I mean *everything*, for my realm. It has always been my duty to watch, to listen, to breathe, to drink, to dance, to LIVE." He stops as he screams the last word into the night, sinking down into the grass and leaning against one of the large bushes. I sigh and follow, honestly happy to be relieved of the heavy weight of the man. "I live for this, for *them*." His arms wave around in frantic circles in the air as he continues to rant, "And they want me, ME to give it all away. And for what? A war? A war that we cannot win." He shakes his head. My hands and feet grow colder as his thoughts turn darker and more desperate. "You know. You *know* we cannot win. And he still controls it all, controls us all…I just do not think I can do it anymore." The poor man begins sobbing, his twisted expression covered by his hands as he weeps. I am stunned, my three closest friends breaking down in the span of one day is too much. My emotional capacity is superseding its limits.

We sit like this for a long while—Gazil rocking back and forth, his head in his hands while I sit with one arm wrapped around my exposed knees and the other lays on his arm, offering the only emotional support I can muster—until I hear a stern voice from nearby.

"Do not fret, Gazil has always been a sad drunk." Rostair's cold words break something in the garden, a feeling of benevolence replaced with harsh judgment.

To his credit, he offers a steady hand to the older man, allowing him a place to rise from his pitiful position and regain his footing. "My Lord, I-I am sorry. You know how the Greentime approaching makes me feel. I just… I could not—"

"Get cleaned up and get to bed, Keeper of Records."

Gazil appears the opposite of how I've known him to be. He fumbles over his words and refuses to make eye contact with Rostair before his attempts to communicate his emotional distress are cut short.

The command in Rostair's voice immediately forces Gazil to straighten his spine. He gives me a slight nod good night before slowly making his way back inside.

I look at my friend, who is struggling a bit to stay on the stones leading to the entryway. "Do you think he can make it to his room alone in such a state?"

My eyes shift to look at Rostair for a moment before concern pulls me back to watch the old man once more. "He should be fine; I have warned the Keepers of the Blue Wing of his arrival. They are accustomed to assisting those in such a state back to their appropriate rooms." He sighs, pinching the ridge of his nose before turning towards me. "You are gracious to comfort him, but know he is a man who has a reputation for being stuck in his ways and stuck in the past."

The words feel like tiny pricks in my heart. Gazil has become a valued person in my life and such words do not do him justice. "It sounds as if the stress of the upcoming ball may be wearing on us all."

These words seem to surprise Rostair as he cautiously examines me. "Are you weary? I hope the responsibilities of being Guest of Honor are not overwhelming you..."

He reaches a hand to graze my arm, the cold causing the skin to erupt in bumps anew. "I am only concerned for my friends," I reply, placing a reassuring hand over his. "All of my friends."

This brings a smile to his face, a sight that sends a shiver through me. "I apologize for our many failures this week." The smile lingers on his face with this statement. "I hope you are not too disappointed."

I shake my head feverishly. "Perhaps I should focus less on my past, and more on my future." I made this same determination before but feel more certain of its validity now, with Rostair edging closer to me, with the stars ushering in a glow of romantic light.

"What are you doing outside at night?" I ask curiously. "Do you not have dozens of new guests to entertain, to perhaps claim one for the season and ask for their favor?" The final words leave my throat before I can filter them in my brain. Perhaps Gazil was not alone in consuming one too many drinks tonight. Rostair's brows lift high on his forehead, and he releases a hearty laugh, the first glimpse of true joy I've seen in his face today.

"I am outside to make my weekly rounds, ensuring all is well." His face grows mischievous as he inches closer to me, pushing us back behind a wall of bushes that conceal us from view. "As for my favor," he brushes his thumb over my bottom lip, "that is something of great value that I do not offer to merely anyone."

My heartbeat gains a manic pace, heat spreading in my core. I feel wetness tinge my undergarments as Rostair looks at me from head to toe. I desperately attempt to keep Mairette's warnings in my mind as I watch him silently undress me with his eyes, his tongue swiping over his bottom lip. His eyes linger on my breasts, the cold breeze causing my nipples to peak through the emerald fabric. A look of animal hunger shades his brow as he turns his eyes to my neck, pebbled with bumps from the cold and streaks of red at his intimate attention. He leans his face close, brushing his nose against my collarbone before offering the barest trace of his lips on my neck, tracing a line from my shoulders to my ear.

When he reaches the side of my face, his breaths coming in rapid spurts, he whispers, "I only offer my favor to those I deem worthy. Do you believe yourself worthy?"

I feel his hands desperately reaching for the bottom of my short dress, grasping the edge of my thighs with one hand while cupping my ass in the other. "Tell me, Centrea." He draws his fingers along my inner thigh, swirling them in tantalizing patterns along my thick leg. "Are... you... worthy?" His fingers sweep along the edge of the undergarments, no doubt feeling the evidence of my arousal.

Mairette is likely just overprotective, seeing me perhaps as the young daughter she never had. I gasp as he presses his palm flat between my legs, pushing me against the row of bushes before beginning a circling motion over my most sensitive spot. The movement utterly immobilizes me, and all thoughts of Mairette are silenced as my body demands more.

With his lips still pressed against my ear, I feel him developing a smooth rhythm between his hand and his breath, forcing small whimpers from me that develop into moans of pleasure. "Tell me, sweet one," he coaxes into my ear, the warm breath of his words shooting even more pleasure down into my core, "do you know how beautiful you truly are?"

He releases his palm from my center unceremoniously before reaching to pull my undergarments down completely. "Gods, your thighs and ass are so gorgeous, so voluptuous, I wish I could see them in the light of day." He successfully pulls the cotton fabric away from my aching wetness and tosses them in the soft grass below us.

I only nod in response before he pulls his head away enough to look into my eyes, "Is this what you want?" The question pulls me back into reality for just a moment as I consider the implications of this act before nodding my approval.

"Please, Rostair."

The second I say his name, my voice more desperate than I anticipate, he plunges his fingers into me, holding me steady with his other hand while he begins another rhythm of thrusts and breaths.

He leans in again to whisper, "This is what I wanted since I first saw you that night in the snow." His thrusts grow more rapid, his thumb reaching up to circle the sensitive area again as he continues, "Your sweet face, your red mark, your courage; it made me want you."

My body is writhing beneath him, gasps of pleasure echoing through the night louder than I intend. He continues to stroke me until I feel a brightness between my legs, the culmination of stokes and thrusts and whispers.

The tension builds and builds before I suddenly shake with pleasure. "I hope this was everything you wanted as well, Centrea." His lips feel like sweet dessert as they give a gentle kiss on my temple. I slump into the bushes and close my eyes, regaining my composure and steadying my breath. When I open my eyes to face Rostair, he is gone. I peek around the corner to see his blue suit slipping into the house, as if our worlds had not just been cemented together.

# A Letter from the Front

*Dearest Sister,*

*War appears to linger on far longer than we ever imagined. It feels as if just yesterday I hugged you goodbye. The memory of your warmth and support often gets me through the days. Strange what months digging trenches can do to memories—some wither away or become almost indiscernible, as if covered in the same muck that I wake up in everyday. Others act like a lifeline. An escape. And gods, do I need an escape.*

*Funny that this whole mess began with a death. The murder of one woman. One Lady of Endoneth. But as mum warned us: Death begets death. Suppose she'd be disappointed by my position here. A ladder climber in the Ice Realm's army. I like to think she would be proud, but we both know better. She never much enjoyed the blood necessary for peace. True peace.*

*But you understand.*

*I wish you could fight alongside us, though I know you have your own mountains to climb. Our family to provide for. And we all serve the Realm in different ways.*

*I hear whispers of the Southern "king." That he left the fighting for the Ice Realm. They say he seeks a weapon from Rostair, something that will turn the tides of this war. Even in his absence, the soldiers from the South far outnumber our own, led by the dreaded Night Flyers. Say what you will about the uncivilized Southerners, their warriors understand how to move in darkness. Like cursed snakes on the hunt. Yet even snakes make a hissing sound to alert their prey.*

*I wonder if this was all inevitable. If the bastard assassin from the Star Realm would always begin this war. If I would always leave home to fight—so young, so eager, so stupid. If this war was always meant to irrevocably alter the landscape of the Mountain Realm, and perhaps our own Realm next. I wonder if...*

*It is useless to wonder, I'm sure. But sometimes, it helps to think that nothing could change the course of this life. Perhaps you feel that too.*

*Yours,*
*J*

The week of the Greentime Ball, all Keepers hold their breath as they prepare the most illustrious estate for the most anticipated event in the Northern realms.

"Centrea!" I anticipated the look of horror, and perhaps, a tinge of amusement on Mairette's face was one that I anticipated.

I knew when I arrived in my room last night, the hibiscus tea already cold on the nightstand, I would have to face her ire in the morning. However, I had not considered the physical repercussions of my after-dinner drinks. My head pounds as I slowly take the morning brew into my hands. Although Mairette appears surprised, she knew enough of my whereabouts to understand what tea would best soothe my aching head, and the air fills with aromatic ginger and cloves.

"He just, I just…" I honestly do not know the best justification for my actions other than, *I wanted him.*

Based on the look frozen on her face, I doubt that would amend the situation. "I was careful," I said with a shrug. "We did not soil my purity; it was merely a bit of passionate, intimate, and soul-altering fun."

She stifles a chuckle at my pitiful summary of the night's events and shakes her head. "You are both adults, and we are nearing a time to declare favor. Who knows, maybe you will be fortunate enough to finally force the Lord to make a choice."

I place the tea down on the table with a loud thud, a bit of liquid spilling onto the wooden surface. "What are you implying? Has he never proposed his favor to another?"

Mairette sits on the sofa opposite mine and sighs. "Well, he is in his twenty-eighth year and has never shown favor to another." My eyes widen as she continues the tale. "At first, people assumed he was just shy, waiting on another to ask for favor instead of initiating himself. However, in his nineteenth year, a young man approached him and left disappointed. Then the assumption was that perhaps he favored women and not men. But when a woman boldly asked for his favor a few years later, he still denied it. Now, all are afraid to face rejection and have accepted his forced position of solitude."

I sit with this information before inquiring, "Do you think he has known another?"

Mairette laughs a bit. "Well, I am certain he has! Intimacy and favor are quite different in this realm." She attempts to explain as confusion contorts my features. "Sex is natural, a desire surely but one that is understood by all. It is when one claims you that honor begins to blur the lines between lust and disrespect. The Lord does lust, it is true. He has taken many into his bed. However, he has never given attention to these individuals. Never taken them on walks. Never given them tours of Endoneth. These actions are beyond what I have ever seen from him, and I have known him since his youth."

She reaches over the table to touch my hands which had started fidgeting in response to her words. "This is why I ask you to protect your heart, protect yourself. We are all in unprecedented territory here. Have fun, but tread lightly."

I look into her eyes and see the comfort of a friend, an older and much wiser friend who wants only the best. "Of course, Mairette."

With my words as assurance, she leans back on the sofa. "Also, please do continue to share the details of these nightly trysts. As Greentime grows nearer, I am sure you won't be alone in the revelry." Her cheeks flush a bit at the admission.

"And what of you?" I grin. "Who are you enjoying in the night?"

Her head tips back and she lets out a howling laugh. "Do you think I have time for lust when there is so much to be done?"

I join in her merriment, the response so consistent with who I know her to be. But a bit of desire spurs inside me. I want her to feel wanted as I did last night.

Mairette jumps from her place and busies herself with her morning chores, namely offering clothing options before preparing my hair and face for a new day. "We shall meet in the main study after your lunch to discuss the Greentime Ball further," she commands as she twists a lock of hair in place. "We are officially only one week away and there is still so much to prepare. The Lord of the estate is taking more of an interest this season for an unknown reason." I feel her eyes cutting toward me. "Yet we must continue to do our part. Your dress is nearly complete, and we must ensure you know all the steps to the traditional dances."

I sigh heavily at the thought of memorizing movements but am glad my afternoons with Mairette have gone back to normal.

Lunch and dinner are held in the common dining hall, though not everyone is expected to attend. However, most guests appreciate the conversation and opportunity to display their social or fashionable prowess. Considering guests' aversion to my presence alongside Rostair's responsibilities forcing his attention elsewhere, I rarely attend lunch and avoid dinners when I can help it. Instead, Mairette often brings meals to my room. Talking with Gazil is usually my sole reason for eating a formal meal at Endoneth, although the constant stares and whispers begin anew each day as new guests arrive. I cannot pretend no other aristocrats have been welcoming. I receive a few nods or small, quick smiles when others are distracted. Yet, no person has ventured so far as to hold a conversation with me, and only a few have asked for a silent dance at various social gatherings. The isolation contrasts the growing attention I receive from Rostair, yet I have learned to tune it out.

The hall itself is large, of course, with high ceilings and seven golden chandeliers that mimic the golden jeweled design on the tiled floors. One rectangular table, long enough to host fifty seats, is decorated with floral arrangements that reflect the seasonal blooms. The walls are white brick and display six large, blue banners, each lined with a specific color and embroidered animal. The first banner is outlined with white and features the silhouette of a running fox, then there's a silver border with a sitting rabbit, black with a detailed crow, green with a butterfly, brown with a roaring bear, and the last of the flags contains a shining golden border with the beautiful outline of a pegasus. On each end of the hall, two towering fireplaces crackle with large fires. Every time I join for a meal in the common dining hall, I tend to spend more time staring into the blazing fires or the embroidered banners than listening to the continuous hum of conversations around me.

I enter the main dining hall today in search of Gazil, wanting to check on the status of his own headache. Pushing through other latecomers, I find an opening and glance around the dining table, searching for the hunched shoulders and grey hair of my friend. It takes me a few minutes, but I spot him slouched low at the corner of the room. His placement alone speaks volumes. Gazil typically situates himself at the center of the room—the best place to overhear the most people, so he says. Sighing, I brave the crowd to find respite in the corner, sliding myself in an empty chair near Gazil. The fine blue cushions help ease my sore body and I turn to see him slowly shifting his head toward mine, each inch of movement clearly causing a constant pounding pain in his head.

"You seem chipper after last night." He winks and quickly grasps his temple in response to the sudden movement, clutching a fresh blue bruise staining his skin.

I see a Keeper in the corner nearby and wave her over to ask for water, "and perhaps some raw eggs, if you could."

The Keeper nods and turns quickly toward the door to the kitchen corridor. While the kitchens themselves are located in the Red Wing, the series of hidden passages help Keepers avoid guests and deliver goods. The great hall to the kitchen is an important passage, and it only takes the Keeper a moment before she places two full cups of water and a mug of eggs before us. I nod my thanks, and the Keeper bows her head briefly before shuffling back to her place, waiting to be summoned by another needy guest. Gazil sends me a withering look before gulping the three yolks down his throat. I wince as he wipes his lips, holding his nose a bit before finally regaining a bit of his composure.

"Last night was…" I honestly do not know how to approach the topic with Gazil, not wanting him to feel embarrassed while assuring him that I feel no judgment toward him and his choices.

"It was a mess, no need to minimize it for my benefit." He finishes the sentence on my behalf.

My hand moves reflexively to his arm, and I shift a bit closer in my seat. "Gazil, you know I treasure you and the transparency of our friendship. Never feel ashamed for who you are or what you do. Never around me." The words leave my lips as a whisper, as I note the increasing number of people flooding the room and finding their seats around us while we sip on our water.

Gazil's eyes grow hazy before he rubs his fingers over the lids. "I believe it is the week of Greentime. It is always a very intense and stressful week. I merely overdid it last night in preparation. Then I stumbled into walls on my way to my chambers, like an utter oaf." He rubs his wrist, red marks lining the skin. He takes a breath and a brief grin grows.

I sense his nerves easing and take the opportunity. "So tell me, sweet friend," my voice a bit brighter and only a bit louder as I attempt to distract him from last night's decisions, "who here do we think will declare their favor today?"

Like all questions of society, my query sends Gazil on another intense and animated rant about favors and names and houses and so on. Apparently, one of Gazil's duties in the realm requires him to record all favored matches each year and list them in an archive for the Lords.

"It is a position I have held for many decades now, the Keeper of Records. And it is not one I take lightly! When the former Lady of Endoneth assigned me this task, I promised her that not a name would be out of place. It took much to please her, but she saw something within me, a potential to be of service to the realm. Using my talents of observation to benefit us all."

I smile at the pride written on his face, the accomplishment radiating from his being as he discusses his work. "It is as I have said many times, dear Centrea: Knowledge is power, and gossip is knowledge."

He squeezes my hand and releases it when a Keeper brings us plates filled with leafy greens accompanied by a grilled filet of meat. Gazil digs into the meal, although I know him well enough to know he is still listening to the world around us, attempting to capture any important news or the earliest evidence of romantic entanglements. I think back to my conversation with Mairette just this morning and consider asking him about Rostair. I shake my head and plunge my own fork into the thick slab of meat. This is not the place to discuss such things, especially about a Lord and an unknown woman with no past. A flash of Rostair in the pool darkens my countenance.

"It is not customary for men like myself to find a match of compatibility, of love..."

Even if I were to gain Rostair's favor, his duty is to the realm. And I am starting to think that perhaps Mairette is right: I may want a romance that is enduring, an intimacy that has the potential to lead somewhere. I fear that Rostair, for all of his many fine attributes, will need to marry for the realm rather than his heart. I chew a piece of brown meat as I contemplate this in my mind, staring up at the noble pegasus embroidered in gold.

I beg Gazil to save me from my afternoon dance lesson with Mairette, but he reminds me of my role as Guest of Honor and insists he must begin preparing papers to complete his own role. "You will love it!" he claims in an attempt to lull me into submission. "I've seen you dance many times!"

His lips curl upwards as he slowly walks away, waving a hand behind him as he says, "Perhaps you will coax even me onto the dance floor this year." I roll my eyes and start toward the ballroom in the Silver Wing, admiring the ombre shift from gold to silver in the tiles lining the wide expanse of hallway.

Mairette waits for me, twirling a bit as she whispers numbers under her breath. For a woman of middling age, she is limber and quick, moving her feet in a daunting rhythm as she recounts the movements in her head. When she hears me approaching, she cuts her routine short. "Good afternoon, Centrea."

I grin at my friend and the courage it takes to say my name freely aloud. "Hello once again, what shall we learn today?" She hands me a stack of folded clothing and instructs me to change in a nearby restroom. "We will be practicing for a few hours, which means you will likely sweat." This is not welcome news; however, I bow my head slightly, grab the clothing, and head toward the room. I am glad Mairette provided appropriate clothing for this lesson. After two hours of movement, my linen tunic and shortened skirt are drenched in sweat.

"You need to move your hips a bit more during the sixth count of this verse." She models the movement for me, exaggerating the way her hips lean side to side before gesturing for me to echo her example. With no music to guide my motions, she counts me in, and I quickly move my feet from left to right before swishing my hips as she instructed.

When I finish the whole dance, she claps her hands in approval. "Well done! Would you like to drink, and we may try it once more?"

I nod, determined to make this run-through flawless. After drinking a bit of water, I slide toward the center of the ballroom, which is eerily empty except for the two of us. The lack of audience gives me confidence as I begin the steps of the dance. This particular solo is upbeat, one that not every Guest of Honor is able to accomplish, but, once Mairette witnessed my potential, she insisted I learn. The numbers echo through the grand space as she yells them out, guiding my movements with the constant rhythm of her voice. The dance itself is exhilarating, empowering. While the traditional dances are more stoic or conservative, the one Mairette chose for me is stunning and sultry, filled with swirling hip movements and turns. As I practice with only her as my observer, I feel compelled to put more soul into the movements, not minding the length of my skirt shifting upward to reveal a bit of unbecoming flesh. The first time this occurred during practice, Mairette laughed a bit and scolded me for my lack of appropriate undergarments before I reminded her that my skirt this morning was floor-length. Regardless, with no one else here, I feel free to show more of myself, of my body.

The dance continues for a few minutes, my heart racing as I sweep my hips in smooth circles and flick my hair from side to side. "You needn't be so sensual, Centrea," Mairette scolds, the mothering side of her returning as the dance routine comes to a close.

I slide my body forward, reaching down with both hands and, just to watch her squirm a bit more, I graze my fingers along the sides of my body, starting at my ankles, lifting a bit of my skirt and pushing in my breasts before weaving my hands through my hair. The movement has the impact I desire, and Mairette rolls her eyes, chuckles a bit, and waves her hands at me. "I know that you know the movements. That should be enough for today." I beam back at her and give an exaggerated bow, raising my skirt to expose myself once more to the empty ballroom around us.

Mairette gathers her things, a checklist for today along with water and a quill, before saying, "We will practice again this week, but be thinking about hairstyles and perhaps something beautiful to paint." She looks at my face and scrunches her brows, deep in thought. "I was thinking a silver look for your eyes, but maybe pink would be brighter."

She mumbles something to herself before leaving me alone in the large ballroom. As much as I hate to admit it, Gazil was correct in his estimation of my love of dance. But, to my own credit, I did not realize dance could be this liberating. The movements typical of a jaunt or waltz are nothing like what I just displayed, and it takes everything within me to take a moment to breathe before rushing to dance on my own again. As I sit in the silence of the room, I look out at the green fields and trees, once laced with snow and now standing tall, unhindered by the weight of the cold ice. The spell holding the room together allows the smell of spring to filter through, while its warmth remains at bay. I sigh deeply and take another sip of water before rising once more to use the space to dance, just a few more minutes.

I held back when Mairette was watching, but, now alone, I dance with reckless abandon, letting out my frustrations and fears with a series of jumpy movements. My head flicks back and forth, mirroring the swishing of my hips and I reach down my hand and snap my body back into place. Mairette was right: The movements are sensual, which only emboldens my confidence and pushes me to do more, hopping from one foot to the other, grasping the sides of my body and touching my hourglass form. The sweat trickles down my forehead and beads of sweat pool between my breasts. I lift the bottom of my tunic slightly to encourage a bit of air as I slow my movements slightly. I look around the room as I pace in a circle, keeping my heartbeat up while also ensuring I am truly alone.

I glance outside and see a glimpse of the gardens, a flash of last night running through my mind. The memory sparks me to move again, so I raise my arms above my head and throw my body in various directions before settling on the ground, my knees thrown forward and my back flush against the cool tiles. My breathing is ragged, heat growing between my open thighs as I picture Rostair whispering in my ear as he trails his fingers along the hem of my dress. My hair billows around me like a crown of brown, my chest heaving. I reach my hands along the side of my chest and down my belly. I picture his silver hair shining in the moonlight as he reached for me, grabbed me as if he wanted me, needed me. My hands tremble as they reach the top of my skirt, slick from the sweat that still coats my body. I close my eyes, remembering the chill in the air, the way he stared at my firm breasts, the way he grabbed my ass in his hand. The heat grows deeper, more fervent as the thoughts flood my mind, the feeling of his hands stained on my body, his words echoing through my brain:

*Is this what you want?*

"Yes," I whisper to myself as I delicately move my hand below the seam of the skirt, hovering over my throbbing center, where Rostair pleasured me the night before. I focus my mind on that moment as I repeat his motions, forcing me to writhe on the floor.

*Do you know how beautiful you truly are?*

My mind is reeling, the pressure of my own touch sending shooting flashes of pleasure down my legs.

*This is what I wanted since I first saw you.*

I sweep two fingers along the aching between my legs, each swipe building closer to release, my hips working in tandem with my hand.

*Your sweet face, your red mark, your courage; it made me want you.*

I press into myself, applying blissful pressure to my core, whispering moans to myself as I get closer and closer.

*I hope this was everything you wanted as well, Centrea.*

Pleasure washes over me in satisfying bursts. I lie on the ground a few seconds before jumping up and looking around to remind myself I am truly alone. The sun is inching its way lower in the sky. I gather my skirt from earlier today and walk toward my chambers.

I walk slowly back through the maze of hallways toward the Blue Wing. My thighs tremble from the effort of this afternoon's dance lesson. I hope the tiredness in my body allows my mind to rest without the interruption of another nightmare. I scan the walls of the hallway as I wander through the Gold Wing, stopping to look into the dining hall. It looks even more grand with no people, no food, only the colossal fireplaces still blazing with heat. I stare up at the blue banners, the threads beautifully woven into the six beasts before me.

"The guardians are beautiful creatures." A mousey voice emerges from the corner of the room as Piré quietly closes the door to the passageway.

"Guardians?" I look at her inquisitively. "I've gathered the connection to the ages." I point to the borders lining each banner. "They represent colors, correct?"

Piré inches closer, balancing a large basket of fruits in her tiny arms. She slowly hoists the basket onto the large table and lets out a weary sigh, shaking her arms a bit before walking toward me.

"You are observant, Miss. Each creature holds meaning to the family of the estate. We are in the Gold Age, and our original lord favored the winged horse." She points toward the pegasus. "You know they are here, in Endoneth, in the stables. I heard a woman made the trek there with the Lord of the house." She attempts to stifle a giggle to no avail, her words continuing at a rapid speed. "I cannot be certain; however, the stable Keepers saw a beautiful companion to the Lord..." she trails off, seeing my cheeks grow the palest shade of pink as she reveals how much those who live in the Red Wing know. "Apologies, Miss." Her head bows low. "The flags, they do, they represent each age of course. I also apologize for the tea. My superior says that we can shift duties after the Greentime Ball. There is much to do. But I will be sure to help with your tea after the event, Miss. I am so sorry. I will try to avoid the gossip; it is inappropriate, I know." The apron lining her brown muslin dress creases a bit as she stares at her tan, leather shoes.

I reach my hand gently beneath her chin and tip it upward, giving her permission to lift her head once more. "Piré," saying her name out loud forces her to look anxiously around the room to ensure we are truly alone, "it is completely normal for people to talk, to gossip, to share information. One of my closest friends speaks constantly about the power of words." I rest my hand on her shoulder as her eyes look deep into my own. "Do not let anyone take away your power."

At those words, the young Keeper straightens her small stature, raising her head high. "Thank you, Miss. It is difficult to put into words how much that means to me."

I nod. "I understand what it is like to be ignored, but know that knowing yourself can be most liberating."

The look on Piré's face is unlike any I have seen so far in Endoneth. A mixture of hope and wonder glimmer in her hazel eyes. "Do you really think there could ever be," her words are light, almost floating into the air as she speaks them, "ever be a world that feels like that?"

I look at the girl, likely only eighteen years of age, staring at pieces of fabric like there is another world, another way. "Feels like what?"

She turns to me quizzically. "Power."

Piré's look of optimism makes a deep impression upon my heart. While I love Mairette providing tea and company, it will be wonderful to see the young Keeper even more after the ball. I decide to spend the evening in, hoping to rest a bit after a long day. The room attached to my main suite contains a large marble bathroom, and the bath tonight helps soothe the soreness in my legs and abdomen. The cotton nightgown hugs my hips and makes me feel ready for the night. I sit near the writing chair to contribute to my running log of the days' events. It appears foolish to put anything between Rostair and me on paper, so I write minimal notes using the most basic descriptions. I look back at my notes on the history of Endoneth, remembering the mysterious message in the margins.

I wonder what "Zeal" could mean. Is it a person? Perhaps the name of one of the fairies I met in passing. Or an animal, the name of a woodland creature? I set these words to paper and look over the ideas.

Another concept comes to mind. I push away from the desk and walk toward the chest of drawers, slowly opening it to retrieve my satchel. When I lift the leather strap in my hands, blurs fade in and out of my mind, my brain striving to develop a memory, any memory from the past. I sling the strap around my bare shoulder and walk toward my bed.

I turn the bag over just as I did only a few nights ago, allowing the contents to fall gently upon the blankets of the bed. Again, I take the scarf in my hands, the shining fabric slipping through my fingertips over and over. Again, I see the dagger, laying delicately, innocently atop the duvet, the handle gleaming, waiting to be yielded. The satchel itself is sturdy, made for long days of exploration and adventure. It does renew a curiosity within me about who owned this bag. Who dragged it through the ice storms mere months ago. Who packed the scarf and dagger safely inside. Who knew this satchel like she knew herself. Again, it feels so familiar to me. I briefly close my eyes and imagine it is mine for a moment, daydreaming of the scarf wrapped around my neck; the daggers strapped to my thighs. The daydream feels too real as if the bag truly belongs to me. I wonder if perhaps Rostair forgot to give it to me, thinking it insignificant. But, there would be no reason to keep it from me.

While at first glance, it appears simple, upon closer inspection, I see beautiful designs along the edges of the leather, drawings of delicate vines etched in a darker brown. The patterns must have been created with an ink of some sort as the designs are not raised or etched. I cannot imagine the time it must have taken to create the precise lines and swirls.

A silken fabric similar to that of the dark scarf lines the inside of the bag. I reach my hand inside to feel the brown lining and hear the crinkle of something. I peer inside but still only see silk. Curious, I run my hand along the edges of the interior and hear the noise again. I feel something hidden inside the lining. My eyes narrow, looking for a way to retrieve the unknown item. The threads holding the lining in place are each accounted for, all but one. Interested, I take hold of the dagger and use the sharp end to pull a few more of the sewn pieces free, creating an opening large enough to fit my hand. Within a few moments, I find myself clutching a worn slip of paper. The paper itself is fragile, as if opened and closed a million times, having weathered the rains and sleet and sunshine of a long journey. The thought of tearing the fragile sheet forces me to work with tedious care to open the folded corners. Once the note is fully visible, I see the ink of a few words smudged leaving an incomplete passage:

*A starry night, away –o— war,*
*Where we the children lay before;*
*These f— words, to one so —r,*
*Hold close to heart while never near;*
*Remember, S—, your purpose be,*
*For realms and —le you — the key;*
*With b— breath I always hold,*
*'Till you return, our brave and bold,*
*For the go— of all should ne'er be sold.*

My eyes feast on the lines before me. I spend hours reading over the lines, copying them down, contemplating what words could complete their phrases and, further, what the phrases could mean. I look at the three completed lines and isolate them as I continue my haphazard investigation.

"Where we the children lay before... Hold close to heart while never near... 'Till you return, our brave and bold..."

I peer outside the window that dominates my bedroom wall to my right, the moonlight bright in the cloudless sky. I sigh, carefully folding the note back into fourths and setting it back into the hidden compartment of the satchel. I drag my tired legs off of my bed, the cold tiles prickling the base of my feet. The satchel is somehow heavier now as I sweep the scarf and knife back in, covering the opening with the leather flap, and place it back in the chest of drawers. As I close the drawer, the words from the passage still passing through my mind, I turn back toward the bed where my copy of the poem still sits. I take the notes in my hands, fidgeting with the edges before finally folding the page in half and pushing it between the mattress and the wooden frame. Until I can complete this work and understand fully what the note says, I want to keep it for myself alone.

My eyes squint as the sunlight filters through a collage of colors.

"Good morning, Miss!" Mairette's cheerful demeanor is lined with a trace of anxiety, likely due to the planning that still remains for the Greentime Ball. Even so, her eyes are filled with the same contentment as every other day. "There is much to do! And I am excited, and relieved, to show you the progress on your gown."

She flashes a smile, the freckles on her cheeks deeper than I have seen them. The sunny weather is likely the cause of this change in their appearance. I notice the changes in my own skin tone, my face and arms deepening to a tanned olive hue. Even Rostair, who notoriously avoids the sun to maintain his pallid complexion, has gained red coloring along his cheeks, stained from the sun. I raise my head off of the feathered pillow to look at Mairette placing a tray on the table between the couches. Her yellow dress is dotted with embroidered fawns on the hem.

"Mairette," I wipe my eyes as I work to stay awake for the day, "do all Keepers need to wear specific clothing?" The question only takes her a moment to process, thoroughly accustomed to my proclivity for asking inappropriate questions.

"Of course." Her words are clipped, chipper yet precise as if she wants to appear more positive than she truly is. "There are standards for Keepers. The lower Keepers must wear muted muslin clothing while upper Keepers, myself included, have a bit more freedom to wear more complex designs or various colors. Above all, Keepers must be comfortable enough to complete a day's work without having to change into a new set of clothing."

As I listen to her response, I step out of bed and into the main section of the room, sitting on the couch nearest Mairette. "Does that restriction cause conflict at times?" I think back to Piré, the emboldened young Keeper and her brown muslin dress, the look in her eyes—so determined and inspired—fueling my own confidence.

Mairette sits across from me, straightening the tea tray on the table and clearing her throat before responding, "Centrea, I am sure you mean well, I do. There is a way of being here. I have explained it once before." She runs her hands through the tight curls of her red hair. "This is what the realm is, and we are so proud to continue the traditions that are passed down to us."

I nod, taking the cup in my hands and sipping the floral blend. "Of course, of course, I understand. I apologize. I do not mean to cast judgment of any sort." She rushes out of her seat and turns to the mirror, looking for the clothing set aside for today. "Mairette, I truly do not mean anything. I am merely curious."

Mairette turns toward me once more, gripping a maroon skirt of linen in one hand and a matching tunic in the other, her eyes a bit red as she says, "Centrea, we needn't discuss it further. What would you like to do with your hair today?"

I look into the mirror as Mairette sets the last braid in place behind my ear, finishing a style that allows half of my hair to fall to my shoulders while the rest forms a crown around my head. While my morning question clearly ruffled her feathers, she continues with her routine as normal, giggling, smiling, and sharing last night's latest gossip. I follow her example, asking my normal set of questions and sharing my opinions on the newest guests.

"The woman in the purple skirt clearly enjoyed the attention of the woman in the green." Mairette nods in agreement. "And did you see the jealousy of her travel companion? Perhaps she asked her to join with the intention of asking her favor."

I raise my brows at her deduction. "I had not considered that." I press my hands to my chin. "How many people leave the Greentime Ball with no person's favor?" I have wondered this for a few days now. I know Gazil has said many times that most wait until the night of the ball itself to request; however, as more established couples have already asked for favor, my interest has piqued.

Mairette turns to rummage through a basket of paints and pulls out a deep red. After examining my clean face, no doubt considering what design to attempt, she dips a brush into the container. "Eyes closed," she says. I do as I'm told, letting my lids shut as she begins her work. "I would say there are perhaps a dozen guests, those who are socially eligible, who leave the ball without a match. Those who are in a declared bond with another or perhaps widowed, they are not expected to find favor at such events. But, for those of whom it is expected, most do."

I feel the cool paint sweep across my eye as she speaks. I am always in awe of the artistry Mairette is capable of when drawing with paints. I open my eyes when she gives the signal. Her precision, like with today's look, is remarkable. Thin red lines frame my eyes before flaring out toward my temples. As I admire her work, I consider what she said, forcing myself to admit how much I may truly want favor for myself. And not just favor from anyone—Rostair's favor.

The thought of Rostair asking for my favor makes my heart flutter. I try to press the feeling down, hoping that I can ignore the genuine interest I have in him and the way he makes me feel—the way a mere look can swirl the pit of my stomach or the touch of his hand melts me. While I know I am an outsider, my social isolation clearly establishes me as someone of little merit. However, there is also no denying the attention he gives me. I notice that it is seemingly more than he gives to other guests, and he has admitted to thinking of me at night at least once before.

Mairette's voice shakes me from my thoughts. "I will see you this afternoon, correct?"

I look toward her, where she's already making her way to the door. "Of course! What is on our checklist today?"

I smirk as she throws back a smile. "Come hungry."

After my latest discussion with Piré, the banners lining the dining hall hold more power than they had before. A phantom breeze rustles the blue flags, the metallic embroidery rippling as silence coats the air in the empty hall. Mairette sits at the end of the expansive black marble table shuffling several pieces of paper and muttering to herself. The intensity has increased even since this morning. The plans for the ball clearly rest heavily on her mind.

"The order of things calls for a very specific seating arrangement." She points toward the empty chairs along the far side of the table. "I need to ensure the social and political relationships never clash and that food aversions are never neighbors..." So many things I truly hadn't considered.

The color of napkins, the size of centerpieces, it all appears overwhelming in addition to the base concerns such as remembering a dance or the appropriate form of greeting. I hear the passageway door flutter open then closed before a plate of food appears before me, the older Keeper slipping in and out of the hall in mere seconds.

Mairette peers over the top of the paper to observe my initial response. "Be sure you look a bit more interested in the chef's artistry on the night of the ball."

I immediately upturn my mouth and hum a small "mmmm" sound.

She laughs. "It is no jest! While I know you appreciate this work, you must be overenthusiastic. People will be observing you more than normal."

If I realized then the importance of this role I may have taken a bit more time to consider my dedication. Not only have I learned so much about the Ice Realm, its customs, and my preferences, but I had not grasped fully the amount of information required to be the Greentime Ball Guest of Honor. The morbid side of myself, one that I notice grows more cynical as I learn of the complications in this world, considers my lack of memories as a potential benefit, the empty pockets of my mind open to store these important rituals and expectations. As the time ticks away and the ball comes closer and closer, the more eager I am to see it pass.

I spend the next hour attempting to eat the delicious meal with intermittent comments from Mairette. Her sweet countenance softens the harshness of her words. Although I know her intentions are for my benefit, an hour of reprimand has pushed me to my limit. Once my plate is swept away as fast as it appeared, I quietly excuse myself. Mairette, a smile on her face, nods profusely and waves me on, returning to the pages of notes and murmured planning.

A silent walk through the halls of Endoneth is a rarity as the days grow warmer and more socialites constantly hover and bustle from room to room, wing to wing, searching for familiar faces and surprising intrigues. I notice Keepers using the halls more often as well, no doubt crowding the passages to attend to the increased number of guests. The Keepers, their hair neatly tied behind their ears and tunics smartly pressed, keep close to the edges of the halls, avoiding any contact with the traveling men and women throughout the estate. My mind is tired from an hour of work, thoughts creeping in about the poem hidden beneath my mattress.

I turn a corner in the Orange Wing with my sights set on a source of knowledge: the main library. Endoneth boasts three libraries, not including the collections of books in the many studies and guest rooms strewn throughout the upper level of the home. The largest of the three libraries is filled to the brim with rows and rows of shelves, books on thousands of topics and millions of stories. The storied tiles of the famed deer and ancient archer that line the windowed wall only represent one of the legends written in the tiles. Other small tales, depicting the mythology of Nourels and the Ice Realm, scatter the floors of the library, although the first I read will always hold a special place in my heart, reminding me of my night in the library with Rostair. That night is almost like a dream more than a memory, but it's one I hold safe.

Rather than scurry around the interior of the library, weaving through tables and chairs to stare down at the epic legends, I instead remain near the edges of the room, running my fingers over the multicolored bindings containing centuries of knowledge.

I have never explored the books in the library, other than the history Gazil selected for me, and I realize now how much I underestimated the power that they wield. Asking questions is always helpful, but reading information from the source offers an additional level of security. I peruse the shelves, eager to find anything about the Mountain Realm. I turn the corner to another bookcase, the binding of each book embossed with shining blues, pinks, and purples. The titles along the shelves depict tales of love and loss, fictional narratives of impossible worlds. Not my initial desire, yet I am intrigued.

My fingers trace over the purple cloth of a smaller work, the silver and pink words spelling, *A Fairy Dream*. I pull the book from its position on the shelf and find the cover filled with butterflies and clouds of metallic. The cursive script of the title is enchanting, the romantic whirls enticing me to open its pages. I fold the book into my arms, cradling it close to my chest as I complete a lap around the library. Patrons of the realm occupy each available chair and sofa, enjoying their own literary treasures or soft whispers of conversation, leaving only room to stand and read. After walking another circle around the space, waiting for a chair to open, I decide to make my way toward my room, hugging the fairy book as I push through the full halls of the Blue Wing. With each room now occupied, the hallways are much more hectic.

Some people linger in the guest wings to eavesdrop on passing discussions. The result is a raucous noise throughout the day and into the night, filling my chamber with the buzz of faint compliments, debates, and swoons rather than the much preferred calm. Occasionally, my presence brings the constant buzzing of talking to a halt, and eyes follow my every move until the novelty wears away.

The cool air of my room welcomes me. The sun sends a rainbow of light through the stained glass into the space. I set the book onto one of the couches and slip out of my clothes, eager to change into something more comfortable. When I finally sit, nestling deep into the cushions of the large piece of furniture, my hands clench the book, curious to see what wondrous stories may be in store. Opening the cover, I lose myself in the story.

*A Fairy Dream: A Legend of the Wood*

*Melara was the Fairy Monarch, a being of great power. Their ability to use magic and control of the elements was unmatched. This story is of their perseverance, their courage, and their love. They were the makers of their own destiny.*

*Caliam was the Fairy Warrior, a being of great loyalty. Their ability to wield a dagger was world-renowned. They were the reason for the supremacy of fairies throughout the realm.*

*Ice Fairies, all sharing similar skin of fair colors, held a responsibility to the earth. The horde worked as one, yet remained individual, like a beautiful symphony of glowing lights, each with their heart and soul and spirit guiding them toward the public good. Melara held their head high, deeply moved by their people and the purpose shared by all. In the brilliant morning light, Melara often walked for hours, peaceful in their contemplation of how to best keep their horde safe from outsiders. One morning, they happened upon another, glowing in a pale blue that complimented Melara's purple hue. Caliam, while known by many in the horde's council, had not met Melara personally, two paths that never crossed. This one walk became another, which became a routine, which became a haven, which became love. One morning, the two leading fairies, their light blazing together like two beacons of hope in the wooded darkness, came under attack, arrows flying through the air...*

A knock interrupts the story, dragging my mind back to reality. "Who is—"

Gazil's desperate voice disrupts my own. "It is me, Centrea. Please permit me to enter!"

The shock on my face certainly shades my tone. "Y-yes, Gazil, please enter." He looks a bit stuck as he stumbles through the heavy door, definitively shutting it behind him and sinking onto the wood.

"You appear, flustered, my friend." I cannot help but hold back a chuckle at his disheveled appearance once seeing he is in a state of sobriety.

"You cannot tell a soul, but I must, I must inform you of something. Something massive!" He begins frantically pacing the floor, his hands pulling at stray hairs in his beard.

My eyes grow wide at this display, and I place the book face down on the table and wave a hand to the couch. "Come! Sit, sit and tell me."

Curiosity has made me insatiable, arguably because Gazil feeds me story after tantalizing story of intrigue. I tuck the short hem of my cotton shift under my knees as I reposition myself, my calves cushioning my body as I wait for his response.

"You know the Lord, yes. I mean, of course you do. I'm more aware than probably anyone of his infatuation with you." He waves a hand at the comment as if this is old news, yet my heart begins pounding at the words. "Well, regardless, our Lord, before his obsession with you, he once had another. Knew another. Knew her so well that most of the realm believed she could be the next leader sitting next to him."

He delivers these words at rapid speed, barely breathing as he shares Rostair's intimate history. "No matter, the woman, she left the Ice Realm soon after the incident where... well... that orphaned the Lord." He takes a moment to pause, perhaps offering this brief silence to honor the fallen lord and lady. "This person, she is *coming here.*" The words sink into my skin, chilling my bones and striking the grin from my mouth.

There are so many questions to ask him, however one precedes the rest. "Does he still love her?"

The drama of the realm is typically my favorite topic of conversation, especially with Gazil who seems to know all. This specific story of romance, however, is not joyous. "I can start from the beginning if that is most helpful." A short nod permits him to continue. "Rostair, the Lord himself, was merely a boy when he met her, Helzaf. She was bright, cheery. The opposite of the charismatic yet troubled lad."

I turn my head and ask, "I heard before my arrival, Rostair was…cold. Has he always been so?"

Gazil dips his eyes to the space between us, keenly tracing the stitched fabric lining the couch. "His parents were strict with him at times, wanting him to grow into a strong leader. They loved him, of course. However, I fear such expectations stirred in him a need to satisfy their hopes, his entire being driven toward their approval. However, she brought out a lightness in him, much like he appears to be with you."

His words are generous, yet remain somber as he continues, "In their late teenage years, they began a friendship, her father a Lord in Tselm, a Desert Estate, and his mother the Lady in control of Endoneth. When their parents learned of their friendship, they saw it as an opportunity for an unbreakable alliance, one that would solidify their families as the most powerful in the Northern realms, a greatly favored alliance. When the leaders told their progenies, it startled them, both old enough to understand duty yet too young to abandon their dreams for something more. However, so it is told, the years of their engagement brought them closer together. The young couple's early adulthood emerged in a period of warfare, halting any thoughts of matrimony, yet they continued to develop their relationship."

He looks at me with a sheepish and solemn expression before resuming. "I, of course, traveled throughout this saga, so I cannot say I saw their love bloom before my own eyes. However, I heard the whispers of the Ice prince and his Desert jewel. The realm adores a good story, you know this."

He rubs the back of his neck. "But the war reached Endoneth more quickly than we ever anticipated, taking with it the lives of Rostair's mother and father and leaving him Lord of a suffering estate. To avenge her hosts, her surrogate parents, and fight on the right side of the conflict, Helzaf rode from our stables toward the South to find their murderer." Tears line Gazil's eyes before he dabs them with the sleeve of his long tunic. "She would send word every week or so at the start. Then every month, then nothing at all for three years."

I cast my eyes downward, feeling the anguish as if it were my own—the loss of parents, of a loved one, a potential partner in life. "I cannot tell you if Rostair still feels for her, but I do know that her presence will likely cause a stir. And I wanted to tell you myself."

He gently pats my shoulder, seeing me process the story slowly. "When does she arrive?" I look into Gazil's eyes as my voice shakes.

He shakes his head. "Of that I am unsure. I heard word of her return through a trusted source who identified her near the border of the Mountain Realm."

I gasp, remembering Rostair's latest update on the war front. "Were you able to hear more? From my... father?"

His face turns even more downtrodden, as if the answer would harm more than help. I nod slightly. Still no word. Anxiety, so often my companion now, swells within me. Is my family safe? Are they searching for me? Was I truly abandoned by them? Banished? Or taken?

Though he holds no answers, Gazil stays with me, and I ring for Mairette, who provides us drinks—lavender tea for myself and a glass of white wine for him. The glimpse into Rostair's past is both helpful and painful, something I wished he had shared with his own lips rather than another's, particularly Gazil who doesn't know him on a personal level. Taking a sip of his wine, my friend turns to me, his countenance far calmer than before. I drink the floral warmth in my own cup and turn to him. "Who were the Lord and Lady of Endoneth?"

He grips the stem of his glass a bit tighter, "The *Lady* and the Lord," he says softly yet with authority, "were two powerful leaders at a time when power was taken for granted. The mother of Lord Rostair was called Gillith, a true child of Ice. Born to a lineage of great leaders before her, namely the first of the Gold Age in our realm..." As the words flow from his mouth, his shoulders lower and his eyes gain a wistful edge, as if remembering a time of great happiness. "She bestowed her favor upon Hepnon for years before her grandfather approved the connection. While it is believed they were not a love match, our leaders were determined, understanding the importance of a winning couple."

Gazil takes another long sip from his glass, relishing in the acidic drink. "Our history is one of great importance." The way he emphasizes *our* breaks a bit of my heart, the implication of my ostracization becoming a bit more apparent with each word. "And our youth do not always appreciate it. It is the reason we make our choices, the reason to support our people, our customs. It is the reason for everything."

He looks deeply into my eyes, tears falling slowly down his rough cheeks. "Thank you for hearing me. This history, it is essential. Hear me. It is *essential* to knowing all that you—that we—are. Do not forget this. I hope you can understand why all has transpired as it has. I hope you can, truly." He places the wine on the table and holds my hands in his so tightly that I begin to feel pangs of pain, yet I cannot tear my eyes from his, the earnest warning in his features forcing my heart to race.

"I love you, sweet friend, please remember this." With these words, he pulls me into a hug, the alcohol lacing his breath and bringing me back to that night in the gardens, where Gazil spewed similar sentiments in his inebriated state. I sigh and pat his back. The poor man is clearly stressed and in need of friendship. I hope he understands the legitimacy of my words from yesterday, that I am his true friend and he is welcome to be his true self with me.

Gazil embraces me for a long while before leaving me alone in my chambers. I contemplate what to do next, if anything. I could question Rostair regarding this past love. Yet, the reality begins to set in that my brief glimpse of passionate romance may be over. I could request he try to gain more information from my father, the Lord in the mountains. Yet, it feels a selfish request as people die daily on the border between us and my potential family.

Instinctually, I set a course for the paper in my bed. Even feeling the paper puts me more at ease, the crisp folds pleasantly slipping from one hand to the next. I open the note and allow the words to refresh me, even with only a few full phrases. It is strange how simple words can bring things into focus. The original note, still tucked safely in the satchel, brings to the surface a tangible past, one that may be foggy, but one that is true. And, while I have learned much about the Ice Realm and Endoneth, made friends here, made a world for myself, a name for myself, it feels less true than the words of a poem.

I begin placing myself in the words.

"We the children... hold close to heart... our brave and bold."

The words of a person beloved, revered even. Though the words were not written for me, they speak to me all the same. Rereading the words gives me hope, joy, purpose. I am brave. And I am bold.

Rereading the words re-energizes me. I stand before my window, looking through the tinted glass to glimpse the beautiful sunset. Even through stained colors, the vibrant pinks, oranges, and purples paint the sky. The navy blue of the primrose flower and the yellow center shine with more allure than ever before. The art throughout the estate is magnificent, yet this window is the most stunning.

I lift my hand to touch the small pieces of glass, so subtly formed with flecks of various textures and tones that are each deftly soldered together with metal. I am in awe at the way each piece of glass is just as exquisite on its own while being a part of a much larger vision. I stand back, taking in the sun as it falls behind the grassy hills.

*I am brave. And I am bold.*

# Eleven

I awaken with a renewed sense of self, thinking through my purpose here. I recall the day I set foot outside of my room for the first time. The first time I allowed Rostair close to me. The first time I shifted my mindset from living for my past to considering my future. Of course, as Gazil's speech on the importance of history made clear, one cannot live independent of the other. However, what little I know of who I was will not deter what I want for myself moving forward. And, after days and days of wondering what my purpose should be, I think yesterday's conversation solidified for me what I want above all else: to be loved as a part of something larger than merely myself.

When Gazil spoke of his people, his customs, his past, he consistently reinforced a unified *our*—*our* history, *our* customs, *our* past. What will it take for me to be a part of that *our*? I lie in my bed, staring at the ceiling, thinking through the following days and working toward this final goal. Perhaps being Rostair's Guest of Honor will prove my position in this realm, prove to the lord of Endoneth of my ability to stand at his side, prove to the people that I appreciate the Ice Realm and its customs, its beauty, its power.

I continue to contemplate this renewed path when Mairette's tender tap on the door precedes her footsteps and the smell of warm orange tea. The scent rips me from my blankets, pushing me toward the couches and table. "Good morning! You must guess what was delivered this morning with the latest guests." Her smile is wide, and her face appears a fraction less stressed from when I last saw her.

I place a hand on my chin as I thoughtfully consider. "Could it be an article of clothing?" I tap my finger against my cheek, donning a look of serious inquisition. "Perhaps, a dress of some sort?"

Her head nods up and down and her teeth gleam as her smile grows even larger. "The dress has arrived! We will have a fitting today as soon as you finish your tea." She pushes the cup toward me knowingly. "We must, of course, ensure the dress itself fits well, and if there are any last-minute additions or alterations to the style, they need to be decided today."

Before long, we stand before the full-length mirror, taking stock of the gown. It is amazing how the designers captured the drawing so faithfully. The shape is exactly as I remember, the dress hugging my broad chest and wide hips, dipping in to clutch my abdomen in the middle. Then at my hips towards the bottom of the dress, the shape flares wide before floating to the ground, a short trail of fabric forming a train that will sway behind me through the ballroom. The fabric itself is luscious, most being a deep green velour that mimics the fresh leaves of the pine trees in the woods. Along the bottom, the hem morphs into an earthy brown while on the top, the color is a sultry blue with crystal flecks of white, like the night sky. I stare into the reflection before me. The dress fits beautifully with only a few slight wrinkles, which Mairette has marked with chalk for the designer to alter.

"Inspiring," she sings as she encourages me to take a spin in the gown. "The Realm will be delighted! Gazil assisted me in developing the concept for the dress. We wanted to capture the essence of nature and the importance of our woods in the Ice Realm."

The crystals sewn into the dress glimmer as I spin, making my appearance all the more enchanting. "Is there anything you would like to add? Something to make it personal to you?"

I contemplate the design. I adore the natural inspiration, and I'm proud of my dearest friends who made it come to fruition. I look behind me at the primrose prominently displayed on my window, the navy glass beaming in the noon light.

Mairette follows my gaze and smiles. "The flower would make a lovely addition, if you please?" She knows more than anyone how important the chamber is to me, how much time I've spent and how much of myself I've discovered in this room. As I turn my face back toward the mirror, my eye catches a glimpse of the chest of drawers.

"And a moth, if it is possible. It doesn't need to be large, but somewhere." Mairette's face in the mirror appears almost as if she is holding her breath. The pause goes on a bit longer than usual.

"Of course!" Her smile returns, yet with less enthusiasm than before. "You will be a vision, Miss. An absolute vision."

My linen tunic and pants feel much more comfortable but far less glamorous than my earlier attire. After placing the appropriate marks for the designer, Mairette shuffles out of the room. I sigh and look out the window, my nerves rising with every minute that passes and brings me closer to the night of the ball, the culmination of much work and thought and preparation.

My mind wanders to Helzaf, what she may wear or when she might arrive. I shake the thought, tucking *A Fairy Dream* in the crook of my arm, and turn toward the door before striding into the hallway. I am unsure where my day will take me, but remaining locked away in my chambers will lead to my own torturous overanalyzing.

The halls bustle with movement, many guests either just leaving or just beginning their midday meal. Spirits are high as any sign of snow has officially melted away, even in the highest sections of the estate, leaving in their wake the most beautiful greenery. The sunshine filtering through the many windows draws me down the main staircase and into the Gold Wing before I venture outside. I follow the familiar path toward the garden arch, the smell of new plants and fresh dirt welcoming me to enjoy the sunny day. The garden blooms with the most vibrant flowers, which look very different from the winter ones. Colors of violet and orange, yellow and pink, blue and red all evoke a feeling of delightful serenity, as if the flowers themselves sing into the warm air, offering a magnificent display of the Ice Realm in spring.

I soak in the warm sunshine as I lazily make my way through the flowers, reading my book as I go. The ways of fairies are fascinating, beings of such great power, yet so small. As I walk through the gravel paths in the garden, weaving in and out of the various walkways and segments, I turn into an open courtyard, beginning to understand more deeply the elation of winter's end. The Greentime Ball itself is where this joy can manifest, where the realm can come together as one, unified in their love of the warmth, the flowers, the peace. The ball has surely gained more importance in the past few years as war rages on just a realm away.

These thoughts swim through my mind, despite my best efforts to concentrate on stories of magic and fairies and love, as I follow the edges of the garden courtyard, passing a number of stone statues in various poses. Many of the statues are arranged in groupings of four or five, figures from the past celebrated here in memorials of carved stone.

I look more closely at a group of statues near the far end of the courtyard. This particular group displays familiar figures of the Ice Realm's Gold Age, all related to Rostair's ancestral past. Each statue is accompanied by a plaque that explains the figure, presenting a bit of history for passersby to consume in quick, digestible bites. In the middle of the group of five, which is organized in a semicircle, is a strong and sensibly dressed female. The plaque below her reads:

*Lady Gillith of Endoneth - Endoneth's Lady raised the Realm into a moment of pure prosperity, building on the work of her father and his father before him. She gave everything for her people. A model of both authority and loyalty.*

"You know, my mother was known for her fashionable taste." The voice behind me fills my heart with inimitable bliss. "She wore these grand dresses—nothing like this statue—these grand dresses with sleeves that doubled her size, making it difficult for her to fit through doorways. But the sleeves always made her hugs warm, engulfing me... in such love."

I hear his voice crack a bit as I turn. He appears tired but pleasant, a few tears threatening to fall from his eyes just before he brushes them away.

"Gazil has told me a bit about her... but I would love to know even more," I say.

Rostair looks at his mother's face and clenches his fist by his side. "Please, do not feel pressure to share. It is a very sensitive topic, I am certain."

He doesn't break his stare at the statue while answering, "Of course not. She is worth keeping alive through our words."

I see his hands relax by his side as he speaks of his mother. "I am sure the Keeper of Records knows much of our history. He worked alongside my parents for many years and honored them with his loyal service." His voice is laced with pain, so much so that I almost request he stop. Almost.

Rostair continues, still looking lovingly into her face etched in stone. "She was powerful, more powerful than any leader I read of in books or perhaps met on diplomatic missions. She knew how to adapt, how to use what was before her and twist it to her will. It was phenomenal to watch, to be a part of. While my great-grandfather and grandfather certainly laid the foundation, it was Lady Gillith who tamed the forest, who returned to traditions of the Green Age to provide her people with what they needed to persevere. The intelligence, the authority she yielded, it intimidated other realms. Sparked rebellions and enemies. Started wars. But she… she led her people bravely and boldly."

The words flow from Rostair like honey, his tone gentle. "You remind me of her. In your spirit, your… curiosity. It overwhelms me at times, if I am honest." The admission takes me aback. Suddenly, his instantaneous interest in a stranger becomes a bit clearer.

Rostair's gentle voice grows rigid. "I know the Keeper of Records has become a great source of comfort for you. It is understandable, as he is quite a charming person." His eyes finally turn to meet my own, a fire blazing behind them, burning with more emotion than I have ever seen from him. "Be cautious, my Centrea. As is commonly known, knowledge is power. And it is often those who know much who are the most apt to wield that power for their gain."

The words tear through me like an arrow through the heart. Even the implication of my friend's betrayal leaves me dumbfounded, frozen in place, my eyes unable to break away from the raw hatred lining Rostair's features. His fists once more clench, a singular tear racing down his chin and falling on the ground between us. For a man so stoic, his emotion flatters me, as if I am the only person in the world to see this side of him. He coughs and turns his back to me, regaining his composure.

"I apologize, the old man often resorts to idle gossip, as you know, and his reputation is unbecoming." When Rostair turns back, his grey eyes are much cooler, filled with concern rather than hate. "I am afraid I must attend to matters of the realm before making more decisions for the ball."

I must still look shaken at his words as he places a light touch to my cheek, a warmth emanating from his hand and weaving its way to my stomach. Flashes of memories pull me from my present fears and confusion and all I see is him. "Sweet Centrea, may we meet again soon?" A wry grin lines his face as he swipes his tongue to wet his lower lip.

The movement has me swooning, a rush of lust sweeping through my body. "Of course," my voice croaks weakly. He touches my cheek a second time, sending shivers through me, weakening my knees as well as my resolve at not completely coming undone in public while the sun leaves us exposed.

He leans in close, his lips tantalizingly near the nape of my neck as he whispers, "Perhaps you could demonstrate for me your penchant for dance?"

Heat flushes my cheeks as he pecks my cheek before leaving the courtyard in a rush.

I stumble into my room as quickly as my wobbling legs will carry me. He saw me. It is difficult to discern whether I feel more embarrassed or invigorated. Of course, my passionate actions were in a public place with the obvious risk of being seen, a fact that likely spurred even more desire within me, if I am honest with myself. And this new notion of an audience has also stirred something within me. Perhaps it is merely that Rostair was the one to witness my pleasure, only fitting as it was his actions that propelled my mind toward seeking it. Yet I must be more aware. It is extraordinarily disrespectful to be seen in such a state.

Despite the licentious nature of Endoneth, public displays of affection of any kind are infrequent and worth noting. Gazil says it is the simplest way to detect a budding romance or future match. Those who touch hands in public, embrace, or find a secluded corner to steal a kiss, are often topics of discussion. Such realities make our meeting in the garden that night all the more treacherous. I must be more careful moving forward, especially if I want to be seen as another member of this realm. Just like the other women here, who want to bestow favor or have favor bestowed upon them, I should conduct my romantic entanglements in a private space.

The thought leaves me reeling once more, and I pace toward the mirror to witness the evidence of my emotional state. Redness still laces my cheeks, and the flush extends down my neck and chest as well. I place my cool hands on my face in an attempt to quell the blush and turn to sit on the nearest couch, thinking through my latest discussion with Rostair and my growing confusion with our arrangement. He never mentioned Helzaf, although I suppose it is likely he is unaware of her return. A thought strikes me as I think through Rostair's disposition, his anger towards Gazil and our friendship.

*Is Helzaf returning at all? Would my friend fabricate a story to my detriment and, if so, to what end?*

The thoughts fly through my mind, soon taking on a life of their own as I revisit that night Gazil flew into my room, pacing like a madman and speaking to me with such recklessness, revealing to me something that would surely deter my pursuit of Rostair, or at the very least give me pause. The spirals of vicious thoughts come like an onslaught, one potential reality shedding new light on another until I am sitting upright at my writing desk, feverishly outlining the several possibilities to justify Gazil's point of view. It appears likely that the men harbor animosity toward each other, if not Gazil then certainly Rostair. However, it is likely Gazil shares this emotion yet cannot fully express it, Rostair's position as his Lord preventing such. I wonder what could cause such resentment, but the number of possibilities quickly shifts my mind elsewhere.

*Could Gazil have invented the return of Helzaf to punish Rostair by pushing me away from him?*

This is a distinct possibility, one that gains merit the more I consider it. I scribble word after word, sentence after sentence, trying to piece together what I know about both figures before growing quite tired. Sighing, I collect the notes, pages of poorly written conspiracies, and place them safely in one of the desk drawers. Regardless of why these two are at odds, I want to believe them both. They have provided me with great joy and solace during my stay, encouraging me to forge my own path and learn who I am in my own way. To have one speak mistruths would be out of the character I know each of them to be—and perhaps neither is lying and I am merely acting out of paranoia. After all, I did also just learn that my secrets may not be as safely tucked away as I would like to believe, that watching eyes and lusting hearts could be looking around every corner, consuming even my most intimate of moments.

# Twelve

The tea tonight is a blend of peach and pear, with bits of fruit delightfully strewn throughout the drink to provide extra bursts of flavor with every sip. I focus on my emotionally gripping book as the realm of fairies fights for supremacy and self-protection. Mairette holds a series of papers, physically checking off lists of actions with a satisfied smile.

"We are ahead of schedule this season," she squeals as she sets the papers on the table and takes a seat near me. "I also spoke with the designer who expressed his profuse admiration at your personal additions. He believes we will have one more fitting before the event itself and that the primrose and moth will provide twinkles of personality to give the gown life." Her head rests against the back cushion as she recalls her conversation with the renown designer. "His work is magnificent, don't you agree? And his willingness to work with the Keeper of Records of all people to develop such a concept, it shows true humility. The mark of a gentleman to be certain."

I place the book on my lap and peer over my mug as I take another sip, a piece of peach teasing my tongue, to see the look of utter awe on her face. The woman is beside herself, as she continues to pour out accolades for this man.

I stifle a giggle and inquire, "How well do you know this designer, Mairette?"

The question reeks of suggestion and encourages a deeper shade of pink to light her freckled cheeks. "Why, I have known him for years!" The implication encourages her to explain further. "He is Lord Rostair's personal designer, and we have developed many important articles of clothing for events such as this." She attempts to force her words into a more serious tone, one of business and professionalism.

I hum in response, reveling in the thought of her romantic interests for once.

She waves a hand in my face. "Centrea, sweet child. It is nothing of the sort." The words sound even less convincing with the look of glee lining her eyes.

"Well, you do know you are always welcome to tell me of your romantic exploits, dear friend." I take another sip of my tea. "It is only fair that you divulge as well!"

Her face turns a brighter shade of pink, her skin nearly burning at the suggestion. She opens her mouth once, then closes it, clearly reconsidering her initial reaction. "You know, I will entreat you to any tawdry story that may arise."

My brows raise and I shift onto my knees at this sudden shift. "Oh? Truly?" I sound like a child asking for a present.

"That is *if* any were to arise." She strikes a dashing smile, and with it smashing my hopes for such a story.

I click my tongue playfully. "You can be tiresome. Why do you not pursue romantic joy? Even for one night, no attachment?"

She contemplates this for a moment before stating plainly, "For Keepers like myself, such attachments may not be merely incidental. There is much more for us to lose." Her eyes sweep low, mimicking my heart as it drops to hear her words. I have seen many sides of my friend, yet this level of emotion is something she only holds when describing her family, which is less and less often.

I look at her. "I hope one day, you will have no need to fear such love."

Mairette's arms swing around me and pull me into a tight embrace. "You mean so much to me, Centrea."

The next morning drags on for far longer than I would like as I sulk in my room, contemplating my task for the day. Mairette, having delivered my tea at nearly sunrise, complained of a sudden "instrument emergency" that would take her attention for the entire day, presenting me with a much-needed break from ball preparations.

However, now I am left with a day of no responsibility and no direction.

Normally, I would search the dining hall for Gazil and have him plan a full day of spying on the latest incoming guests and wandering the grounds. But, after Rostair's words in the garden, my inclination is to give our friendship a bit of space. Additionally, I am certain Gazil is experiencing his own influx of work as I have noticed many people taking their chance to offer favors before the ball.

There are only four more full days before the fateful date, and I count them in my mind to keep track of the order of things: one dedicated to another dance rehearsal (minus my own improvisation), one dedicated to another dress fitting, and one dedicated to a rehearsal of some sort. The rehearsal is meant more for the many, many Keepers and entertainers for the night, but, as the Guest of Honor, my movements are also part of a highly choreographed night. The final day, the day before the Greentime date itself, is a complete day of rest for everyone before the reveling begins.

According to Mairette, this is very necessary for the minds and bodies of all involved. On this day, all guests must eat in their own quarters, snacking on meals and fruits supplied the day before, to allow the Keepers of the kitchen to rest as well. It is the day I am most looking forward to as the stress of the Greentime Ball is beginning to make me perpetually anxious, hardly able to sit still as the responsibility of my role weighs heavily on my mind.

It is this anxious energy that drives me from my room, where I avoid the main food hall and instead head outside. The breeze cradles my face as I open the doors leading to the green patches of grass. Beyond the gardens, I walk along a small gravel path, watching dozens of people play field games.

One group uses wooden mallets to hit a small ball through hoops along a designated path in the grass. Another flings a large carved branch through the air, attempting to land it the farthest away from a steel post. Further down the path, two men toss a ring adorned with ribbons of all colors onto a four-pronged wooden post several feet away. One of the men cheers as he lands his ring onto the farthest and shortest prong, eliciting a disappointed huff from his companion.

The scene of merriment brings my spirits up slightly, hearing the laughs and cheerful chatter of the Ice Realm guests. I notice, heartily, that my presence has barely distracted the socialites from their respective occupations, only a few lingering glances and one particularly loud gasp.

I round a large tree protruding from the vibrant green of the courtyard, leading me to the archery field fence. Since my memory attempts with Rostair last week, I have not returned to shoot at the targets that face away from the sports courtyard behind me. The field itself contains five large targets made from muslin and hay, all lined yards away from a wide gazebo filled with bows and arrows of various sizes.

The metalwork of the fine structure is woven into intricate scenes of people hunting great beasts of the woods. The top of the gazebo provides a welcome shade from the shining sun, allowing those who practice a better chance of landing near the bright red center of the target. There is only one other guest practicing her shot, a sprightly woman of slender build. She is dressed in a dazzling purple tunic, black pants, and a short lilac skirt draped diagonally over her upper thighs.

As I walk toward the gazebo, I see her nock a yellow arrow onto the string before pulling back to rest the arrow's feathers near her cheek. She waits there a few moments, and I find myself waiting too, holding my breath as she straightens her spine and aims. I'm shaken from my trance as she releases the arrow and a loud thunk echoes through the field. Her blonde hair shakes as she pumps a triumphant fist into the air. I follow her look to the target and raise my brows in admiration. A perfect shot, centered in the red dot of the target.

"Well, hello," a voice says, and I turn back to see the woman sauntering toward the edge of the gazebo. "I did not realize I was performing for onlookers." She emits a bit of a chuckle before offering a hand. "Yekmasha." I take her hand quizzically. "You may refer to me as Asha, if you wish."

My mind is blank, as if I have never spoken with another human before. None of the guests have ever told me their names, and none, other than the occasional dance partner at an event, have ever ventured to speak with me. Outside of Rostair and Gazil, no person in this high society world has given me any form of friendship.

Noticing my increasing nerves, she continues, "I believe you are known here as Centrea, correct?" I nod, still processing the shock of this conversation.

"Yes," I begin hesitantly, as if I've forgotten how to speak. "Centrea, that is correct." I attempt a smile, which no doubt appears half-hearted.

She returns a smile of her own, an utterly sensational sight as her golden skin seems to glimmer with the rush of pointed emotion. "You have caused quite the stir in this realm, I have heard. We in the Sun Realm do not often worry much over the gossip that travels over our borders. Yet, the mysterious appearance of the 'woman of the wood.' Well, that sounds utterly fantastical, does it not."

Hearing that nickname sends another shock through me. Of course, I am under no pretense that others don't use the phrase in their murmurs, but none have done so in front of me, and so boldly.

"I apologize." Asha's perfectly manicured, blonde brows furrow in concern. "I did not mean to offend. Centrea is the only name I will utter from now onward." Her words touch me as does her sensitivity to my reactions. "Please tell me," she continues, the crackling in her voice causing my heart to thump loudly in my chest, "would you like to join me in my practice?"

I accept her invitation and am reminded me of the skills I displayed at my last attempts at archery. While Asha is clearly more precise in her handle of the bow, I also hit the center of the targets many times in our hours of practice. And she contains as brilliant a personality as her appearance. The two of us together highlights my distinctive features: my wide waist and hips, my average height nearly cowering at her tallness, and the ink splattered along my hands and face appearing particularly messy in comparison to Asha's perfection.

Asha chats merrily as we practice. "This is my third time attending the Greentime Ball. The first year, I found myself approving the favor of a young woman who clearly set her sights on another, wealthier Lord and used me as some sort of remarkable bait in her schemes. The next year was much lighter, as I avoided favors and drama and drank enough alcohol that I awoke the next morning passed out under a desk in the main study."

Her laugh emits a terrific sort of glow as she continues. "While travel is wonderful, I enjoy my home more than any other realm. The Sun Realm is filled with sparkle and gold." She pulls the string of her bow taut before releasing it with a satisfying *whoosh*. "Our buildings are lined with metalwork of all kinds, decorating the pale stone. These brick buildings cannot compare," she states matter-of-factly before settling another feathered bow into its proper place. "My father is an architect, you see. The most renowned in the Nine Realms. He sees the potential for beauty in the most mundane. It is truly inspiring."

The Sun Realm sounds inspiring from her descriptions: golden palaces, days filled with sunshine, and large lakes of the clearest blue waters. "I hope one day to witness such beauty." I sigh thoughtfully as I daydream of such an adventure.

I notice Asha hesitate as she raises the bow in front of her, as if thinking about her realm, remembering her people and their importance. A look of darkness shades her eyes for a moment, before she smiles and whispers, "I would very much like that. For you to see the realm with your own eyes." With that, she releases the arrow and strikes the center once more.

I nod my approval at her efforts. "You are quite well-versed in archery. You rarely miss a shot!"

She turns her head slightly, watching me out of the corner of her eyes, the darkness returning momentarily as she says, "Well-trained, yes. I am a master of the bow indeed."

After hitting the target once more, I sit on one of the metal benches beneath the shaded gazebo and press into the soreness in my arms. "It may hurt worse in the morning." Asha's voice is laced with a harmless giggle. I recognize the truth in her words already, the muscles in my arms nearly screaming from their sudden labor.

I nod grimly. "If you would like, we could ring a Keeper for some refreshments?" I offer, my avoidance of the dining hall now evidenced by a growing hunger burning in my belly.

Asha flashes another smile, the waves in her hair essentially glowing as she shakes her head from side to side. "No need to bother them during such a stressful time. There are other ways of finding sustenance. Come."

Again, she offers her hand, this time to pull me from my place on the bench and toward the gravel path. We walk side by side, my hand nestled in her arm, as she whistles through the courtyard. If the groups of sporting guests ignored me on the walk to the shooting grounds, they were certainly looking now. The number of gasps, whispers, and stares seem to only embolden Asha as she holds her head high and marches toward the house.

Once inside, she points toward the Red Wing. "The kitchens, I believe they are this way."

My mind grows worried at the implication. "Asha, we are not allowed entry into the Keepers' wing. It is for their eyes alone."

She scoffs a bit and places a dainty hand on my arm. "Centrea, we should not worry. I must admit, there is much I fear, but the wrath of the Ice Lord I do not."

The worry in my bones intensifies as we near the forbidden wing, the tiles beneath our feet fading from the golden flecks to thorns of red. Asha sees my panic and sets a reassuring hand on my back. "There really is no reason to worry, my friend. It is a silly rule to maintain a sense of order. That is all!"

I nod absently, still riddled with a sense of unease as she places her other hand on the archway lining the red corridor ahead. My feet feel like lead, my hands tingling a bit as I wring the sides of my yellow skirt.

"You know," Asha gently cradles my forearm in her hands, coaxing me to inch my way forward into the hall, "I had a friend who understood stress in a way I could never quite manage. As youths, she would offer habits, little tricks to overcoming fear."

My heart thumps erratically with each step, thinking about what Mairette, what Rostair, would think of me violating this space with my presence. "She would say, 'One step forward, and you will be in a different place than you were before as a different person than you were before—and perhaps that place and that person will be able to handle the burdens you face. If not, take another step until you find the place and the person who will.'" Her throat sounds as if it aches with each word, choking a bit at the remembrance of her former friend. "Just one step, then another."

The visual is bound to look absurd, two women clinging to each other as they walk down an unassuming and utterly innocuous hallway. Once the tiles are bloodred, the glimmers of gold long gone, I begin to regain my sanity, the anxiety of what may happen passing away, replaced by utter curiosity and awe.

While the hall is dim, no windows flooding the space with natural light, the small lanterns allow just enough light to display the wonder of the wing itself. The walls of the walkway are covered from ceiling to tiled floor with pages upon pages of artwork. Unlike the other wings throughout Endoneth, with the manicured and carefully curated artwork tastefully placed, the art is plastered to the walls in a gloriously haphazard manner.

The images lining each page follow no particular pattern or form, each its own style. Some artists used traditional mediums—chalk, paint, pencil—while others' inspirations manifested in alternative forms, such as mud, dust, and even smears of food. My eyes jump from page to page, consuming each as if I had never seen artwork before.

Asha's smirk gives away her delight. The words "I was right" are essentially written on her lips. I ignore her self-satisfaction as I continue to peer down the hallway, the lighting barely illuminating the space and forcing me to squint slightly. As we walk through the hall, we pass door after door with lazily painted signs that read various rooms:

*Main Dining Hall... Ballroom... Blue Wing...*

The names go on and on, down the narrow corridor covered in artwork. "Last year, during one of my wine-induced trances, I slipped into one of the passageways that led me here." Asha points a hand toward a slab of wood tacked onto a door that reads, *Second Library*. "I remember a feeling of cozy warmth when I entered through, as if the worries of the outside world—of wealth and skill and expectation—were all left behind." She twirls a tendril of her shoulder-length hair around her finger as she sighs. "When you look at these, do you not wonder if there is more to life than that." Her words are more a statement than a query as she moves her eyes over the many works of art.

Suddenly, a door behind us opens, and an older Keeper sees us instantly, readjusting the basket of yarn on her hip as she walks sheepishly toward us. We smile a bit before allowing her to pass. She hurries along the corridor, rushing to the end before disappearing down a flight of stairs.

I look at Asha and sigh. "Well, now I *know* Mairette will hear of this excursion by nightfall."

The disappointment in my voice doesn't appear to deter her. "Let us continue. There is nothing to lose now, correct?"

She grabs my ink-stained hand in hers and follows the path of the Keeper, our footsteps echoing through the hallway, announcing our movement down the steps. The stairwell is also covered with artwork as the spiral steps lead us deep underground. There are a few areas of the long walk down that are so dark I nearly trip over my feet, and I notice softer footfalls on dirt replace the pinging sound of tiles underfoot is replaced by the sound of crumpled dirt.

After minutes of walking, we are surrounded by soil, some still covered by pages, until we reach the end. My breathing grows heavy with the many steps downward and hitches once more as my eyes adjust to the darkness of the space. Before us appears a large expanse filled with Keepers settled into various couches, chairs, and chaises. While the ceiling hangs low, beams of wood holding the structure of moss and soil together, the space is enormous, spanning the size of the entire Gold Wing. The Keepers pay us little mind as we shift away from the stairs and toward the nearby corner.

"Have you seen this place before?" I ask Asha as the slight murmur of voices mingled with the smell of sweet teas and earthy soil assault my senses.

"Never," she breathes, clearly as speechless as I. The walls of the space are lined with the same lanterns seen on the floor above, and a crackling bonfire provides additional light at the center of the room. Large openings lead into various spaces on both sides of the main hall, one that appears to be a dining hall and the other a recreational room. The most urgent and hustling sounds come from the room across the stairs, a massive kitchen that supplies all food for the entire estate. I can only imagine the number of Keepers working in the kitchen and the amount of stress that accompanies the job.

Suddenly, I see the brown tinge of a muslin cloak before me. "Here," Asha says, "we would not want to raise unwanted attention. We are guests here after all."

I grasp the cloak from Asha's outstretched hand before throwing it over my shoulders. Asha points toward the kitchen with a playful smirk. "Shall we venture in?"

Pangs of hunger sweep through my stomach once more, reminding me of the original purpose of this journey and I nod, placing the hood of the cloak over my head. In a few steps, we enter into a kitchen as large as the enchanted ballroom. White marble countertops sit atop metal counters lining each wall, and several kitchen islands stretch in a cross shape, meeting at the center of the room.

The open space of floor, the only flooring covered with plain white tiles in the basement wing, is barely visible as Keepers continuously scurry this way and that, carrying either ingredients or entrees in various stages of completion. A few Keepers carry firewood, swinging open the metal doors of the counters with protective gloves and tending to the small fires that blaze beneath the marble, helping the cooks heat various vegetables, sauces, and meats. Other Keepers take the finished food through doors to passageways, heading to the guests no doubt gathering in the food hall. I see Asha's face from the corner of my eye, her mouth agape and face utterly astonished at the busy space.

I turn to my left and find another friend. Before I can stop myself, I reach my hand forward, "Piré! How are you?"

The young face brightens at the sound of her name—a quite different reaction from the concern she usually shows when we are in the upper floor. Her eyes brighten further when she sees my face hidden in the folds of the cloak.

"Miss, hello! What are you doing in the Red Wing, eh? This kitchen is a bit of a busy place. Would you like to come to a calmer section?" Her high-pitched voice moves almost too quickly to comprehend.

A hand settles gently on my shoulder, and I hear Asha's voice straining to speak loud enough to be heard over the hustle of the kitchen yet soft enough to go unnoticed by the many Keepers passing by. "That sounds lovely. Before we venture forth, could we trouble you for something small to eat?"

Watching Piré sweep through the kitchen is like witnessing a dancer on stage. She weaves gracefully past the bustling Keepers to scoop up a few pieces of fruit and bread for Asha and me to consume. Her movements take only moments, as she swoops to the center island and back with ease. She ushers us with a smile toward one of the many tables sprinkled throughout the main gathering space and, after much convincing, takes a seat with us. Our backs to the kitchen, still close enough to hear the yelling of head chefs and responses of lower Keepers, Asha and I dig into the sampling of fruit and bread, the bursts of fresh juice rejuvenating my senses.

Piré begins a tour of the wing as we sit, pointing out minute details of this gathering room as we munch on warm slices of sourdough. "The Red Wing is a sanctuary for us Keepers. Our sleeping chambers are just to our right. We each share a room with two other Keepers. The Head Keepers have their own spaces, separate from the rest. We are currently in the main gathering arena, where many stop by between the various tasks that fill the day. That way," she discreetly points toward the far end of the wing to our left, "is the Red Dance Hall. We hold the most wonderful events there—celebrating seasons, weddings, or the occasional departure." Her eyes dazzle in the dim light of the lanterns, the pale glow of blue light shimmering as she describes the Keepers and their celebrations. "Of course, we all labor for the Greentime Ball, which is why the main space appears rather vacant at the moment."

I hold in a gasp, peering around at the considerably full room and wondering what a normal day looks like if this is considered vacant. "We will hold our own Greentime celebration exactly a week after the ball; it is always grand!" She points toward the next room, the archway nestled between the staircase and ballroom, and says, "That is the Collective Art Space. All Keepers are welcome to use the tools kept there. I am sure you will love it, Miss." Her voice lowers as she twitches her eyes side to side before saying, "The Lord never visits, which allows us a bit of a reprieve from… expectation. The space is bursting with creativity, completely unhindered."

Asha eyes her cautiously, swallowing the final piece of bread as Piré moves on, more careful with her words than before. "Finally, the last common space is there." She directs our eyes toward our left side, where there is an archway between the kitchen and dance hall leading to another room of tables and chairs. "It is the main dining hall of the Red Wing. This is where Keepers gather for the main meals of the day, our first before sunrise and the second after the guests' main dinner meal."

As I finish the final piece of citrus, the taste sparking a bit of joy in my heart, I nod to Piré. "This place is absolutely wondrous."

The words bring a wide smile to the young Keeper's face, her pale skin luminous with pride. "Come, come." Her long curls bob up and down as she rises. "Let me show you something I have been working on for the last month."

Asha and I follow Piré as she turns and quickly slips through the tables and chairs, leaving behind small curls of dust from the soil beneath her leather flats. We pass the wide expanse of the main room and reach the archway to the Collective Art Space. Even standing at the entrance, I see the immense beauty forged here. The room is as large as my chamber, each wall lined with shelves stuffed with art supplies—paints and brushes and coals. A large drafting table sits at the center, covered in canvases, papers, and fabrics, some filled with partially completed works while others remain empty, waiting for the inspiration of a Keeper to take hold.

Asha steps into the room first, eager to see some of the pieces up close. "These are quite impressive. Who creates here?" Her thin fingers hover above the pile of artwork and she turns to Piré for a response.

I walk the perimeter of the room, scanning the various shelves of tools as I hear the young Keeper's response. "All Keepers have access to this room and its contents. This... this particular piece is by Ganevel." I hear the sound of crinkling paper as she describes the artist of a particular piece to Asha. "He is an elderly Keeper who came to Endoneth from the Desert Realm fifteen years ago—a formerly enslaved male, so I understand. He utilizes this space often and, in fact, many of the pieces in the Red Hallway are by Ganevel."

After walking around the room, I join the two women at the large wooden table, glancing at the art for myself. Asha was correct in her assertion of talent; each incomplete painting or drawing is filled with thought-provoking and exquisite images.

I lock eyes with Piré before taking a page into my hands. "May I?" I inquire, acknowledging my position in this place as a guest, an observer. She nods her head with an appreciative smile. I look at the parchment before me, outlining the rectangle with my fingertips before scooping it into my hands.

I hold the parchment in front of me. The image is of a full moon set in a stunning night sky, fading from the deepest indigo to a pale blue. The stars are so realistic, I can almost see them twinkle in the moonlight. The moon and stars shine down upon a field of long grass that appears as if it's blowing in the wind. The shadow of a figure stands amongst the green blades, standing tall, a set of knives hanging at their side.

A scrolling script at the bottom of the page, highlighted in bold, yellow paint, reads: *Long Live King Alcor*. The name strikes a burning through my chest, like a lightning bolt sent straight through my heart. I see Asha from above the artwork, looking curious at my sudden intense attention.

I turn the page around and ask, "Who is depicted here?" When Piré reads the words, her pale face turns almost ghostly before turning toward Asha whose brows lift as she sees the painting.

Piré's voice is so low I am nearly touching her face as she speaks. "There are Keepers who... well, they are hoping the King in the South is successful."

King in the South? I run my hand through my hair, careful to keep the hood of the cloak safely on my head. Asha's face is still frozen in shock, shifting her eyes from the words to Piré to the words again, and I am sure this revelation is something much more dangerous than I could ever understand.

I lower the parchment a bit, turning it away from the room's entrance. I see other posters with similar writing, the yellow script forming phrases like, *The King is Coming, Support our Sol,* and *Keepers for Kings.* A moment of heavy silence blankets the room. The chatter of Keepers outside continues, punctuating the wordless minutes between us.

Eventually, Asha moves to pull the painting down onto the table. "This is quite a dangerous position to take." Her eyes never leave the shadowed figure. "However, all people are welcome to their own... opinions."

I let out a heavy breath, not realizing how long I had been holding it. Piré appears even more relieved to hear the acceptance, or at least indifference, toward the artist's declaration.

The room suddenly feels very public, open to prying eyes. The tension of war and the opinions of various realms felt so far away when Gazil spoke of it all those weeks ago; even when Rostair mentioned fighting on the border, it was at least somewhat removed. This, I see now, was naive. The Keepers who made these posters certainly feel strongly about this war, about this "king." I suppose it is likely many know warriors on the front, fighting for one side or the other. I wonder what Asha thinks about this conflict, being from a neutral realm like the Sun. Although I met her mere hours ago, I feel a desperate need to know her opinion, trusting her to know the right way to think. But she remains silent, keeping her opinions of the words to herself. Piré is also notably silent.

I glance at the picture once more, "May I keep this?" I did not think the young girl's face could grow paler, but my question leaves her deathly. She looks to Asha yet again, eager for the older and socially superior woman to answer for her.

Feeling this desperate and nonverbal request, Asha sighs. "Centrea, you cannot be seen with such a phrase. Even possessing this, even muttering such words aloud in Endoneth... it could be seen as an offense worthy of death." Her eyes meet mine, pleading with me to see reason.

Before I can answer, a hand taps my shoulder, and I hear a familiar voice. "Miss, whatever are you doing here?"

Mairette looks horrified. She shakes her head at Asha as Piré slips away, hoping no doubt to save herself from Mairette's wrath. "You should know better than to lead her here. This is, what, your third season?"

Asha bows her head in embarrassment as Mairette continues, "You are both highborn. This is a place for Keepers; it is sacred to us." She glances at the pages on the table and her eyes become wide and even more frantic. "You both must leave, leave now." She turns on her heel and walks toward the stairs, confident we will follow behind as instructed, which Asha does. I follow soon after, but only after I fold the parchment with the shadowy figure and stuff it in the waistband of my skirt. On our brisk walk out of the Red Wing, I take closer notice of the artwork lining the hallway. I spot several crescent moons and skies full of stars.

Asha and I part ways soon after emerging into the Gold Wing. "Perhaps we may learn more about one another over tea tomorrow?" she asks. Her smile cannot hide the exhaustion behind her eyes.

We both need time to sit and process our trip through the Red Wing. As soon as I reach my room, I grab the poster from my skirt and smooth it out atop my writing desk. The words nearly glow in the evening light, and the silhouette of the king casts a spirit of foreboding in my usually comfortable space. I wish I could know more about this supposed king and his motivations. All in Endoneth fear speaking of such issues, perhaps because of the king himself. All I have heard, all that I know, is the threat that looms over this realm and its people.

Mairette's words echo as I look into the shadowy figure once more.

*An enemy, someone meant to destroy you... Red is on the horizon.*

The Southern King and his people, they seek only power, and such a thing is quite dangerous when misplaced. I shake my head and grab the painting, folding it again before rushing to the chest of drawers on the opposite side of the room. I take the open the satchel from its spot in the drawer, placing the folded artwork inside and shutting the drawer shut. A thunderous pounding wracks my head as tears rise to my eyes. I make a whispered wish that Rostair's armies succeed in stopping the Lord of the South, this Alcor, from setting foot in the Ice Realm, in Endoneth.

I move to the bed in my chambers, reaching for the hidden poem. I squint at the unfinished words, hoping the rhapsodic lines will offer comfort and a decent distraction. With each new piece of information I learn about the Ice Realm, about Nourels and its people, the more decisive my guesses become. I place the poem to the side before pulling a fresh page in front of me and dividing the blank canvas into eight segments. At the top of each section, I write out the missing word with the words before and after. With these phrases written out, I list words that may fit:

away —o-- war,
- won
- among
- some
These f— words,
- fire
- fine
- forced
one so —-r,
- far
- err
- fair

Over and over, word after word, I feel myself growing closer to the original lines. After an hour or so, the poem is more complete than before:

*A starry night, away <u>from</u> war,*
*Where we the children lay before;*
*These f— words, to one so —r,*
*Hold close to heart while never near;*
*Remember, S—, your purpose be,*
*For realms and —le you — the key;*
*With <u>bated</u> breath I always hold,*
*'Till you return, our brave and bold,*
*For the <u>good</u> of all should ne'er be sold.*

The good of all to never be sold. I wonder what the poet means by this. But, before my mind can wander far, I hear the light rap on the heavy door follow swiftly by Mairette's voice, "Miss, would you enjoy tea for the night?" She opens the door without waiting for my response and takes long strides toward the table.

I shuffle the papers around to obscure the view of the poem, placing a few scribbled drawings at the top. "Mairette—" I start, knowing my friend will likely be livid after the visit this afternoon; however, she holds up a hand to halt my words.

"Centrea. I need you to hear my words. The Lord in the South, Lord Alcor," the words force her face to twist, her voice trembling as she continues, "he is no King, and he is responsible for the loss of much at Endoneth. So, so much."

My heart drops, tears prickling my eyes as fear dominates Mairette's voice, her entire disposition. This reaction only validates my reaction to the portrait, the sense of foreboding becoming even more prominent. "Centrea, you are so special to me. I am not upset to see you in the Keepers' wing, for seeing the paintings or speaking with lower Keepers. I am upset that you may be placed in a position of danger. Do you hear me?" Her voice grows more desperate with each word, the tears now flowing from her eyes down her face, her nose running as she attempts to regain her composure.

I run from my place on the bed to my friend, guiding her toward one of the sofas before assuring her, "Do not fret, Mairette. I believe you. If anything, I am as scared of this man as you are." The words seem to calm her slightly, the affirmation of my position acting as a salve for her weakened state.

Mairette's breathing steadies, and her hand on my arm is now a gentle grasp rather than a wringing grip. I reach for the tea on the table. "I do apologize for my wandering into the Keeper's sacred wing. I understand there are ways of living in Endoneth, and I've disrespected those…"

She squeezes my arm and turns to me, "That is mainly a rule the Lord himself follows. There is no true 'tradition' to isolate the Keepers of the estate. It is just the way of things here. We have our place and the guests, you have yours."

I pause and contemplate this statement. "But… " I begin slowly, "how do you know that I am not merely a Keeper from another estate or, somehow, another realm."

She looks at me with great sympathy, a look that I have not seen in a long while from Mairette, similar to the way Asha looked at me out in the archery field, before explaining, "The clothing you wore, it was filthy and torn, yes. But it was quite expensive. More expensive than those of a typical Keeper, even in the finest of homes." She pauses, as if wondering to herself how much of the truth, of the other realms, my mind can handle. "Your clothing, your belongings, your taste in food and drink, would indicate someone of high status, someone who is likely missed. The Lord... he... he has been in contact with leaders from the North, some from other realms as well... searching for... well, for anything helpful." She chooses her words so carefully, I wonder how much of this she is meant to share with me, particularly the parts that required a bit of sleuthing to find.

Rostair, who was known for his coldness and stern leadership before my arrival, must not be a leader who appreciates knowledge shared without his approval. This warms my heart, my hand grasping Mairette's which is still gripping my arm. "Thank you for telling me this, Mairette. I know there is still much that I do not know, and largely much that you do not know about me either. I just hope... I hope that in the end I am someone that I would be proud of."

Her face contorts into a look of utter pain before she says, "You will always be someone I am proud to call friend."

I hope I am right.

# Thirteen

The nightmares continue throughout the night. Echoing voices scream, "Long live King Alcor" and "Support our Sol" and mingle with the memories of my Endoneth loved ones, each warning me to avert my eyes from a hooded figure running toward me. The man, the same man I saw in the artwork from the Red Wing, moves swiftly through a fog in the dream. His eyes burn a crimson red, and he quickly approaches as he glides over the ground, seemingly floating in the mist, creating a horrifying sight from which I cannot escape. When the figure speaks, its voice emerges like more of a high-pitched screech with each word punctuated by long gulps of air, as if each syllable requires an extraordinary amount of strength. "I'm... here... for... you."

I wake the following day with an unusual burst of energy, my body maybe overly grateful for escaping the shadow in the nightmare. Stretching my arms wide and emitting a loud yawn, I look toward the stained-glass window, the sunlight barely trickling in through the colored glass. As my head turns, I let out a slight yelp, seeing a figure huddled in the red chair near the bed. At my sound of surprise, the figure shudders awake, his grey eyes looking shaken and tired. Rostair looks more stressed than Mairette has been while planning the ball. His eyes are bloodshot and hair is terribly disheveled. His choice of clothing, a plain black shirt and black linen pants, also alarms me, the simple appearance quite uncharacteristic.

"Rostair, are you well?" I lift my head, suppressing another yawn as I see the frantic look flashing across his face.

Rostair sinks deeper into the velvet chair, letting out a weary sigh before peering up at me beneath heavy lids. "It was a long night, has been a long few nights, if I'm honest." His voice mirrors his appearance, the usual charm gone, replaced with doubt and grief. "You know, I inherited this position during wartime. Of course, my mother prepared me as best she could for the moment I became Lord, but sometimes... there is no warning...  You must... well, she had to make... the decisions were difficult, and she had so little time to make them before..." Rostair balls his hands into fists so tight I see small trickles of red begin trailing down his palms.

I rush to find a washcloth and pry his hands open to assess his self-inflicted wounds. Whimpers of despair escape his lips as he continues his attempt to develop a coherent sentence. "The death... the death of my people. It is... too much... and now... he... she... they approach, and I-I cannot ascertain... cannot plan... cannot... cannot..." The frustration riddling his mind forces the words to come out in desperate spurts, his face flushed and eyes beginning to brim with tears. Seated at the edge of the bed, I watch this man whom I have grown to admire, whom others revere, spiral into emotional turmoil. "I just... I know she thought she had more time. And I cannot help but think..." His head falls into the red-stained washcloth. He need not finish the sentence for me to understand his fear of death, of its fated arrival.

I wait, too stunned to move or speak. Rostair remains hunched over, his head in his hands, his shoulders moving up and down with silent whimpers. "I just need to... focus on... the ball. The war may come in a matter of days, but... they will keep them at bay, I am certain." The words, muffled as they barely escape through his fingers, are more to convince himself than me. I am unsure if he fully recognizes my presence, still merely staring at the plain linen of his black shirt as he hides his face.

He continues to mutter whispers into his still-bleeding palms, too quiet to discern. While I await some sort of acknowledgement, his last phrase sinks in.

War is close? The last I was aware, fighting was at the border, still many miles away. However, the battles could potentially reach Endoneth in days. Fear strikes deep in my stomach as the terrible premonition Mairette delivered during the ritual bitterly returns to the front of my mind.

Could this be the red on the horizon? The enemy coming to harm those I have come to love? Rostair's hand on my leg shakes the fearful thoughts from my mind as he looks up from his hands and stares past me. His look is vacant, so worn and tense; I can only imagine what the last few war updates brought forth.

"Is there anything I can do?" The words scrape across my throat. The alarm of Rostair's abrupt visit has dried my mouth. He still stares behind me, finding it almost difficult to return to the present, to the horrible reality of war and death.

"Rostair," my hand cradles his cheek, now stained with streaks of blood and dried tears as his stoic figure remains unmoved, "we are safe here, just like you said. We are safe here and all will be well."

Despite my lack of conviction, the words appear to pull him from the haze of sorrow and concern. His eyes flick up to meet mine. "Of course, of course. Endoneth itself is blessed, protected with an ancient magic. And, while not impenetrable, the intruders would make their presence known long before reaching the home itself. In theory, anyway." I wipe my thumb over his cheek as he continues, again attempting to convince himself of the protection. "I procured the spell, the enchantment, after... well, after my parents..." His voice fades away and I nod in understanding, soothing him into a sense of security.

"I am sure the enchantment will protect us all, Rostair. Do not fret. There are also guests among us who I am certain are well-versed in conflict. They would also no doubt protect us." My thoughts turn to Asha, a self-proclaimed master of the bow. Would these guests, Asha included, actually risk their lives in defense of the estate and the near strangers out of a sense of honor or nobility? I am unsure. However, this thought convinces Rostair, and, as he nods his head and moves to rise, he appears at least indifferent to the worries he brought with him this morning.

We take the opportunity to forget the conflict, talks of wars and plans of escape completely out of the question, for the rest of the morning. Mairette, a bit shocked to see Rostair in my chambers so early on the week of Greentime Ball, brings a green tea blend, nodding a bit embarrassingly toward my guest before offering to retrieve an extra pot.

I push my own mug across the table toward him. "You likely need the comfort of a warm beverage more than I."

He smiles and slides the glass toward me once more. "We both deserve warmth. Besides, we are not discussing the pains that may haunt me this day, remember?" I nod gingerly, placing the mug to my lips and sipping. It takes Mairette only a few moments before she reemerges with another set of tea alongside additional handheld sandwiches and scones.

"Thank you so much, Mairette." I take a small, raspberry scone into my hands and lick my lips before remembering. "Oh, and I will be ready for our dance session this afternoon, of course. If you could bring the appropriate attire, I may ready myself here."

She grins slightly, the tray that formerly held Rostair's tea kettle resting on her hip. "Of course, Miss. I hope you have practiced." Her note is filled with humor; however, I know the stress she must feel with the date of the ball fast approaching. I wonder if she is aware of the looming threat, of the potential for her long-awaited and thoughtful event to be interrupted by those who mean us all harm. I look to Rostair who merely sips on his own cup of tea, clearly not intending to send a warning of any sort.

I turn back to Mairette who is now tensely tapping her foot on the tile floor. "Of course, I have taken time here and there to memorize the movements. You shall see!" I flash a smile, and she returns one of her own.

She nods curtly at me, then gives a short nod to Rostair before spinning around and rushing toward the corridor. I bite into the scone, the bitter raspberries tamed by the subtle taste of lemon, and consider Mairette, the Keepers below us, and the war on the horizon. Instead of pondering the intricacies of war, Rostair grins and squints his eyes as he reaches for his own scone.

After filling his mouth full of blueberry scone and swallowing, he finally speaks what is on his mind. "So the dance, eh?" The grin grows to consume his face and my blood bubbles to the surface of my cheeks. I cross my legs, squeezing them together as he continues his teasing. "We all need a release every once in a while, trust me. It is stressful to lead an entire estate on my own. However, my sources of stress release are typically less... rhythmic."

His smile is more than welcome after seeing him at his lowest point, even if it leaves me feeling more exposed than I ever have. He refuses to pry further, saying, "It would be uncouth," despite enjoying recalling the memory for himself. He coolly shifts the conversation to other forms of preparation, interested to hear about my impression of the Ice Realm's many traditions and my place within them.

The few remaining hours of the morning are consumed by talk of the Greentime Ball. The discussion of my dress is of utmost interest. I attempt to describe the dress as best I can, yet ultimately, in my own estimation, fall short.

The entire time, Rostair grins and nods intently, taking intermittent bites of sandwich and scone between clarifying questions: "What sort of threads hold the fabric pieces together?"

"How many stars appear?"

"What shade of brown is used?"

While I admire his interest, it astonishes me the details that concern him, questions I never truly considered noteworthy. I heartily respond to each eager question, smiling and laughing with Rostair as if we are old friends, as if there is no war in the realm, as if there is no Greentime Ball or responsibility as Lord or Guest of Honor. And, after fully exploring the visual of my ball attire, he finally relents his questioning and we resume discussions of balls and dancing. As we continue our conversation, the topics of favors and romance, of affairs and intrigue creep along the tip of my tongue, as they have been ever since Gazil brought them to mind.

Would Rostair bestow his honor upon any person this season, and, if so, could it be me? But the possibility of Helzaf truly coming to join her former love alongside the possibility of Gazil's desperate attempts to deceive me into abandoning my affections toward Endoneth's Lord ultimately halt my inquiry. And so I sit and laugh and talk with a friend, reading a few stories from *A Fairy Dream* as the minutes tick away and reality slithers back into view.

I feel Rostair knows me in a way no other person has, and it lightens the weight that has settled on my chest since hearing about our uncertain future. It takes everything within me to keep my promise to him, to not mention the war or its consequences until the clock strikes twelve. But, when twelve o'clock makes its unwelcome arrival, I am glad I kept the promise.

Today is the final rehearsal for my dancing solo before the Greentime Ball. I did not lie to Mairette when I informed her of my dedication to memorizing each set of movements, and, as I completed the dance for the first time this afternoon, she glows with appreciation and pride. "Amazing, Miss! Utterly gorgeous. Oh, I cannot imagine how you will look in the gown they have designed for you. Ahh, it shall be stunning!"

It may be the mounting expectation of the ball only three days away, but Mairette showers me with more accolades than usual.

"Again!" Her smile shines as she requests another show. I gasp a bit, gulping down air enough to catch my breath and start the routine over again. The beats are subtle yet consistent, allowing me to glide into various motions, spinning and jumping through the sunlight of midday in the ballroom.

"Chin up here!" I hear Mairette yell over my shoulder, keeping a close eye on each facial expression and micromovement. When the song is finished once more, her face is practically glowing with delight. "I have truly never seen someone perform this dance more naturally!" She swoons, "It is as if your feet were made for these sudden yet sultry movements." She bends down to grab hold of a water container, offering me a generous gulp before requesting one last run of the entire number.

My heart is bursting inside my chest, my breaths echoing through the ballroom in exaggerated heaves. I hear claps joining the sound and turn to see Asha walking toward Mairette and me, avoiding the droplets of sweat on the tiled floor. "Magnificent." She grins. "It is captivating to see you dance." She rests a gentle hand on her exposed hip, the waistband of her skirt as low as could be, and looks around the room.

Mairette, seeming less pleased with the sudden arrival of Asha and her critical eye, nods toward me. "Be sure to keep practicing before the grand event. You must not grow indifferent before such an important night."

She barely acknowledges Asha before rushing to the end of the ballroom and through a passage door into the Red Wing. Asha looks after Mairette with a look of slight disdain before redirecting her energy toward me, still steadying my breath from the exertion of the dance.

"I was told you would be practicing for the ball, and I thought I would remind you of our arrangement to enjoy a kettle together." Her words appear innocent enough. "I can host you in my chambers, if you like?"

I nod my head and slowly eek out, "After… a bit of… cleaning and… new clothes."

Asha laughs and nods. "Yes, please do! I enjoy a sweaty woman myself, but perhaps not in my friendships." My cheeks redden as I gather my water container to leave. "I shall accompany you, if you do not mind," she adds as I begin walking toward the exit. "Then we can walk together to my quarters in the Green Wing." I look back and nod in agreement as she walks briskly to join me when I reach the archway.

As we venture through the halls of the bottom level, I listen to Asha describe her favorite aspects of Sun Realm architecture, a subject I can see means a great deal to her. "The ornate rooftop tiles that you see here in Endoneth are beautiful to be sure, but in my realm many of the livable homes use the roof as an additional gathering space for families and friends to spend time. Some have linens draped along pillars to create an awning of sorts, to protect from the sunlight."

She waves her arms dramatically as she describes the various linens and their origins, many woven in the Ocean, Valley, and Green Realms. "Each realm has a different technique and produces very different designs in their fabrics. I quite favor the Ocean Realm fabrics. They utilize unique materials from the sea that shimmer delightfully."

We climb the stairs toward the Blue Wing and, as we turn the final corner toward my chamber's hall, we halt abruptly, nearly colliding with Gazil who jumps to the side at the last moment. His look of shock is quickly replaced with a glimmer of grief. He opens his mouth to say something to me but shakes his grey tousled hair and moves past us toward the stairwell. I nearly reach my hand to stop him, to demand he reassure me of his loyalty and friendship, to dispel the rumors circling in my head since Rostair's pointed warning. In some ways, it is a relief that Gazil moves past us so swiftly, relieving me of the choice to confront him.

I sigh deeply, forcing Asha to look at me sympathetically. "I know the old man is a friend of yours." She turns her head toward the stairs then back toward me before grasping my hand in hers. "Come on, let us gather some clean clothes so we may take tea."

I feel renewed once dressed in clean, dry clothes, having washed away the film of sweat that developed during the rehearsal. While I flit this way and that, preparing myself for the evening ahead, Asha sits on one of the two couches, a book in her hands as the fireplace continues its low roar, burning less intensely than in the winter months yet still maintaining a steady purr of warmth. "The tales of fairies are most marvelous," she notes, turning the pages viciously. "They are most noble creatures, filled with magic and courage."

I look into the mirror, checking the navy linen tunic and brown satin pants. I eye the speed with which Asha consumes the words on each page. "How can you comprehend the story itself at such a pace?"

She chuckles at the notion and says, "It is one of my many talents, Centrea. Fast reader." With that she shuts the book and stands. "Shall we?"

I follow her through the door and back into the blue-tiled hallway. While I usually make my way toward the lower level or the libraries and studies of the Orange Wing, we move toward the Green Wing. Its halls are beautiful. Unlike much of Endoneth, where floor-to-ceiling windows abound, the Green Wing's walls are utterly devoid of windows. Instead, as soon as the tiled floors shift from blue patterns to green, I notice sun emanating from above, the entire ceiling being one continuous skylight.

"Perhaps after our tea, the sun will have set," Asha notes as she notices my interest in the windows above. "The stars shine brightly throughout the halls at night."

I suddenly feel a sense of embarrassment for not visiting the wing sooner. Even on my initial tour with Rostair, we never ventured into the wing itself, he merely pointed toward the direction of the additional guest rooms and assured me I would always maintain my room in Blue. Many guests, like Asha, who abide here were latecomers of the season, often arriving just this week. However, as I gaze around the beautiful evening sunshine, I wonder why other guests do not utilize the wing more often.

Almost as if sensing the question in my mind, Asha says, "I believe the Lord Rostair does not favor the stars. He believes that most guests likely feel the same, I suppose." We continue walking through the halls, turning left then right before stopping in front of a large door. "I, however, adore the stars and the night sky." Asha flashes a smile as she turns the large knob at the center of the door and invites me in.

The room is cozy, nearly half the size of my own. Against the left corner is a large bed with a bright green quilt. On the opposite corner sits a small couch and green leather chair set around a circular table. The tiles fit together to create a large design, rather than each individual tile holding its own; the intricate shades of green come together in the center of the room to form a large tree. The tiles nearest the door are carved to resemble bark, and the tiles representing leaves contain small bumps to solidify the illusion. Asha removes her boots and places them to the right of the door, looking at me expectantly. I follow her lead, unlacing the brown boots and setting them near hers. She rings a small bell to the side of the door and saunters toward the couch and chair.

"You may make yourself at home," she calls over her shoulder, sinking into the couch and letting out a contented sigh.

I make my way toward her, eager to take a rest after an intense day, both physically and emotionally. I've intentionally kept my thoughts away from Rostair's visit this morning, which has successfully prevented me from considering the realities ahead, and I wonder now how much other guests know regarding the war and their potential places in it. I look at Asha, a woman I have known less than a day but feel like I've known forever, and consider how much to divulge.

Again, she appears to read my thoughts and answers, "I realize there is much struggle in the Ice Realm. However, I am sure many guests, myself included, knew the risks of attending the Greentime Ball and chose to make an appearance despite this." Her eyes glance toward me; wisdom oozes from them and calms my nerves. "Many would not venture into this realm had they no faith in Lord Rostair's ability to protect his estate and its people."

This matter-of-fact statement eases my anxieties even further. "What do you know of this war?" The words leave my lips before I can truly consider their implications. The posters in the Red Wing surely prove there are monarchists in our midst, and it is likely some guests share their sentiments. Asha takes a moment to consider her answer; I can see her working to develop an appropriate version of events.

"This war is years in the making. I am certain you have learned of the two sides—those who support Rostair and the other Lords of the Northern Realms and those who support the Poet King from the Star Realm." She thinks through her next statement. "It is a conflict that is above all about power and protection. Both sides believe their way of ruling is correct, that it will protect as many people and their ways of life."

She pauses once more, the lingering silences between snippets of responses becoming nearly unbearable as I settle on the edge of the green chair. "Centrea, it is most appropriate to avoid this topic with others. You cannot be sure who to trust in a place like Endoneth. I am sure you realize this." Her response gives me pause, uncovering the stupidity of my queries to a stranger.

She again sees my concern and responds directly to my thoughts, "I can ask you to trust me, but cannot force you to do so, of course. I am sure it must be jarring to awaken in a foreign place with no recollection of who you are or what you are able to do. Just know this..." she squints her eyes, almost as if pained by something, before continuing, "you are... you are special. Do not let them deceive you into thinking any differently. Give nothing away, do you hear?"

Her cryptic words confuse me further and I open my mouth to ask her if she knows me, knows my family, knows my father. However, a knock on the door pulls us from the conversation as a Keeper brings a tray into the room and sets it softly on the table.

Asha looks toward the Keeper and whispers a quick, "Thank you," before moving a hand forth toward the kettle.

The young Keeper, a plump, tanned, and black-haired woman, bows ever so slightly, never taking her eyes away from Asha. The tension between them is palpable and I feel the sudden desire to leave the two alone. The Keeper seems similarly interested in a private moment with Asha, staring at Asha's hands as she pours us both a cup of warm tea.

Perhaps noticing the Keeper lingering or acknowledging the sexual tension for herself, Asha says, "Not tonight."

I avoid looking at the Keeper as she sulks toward the door, her head a bit low and stride somber.

I look back toward Asha, my brows high and mouth a bit agape, "Spending the night with a Keeper?"

She ignores my curiosity and sips her mug. "Never you mind, Centrea."

I giggle a bit before tasting the sweet honey tea for myself. It is nice to see that not all guests are averse to being friendly with Keepers.

The last hours of the evening pass in an instant it seems. I lean my head against the back of the leather cushion and peer outside the ceiling, the stars as dazzling as Asha mentioned they would be at night. How I desperately wish my chambers, as beautiful they may be, included this feature. However, I think of my elegant stained glass and know that I would miss the rush of color during the day and the image of the primrose watching over me at night.

I weigh in my mind which I would prefer until Asha's yawn brings me back to the present. "Perhaps we should ready ourselves for the night. The final day of preparations is known to be one of great business for the Guest of Honor."

My eyes stay fixed to the sky. The strongest stars brightly twinkle in and out of vision, leading the faded sparks, stars that live farther from our world, together to form constellations.

"You seem to enjoy the stars." Asha's voice reaches my ears as an almost ethereal noise, humming in the background as the stars sing their own songs to me. "They hold many meanings. I do not know the particulars, but an old friend once knew. She would tell me about the stories of the stars, about how each star held its own past and that the stories were ever changing, not fixed in time but waiting to be interpreted."

My eyes move from one bright light to the next, allowing the information to sweep over me, and watching the stars shift and glimmer to deeper shades of yellow, orange, and white. I wonder how many know the stars in such a way and what they are telling each of us without us even realizing. What would they say to me now, with the most important event mere days away; with war on our doorstep; with my memories still swirling bits of fog? If I can trust anything, it would be the stars. Unlike people, they would never lie. I can feel that with great certainty.

That night, after wandering through the halls of the Green Wing before managing to stumble across blue tiles, I enter my room in a state of pure exhaustion, too tired to even sip Mairette's nighttime tea. My state of weariness is not enough to stave away nightmares, though, and this time they're bolder and clearer than before. Fields of green shine brightly in the sun. My pale-yellow dress echoes the realm's glee at the arrival of Greentime and the final touches to prepare the ball to be the most extravagant to date. I sit amongst the blades of green, while guests and Keepers hover nearby, occupied with their respective responsibilities.

Rostair suddenly towers above me, reaching his hand low to grab mine and pulling me into a tight embrace. "You are the one I favor, dear Centrea. You must have known all along." The words come in rasped whispers, the cool feel of tears lining his cheeks as he presses his face against mine.

His closeness ignites such a longing within me, that the pit of my stomach soars at his proclamation of affection. The sun abruptly dips low from its place high in the sky, creating a stunning view of millions of stars surrounding us. The stars leap from the night sky, forming curtains of twinkling lights that surround Rostair and me as his arms squeeze me tighter, his hands running from the nape of my neck to my lower back in soothing strokes. The stars linger around us, a layer of protection from the outside world, from the realm, from disapproving onlookers, from lost memories and honor-bound obligations. The warmth of his chest consumes me, spreading throughout my body and engulfing my every fear in its wake.

A liquid warmth falls from his chest to my abdomen and onto our feet. In an instant the notion of security shatters as Rostair lets out an ear-piercing cry, his white hair flying back and his mouth twisted in pain. I look down at my yellow dress, now stained with warm, red liquid. The blood seeping from Rostair's chest pools at our feet, amongst the grass and flowers.

Stunned, I leap back, attempting to assess his injury and help heal him. However, once beyond my reach, he is on the ground without a warning or fall. He lies lifeless, his legs broken into crooked shapes behind his torso and his eyes rolled back into his skull. I heave forward at the sight, clutching my stomach as my eyes scan the injuries that multiply with each second, the source of which is nowhere to be seen.

A blast from up ahead pulls my eyes forward, and the stars and Rostair's dead body disappear. The sky is painted black and the grass below a deep red. I attempt to move, to rush away from this horrid place, but cannot. Ahead, the hooded figure, the one from many nightmares before, emerges on the horizon, clad in armor and holding a sword. Unlike in other dreams, the face of the figure is clearer, his icy-blue eyes filled with evil intent, partially hidden by sweeping strands of black hair. With each step closer, my heart falls deeper into despair, as if I await a death that is unavoidable, immovable. With a flash, he is before me, his sword held high above his head, a grin lining his face.

A flash of lightning follows the roar of thunder that wakes me unceremoniously from my sleep. I lift myself from the bed, testing my ability to move freely about the room. Pounds of rain hit the stained glass in gushes. I walk to a water basin and splash cool water on my face, attempting to wash away the memory of Rostair and the shadow figure. I slowly walk back toward the center of the room, the tiles beneath my feet providing an additional source of coolness. Pacing with intent, I march between the various spaces in the room—first retrieving the poem from beneath my mattress, then pulling a clean sheet of paper and quill from the writing table and finally settling into the sofa closest to the fire.

I reread the words *'Till you return, our brave and bold* until my heart returns to a normal beat. I picture the author speaking to me. I am safe. I am protected. And I belong to people out there, people who care for me.

And, what if... what if they are in search of me? My true family? At this thought dozens of possibilities fly from my mind. I run back to the writing desk and pull the drawer completely out of the socket, bringing it to the table between the couches, filled to the brim with notes and possibilities.

I take out each paper, one by one, and delicately place them into piles. The most pressing notes I put in the center, where the painting from the Red Wing, Mairette's premonition, and Gazil's description of the realms all fall into place. I read my memory of Gallen and add it to the pile, thinking perhaps he is connected to all of this. After sorting my notes, I place those of least importance back into the drawer, mainly my ramblings of emotions over Rostair and the way of the Ice Realm. I then read each segment of notes carefully. I read over the descriptions of the fairies in the woods and their fallen friend, of the power of the pool and my sudden burst of memory, of the birds that gathered on the platform at Rostair's beck and call, of Mairette's foreboding of an unsuitable connection.

On and on, note after note, until I reread the dreaded words from that night: There is someone coming for you... An enemy, someone meant to destroy you and those you have grown to care for, to love... Red is on the horizon.

I know that I am someone of importance, someone from the Mountain Realm with value. Whether only to one person or to many, it is no matter. It is enough to have an enemy in the Poet King of the Star Realm. I wipe my eyes with the heart of my palms.

Tears sting the corners of my eyes as I think of the warm feeling when I remembered Gallen and his love for me. I now feel desperate to remember, as if my former failures to recall memories mean nothing.

I can no longer wait for a message that may never come. Cannot stand to face the many guests who snicker and judge. Who claim to know my father or my realm yet refuse to share such knowledge.

I need to return to the pool, to the cavern of magic. I stand, ready to burst into the early morning light. Anxiety propels me, my mind refusing to rest until I make something happen, to fix what was lost. The thought of the pool and the memory it spurred bring out something within me. I have been so idiotic, distracted by thoughts of a ball and Rostair, of favor and social standing. It all seems pointless in this moment.

"I should have returned weeks ago," I whisper through clenched teeth.

I quickly rush to find more comfortable clothing, something that would serve me well on the long walk to the stables then for the ride on the winged horse. I halt for a moment, bitterly realizing my ignorance of the way itself. I sigh and think of another solution. Perhaps I may ask Rostair to accompany me once more during the day of rest before the ball. The thought settles into my brain for long enough to ease the rattling of self-loathing and anxiety.

"Yes," I touch my hand to my chin thoughtfully, "surely he will accompany me."

Mairette saunters into the room a few hours later, a massive stack of papers in one hand, and a single cup of warm tea in the other. "I apologize, Miss," she says breathlessly. "This is all I could muster this morning. I fear I am already behind on preparations for the day."

I look outside the window and barely see sunlight. I wonder how many tasks she has already completed and at what hour she woke to complete them. Looking back to Mairette, I notice how unusually frazzled she appears, her eyes red and her curls braided carelessly in a knot atop her head, stray pieces flying out in numerous places.

"Sweet Mairette, take one moment to sit and rest, for me." I pat a spot on the sofa and take a seat on the table while shifting my own stack of notes behind me, out of her view. Mairette barely notices, setting the cup down next to me with a thud, a bit of the liquid spilling out. She uses her now free hand to shift through her papers, pulling the page on top to the bottom and scanning the fresh words with feverish speed.

I stifle a laugh, leaning over to grasp the tea and breathe in the fresh peppermint. "Is there anything you need me to—"

Mairette interrupts, "Centrea, there is a precise list of items that need to be completed before midnight tonight." Her direct address catches me a bit off guard, even when Asha warned me of this very reality just last night. "First, I would advise you to finish your cup of tea." I bring the cup to my mouth and begin my first task, a bit hesitant to know what else is in store if drinking my morning tea is included in the list.

"Next, I need you to meet with the dress designer for your final fitting. I would accompany you, however there is just much to accomplish in the limited time we have left. After the fitting, you must walk the ballroom and approve the greenery with Lord Rostair. This will hopefully be brief; however, the Lord is known to be quite… particular when it comes to these events." She pauses, licking the tip of her thumb to flip her current page to the other side.

"After this, you must choose a plant from the garden to have placed by your Seat of Honor. You also have a number of additional tasks to complete at your leisure." I nearly spit the tea from my mouth at the word, knowing there will be no such leisure afforded me while I complete the tasks. "You must help choose the order of music, the reading of words, and review the remaining guests who are without favors." Mairette sighs deeply at the end of her soliloquy, looking at me for the first time since arriving this morning. "It may seem too much, but I assure you—"

This time I interrupt. "The tea is finished, now onto the fitting, correct?"

I smile meekly at Mairette who wears a look of deep appreciation. "I shall send for him now."

Soon after Mairette's departure, Komik arrives, and I understand Mairette's interest in the designer. He is stout and cheery, easygoing and fashionable. His blonde hair is cut short to his head with a broad mustache curled at the ends.

"Splendid!" his voice booms low. His round rosy cheeks force his eyes to squint when he smiles. "The dress is complete. I do not see a need to alter it further."

I beam at his work. The addition of the primrose at the bottom adds a bit of color to the brown and the delicate embroidered moth rests on the shoulder.

"This work is fantastic. Thank you, truly." I turn in a circle, feeling the smooth fabric swish against the blue tile.

Komik's eyes exude delight. "You are welcome to enjoy a few glorious moments of rest before Mairette ushers you to your next engagement."

I nod appreciatively toward him, noticing the flush of red that tinges his cheeks when he speaks of Mairette. "She is a wonderful Head Keeper, is she not? I am just fortunate for her friendship." The delight pours from his words.

"We are all fortunate, indeed," I respond. Before I can censor myself, I continue, "And I believe she deserves someone of equal caliber." I nod toward him and smile.

Komik averts his eyes and shuffles awkwardly before nodding in agreement. "Please, enjoy the remaining hours of your day. While it is a stressful position, the Guest of Honor, it is one not many are fortunate enough to experience firsthand. Enjoy every moment."

And with that, he pushes the door open and strides away.

I take Komik's advice and leisurely undress and hang the gown near the mirror. Before I meet Rostair for our walk-through, I contemplate my request to return to the cavern. I will surely find an appropriate moment to make such a request, but how do I ask. I wish to avoid the circumstances of our last visit, if possible.

The notion of myself and the Lord of the estate swimming with no clothing is surely not something I would like to revisit amongst the guests and Keepers who will likely be present. I walk toward the chest of drawers, the breeze of the cool air tickling my bare skin. I choose a purple skirt that ends just above the knee paired with a cropped, cotton tunic that leaves both my shoulders and midriff exposed, allowing my tanned skin to glimmer in the growing light of day.

I tie the top of the tunic as I peer into the mirror, whispering to myself over and over, "You are brave, you are bold, you are brave…" I spin on the heel of my leather boots and hold my head high as I venture to meet Rostair in his favorite room.

The ballroom looks almost unrecognizable with the Greentime decor covering every inch of flooring and climbing up the four columns that outline the room. The Keepers must have worked all night bringing in a great number of flowers, palms, and branches. Even the floor itself is decorated meticulously with rows of flowers and potted trees, leaving a path to enter the busy room and space for dancing. As I continue walking, it feels as if the room elongates, allowing space for more and more plants and art fixtures. I wonder how strong the enchantment on the room must be, as the ballroom grows to at least ten times the size it once was.

At the end of the long space sits a stage, the dark wood contrasting the fantastic golden tiles with stunning effect. I walk through a path of trees and bushes before I reach the stage. Atop the riser there appear two massive chairs, sitting like thrones on the wooden platform. I lean forward, placing my hands on the warm wood to look a bit closer. Both thrones had been carved from massive blocks of ice, delicate designs etched like marvelous statues. The largest is placed at the center of the stage, the material glimmering in the sunshine, while the second sits nearby, a bit smaller yet no less artful in its carved markings. Despite the warm air, neither chair melts, both standing firmly upon the plats of wood, exuding excellence and authority.

"Here is where we sit." I turn quickly to see Rostair's solemn face. The last we met, there was much on his mind, a fact that forces me to hold on to my request a bit longer, not wanting to trouble him further.

*You are brave; you are bold.*

The words ring a bit hollow as I see the pain in Rostair's posture as he turns to survey the scene, nodding his approval at certain plants and configurations, while wincing at others. Within moments, he seems to have noted nearly twelve issues with the decor and briskly walks toward Mairette, who has just scampered into the ballroom to see its progress.

I walk along the edge of the one wall, getting lost in the beautifully coordinated flowers as Mairette and Rostair speak tersely about a group of statues. "We cannot include these. We must be reasonable," Rostair's voice rasps.

Mairette refuses to retreat. "This is the way it must be, Lord Rostair. It is tradition to include references to all nine."

I come across a wall of flowers, the various colors placed together to create the outline of a white, winged stag. The room smells sickly sweet, with hints of floral and fruits and soil mingling together. A few paces beyond that I hear the trickling of water pouring into a small pond, where glowing green fish swim in small circles. I hear their two voices move on to discuss the particular shade of green of the wall of bushes that line the far end of the hall just beyond the stage and thrones. As I eavesdrop, I understand a bit more about who Rostair was before my arrival and discover that the word "particular" was a gracious euphemism on Mairette's part.

I attempt to ignore their conversation, which has shifted toward the level of enchantment placed upon the room and whether it is enough to keep the flowers from wilting, and instead turn toward the formerly contested group of statues. Similar to those in the garden courtyard, the nine statues are carved from impressive marble, and lines of gold and silver are included within the stone. Each presents anatomically correct plant figurines. According to the silver plaques attached to the base of each statue, each represents a plant native to one of the nine realms. I look inquisitively at each statue, attempting to sear the plants into my memory, helping me further develop an understanding of the Nine Realms and their unique characteristics.

*Ice Realm - Sarcodes Sanguinea*
*Mountain Realm - Picea*
*Green Realm - Dahlia Pinnata*
*Desert Realm - Salvia Dorri*
*Sun Realm - Tagetes Patula*
*High Realm - Ageratum*
*Valley Realm - Convallaria*
*Ocean Realm - Plumeria Rubra*
*Star Realm - Oenothera*

The words mean little to me, as if a foreign language. The statues themselves offer a beautiful look into the different landscapes. The small petals of the Desert flower are clearly meant for a dry environment and the plumeria rubra meant for more tropical weather. I scan the remaining flowers, impressed by the sculptor's ability to capture the intricacy of each plant, and halt when I examine the Star Realm flower more closely. I would recognize the shape of the flower from miles away. Delicate petals form a rosette at the center of the flower, surrounding stamens that jut out from the center.

"A primrose," I whisper in awe.

The rest of the world disappears around me—the frantic shuffling of Keepers, the continued conversation between Rostair and Mairette, the murmured discussions of guests enjoying the sunshine outside—fading to nothing as I stare at the flower etched in stone, the petals glittering in the sunlight that flows through the enchanted walls. The object that decorated my chambers for months, it was as if a part of myself stood before me, reminding me of who I've become while simultaneously encouraging me to push myself beyond this comfortable ignorance.

I stare and stare and stare, hoping to find a kernel of truth in the wrinkles of the flower petals or the lines creasing its leaves. I am left instead with the symbol of Star, our enemy in this war, and its Lord. I shake the connection away, rather choosing to revel in the notion of finding a part of me that moves beyond my past, something I've allowed to shower me in times of depression and joy, anxiety and peace, anger and grace. The primrose is so much more to me than a mere symbol, it represents the hardships and the triumphs of my life for over half of a year. And, as I have grown to love many who abide in this estate, I have also grown fond of the window through which I've seen this world.

"We should continue to make the rounds, Centrea." Rostair's voice startles me.

My hands, which were gripping tightly to the edges of the statue, quickly release the cool marble and instead grab the sides of my skirt, twisting the fabric between my thumb and index finger as he waits for my response. "Of course," is all I can manage.

When I finally rip my eyes from the nine statues, Rostair barely glances toward me, his head flicking left and right as if still assessing what portions of the ballroom need altering.

"This seems to be quite important work," I note, bringing my hand to his arm and beginning to follow his lead through the forest of flowers.

"Yes." The initial answer is concise and stoic. "There are many traditions to follow, much to organize and coordinate. I have a reputation to uphold and, especially now, I need to assert my authority and present Endoneth as a place that will always be one of glory."

I sense a kernel of fear behind this explanation, the looming conflict certainly causing more stress than usual. He places a warm hand on mine as we continue to weave through the pathways, pausing at times to note a specific structure or plant that Rostair deems unworthy of the celebration.

"We all must look our brightest during the Greentime Ball. Every pawn must be in its rightful place. Every flower, every tile, every light. It all must be utterly and wickedly spectacular." I admire him for his passion. He desires a place of excellence, likely a standard started by his great-grandfather. I wonder how tiresome such an expectation must be, how often Rostair feels obligated to uphold what was done before.

A few hours pass and I feel numb to the look of plants. All living things become green blurs before me as we twist and turn through the room several times through. We stand before the stage for the fifth time today, Rostair fiddling with the collar of his ruffled, red tunic and muttering something about the placement of the chairs, when I finally work up the courage to ask about our day of rest tomorrow.

"Rostair, I wonder if I could ask you to consider a favor."

He looks at me from the corner of his eyes before turning to face me fully. "Why of course, dear Centrea. Anything."

I am pleased to hear his willingness to listen, and it gives me a confidence boost. "Tomorrow I understand the entire estate enjoys a day of rest. And I would like to return to the… the cavern that… you know, the cavern."

I feel the betrayal of a blush rush to my cheeks as I fumble over the words, the enticing memory suddenly slamming into my mind and forcing my heart to beat at twice the normal speed. I look down, hoping Rostair ignores the blush and focuses on the question itself.

He clears his throat, pulling my chin gently upward so that my eyes meet his. "Centrea, of course. I would love nothing more than to return. Perhaps this time our trip will be uninterrupted."

The hand on my chin traces the line of my jaw and down my neck. The touch, the first intimate moment since arriving at the ballroom today, eases my anxiety, which was likely brought on by my own fear of rejection and only made worse by the tension clouding the air during this ballroom visit.

My shoulders lower, my muscles relax, and I relish in Rostair's nearness. "Thank you," I breathe, "I have wanted to return since our last adventure."

He smiles at this, his fingers brushing my collarbone. I inhale sharply. "I have wanted to return also." These words leave his lips in a whisper, his face leaning forward so I may hear more clearly. "I look forward to our meeting."

Later, while walking the garden, I wonder what sort of plant Guests of Honor typically choose to sit with them on the wooden platform. I attempted to elicit a useful response from Mairette before leaving the massive ballroom, but she barely paid me mind.

"Centrea," she said as she drew a delicate check mark near a line of scribbles on her latest stack of papers, "it may be whatever you wish. Some choose a plant that is meaningful to them. However, most choose based on aesthetics. I would suggest you trust your intuition."

A heavy sigh escapes me as I remember her half-hearted suggestion as I round a corner of the gardenscape. I look from one beautiful flower to the next. The choice should be a simple one. And with how little guidance Mairette provided I assume it is truly the least important decision of the entire event. Another sigh, another corner. I could choose a plant to match my gown, something that matches the rich colors that Komik so wonderfully wove. But the rows and rows of flowers do not assist me in my quest.

By my third sigh, I've entered an interesting part of the garden. Surely, I have seen this section before. I have spent many hours walking through every inch of this garden, but I had yet to notice this patch of bushes. I hesitate before stepping forward, the healthy green grass of spring suddenly crinkling beneath my feet, brittle and brown. I look around and see dark green bushes filled with dark plants, flowers of the deepest blues and purples. I reach out a hand to grasp one before it withers before my eyes. I try to run my hands along the leaves of the trees as I pass by, just as I do during my walks, and each drops low, the branches losing their leaves and shrinking until only trunks remain.

My jaw opens wide with concern as each plant seems to die away as I approach it. My mind reels, my vision growing blurry as I try desperately to rationalize my predicament. *How is this happening?* I reach a shaking hand toward a dark rose, hoping I feel something, even its thorns. Just before my fingers reach the black petals, it slips away, its bush following. I scream in frustration, my voice echoing through this mysterious layer of the garden. Gusts of wind cloud my senses, causing even more confusion. I hear something, a whisper, say, *It is foretold.*

I look around to find the source of the fiery voice. Its curious phrase is like a siren, beckoning me to find the source.

*It is foretold, young one. Come to your senses.*

My senses have never been more muddled. Before I know it, the wind grows to an angry torrent, pushing me into plants that die before me and blocking any sound from reaching me besides the voice repeating the same phrase over and over.

*Come to your senses... come to your senses... come to your senses.*

I fall to my knees, the coarse hay-like grass cutting into my knees. My hands reach up and hold my ears as I scream, wanting this to end, wanting to be back to where I once was—confused over a plant and a man and a cavern.

Suddenly, I feel a tug on my shoulder,

"Centrea!" The voice is fervent, fearful. "Centrea! Please, get up!" My eyes are closed so tightly my head hurts from the constant strain. I feel the grass below me, hear the sounds of birds and concerned chatter. When I finally look around me, I notice a small crowd murmuring to one another as I lie in the center of the statue-laden courtyard hugging my knees close to my chest.

I see Gazil out of the corner of my eye, his hand reaching out for me and his face filled with the utmost concern. "My dear Centrea, please say something."

This last statement is quiet compared to his earlier words as he notices my head shake from side to side and my arm push my tired body from the ground. It is only then that I see Gazil more clearly. His hair is disheveled and jaw a bit swollen. Now I am concerned to see my old friend hurting. Although we have not spoken for days now, I still see him as one of my closest friends, someone worthy of protection and support. With his help, I lift myself from my position and wave onlookers away as he guides me to a nearby stone bench.

I notice his delicate state as we walk arm in arm. His poor head is a bit scratched and bruised, his leg limping a bit as he attempts to walk naturally. The sharp intakes of breath with each step only verify the limp and pain. What on earth happened to my friend? Someone who, at one point, shared the most minute details of his days with me.

As we sit, I rasp, "Gazil, you're hurt." I know he hears the question within the statement: *What happened?*

He rubs his chin, pulling at the braids of his beard as he contemplates his response. "I could ask you the same. I have never seen someone in such a state." He avoids maintaining eye contact, as if attempting to shield me from how horrifying I must have looked and sounded.

"I do not..." I pause. I do not really know what to say. I am not sure if I completely know what happened or how I came to be pulling at my hair and screaming in the middle of Endoneth's gardens. "I am unsure what occurred. Perhaps I fell asleep and walked during a dream. You know how they often cause me such distress." This was a pitiful answer and Gazil knows. He nods anyway, appeasing my sense of control for a moment.

"I got lost in the woods last night, while I was not in my clearest state of mind." Ahh so he was intoxicated, and so soon before the Greentime Ball—bold.

Although I understand the stress of the upcoming event, I am shocked that Gazil would be so reckless.

"It looks much worse than it feels, mind you. Only scratches and bumps, nothing more." It certainly looks much worse than he claims, however I push my concerns aside, noticing how nervously he rubs the back of his neck, and focus on the remaining tasks for the ball.

"I still must review music and words and the favor-less guests for the ball." I sigh, gripping the bridge of my nose with a furrowed brow.

I feel Gazil straighten and when I look his way, he wears a bright smile and eagerly asks question after question regarding the preparations. I answer every question, explaining my experiences in the maze of the ballroom, the awe I felt at the enchanted space, and list again the number of tasks I have left to complete. He nods contemplatively when I complete my rant, and I am satisfied to have my companion back after a few days' distance. I realize now that, while Rostair means well, his concerns cannot be warranted when it comes to Gazil, who is such a steadfast friend.

"Would you like to see the archives?" he asks with a bit of a smirk. "I know you must make a list of guests who have yet to match together, all Guests of Honor must. I typically place the task on an apprentice; however, I know we both could use a reprieve from this madness."

He waves his hand around at the people, sharing looks and whispers as they pass by us, as they have since he led me to this bench. He is right—I despise the gossiping at my expense, the continued discussions amongst strangers as they contrive my story and my intentions.

"Let us go." At my response Gazil's smirk grows into a tight-lipped grin, and he grabs my hand and pulls me forward, grimacing a bit at the sudden force on his arm.

I gently rub his arm as we walk arm in arm toward the estate entrance. "You must be more diligent with your alcohol, Gazil. I cannot have you looking less than fabulous for the ball."

He squints his eyes tightly and sticks out his tongue at the notion of looking less than perfect at the important event. "Could you imagine? Me? With my repute for fashions of the most elegant sort? I would never live such a thing down." I laugh at his confidence, not in jest but in appreciation of his eccentric and bright personality.

We wind our way through the Gold Wing, and with each step, Gazil appears more and more depressed. The look on Gazil's face, so downtrodden and unusually grim, rings alarms in my mind; however, I am certain the stress of the ball as well as the rumors of his drinking escapades have made his days much harder than usual. We climb the stairwell slowly to allow him breaks as he rests his weak and healing body, before turning toward the Orange Wing and entering a corridor near the studies. Down this almost unnoticeable hall, there are formal portraits of leaders and important patrons of the Ice Realm.

I see Rostair's family line proudly placed at the end of the hall nearest to the large arched door. His mother's eyes seem to follow my movements as I reach the end of the hall, her stern facial expression encouraging me to straighten my back and fold my arms neatly in front of me. A mosaic of brightly colored tiles surrounds the archway of the wooden door, broken into the smallest pieces to create intricate pictures. Women and men in bright-orange-colored robes work in various capacities throughout the archway's rectangular segments—some reading through rolls of papyrus, some transcribing old texts, and others are posed as if in a heated conversation.

"All the tasks of our scribes." Gazil notices my interest in the mosaic. "I was not officially trained in the laborious school of the scribes. Many even travel to other realms for a more rigorous education or perhaps a specialty of some sort." His arms are folded thoughtfully behind his back as he examines the mosaics. A glimmer of pain laces his eyes. "It is such an honorable and integral position of the realm. Knowledge, as you know—"

"Is power." I complete his sentence for him, a glimmer in my eyes as I attempt to peer through the small, square window of the door.

Gazil chuckles. "You are learning quickly, Centrea." His voice is endearing yet shaded with a bit of sorrow. He pulls a large, rugged key from his pocket and turns a glass doorknob to creak the old door open on ancient brass hinges. As soon as the door swoops open, a rush of air, thick with the scent of dust and books, hits us.

The room is smaller than I imagined, smaller than the estate's main library and barely larger than the art room of the Red Wing. Two rows of tables and chairs fill most of the room, and papers and various old books are strewn throughout. The walls are covered from floor to ceiling with drawers that are labeled with numbers and letters.

A rustic ladder leans in the corner, providing scribes with a way to reach even the highest drawers that are nine or ten feet high. We are the only two people in the room. There's no sign of orange-robed scribes or intrigued guests.

Gazil chooses an empty table and invites me to sit as he gathers the list of guests. "This should only take a moment," he claims as he opens one drawer before shutting it abruptly. "I updated the list just this morning; however, the scribes tend to tidy the room up every hour or so and sometimes place books or documents in the wrong drawer."

Considering just how many papers are required to keep an estate like this running, I could imagine it would be quite the challenge to keep the storage system organized. It takes a moment, but he finds the list and turns to place it on the table in front of me, his expression moving from sorrow to desperation. The list is extensive, nearly fifty sheets of paper, written front and back in tiny print. I squint my eyes to read Gazil's handwritten notes, brief explanations of the newly favored couples and their significance. He absentmindedly hands me a magnifying glass, which I grasp thankfully as I flip through the pages. Gazil merely sits at my side, frozen, his face staring at the other side of the wooden door.

"Which are the guests with no favor?" I attempt to break him from his eerie silence, "I realize that is my main task here, correct?"

He blinks his eyes carefully and responds, "That is your task, sweet Centrea." The statement is lifeless, almost hollow.

The sound breaks me. "Gazil, are you quite alright? I must know." At first, I found his behavior a bit strange but thought the pressure of the ball could be the source of his stress.

However, I feel his behavior is becoming worrisome. My friend who would typically awaken at the sun's dawn and never emerge from his chambers poorly dressed or blemished. My friend who enjoyed sharing the latest gossip and pointing out the latest winter trysts. My friend who is fierce and intelligent, so well-traveled and knowledgeable, is fumbling through the stack of paper with a sort of caution that is so unusual, so unlike him. His eyes never turn to meet mine, his head shaking slightly and every so often glancing at the door. The longer the silence continues, the greater my worry becomes, a strange sense of unease resting heavily on my shoulders. Is he waiting for something? Or perhaps, wondering if someone will enter the chambers.

"Centrea." The tone of his voice causes my worry to peak, a snarl of terror taking root in my chest as he stares at the pages before him. "You know how dearly I care for you. You are truly one of the most genuine people this estate has hosted, perhaps the most genuine, and kind, and wonderful..." He trails away toward the end of his statement, becoming flustered. "There is almost nothing that I would not do for you. And I knew on the day you helped me when I was at my lowest point, I knew that we were destined for more than balls and dinners and drama."

Suddenly his back straightens, and his eyes finally look my way, a look of purpose shining on his face. "If I asked you to do something, perhaps something reckless or irrational, would you consider it... for me, that is?"

A blush rises to his cheeks, sweat lining his brow, yet his stare remains constant, confident. I could see why in his youth he was able to woo any number of lovers.

"Centrea." He turns to face me fully, placing a trembling hand on my arm and ushering me to sit on a cushioned chair near the table, the papers still sitting in a pile. "Please hear me. I am tempted to leave this place, and I would like for you to accompany me."

I recognize the sensation of my mouth gaping open. This is indeed irrational. Before such an important event? Something both Rostair and Mairette, along with hundreds of other Keepers, have restlessly prepared for day and night? Something to distract the realm from the war nearby? Then there is the notion of me leaving with Gazil alone. This sort of talk, the insinuation of his words, leave me speechless. He is at least somewhat aware of my feelings for Rostair, perhaps not as much as Mairette, but certainly enough that he understands the ridiculous nature of his request. He also understands what such an act would do to both of us, our reputations, our plans, all ruined.

*What could he possibly be thinking?* I wish I could voice these words, but my tongue is too dry.

He stares into my eyes, unflinching, "Centrea, please. I love you."

Obviously, I've never thought of Gazil as anything but a dear friend, and I never considered him feeling anything but platonic affection towards me as well. Such a notion catches me off guard, throwing my sense of reality into a frantic state. The words are piercing, and hearing them from his mouth repulses me. My mind reels. I do not mean to demean him for his age or the lovers he has previously taken, but I have never looked at him as anything other than my friend, a wise and trusting friend. The seconds move slowly, time creeping by as if forcing me to live through this moment for as long as possible. Has he felt this way for a long time? Notes of betrayal add to the toxic mixture of feelings flowing through my body. How could I express all that I am thinking to Gazil, this fragile man holding his breath as he waits for a reply.

My silence says volumes and his eyes grow wide. "I merely meant—" Gazil's explanation is interrupted by the lock turning inside the door and a creaking as a scribe shuffles into the room, appearing utterly unfazed by our presence and moving to a table toward the back to review an old tablet with some sort of shapeless symbols.

At the appearance of this scribe, Gazil tenses, his movements becoming less confident and the blush extending from his cheeks to the back of his neck. I glare at the paper on the table and attempt to read the words, yet they mean nothing as the letters seem to swim together. I glance toward the young scribe who merely continues with their work, either too busy to worry or just unwilling to care.

Despite the strangeness of this encounter, I feel sympathy for Gazil, for his heartbreak and lack of proper support. The reality hits me that I would typically be his shoulder to cry on, yet I no longer feel it would be appropriate. I reach for the last paper of the stack and roll it into a tight and protected scroll before tying it with a small piece of string. As I stand to leave, I place a steady hand on Gazil's shoulder, his eyes still staring hopelessly at the table, hoping perhaps that he could take back his assertion, that he could turn back time and make a different choice. As I walk slowly toward the door, his soft, quiet sobs fill the space. I do not look back. I cannot look back.

"You will always be my friend, Gazil. Always my friend."

A small tear falls from my own face as the wooden door to the estate's archive shuts behind me.

I am reminded of Gazil's pitiful expression as I stare into the soft crackling of the small fire in my chambers a few hours later. I have been unable to move since the encounter, which shook me up a bit. I consider dozens of possibilities to explain the scene from the archives. He wanted to leave Endoneth before the ball, an event he claimed to value.

Perhaps he knows of Rostair's intention to ask for my favor that night? Perhaps he knows more about the war than even Rostair, wanting to leave before the fight reaches our doors?

Many possibilities that do nothing but raise more questions bounce around my head. But nothing explains this sudden shift in his demeanor. I sigh, drowning in my own thoughts as they spiral out of my control.

Is it possible that I am the cause of this change in Gazil's perception of me? I think through each of our afternoons together, our meals in the dining hall or many discussions in the studies. Never did I imply romantic feelings, or did I? My brows scrunch in frustrated concentration. I thought I learned everything necessary to integrate into this world, but that was perhaps foolish.

Clearly, there is something I misunderstood, and it cost me my friend.

I groan as my face falls into my open palms. Even subjects that usually bring me delight—fairy stories, garden walks, Rostair—all somehow lead me to Gazil and a deep sense of shame. I retrieved the poem from its designated place under my mattress as soon as I entered the room, reading the words over and over to find some sort of solace in my despair. It soothes me.

I wonder what the author of the text would say to ease my heart.

You have the potential to handle anything? Never allow the folly of others to extinguish your passions? Men are incompetent?

The thought of this author's advice brings me a slight spark of joy in the shadows of this despair. I look toward the stained glass, the sun setting far faster than I anticipated. There are still tasks to be completed, but I feel too empty to care. I wish Mairette could join me for tea, but she is immensely busy with last-minute preparations, and I would be selfish to trouble her with senseless drama. The final flecks of sunshine color the tiled floors. I read through the poem once more before rising. I place the paper back in its place under the bedding and lay down atop the fluffy blankets.

I think about my outing with Rostair tomorrow. I try to remember how long we stayed in the water the first time we visited the cavern, as I assume the time spent in the magical pool impacts its desired effect. What will I remember and how will it change me? The thoughts float through my mind until I drift to sleep.

I wake to the sharp sound of the door slamming closed, the soft clinking of a tea tray set upon the table, and Mairette's sensitive touch on my calf.

"Centrea, I apologize. I understand it is meant to be our day of rest..." Her voice is unusual, unlike anything I have experienced from her before. Even in her most vulnerable and emotional moments, Mairette is certain. Confident. Concise. Now she is stumbling over her words. And a new ring to her voice carries through my chamber: fear.

My eyes open and shift to her form, which is still a bit blurry as I adjust to the morning light. "It is just... I have something I must tell you." She raises her hand to stroke my cheek, motherly and caring.

Her words are careful, as if in my fragility I may fall apart at the seams. Now I am truly concerned. All my closest friends seem to be exhibiting the strangest behavior mere hours apart from one another. My breaths begin coming in short huffs as I think that something must have happened to Mairette's family or Rostair. Or perhaps the war is finally here, and we must evacuate. The second I think of this possibility, the more convinced I am of its validity.

Raising onto my arms, I ask Mairette, who is perched delicately on the edge of the bedframe, "Is it the war? Is it here?"

She shutters at these words but shakes her head. "It is not that, not quite yet, Miss." Her face is a lighter shade of pink which dulls the shine of her usually vibrant hair and eyes. "It is your friend. The old one, Gazil."

My heart stops. Did he tell people of our horrid interaction, of my rejection toward his advances? Or, even worse, did he tell others that I instead agreed? A blush creeps its way up my chest, neck, and finally my face.

"What has he done?" My voice is sharper than I intended, and it takes her aback a bit, her hand resting startled over her heart.

"I do not think you understand. He was found this morning in the garden..."

Fallen?

Drunk?

Asleep?

# Fifteen

"Dead."

I hold my stomach and heave forward. Mairette's hand gently strokes my back. Many feelings roll through me at once: anger, fear, pain, sadness. The next thirty minutes continue in a blur. Mairette explains little of the details about poor Gazil and instead attempts to ease the news with citrus tea and a warmed blanket by the crackling fire. She slowly prepares my clothing for the day—a thin cotton shift in dark black with soft dark embroidery climbing the sides of the dress. I have never seen her move so slowly in the morning before, tiptoeing from one side of the chambers to the other to create a space that is warm and safe. Her presence is one of great comfort and familiarity as the news of my dear friend sinks in. I appreciate the care with which she moves about the room, asking delicately if I would like to style my hair or color my face for the somber day ahead. By the end of the first hour, I am awake. The first hour in this place that I am without one of my confidantes. I am ready to face the day, no matter what lies ahead.

"The day of rest is no longer, I am afraid," Mairette notes as we walk slowly toward the door. "The Lord of the estate has prepared a wake, as the deceased is—was—a member of the Royal Council as Keeper of Records." Her face is solemn, though she attempts to appear put together for my sake. She places a firm hand on my back as I pull the door open and enter the Blue Wing.

The world spins on, even as Gazil lies somewhere in the estate, cold and still. Mairette, thankfully, remains by my side as we weave through crowds of guests, some dressed in mourning colors while others whisper to one another, looks of realization and horror spreading across their faces. It feels almost surreal. I think about what Gazil would say at the sudden and mysterious death of a senior member of the estate.

A jealous guest makes a move the night before the largest event in the realm? A point is being made, Centrea.

Guiding me through the halls, Mairette stays calm, whispering to me every so often and drowning out the incessant chatter of others. "Lord Rostair will explain the circumstances of the discovery." She uses any words but the brutal and blunt truth.

The closer we get to the familiar study, the thinner the crowds become, people staying far from the leader of the estate. The reason for this becomes clearer as we reach his study door. Loud clashes of books and glass shake the walls. I place a cautious hand on the wood, and Mairette looks at me with sympathy before she turns around and leaves me for the first time since waking me this morning.

My heart slips into my stomach as I press my clenched fist against the door. The knock seems to pause the chaos going on inside. A few moments later, the door creaks open enough to reveal Rostair's face, his hair disheveled and cheeks flushed with rage. When he notices me standing before him, his demeanor shifts, spine growing taut and his free hand attempting to comb the stray hairs atop his head.

"Centrea, please." He opens the door with enough room for me to barely squeeze inside. I immediately scan the study and see a number of broken trinkets, stacks of books overturned, other books strewn across the floor amongst smatterings of broken glass. Rostair appears frantic, his hands clinging to the roots of his hair, his eyes puffy and red, and his clothes plain and disheveled. He appears out of sorts in a way that sucks the oxygen out of the space, as if Gazil is truly dead.

Gone.

Forever.

Breathing becomes difficult. My head dips dangerously low as the room seems to flip around me. I reach for the chair near the edge of the room, wading through the fallen books to find respite in the sea of swirling shapes and darkening corners.

"He is... he is important to... to the realm." Rostair paces with large steps, circling the study. "He cannot be gone, he cannot."

He slumps into the chair next to mine and attempts to steady his breathing, taking in long, drawn-out inhales and waiting a moment before releasing them.

"He was more than a member of the estate... more than just... the Keeper of Records." His words still come in segments as he gulps down bursts of air. "He was... he was my uncle." His head lands into his open palms as he gives way to silent cries.

My eyes grow wide at this admission. Gazil? A member of the Lord's family? "Zeal, he... he understood people. He... he always knew people. And... and my father, his brother. My father knew he would be a great source for the estate, for the realm." The words are muffled yet I hear the term of endearment with clarity. Seeing Rostair in distress propels me from my seat and to his side, rubbing his arm and leaning his shoulder against my hip.

*Zeal...* Curiosity pricks at the back of my mind at the nickname. Yet, with Rostair in such grief, I push back the impulse to think further on it.

"Please, tell me about him." I gently stroke the matted hair to soothe his pain.

"You knew him better than most, it would seem." His words are biting, although I know he does not mean them maliciously. "I know... I know he would have loved to see you thrive," he says with confidence. "He always cared deeply for others, even when he seemed to only care for their drama or the latest fashion trend. He... he really did care."

Rostair lifts his face, and I see the look of admiration for his uncle. "I never claimed him as my family to protect him. Yet, this proved too difficult a task, it seems." He wraps an arm around me and pulls me onto his lap, hugging my body into his as if my presence provides him with comfort that close proximity affords. "I know that he was not the most honorable of men, and he often romanticized reality, but he surely meant no harm. Never to my knowledge in any case." One hand runs across my back while the other traces the outline of my knee.

I think of my discussion with Gazil just the night before, his declaration of love and desire to run away, to leave Endoneth and its people, Rostair included. Never will I admit this to him, not in this state. So, I continue to listen in silence, my face buried in his wrinkled cotton tunic as he talks about his uncle, a man who was not blameless, but who surely understood the meaning of fun.

After about an hour of telling stories about Gazil and his antics, Rostair turns silent, seemingly contemplating what to do next or merely reflecting upon someone important in his life, the final speck of family left. We sit like this for a while—together in a chair in his study, my arms holding him tight, my face buried in his tunic, and his hands scanning my body, providing some comfort in this unfortunate situation.

I finally gain the courage to ask the question on my lips since Mairette woke me this morning. "How did it happen?" The words are whispered into the air, and I almost wish I could take them back, understanding in that moment how Rostair would likely not want to discuss the details so soon.

The question does not faze him. He continues tracing the segments of my spine with his fingers, moving his hand beneath my shift to touch my bare skin. "He was found in the garden, a head wound. Perhaps caused by a rock." A gasp leaves my throat, and my heart sinks even further than when I first heard the news itself.

A murderer is here in the estate, killing members of the household. Did the killer know of their familial relationship? Or could this have something to do with his position? Or, even worse, is this the first of many deaths to come, the enemy attacking us from the inside?

"Who was it?" I croak out angrily, spit flying from my mouth.

He looks at me gently. "We are looking into leads. However, there is little to be done." His eyes fall to the floor, yet the hand on my spine continues its exploration of my back. "Today is meant to be restful, and so it shall. We will celebrate Zeal's life, then we will enjoy our final night before the formal dance. It will be spectacular; I just know it!" His words are uncertain, as if said more to convince himself than to reassure me. He smiles weakly, distractedly.

Despite the preparations that need to be made for the funeral, Rostair and I remain in the leather chair in his study for another few minutes. My hand combs through his tangled, silver locks and his tenderly caresses my back and legs as I sit on his lap. There is no pressured feeling of lust or passion. Our touches are more reminders of our support rather than invitations to intimacy. I prefer the former at this moment. Rostair's embrace is like a blanket of protection against the onslaught of grief and loss. His breathing is even and warm against the nape of my neck as he nuzzles against me. I melt in the closeness of him, of our shared pain. Gone are thoughts of the caverns, of restoring my memories and assuring my purpose. At least, gone for today. Today is about remembrance, but a different kind. Remembering a person who meant a great deal to me and to Rostair and to many in this realm, I'm sure.

We sit in peaceful silence, knowing that the day would certainly bring long discussions about what occurred in the garden last night and what the consequences will be for the future of Endoneth and its guests. Thinking about those difficult considerations makes me enjoy this silence all the more. And if this is how I am reacting after only knowing Gazil for months, I can only imagine Rostair's thoughts. I look to him, his eyes closed and face blank, no trace of sorrow or joy or anger. The only evidence he is awake is the continued movement of his hands, although I begin to wonder if he is able to continue those even in his sleep.

He sighs, breaking the comfortable silence, before opening his eyes. The gaze of his cool, grey eyes intimidates me enough that I look away, instead focusing on the clenching of his sharp jaw. "I should rise," he says plainly, as if finishing one official meeting to attend another.

With the hand on my legs, he pushes my feet toward the floor, shifting my body into a seated position on his lap before pressing the hand on my back, urging me to stand. My shoes land on the tile with a loud clopping noise as my body flops forward. Rostair flexes his hands at his sides as he follows closely behind me, slinking past the chair and toward his cluttered desk. The mood shifts instantaneously from warm and safe to cool and stale.

I cautiously approach the desk as he takes his place in the armchair just on the other side. The desk is like a barrier between our bodies, once almost in sync and now feeling realms apart. I become suddenly aware of myself, my blushing cheeks and fidgeting hands. All the while, Rostair busies himself with papers and quills, tidying the bits of broken vases and ripped papers from his earlier outburst.

"We must carry forth," he states, voice vacant. "The wake shall be in the evening. This should provide enough time to prepare while also ensuring we have space to conduct a thorough investigation of the events of last night."

I glare at him, standing like a child before her superior awaiting direction as he continues to list the important tasks for the afternoon, not once lifting his eyes to meet my own or even nodding in my direction. "Is there anything I can do?" The words jolt him to attention, his hands pausing their business to answer, as if suddenly remembering my presence.

"Ah," he starts, his words more affectionate than before, yet still miles far from the intimate words shared on the armchair, "yes, Centrea. Yes, Mairette should present some options for you. I believe… our customs may be foreign to you. Well, of course, I suppose any custom would be foreign, unfortunately." He stumbles through the words painfully. "In any case, you certainly may present words in the form of a written letter or poem, if you would like. It is customary to bury the dead with such things, so they may enjoy the words of their loved ones in the afterlife."

The word *dead* hangs heavily in the room. Rostair returns to shuffling papers, jotting down notes, and further preparing for his uncle to be buried. I shift backward, now feeling like an intruder in his personal space. "I would be honored," I mumble as I turn toward the exit. He continues to jostle books as I open the door. I wait there a moment, one foot across the threshold into the hallway, waiting for some response. None is given.

Grief is an odd emotion. As if the theme of the day, this phrase returns to my mind over and over as I walk the halls of Endoneth.

I find Mairette mere minutes after leaving Rostair's study. She does not say it, but I am certain she made an effort to be close in case I needed anything. When I ask about the wake, she shares much of the same information as Rostair did, and I gather that I must hastily write a letter of sorts to Gazil before the beginning of the processional tonight. She holds my arm gently and guides me to one of the studies, insistent that sorrow is better felt amongst company.

I do not admit this, but I feel she wanted to protect me, doing so by placing me in an open and public space to limit the chance of another attack. Once she settles me into a writing desk on the far side of a particularly crowded study, she rushes to procure me tea and light sandwiches before departing to assist with the last-minute event. The whispers of guests continue as they had before, yet now they discuss another element of my mystery, a friendship with the dead.

"Do you think she knows the culprit?"
"She must have an idea of what took place?"
"I saw her with him just yesterday. They were walking together with such purpose, did you not see?"

I roll my eyes to placate the tears threatening to burst. Focusing on the blank page, blocking out the curious onlookers and their unfiltered thoughts, I consider what to write.

What does one even say to their departed friend? Especially a friend who more recently revealed himself as something different? A friend I wanted to trust but whose recent behavior made me feel out of sorts.  I only knew Gazil for less than a year, yet the hectic conversation of last night felt like a deeper sort of deceit, a wound that unexpectedly threw me off-kilter. Each sweet memory is now clouded with suspicion, a violation of my affections and a manipulation of my deep affections for him, twisted from pure and platonic to sexual and duplicitous. Yet, I still miss him, at least the friend of before. In truth, the Gazil I knew and the Gazil of yesterday seem like two different people to me deserving of two separate messages for the afterlife.

What does the afterlife even look like? What happens there? These philosophical ponderings are not a helpful addition to the overwhelming emotion currently in my mind. I shake away thoughts of where Gazil is and think harder about who he was, both to me and to the realm.

Streams of words come to mind, and I place them on the page recklessly, no thought to proper spelling or punctuation. Mimicking the thoughtless guests and their uncensored gossip, I write directly what is in my head, every angry word and confused question. I write about my happiness and feelings of familiarity as well as the ways those feelings now ring hollow within me. I write about who I now know him to be, an uncle to the Lord of Endoneth. How this discovery only doubles my anger and confusion. I write feverishly, as if the world around me has melted away and all that is left is myself and the ink. After several pages sit drying, heavy with ink and words and sentiments, I stand and stretch my arms above me, looking to the ceiling and back down to the tiled floor to reset my body.

"Centrea!"

The yell comes from the entrance of the study, and I turn with the rest of the guests to see Asha running through aisles of tables and people to reach me. Guests huddle together into circles to debrief the sudden appearance of the strange woman from the Sun Realm and her curious relationship with me, the black sheep of the estate. Asha continues toward me, unbothered by the discussions at her expense. "I have been searching the entire estate, dear friend." She cups my full cheeks in her hands as she whispers, "It is a horrific loss and there are no words to express the sorrow I feel on your behalf. How are you?" The words roll over me like warm water, washing a bit of the fear and sadness away. I scoop her into a strong embrace, and she nods her understanding on my shoulder as she reciprocates. I nearly engulf her slender frame, my broad chest and arms squeezing her tight. The visitors are emboldened to speak even more passionately of their opinions regarding my behavior, my friends, my presence. It is all too much, especially today.

"Would you like to walk for a bit? See one of the galleries?" Asha pulls my shoulders back a bit to see the look on my face. I offer a slight nod which is all she needs. She takes my arm in hers and pulls me toward the door. I manage to grab my pages of ramblings just before we are navigating through groups of staring guests. I ignore their sneers and judgments as I follow Asha away from the Orange Wing and toward the stairs. We walk in silence, the only sound coming from the passersby, all either intrigued or seemingly grieving. I wonder to myself how many tears are genuine. How many of these people really knew Gazil? But, then again, did I truly know him?

The stunning gallery of glass is the first place we are alone, though the echoes of voices seem to follow us. The setting sun forms an alley of rainbows as Asha and I pace slowly past each glowing creation. "You need not talk. However, I am here to listen, if it is what you wish." Asha's whispers are kind and generous, her arm holding me up like a crutch. Since leaving Rostair's study, the stress of writing and listening exhausts me far more than I expected. In this moment, Asha is my rock, this person I have known but a few days. Poor Mairette has no time, having lost her own day of rest to prepare for a wake before managing the Greentime Ball tomorrow, and Rostair is battling his own loss.

"It is difficult to put into words what I feel or what I want. I tried to write it down." I hold the pages up a bit and rasp, "It is difficult."

Asha continues to cradle my arm as we look at the glass artwork, each the culmination of hours and hours of energy and imagination. They put my words to shame. I hope when Gazil reads the pages, that he understands more than I.

"Asha, what do your people believe about the afterlife?"

She turns to me, her smile sympathetic yet proud. "There are three places one could go," she begins. "The first is toward the Western sky, where hosts of stars guide you toward an everlasting sea. Here, you live on islands of perpetual pleasure, each with a distinct form: lust, food, drink." The gold of her eyes gleams in the dimming light, and she pushes back a loose tendril of hair behind my ear. "In the North, you can choose to live amongst the birds, in havens built of clouds. The stars are believed to understand human voices and present gifts of fealty to those who chose to live selflessly."

We steadily walk toward the end of the gallery, toward a sculpture of a beautiful swallow lost in reeds and snow. "And the third?" I ask, her tales bringing me closer to sanity and perhaps further from grief.

Her head tilts to the side as she observes the glass. The swirls of blue and white are magnetizing and inviting set against the golden tiles. "The third," she breathes in deeply, reaching her fingertips toward the pointed beak, "the third is below the earth. You choose to live amongst the glow of tree trunks and mystic creatures. Your family may join you in any of your choices. And, if someone you love chooses another world, you have one chance, just one, to join them. This is why you must ensure that those you love, the ones you want to have with you for eternity, that you all choose the same path."

"And what path will you choose?" Asha's grip slackens a bit as my arm rests at my side. "I have always loved birds, the way they chase their dreams and fly away from those who wish them harm. I believe we have much to learn from them." She settles her hand on the cool glass and smirks. "Would it not be wonderful to live amongst the birds?"

The pages in my hand are nearly an extension of myself by the time crowds gather for the wake. Asha follows close behind me as we walk outside through the front doors of the estate. Crowds of hundreds are organized in rows and rows roped off into several sections. The sky is dark now, the stars flooding the courtyard with a dim light that filters through the trees. I walk toward a wide aisle in the center of the sections that leads toward a casket and find the first pair of open seats. And, with my entrance, the whispers begin again, this time directed toward my words, conjecture after conjecture regarding what I may have written to Gazil to carry with him into the next realm.

As we sit, Asha places a reassuring hand on my knee. "The processional should begin at any moment," she says.

I look around, noticing the empty seats filling quickly. Music begins playing, the sharp strumming of ten stringed instruments booming through the courtyard, quieting the crowd. Rostair moves toward the center from his seat on the first row to stand in front of the bejeweled casket. Dressed in a glimmering black suit with a lace overskirt, he looks far better than he did when I left his study. His hair is slicked back into a tight bun at the nape of his neck, and his skin glows in the moonlight. The smile on his face, filled with passion, ignites me, bringing me even further out of my own head and into the world once more.

"This is an exceptionally sorrowful day," he begins, his voice authoritative as it fills the perimeter of the courtyard. "A particularly exceptional sorrow for our annual day of rest. However, the Ice Realm and its people have always been resilient. Even now as death knocks its heavy hands, we remain steadfast in our loyalty to our realm, to who we are."

Nods and murmurs erupt through the crowd, some peering toward Asha and me as we listen.

"Gazil, our Keeper of Records, was a most loyal member of our court and someone, a member of the enemy camp, wanted his death to deter us. We will not be deterred!" He pumps a stern fist in the air for emphasis, and the crowd joins in with loud *Hurrahs*. My heartbeat accelerates, excitement flowing through my veins as Rostair encourages his people, finding a silver lining in this terrible circumstance. "WE WILL NOT BE DETERRED!"

The crowd roars, leaping to their feet. Even those from other realms, those in Mountain and Desert, join in the excitement. Standing to my feet, I feel weightless, as if part of something important. Asha remains seated as she observes the people around us. The courtyard is electric, filled with hope. Rostair lifts both hands above his head and a hush settles through the audience of hundreds.

"Now I know that this man, this man of Endoneth, he was valued by many amongst us. If you have words for him, now is the time to include them." Rostair returns to his seat as a number of people stand with pages in their hands and begin forming a line in the center aisle.

Clenching my own pages, I move to join the line, inching slowly forward as person after person drops their written letters into the casket. When I reach the front, I notice the intricacy of the box, covered in detailed patterns built out of small tiles and jewels. For Gazil, the tiles are beautiful shades of green and blue to create a detailed map of the realm, like the map we reviewed together in the library. Sapphires and emeralds outline the map, rows and rows of jewels. The casket is opened just slightly, enough to allow the guests to slip their words into it. I stuff the pages of my thoughts, my internal dialogue, into the casket and send a silent prayer that he receives them.

When I turn away from the casket, a curtain of blonde catches my eye. Sitting next to Rostair, whispering into his ear, is a woman. The figure is unfamiliar, with strong features and fire-red eyes. Her black dress is cut low to her navel, accentuating large breasts and a wide stomach. She shoots a look at me, and our eyes meet, hers squinting into slits as they trail up and down my body. A cunning grin creeps onto her pale face as she presses her lips to Rostair's ears once more. Whatever words pass between them causes him to squirm in his seat in discomfort before lifting his head forward and finding me. She places a possessive hand on his thigh and reality dawns on me: This is his former lover.

This is Helzaf.

# Sixteen

The walk back to my seat is excruciating; it feels as if a spotlight shines on me, each step revealing me to a fresh row of guests, hungry to see what I do next. I wish more than anything I could see Gazil, to ask him about Helzaf and these guests and how to properly prepare for the ball tomorrow. Asha's look of concern reveals to me the devastation that lines my own face.

"Do we need to leave early?" she whispers into my ear, the hair blowing against her breath.

I shake my head slowly, eyes glued to the blonde hair of Rostair's friend, if that is the term. We wait for hours, the music of the stringed instruments filling the time, some joined by low hums or the occasional lyric. All the while, Helzaf and Rostair share words between just themselves, as if the remaining courtyard were empty.

Jealousy oozes from my pores as guests continue to slide their letters into the casket. It feels ridiculous to be so impacted by the appearance of one woman during the wake of a dead friend. Yet the jealousy is almost easier to face than the grief.

By the end of the night, the instruments slow and Rostair rises once more. "Thank you for your words." He bows and walks away from the casket, down the center aisle, and toward the estate. When he passes our row, he looks directly toward me then gives a subtle nod and my heart lifts.

If the walk to Asha was excruciating, the walk into the estate is hellish. The rows and rows of people take over an hour to dissipate, most moving toward the guest wings while others head for the dining hall for a late drink of wine. The events of today have left me empty, sullen, and tired. While Asha insists upon spending more time in my chambers, I convince her to join me on only the walk to my room before going to sleep herself.

Alone in my chambers, I replay the day over in my mind. Notes of citrus swirl through the air from the tea sitting in the center of the room; however, my body feels too numb to enjoy it, and I leave it to act as a perfume for the room. This is the first moment of true solitude I've had since falling asleep last night and it feels nice to not care. To not care about how Rostair feels. To not care about the gossip. To not care about appearing weak or upset or scared. It is also the first moment I can truly be alone with my thoughts without prying eyes and listening ears. I rush from the closed door to the bed, changing from my funeral attire to my nightgown before reaching for my favorite source of comfort.

The crinkled page invites me into its story, the words creating another world, a source of escape. *Our Brave and Bold*. A knock interrupts the words.

"Centrea?"

The voice sends a smile to my face. "Please, enter!" I pull at the lace lining the sides of my nightgown, attempting to appear calm, yet my blush betrays me. I shove the page beneath my pillow and cover my legs with a blanket.

Rostair skips into the room and my heart soars. His smile sends my heart into a crazed rhythm, and I hope for the closeness I felt just this morning. "I apologize for today. I realize this must be a difficult day for you."

He stalks toward me, resting upon the velvet chair and tossing his head to the cushion. There are so many questions, but now all I desire is to clasp his hand and pull him close. "There are likely many confusing realizations from today. And I know I promised to bring you to the caverns; however, time merely slipped away from me."

The caverns. I had nearly forgotten about his agreement the day prior. "Perhaps it is for the best," I answer, clutching the blanket in my hands. "I cannot imagine what the day must be like for you. Losing a member of your own family. I do hope you're doing OK."

He shakes his head in response. "It was a difficult day. It reminded me of a similar day from my past, which brought back unpleasant memories." He stretches his legs on my blanket, and a darkness fills his eyes. "But it was made better."

The shadow of a smile haunts his face. "An old friend arrived. A friend I once believed was gone forever. She returned to me, for me." He grasps my hand in his. "I do not want you to misinterpret my words, Centrea. She is just a friend. Nothing more."

A great burden lifts from my chest, and I breathe a heavy sigh of relief. "Why did you not mention your relationship to Gazil during the wake?"

The question takes him by surprise, yet he smiles deviously. "You are quite perceptive, my sweet. Gazil's role for the realm required anonymity. To pass from realm to realm undetected one must be like a fly on the wall. Unnoticed by all but also able to stand out when need be. Zeal had a flare for the dramatics."

I laugh and roll my eyes, and Rostair soon joins me.

Chuckling, he finishes, "But he was loyal, almost to a fault." He pauses for a moment before adding, "Unless he had a bit to drink, which was quite often, I am afraid. Then his recklessness often overcame his loyalty."

I think about our last night together and nod. Alcohol must have been his folly, one that may have led to his demise.

I lock eyes with Rostair, his features now soft. "Do you know any more details about how it happened?" I ask. The thought alone is nauseating, but I must know.

Rostair shakes his head. "My medics are considering all possibilities. However, it was likely just a bad fall made by an old man who had the misfortune of striking his head on a rock. One with an attachment to wine." So, it was the alcohol.

A tear falls down my scarred cheek and I quickly brush it aside before more follow. "I saw him that afternoon. He was not well. I could have, I should have ensured his safety." My voice cracks and I begin trembling, pulling my legs to my chest as I recall his slurring words and irrational request.

Rostair jumps to my side, slings his arm over my shoulders, and eases my concerns with soothing coos in my ears. "This is not your fault, sweet one. It is merely a matter of man. It is something no person can predict or prevent. Do not fret." He continues to voice these soothing phrases as his hand rubs against my quivering arm.

When my shivering body stills, he pulls me close. "Did he seem unlike himself last night? Anything that would cause concern?" The question nearly causes the trembling to return, but I manage to remain calm, my hands clutching the edges of the gown.

"Nothing of note," I say, hoping to salvage my friend's legacy. "He led me to the archives, we reviewed the list of couples and favors, then he said he wanted to work on something personal." I hug my legs close, my heart thumping in my chest.

Rostair nods and continues to rub my arm. "I just... I want to know you are alright." He moves his hand to my waist, holding tightly to the wide curves.

Did the Keepers in the archives say something to him regarding our conversation? I don't recall any person close enough to hear, yet there were certainly those who witnessed the fallout. The tears. My abrupt exit.

I turn my face to look directly into his eyes. "Rostair," his name sounds like a ballad on my tongue, "I promise you. I am unharmed."

Physically, at least.

I fall asleep cradled in Rostair's arms, too tired to touch the orange tea Mairette left on my desk hours before. As soon as I drift off, I hear the drum of voices running through a blizzard of white. Dressed in red, the crowd clammers toward me, screaming incomprehensibly as I desperately dig my shoes into the ice and spring forward in tight bursts.

"Sol is near, the king is clear! Sol is near, the king is clear! Sol is near, the king is clear!"

Jeers echo in my ears and I try my best to thwart them, pushing my palms against the sides of my head to block them out.

"Red is on the Horizon! Red is on the Horizon! Red is on the Horizon!"

The chanting takes on a crazed rate, the voices chittering quickly until the words become one high-pitched sound. I grit my teeth as I push harder, the corners of my forehead splitting from the excess effort. My eyes clamp shut as I concentrate on anything but the noise. Even with my eyes closed, I see a blazing light burning in front of me. I fall to my knees, my legs giving way. When I try to move or open my eyes or scream, I cannot. The dream holds me hostage to witness the muffled voices of the screams. The warmth fills me, scratching at my skin, creeping through my blood.

When I nearly lose hope, when the screams seem perpetual, when it seems there is no way out, a quiet voice begins to fade in, breaking through the horrific chanting.

"Sol?"

I hate to remove my hands. The screeching of the high-pitched chants causes my mind to split in pain, but I want to find the source of the voice.

"Sol?"

The feeling returns to my toes, my feet, my legs. I attempt to stand, which is difficult with my hands still glued to my ears. I stumble forward and something, someone, breaks my fall. Their cool body eases the pain.

"Sol."

The voice—husky, low, familiar—whispers in my ear.

"You are the key."

I jolt upright in my bed, my head moving fast enough that my chambers swirl in my vision. Rostair is gone. The room is dark, the sun still hidden below the hills. Breathing consistently in and out, I wipe the sweat from my brow with the edge of the blanket. I still hear the phantom ringing in my ears, a cruel souvenir. In addition, I still hear the stranger's voice, the low vibrato of his words mingling with the ringing, sending it to the background as it consumes my mind.

*You are the key.*

Swinging my feet to hit the cool tiles, I slide myself off of the bed and begin pacing. I consider calling for Mairette, asking for tea or a listening ear but the notion seems less than appealing. Walking from one wall to another, the tiles grounding me as I think, I try to replay the nightmare in my mind, wincing through the thoughts of the pain to recreate the voice of the man. This must mean something, it must.

*Sol. Sol. Sol.*

What did it mean? I wring my hands together in frustration. Sighing, I pause my pacing to retrieve the poem from my bed. Squinting at the page, I move back and forth again, from wall to wall of my bedchamber. I read the words over and over until something catches my eye:

*Remember, S—, your purpose be,*
*For realms and —le you — the key;*

I rub my eyes and head toward my writing desk, the sun just breaching the top of the horizon. The soft haze of morning barely filters in through the stained glass as I reach for ink and a quill.

At the bottom of the page I write, "Sol. You are the key."

My head twitches to the side, my hand rubbing the back of my neck as I stare at the words. I hear the voice of the man from my dream as if he were standing before me once more:

*Remember, Sol, your purpose be,*
*For realms and people you are the key.*

# A Letter from the Front

*Dear Sister,*

*I am uncertain of what you know. Uncertain of how much Lord Rostair chooses to indulge or how often those in the estate - guests and Keepers alike - are updated on our whereabouts. I do know that letters are stagnant. Ironically, the closer we come to the Ice Realm border, the less we hear from those in the Realm itself. The younger messengers are frightened to set foot outside the trenches they spend all day and night digging. Even the military orders are sparse, leaving us to make hesitant movements with little guidance. Truth be told, this letter may never reach your capable hands.*

*Though I must try to reach you. For my sanity, if anything.*

*Many have perished. Needlessly, so it appears in retrospect. So many, in fact, that I have been promoted: The Third General's Second-in-command. Better than the lay soldier, I would say. And one more rung up the ladder. The Ice Realm has never been a place of ease, yet we are getting closer, so much closer to a better life. Me, a warrior in the army. And you…well you were truly built to lead. I can see you being a person of great value to those in Endoneth. In the Realm. Hopefully, our other siblings find their way as well.*

*With my new position comes new information. Now I know your aversion to gossip, however the spirit of the Greentime season makes me want to divulge. The Lord's romance, you remember? The woman of brightness and joy, with the golden hair from the Desert Realm?*

*She is alive and she wants revenge. I have never seen a look so sinister in any human being. She hurts for the fallen Lady of Endoneth, for the Lord's pain. The lust for vengeance has made her into someone else entirely. Someone capable of maniacal evils. And, from what I hear, she is coming to Endoneth.*

*Now I know you grow anxious around the Greentime so take care of yourself. You do not need to worry about what others think of you. Just shine.*

*Yours Always,*
*J*

The Greentime Ball is an illustrious celebration of life and love. Dancing, eating, drinking, and merriment precede a short season of sunshine and pleasure. The Ice Realm becomes host to any deemed significant in the Northern Realms, eager to make their mark and prove their position.

Mairette brings the morning tea after I completed the new phrases of the poem. Now beams of sunlight bleed through the glass window, the primrose standing like a beacon in the center. I sip the sweet strawberry tea as I watch Mairette frantically sift through pages regarding tonight's event. I am surprised she stayed after setting the tea tray on the table, but, every so often, she quiets her mumbling to look my way, perhaps checking to ensure I look better than I did yesterday. Or perhaps reassuring herself that I will be able to make it through the night. Regardless of her aims, she stays as I sip on the smooth taste of fruit, sinking into the couch nearest the fireplace.

When I am halfway through my cup, Mairette clears her throat. "Are you ready for tonight, Centrea? It will be a beautiful night, that is certain." She offers a small smile with her words, attempting to cheer me into a state of excitement.

I nod my head. "When will I need to be dressed to be presented?"

I hope to stay in my room as long as possible. I know both Rostair and Mairette will be busy with the ball, Asha will likely be readying for the event herself, and I wish to be alone with my thoughts, especially when I am soon to be reminded at every turn of the drama Gazil loved so much.

"You should have all morning to rest." Mairette gives me a warm look, stepping closer to me as she continues, "I will come with your gown and the colors for your face after lunchtime. You are welcome to do whatever you wish until that time."

She turns again to the pages, murmuring names and times to herself before stepping away from the couch and closer to the door. "Mairette?" I stop her just as she places her free hand on the door. "Thank you for being here for me. For everything, really."

Tears brim in her eyes as she grins and says in a hoarse tone, "Sweet Centrea, it has been an honor." After a moment, she sighs deeply, reaches for the door, and slips into the hallway toward her next task.

The morning floats by in what seems like minutes. I enjoy the rest of my tea and attempt to rest. Carrying the stress of the past few days has worn on me. My muscles are tight, and my mind is in treacherous knots. I close my eyes, then breathe slowly and letting my whole body become weighted and limp.

I want more than anything to stop the thoughts rattling around inside and to focus on simpler things, like the sound of the simmering fire, the feeling of the soft couch beneath me, or the smell of berries that still clings to the air. The events of tonight, stressful and choreographed they may be, will come and go. Tomorrow morning will bring a new day with far fewer stressors. A day to truly mourn Gazil. A day to revisit the caverns and explore the magic of the pools. A day to decipher the remainder of the poem, still waiting beneath the feather mattress of my four-poster bed.

The simpler things will come. Yes, beyond today. My own reassurances allow my lids to close and a soothing numbness to overtake me. The sleep is restful and pure, not plagued by nightmares and screams.

I awaken to Mairette's gentle hand upon my shoulder as she whispers, "It is time."

I assumed preparing for the ball would be hours of work; however, I had not considered how involved becoming *presentable* would be. Rather than just Mairette combing and braiding my hair as usual, several Keepers flood into my room to assist her. Soon after I stand from the sofa, my typically open and spacious chambers are now cramped with people and fabrics and baskets filled with numerous tools and paints. Mairette directs them like a conductor, while the lower Keepers perform like instruments in a dazzling orchestra. I merely stand by and watch the magic bloom before me. She is the only voice that quickly and delicately points them to each task, the Keepers nodding their heads in submission as they flit throughout the room. One young Keeper approaches me and begins to remove my clothing, still the nightgown from the previous night. The lace that decorates the sides tickles my bare skin as it falls to the floor. Like a warrior on a mission, the Keeper collects the fabric in one hand and hands it to another. Then Keepers wipe my body, cleaning the grief and dirt from the previous day. Another Keeper pulls the decadent ball gown to hug my body.

I had almost forgotten how stunning the work of art looked on my body until I peer into the floor-length mirror and gasp. The final touches and alterations made the dress perfectly hug my wide curves, the colors effortlessly accentuating the sensual dip of my breasts and jutting hips. The glimmering fabric brings a smile to my face before I am pulled onto a stool to prepare my face and hair for the night. A Keeper, this man older than the others, pulls a pale sheet of muslin around my neck before preparing a small table of paints to decorate my face. His hands move quickly yet are so precise. I cannot help but stare in wonder as I watch him work, completing tasks that appear second nature. Mairette takes a moment away from the Keepers on the far side of the room to see me, whispering quiet instructions while moving her hands in waving motions around my face. The Keeper nods as she describes her vision and, without a word to me, she leaves, attending to another group of Keepers holding a number of hair pins and brushes. The older Keeper squints his eyes and holds a thumb in front of my face, tilting his head from side to side as if I am a blank canvas and he a master artist.

The painting itself takes hours. The older Keeper swipes various brushes this way and that over my face, and every so often, Mairette returns by his side and whispers a few words before leaving again. I am thankful for the hours I used to rest this morning as this chaotic dance of Keepers and their tools brings a manic, yet beautiful, energy into the space. Soon, as the painting Keeper finishes the final touches on his masterpiece, I feel the hands of others running through my hair. I hear Mairette's quiet chirps of instruction before brushes begin pulling various clumps of hair in different directions. I close my eyes, attempting to focus on my breathing as the Keepers work. I am constantly met with abrupt pulls and brushes, the cool feel of gels or pricking of pins. This process also takes time, perhaps not as long as the painting, yet I could not say for certain. The sun is my only guide, and it is indeed becoming darker by the minute. Before long, two female Keepers pull me up by my arms and twirl me around to face the mirror.

My image stuns me. Had it not been my dress upon the woman in the mirror, I would not believe it was me. The paint on my face is a stunning mixture of greens and blues that fade into a clean white color at the top of my forehead. My eyelids have a bright yellow color that flares out to my temples, outlined by dark black kohl. My lips are a pale pink that radiates in the sea of greens and blues. Rather than cover my scar, the painter used a dark red paint to highlight it on the side of my face, a gorgeous reminder of my perseverance and strength. On top of my head, my hair sits in a gorgeous collection of intricate braids, with strips of silver, green, and golden fabric woven in. The hair in the knot falls down my shoulders, a mixture of stray braids and curled hair mingling with the top of the dress.

"A vision." Mairette looks into the mirror just behind me, beaming at her work. "Please do not become emotional; paints can only withhold so much." She smiles sincerely and grasps the sides of my arms. "Are you ready?" I nod at my friend who has supported me and prepared me for this moment, for this night. For the first time since the Keepers entered my room, I speak with an air of confidence, of authority, of grace.

"Let us dance."

# Eighteen

I hear the strumming of instruments as soon as my glass shoes hit the hallway tiles outside my chambers. Mairette, who stands with several Keepers carrying baskets of used brushes and additional strips of fabric, gives a slight nod and a reassuring hug before heading toward the entrance of the Blue Wing passageway. "I will see you in the ballroom," she says reassuringly. "Take your time and breathe."

Watching her figure slink into the hidden wall door, I take a moment to gather myself before turning toward the stairwell. I notice as I round the various hallways of the wing that music fills every space, and musicians are stationed strategically throughout the maze of halls to ensure a song can be heard regardless of one's location in the estate. I pass at least three different Keepers, some more skilled at the stringed instruments than others, plucking away as I walk slowly, holding the skirts of my gown to avoid dragging them along the tiles. As I pass by the various guests and Keepers, I hear small gasps and whispers. Unlike the usual sneering and judgmental murmurs, these are sounds of surprise and admiration, even whistles from guests impressed by my appearance.

Perhaps they are unable to identify me, unrecognizable as a decorated beauty, one of the realm. However, the rosy red of my scar no doubt reveals my identity—the marring of someone with a secret past that may keep me from ever fully integrating into this Estate of Ice. I shake away the negative thought, pulling my shoulders back and driving my chin forward. I am every inch a part of this world, the Guest of Honor, Rostair's chosen favorite.

Bright lights descending from the ceiling illuminate the spiral staircase. The blueish glow feels ethereal as the music of strings fades and the sound of a harp takes its place. The source of the music appears at the end of the stairway, where a beautiful Keeper with pale-purple hair waves her hands across the large harp with ease. Her silver dress gleams in the moonlight as she moves her head back and forth, eyes closed, feeling the movement of the notes. I smile as I walk past her and survey the entry hall of the Gold Wing, which is decorated much like the stairs. Keepers spent last night elaborately decorating the space with strings of lights and cascading flowers. This room follows the golden theme as golden flakes of paint dust each petal of every flower. I imagine it took months to prepare flowers for this one space alone, flowers covering every inch of the ceiling. The lights are placed in such a way that make the gold of the tiles glimmer even brighter, and the glowing bulbs overshadow the light from the starry windows. The decor is so breathtaking, I almost forget the hundreds of other people scrambling to join the festivities. The farther I walk through the wing, the louder the voices around me become. Guests dressed in their very best chatter away, drowning out the harp's song. My knees begin to tremble as I see more and more people gawking at me as I pass. Although the crowd grows, the colorful attendants create a path through the hall, leading me with wide eyes and fidgeting hands to the ballroom. I nearly turn to leave, ignoring my responsibilities and returning to my bed and my fireplace and my poem. Instead, I trudge forward, pressing my hands into the sides of my dress to stop their quivering. Just before I reach the threshold, I feel a tug on my arm followed by the brush of a soft hand in mine.

Asha's dress is stunning; the light-brown fabric shimmers with a glittery floral pattern. A long sleeve that billows at the end sheaths one arm, and a high slit on the opposite leg exposes her toned thigh. The color brings out the caramel of her skin, and her face is decorated with a thin lace elegantly adhered across her forehead and down to the tips of her chiseled cheeks.

"Is it not glorious?" Her eyes scan the ceiling above us, where the golden-tipped flowers shimmer in the light's glow. "How are you faring? Are you just arriving?"

Her questions are rapid and fervent, laced with concern and care. I place my hand on her arm, which is still entangled in mine. "Asha, you look like a dream."

It is true, and the answer allows me to avoid admitting my nervousness, which hopefully she sees as a sign to also avoid such discussion. She tightens her hand in mine and smiles, then says. "Would you like to take a moment to look at the beautiful decorations before braving the ballroom? I understand, one's first ball can be overwhelming."

I smile in return, suddenly feeling less alone. "Shall we enter together?" I offer, pulling her arm a bit closer.

Her smile falters slightly, but she nods.

The entrance to the ballroom is more extravagant than ever, the archway covered with green vines of fresh fruit and carpets of various patterns lining a path toward the first layer of plants. The party is in full swing. Men and women take to the dance floor while others explore the various paths and courtyards hidden throughout the expansive room. A man dressed in a velvet green suit stands on the inside of the entrance, looking at me and Asha as we step forward. Asha takes a small step backward, her hand slipping ever so slightly out of reach. She gives an apologetic grin before looking toward the floor.

The man in green looks at me, a serious expression lining his stoic features. "How would you like to be addressed, Miss?" His cold voice is blunt.

I quickly scramble for a response. "Centrea."

The word is not as confident as I would have hoped, yet as it leaves my lips the man's brows shoot upward and he bows reverently.

"Oh, of course, I do apologize, Miss. Of course, of course," he continues muttering to himself as he returns to his place at the edge of the archway. With a loud, booming voice he states, "Presenting our Greentime Guest of Honor, Miss Centrea!"

The introduction halts the dance as anyone within earshot bows their head toward me. Heat stains my cheeks as I clumsily attempt a bow in return. The moment lasts seconds before the announcer continues his work. "Presenting Yekmasha of the Sun Realm!" The dancing continues and the blush recedes from my face. Asha grabs my hand once more and pulls me past the dance floor toward the stage in the center of the far wall.

As we pass through the crowds of faces, some are familiar and others I am unsure if I have seen before. A set of deadly red eyes catch my attention. Helzaf peers from one of the groups to catch a glimpse of my walk through the room. When our eyes meet, she twists her lips into a wicked grin, her face filled with nothing but hatred and vitriol. Perhaps she returned to Endoneth intending to see Rostair join her with open arms. My presence would be most unwelcome in such a circumstance, to be sure.

I flash her a smile in return, refusing to back down from this battle. Helzaf laughs broadly, the green tint of her lips glimmering as she tosses her head. The sound of her laugh reaches my ears despite the flurry of voices, penetrating through a sea of people to reach me with a shrill noise. She turns on her heel to join a group of chatting women as if our encounter never occurred. The chatter of the crowds resumes, and Helzaf's evil laugh dissipates like a waft of odorous air. Irritated, yet undeterred, I press onward. Asha continues to walk alongside me through the haze of people and plants.

*He chose me*, I remind myself as we venture further into the center of the hall.

*Be brave. Be bold.*

My heart skips a beat when I see him, beautiful and regal in a tunic of fine green silk and a long skirt of golden lace. His hair is braided back into a knot that sits at the nape of his neck, and strokes of golden paint start at the top of his forehead and extend through the middle of his hair, creating a striking contrast with his natural silver. Rostair's eyelids are painted with the same gold that shimmers below the lid as well. His lips glow in the moonlight, more inviting than I have seen them.

When he hears me approach, he stands from his throne of pure ice and walks to the edge of the platform and waits for the song to end before addressing the ever-growing crowd of people.

"Good evening, members and guests of the glorious Ice Realm. Endoneth welcomes you, and I do hope you feel at home." He glances quickly at me before moving on. "This year, the Greentime Ball is a symbol of our triumphs and further hope of success against those who wish us harm."

This political statement sparks whispers throughout the room, some guests clearly attending for pleasure rather than political allegiance. "We have a special guest amongst us, a person of curious beginnings and an even more curious future. Who knows what may become of our elusive new friend. Centrea, my Guest of Honor, please do come up and join me."

His hand stretches toward me and guides me onto the stage. The two lanterns to the left and right of the stage glow a strong purple and blue that mingle stunningly with the stars of the night sky that seep through the enchanted walls. I see Helzaf brooding out of the corner of my eye, her arms crossed and a deep frown replacing her once smiling face, yet a glimmer of mischief gleams in her eyes. When I stand beside Rostair, looking out into a crowd of hundreds, a warmth spreads through my body, a feeling of contentment like I have not felt since arriving at Endoneth. The people in the crowd lower their heads in respect as we turn and sit upon our ice thrones.

Rostair clasps my hand in his, and there's a wild sort of excitement in his wide, grey eyes. "I hope you are ready for a night you shall never forget," he says confidently.

I look at the groups of people, hear their whispering words, and see their prolonged glares. Of course, the ball will be a winning event; with a planner like Mairette—how could it not be? And my confidence in her abilities may be another reason for my continued nervousness. I would hate to ruin this hallowed tradition, this fantastic celebration, especially after Gazil's death and the war upon us. This is important; I realize this more than anything now that I sit upon the icy throne holding the hand of the Ice Lord himself. I look at Rostair; he appears completely undeterred, filled with anticipation for the night ahead.

His eyes scan the room, like a hunter eyeing his prey, sitting at the edge of his blue chair to ensure every person plays their role. It is fascinating to see him in this position in front of hundreds. The culmination of years of preparation and patience, his position as Lord is to see his people happy and safe while trying desperately to maintain this sense of ease while the world outside these walls burns. I wonder if there is a kernel of fear beneath the layer of confident armor. I wonder if he spent his day staring at military maps and handing out orders while I sat on a stool like a doll. His hand tenses in mine for a moment, which sends a jolt of energy through my body, returning me to the present.

"I am excited to see you dance, sweet Centrea." He continues looking out into the crowds before us. "I believe it will be a fabulous show."

He smiles to himself, perhaps thinking about my dance or perhaps reveling in the joy of Greentime. I respond, "I am excited to show your people. I want to have a place here, to be a part of something."

This response rips his face from the people and instead he focuses on me, a surprised grin turning the edges of his lips upward. "Is that so?" The tone of his voice is playful, filled with glee.

Before I can respond, Mairette's figure emerges through the crowd of people. She is wearing a dress of pale pink and green, with yellow flowers embroidered into a wavelike pattern across the chest. She appears more at ease than I have seen her in days, almost as if seeing the fruition of her many hours of planning and effort has given her a renewed feeling of peace.

She beams, her pearly white teeth absolutely exquisite in the moonlight as she looks up toward me. "My beautiful friend," her words are so gentle and pure, "are you quite ready?" She gestures toward an open space in the center of the room, a path created through a parted crowd of guests, all looking eagerly toward me, to witness what I might accomplish, what I could achieve.

Nerves swell in my chest as I stand, and Rostair's hand presses into mine reassuringly. "Soar, sweet one," he whispers softly as he releases me.

The phantom of his touch is enough to help me press forward, thinking through the order of the dance moves as I walk slowly toward Mairette who waits patiently for me to descend the platform. I see Asha giving a wave of support, her eyes gleaming with intrigue. I feel my palms sweat and I press them against my gown, hoping once I begin that the tension leaves my mind and body.

Before I can truly gather my wits, the music begins, a slow stream of violins accompanied by a deep cello. Instantly, my body reacts, the muscle memory enough to take control and swish my hips in time with the beat. I catch small glimpses of Mairette as the song continues, clearly rehearsing the dance in her head and providing subtle reminders of each next step. Soon, I realize I need no help; the moves come naturally as I continue the dance.

My dress twirls gently with each strong move while my head rolls from side to side when the dance suddenly pulls me from one move to another. As the song reaches the second minute, I am lost in the dance, putting my body completely into the performance, ignoring the gasps and smiles from the crowd. I think the impression is a positive one, but I realize I do not care as much as I once did. I smile unabashedly. Every anxiety I have held, every tear

I have shed, every fear of the future, I put it all in the dance.

Suddenly, I can't hear the voices of guests or see Mairette's guiding hands. I only hear the vibrations of the music, I only see Rostair's eyes as he traces my every move, consuming each subtle shift of my legs or twist of my hips. As if undressing me in his mind, he lightly licks his lips as I grin toward him, unashamedly performing for only him. The floor is empty, and there's only me and Rostair. He nods in approval, a movement that sends my heart soaring. The toes of his pointed shoes follow the beat, as if wanting to join me, to lean his body beside my own and feel the music as I do. I raise my arms above my head, hearing the climax of the song roaring in my ears before landing in my final pose.

The entire room erupts, guests having poured into the ballroom during the show, clamoring to see a glimpse of the Guest of Honor and her mystical movements. My chest moves up and down as I breathe heavily, holding the pose for as long as possible, capturing this moment, this feeling, to keep forever in my memory. Power surges through me, the breaths still coming in short bursts as the hundreds of hands continue to shower me in praise.

The sense of approval, of belonging, it's intoxicating.

I raise my chin to look at Rostair who is leaned back in the throne, leg propped up on the seat, and wearing a wicked grin. His chest moves rapidly in time with mine, his breathing just as labored as my own, as if he, too, danced before all of Endoneth. His nails, covered in a golden sheen, dig into the arms of the throne, threatening to tear chunks of ice away from the masterpiece.

Instead, as the crowd quiets, the claps slowing to a meager few, he stands once more before his guests. "We greatly admire the dazzling performance of our Guest of Honor. I believe I am not alone when I say there has never been such a dancer to grace this ballroom." His voice steadies as he continues to address the people who surround the stage, peeking out of the mazes of greenery and small courtyards to hear his announcement. "Let us now prepare for our traditional gifting."

With this he nods toward me, encouraging me to leave my position in the spotlight to return to the stage, and place myself upon the smaller throne near his own. "If any person would like to present our Guest of Honor with a gift of green, please step forward."

When I finally reach my seat, the walk to the throne feeling like its own journey, a line of guests have already gathered to greet me, waiting to enter from the side of the stage with beautiful flowers in hand.

The first guest approaches the stage, and I peer down to welcome them as they pull from their long robes the stem of a single flower. My breath catches as I look more closely at this gift, the onyx petals of the flower shimmering in the moonlight.

"For the Guest of Honor," the man rasps with a smile.

He places the primrose on the stage, spreading his arms out to the side as he bows his head before me. The single flower sits on the wooden platform as the guest walks away, leaving his plant like an offering to me. I nearly reach out to pick it up, to hold the black petals close to me, feeling a sense of kinship to the magnificent flower, alone in front of a crowd of strangers, begging for a place to belong. The primrose's loneliness is cut short as the next guest moves from their position in line to stand before the platform.

Dressed in a short green skirt, the woman pulls a potted plant from behind her back. My eyes widen as she plops it down beside the other flower, the gleam of another primrose standing tall as this guest gives her own bow of supplication.

One after another, each guest approaches the stage, presents their plant, and offers words of respect along with a bow of their head. And with each guest, the collection of primroses grows. Some flowers stand alone, while others are planted inside pots or vases of water, however each is the same shade of dark black, each exuding the same powerful energy.

I look at Rostair to gauge his reaction. He sits with his feet firmly set on the ground, his hand gingerly tracing the lines of his jaw as he witnesses each guest place a new flower in the ever-growing pile of primroses. I think back to what I know of this traditional practice; the flowers are supposed to mean something.

"Are the flowers usually of the same kind?" I whisper to Rostair as the next woman places a blue vase on the stage.

He continues to glare at the flowers. "Not typically," he responds, distracted by the display.

The answer does not instill a sense of calm in me as the dozens of primroses turn into hundreds within the span of an hour. At the end of the line, I see the swish of Asha's golden sleeve, her own black primrose held half-heartedly in her hand. She refuses to meet my eyes as she places the final flower atop the rest. When she steps back, giving a small bow, her gaze toward the tiles, the flower topples from its precarious place on the mountain of plants.

Gasps travel throughout the ballroom as the primrose falls to the ground, leaving its honored position on the decorated platform amongst its kin. Asha grimaces and shoots a concerned glance at Rostair who stifles a laugh at the scene.

"They are certainly never to touch the floor. A bad omen." Rostair's whisper squeezes any lingering joy from my system.

Returning her eyes to the floor, Asha steps back into the crowd of guests, attempting to ignore the flower that sits alone on the floor in front of the stage.

"Many thanks, blessed guests of Endoneth. I trust our Guest of Honor accepts these gifts with great... appreciation." The final word from Rostair's voice echoes through the space as every face looks toward him with anticipation. "Please, do continue the merriment. Keepers, the food, if you will!"

With this request, Keepers emerge from the shadows of the ballroom carrying trays of delicacies and fine drinks. Guests clap gently as they begin dancing, drinking, and talking. As soon as the attention is fully removed from the stage, I sink into the throne, relaxing the tension that built during the long gifting ceremony. I attempt to bat away confusing thoughts about the black flowers now lining the stage, almost completely covering the wooden platform floor. Mairette sweeps in front of the stage in a flash, picking up the wayward flower and placing it in its rightful spot with the others.

Observing Mairette's face, the way she refuses to look directly at my face for the first time tonight, I begin to realize the significance of the collection of primroses and Asha's disgraced offering. This is meant to be a time of celebration, of greentime and sunshine and joy. A festival of diversity and unity. Yet the ocean of black petals reflects a singular message from the ball attendants, coordinated and preplanned.

And, while Mairette attempts to perfect the scene, the omen of the fallen flower remains.

# Nineteen

The night continues despite my minute fears spurned by the presence of my favorite flower. It is likely that someone, Mairette or Rostair, even Asha, informed the gathering attendants of my appreciation for this particular bloom. Obviously, the purpose of the gifting is to provide meaningful offerings and, for those who know little about me as an individual, the knowledge of my most beloved flower would provide a heading.

But there was something about the way Rostair stared, the way Asha tilted her head toward the floor, the way Mairette avoided my eyes that only increased the sense of dread within me.

I shake this away and attempt to enjoy the smile on Rostair's face as the people dance and eat and gossip. The ball itself is marvelous. The musicians continue alternating songs to display a variety of sounds that echo through the large hall. The magical enchantment that protects the large windows from the outside air also links its energy to the various lights placed throughout the room. As the music ebbs and flows, so do the lights, growing brighter and dimmer to meet the tempo. The colors also change to reflect the emotion of each song. An upbeat romp encourages the lights to burst with bright pinks and oranges while a slower ballad colors the lights in dim blues and purples. Watching from the top of the stage is like witnessing magic itself, bottled up inside this one room. I cannot help but notice the various couples enjoying swift and gentle kisses in the shadows of the plants and bushes, a few declaring their favor for the first time this season. I wonder if Rostair will choose to declare favor this year. It would bring me tremendous joy to receive such an invitation, to feel like his eyes are for me and me alone.

Gazil did say the night of Greentime was a popular night for such declarations. I sigh at the thought of my friend, sadness oozing from my shattered heart at the thought of him missing my dance, missing the dress he helped create, missing the pile of my favorite flowers, missing the drama of the couples swirling about the ballroom.

Rostair must notice my downtrodden face, as he reaches for my hand in the short expanse between our two chairs. "Is it not glorious?" I feel his thumb tenderly passing over the top of my hand.

"Magical," I answer, the lights shifting from a muted red to a fearsome turquoise.

"Enchanted," he quickly corrects with the slightest smile, "you remember?" His eyes turn toward the lantern in the corner.

I nod, recalling our first tour of the estate and his brief explanation of the spell cast upon this place. "Where is the source?" I look at our hands, joined together atop the arm of my throne. "Where did Endoneth acquire such power?"

I believe the question to be innocent enough, yet Rostair's spine stiffens slightly. "It is a long tale, perhaps for another night." He flashes his charismatic smile at me once more and his thumb continues to move across my hand. The stars twinkle above us, singing their own song as the night wears on.

"You are like no one I have known before, Centrea." His voice quiets to a whisper, heard only by us despite the numerous men and women dancing around the stage.

With the introduction of wine, the party becomes rowdier, more debaucherous. Stolen kisses in the shadows become passionate in the middle of the floor, couples moving closely together as the music pulses through the air, a sense of sensuality felt by each attendant. He moves his other hand to grasp my chin, his touch gentle yet firm as he turns my head to face his chair. "You are… different. Someone with purpose and grit."

My heart aches to be closer to him, to ignore the crowds of people, ignore notions of respectability, and sit upon his lap, hugging his chest close to mine. "Thank you, Lord Rostair." The sound of his official title is strange as I say it aloud, yet the words brighten his face.

"Would you like to share a dance, my Guest." His words sound like more of a request than a question as he stands and pulls me to his side. I lean into his warmth, the silk of his clothes sliding delightfully against my gown.

He leads me toward the dancing, a number of couples in the midst of their own waltz. Effortlessly, Rostair spins me around his finger before pulling me close in time with the music. The ballroom spins in delightful streams of light as we dance. His hand in mine is protective, possessive as the other hovers tantalizingly close to my rear. I wish I could shimmy his touch ever so slightly lower as we glide over the tiled floor. Yet, his hand is firmly placed on my lower back, his fingers grazing my dress over and over. I look deeply into his eyes as we waltz, the grey blazing like small fires, yearning for something that perhaps I could provide. Our dance seems to last a lifetime and a second at once. When the music ends, he extends his arm to bow before me, presenting me with an obligatory thanks. He refuses to let go of my hand as he leads us back toward the stage. As drinks continue to pour, the guests become bolder, speaking louder and with reckless abandon.

"Do you think she is the one?" "She has him, heart and soul." "Do not be ridiculous, he is the Lord of the estate!"

The gossip circulates through the night, and, for maybe the first time, it brings a bright smile to my face.

A young Keeper approaches Rostair as we return to the platform, offering him a goblet of wine before whispering quickly into his ear. His face remains solemn, yet his brows furrow slightly. Taking a small sip of his wine, the flicker of his eyes masks any sense of emotion. It is difficult to know if the message was regarding the war or the ball or any number of important topics. Instead of wondering, I take his hand and pull it onto my lap, tracing my fingertips along his palm. The distraction takes him by surprise but causes his shoulders to ease and his eyes to dull, just a bit.

Settled back into our thrones of ice, Rostair looks at me. "You have placed a charm on some I see." He nods to the guests in the crowd, to those who continue to voice their opinions of me through slurred words. His observation makes my expression glow brighter, filling me with a new sense of confidence. Perhaps he waits for me to approach him, to ask him for his favor, if he will not ask for mine. Even if he does not anticipate such an offer, I feel inclined to try.

Clearing my throat, I look at the Lord as he sinks into the comfort of his seat. "I have felt for many months now that I wish to remain here. To learn who I was and perhaps gain a more complete concept of who I can be for Endoneth, for... well... for you." A flush of red spreads over my chest, threatening to flood my face.

The words encourage his smile to grow, filling his face in an almost unnatural manner. "Why, Centrea. This is the most pleasant news." He grips my hand harder, the edges of his rings cutting into my skin.

He has never been so rough. I attempt to look into his eyes, yet his gaze remains glued to the rush of the crowds before us. What prompted this change? The words of the Keeper? The dance? The wine?

"It is marvelous, being completely in control of so many." His face is nearly glowing with a sick sort of satisfaction as he continues. "Even those who seemingly do not belong to me." His grip tightens, the metal of his rings sinking into my flesh.

I bite my lip to keep from crying.

"But this proves I can take anything I want." His voice is dark and cold and menacing.

I squirm a bit, a sense of unease falling onto my shoulders, his face frozen in that eerie grin. The sounds of the party become suddenly overwhelming; the strumming of the musicians mixes toxically with the voices of the attendants.

Helzaf's shrill laughter breaks into the mix, causing the sounds to echo through the ballroom with a crazed sort of frenzy, her voice leading the charge. Rostair's eyes lock with mine, the grin stained onto his face.

"Whatever is the matter, dearest?" The tone of his voice has never seemed so insincere. "I realize the Greentime could seem overwhelming, but you should not fret. Our night is merely beginning." A small chuckle escapes him, starting from deep in his chest before erupting through his throat.

The world seems to turn upside down as my mind races.

I have no time to think through the noise and Rostair's unnatural behavior before the roar of breaking glass fills the space, a whoosh of air pushing from behind the thrones of ice. I feel a mixture of air and shards of glass hit the back of my neck before I spin my head toward the source. The guests throughout the room scream and run toward the arched entryway. I see the shadow of a man walk slowly onto the golden tiles, his boots crunching the broken glass of the once-enchanted windows. His face glows with the pale purple and blue light of the lanterns in the corners of the ballroom, flickering slightly.

The man surveys the scene before him: the running guests, the glowing lights and decorative plants, the stage and thrones. Soon, his blue eyes lock onto me, his face growing pale as he rushes forward.

"Sol?" His low voice grows desperate as he begins to run. "Sol?!"

Rostair stares at me, his devious grin painfully wide. "Well, Sol. It seems your friends have arrived."

# Twenty

The chaos of the last few minutes leaves me stunned, stuck to the throne, hand still clasping Rostair blindly as I attempt to piece together what is real. With each passing minute, Rostair looks more and more manic, his devilish joy forcing his face into a demonic expression. Hatred fills his eyes as he twists my hand even harder than before, toying with the man running toward us.

"You know this brat of yours has been quite accommodating here, Alcor." He seethes as he says the man's name out loud. He yanks my hand as he stands, glaring down at the warriors from our pedestal.

Soon, I see the striking blond hair of Helzaf rush forward, blocking Rostair from the approaching the small army of five. The warriors are dressed in rich blue tunics that extend to their knees, cut in the sides to allow free movement of the black leathers covering their legs. In the center, the shape of a flittering moth is outlined in red. They each hold a knife in both hands, scanning the room for any sign of a threat, all but their leader.

Rostair called him Alcor, and the name pricks at the hollow of my stomach. The picture of the shadowy figure comes into full view in my mind, and the posters from the Red Wing come to life before me. His icy-blue eyes hold a sort of hypnotic wisdom, a man who has experienced deep loss as well as victory. He wears this openly, inviting anyone, even his enemies, to see his true self in all of its flaws. He grips one of his own knives in one hand, and the other extends toward me as he runs, the rush of cool, spring air flushing through the loose wisps of his close-cut hair. It all comes rushing through me as he reaches the edge of the stage. Rostair's arm painfully possesses me, refusing Alcor of his prize.

*The King is Coming, Support our Sol.*

The banner from the Collective Art Space burns in my mind as I recall the yellow script, Mairette's warning, my nightmares, that voice, calling to Sol, to *me*. It is all too much. My mind is torn in two: part of me wanting to cling to Rostair, to my life in Endoneth, to the hopes I placed in who I could be, while the other part wants Alcor to carry me far from this place, to another realm.

"Release her, you monster!" Alcor bites each syllable as he yells toward Endoneth's Lord.

Helzaf's shrieks of laughter rip into the air. "Our Ice Lord, he does enjoy playing with his *prisoners*."

The word cuts into me, her red eyes slicing through me with sickly precision.

Prisoner.

I turn my chin back to the emptying ballroom and notice Keepers slowly making their way toward the stage, shoving past running guests. Unlike their normal stature, attempting to melt into the shadows, unnoticed by the many socialites who stalk through the halls of Endoneth, the Keepers raise their heads, standing tall and rushing to the scene of great tension. I realize with a confusing rush of emotions, they run to me. To me, their Sol.

*The King is Coming, Support our Sol.*

"This?" Rostair raises my arm like I'm a doll, like I'm his personal toy.

Nausea burns in my throat as the realizations keep snaking their way into my mind. The way I gave myself to him, allowed him to do as he pleased. How I *enjoyed* it.

My knees tremble as Alcor reaches to climb the stage before Rostair tsks, "Oh no, you are mistaken, sir."

A voice from behind Alcor rises in indignation. "That is *king* to you." I recognize him, the voice of a dream. The man raises his knives and wipes a bit of sweat from his pale-blue forehead.

"Gallen?" my voice cracks as I dive deeper into a confusing mixture of personal despair and enlightenment. The man's eyes spring to life at the mention of his name, his bright blonde hair luminous in the light glow of the lanterns.

I hear Rostair sigh impatiently. "This impudent behavior is a waste of my time, and on the night of our Greentime Ball? Now, I know you Southern Lords are ignorant of the importance of the Northern customs; however, you surely understand the magnitude of your horrid interruption." His hand moves to grab my arm with a deathly grip. "This… Southern harlot. I know you would not risk her life, young *King*." He spits the title out like spoiled fruit, clearly unimpressed at the man standing mere feet away.

Tears begin rolling from my lower lashes despite my best efforts. Each drop feels like a warm betrayal falling to my feet. Alcor looks desperate to reach me, Gallen not far behind. I see the other three quickly running in various directions, containing the ballroom, gaining the upper hand as they wait for their moment to strike. That is my hope, I think. My mind still wavers between what I've known for nearly a year and what I've forgotten.

Alcor ignores Rostair's taunts, scanning my body as he holds the knife above his head. "Sol, have you been harmed?" Gallen reaches him, holding his knives close to his sides as he whispers something low, Alcor nodding in return. "Sol. Look at me, please."

It takes a moment for my brain to register the word, the name. I meet his eyes, the icy blue as clear as a mirror. "Alcor?" The name feels both foreign and familiar.

"Agh." Rostair whips my body toward him, my head knocking hard on his shoulder. "This family reunion is tiresome. Now, darling Centrea, I mean *Sol*," the maniacal grin returning to his face, creating someone I barely recognize, "would you like to tell your darling brother of our... intimacy... or shall I?" My face burns, the tears flowing faster.

A blur of pale blue rushes into my periphery, screaming and slashing. Rostair clutches his leg, falling to the floor and dragging me with him. "Blue-skinned shit," he screams in frustration as Gallen jumps to my side, swiping swiftly at the hand holding my arm.

Before I can blink, Rostair releases my arm to stuff his bleeding hand in his clean silk shirt. The feeling of freedom is fleeting as I am suddenly rushed into Gallen's chest, the warm feeling just as I remembered it after the cavern pools: warmth and love and safety.

My tears continue, but for another reason. Not for embarrassment or betrayal, not for the pain. Tears of pure happiness. He whispers into my ear sweetly, "It is all for you, Sol. Always."

The words flood my heart with a welcome and bright sensation, one difficult to put into words. He smells like salt and citrus. And even as the world around us falls into further turmoil, his kind face offers a sanctuary to escape. I hold onto the blue sleeves of his tunic as he guides me to the edge of the platform.

I still hear Rostair's bouts of anger, calling for guards to line the halls, to prevent the success of this rescue. The unfamiliar force of men and women, holding long bayonets of silver and dressed in blinding white uniforms, underscore the absurd nature of the past hour, of the past few minutes. They represent my ignorance of Endoneth's true nature, hiding in the same place I called home, while I was none the wiser.

Gallen pushes me toward the King from the South, his eyes having never left me until I fall from the stage and into his arms. "I am so sorry, Sol. I am so, so sorry." He brushes stray hairs out of my face and takes me in his arms, reassuring himself of my safety. The tender moment is broken almost immediately as he nods to his fellow knife-wielders, and they burst into action.

Alcor catches my attention, grazing my arm with his hand. "Can you run?"

I barely have time to nod before he presses me forward, his hand offering me support without pulling me himself. The subtle offer of independence validates his trust in me and further convinces me to trust him.

The warriors stay behind as we press forward. Gallen briefly looks back to watch me retreat before facing the spears of three guards. "Run!" he calls after us, a sign of encouragement rather than a command, reassuring us to push on, to trust their ability to face the dozens of guards now lining the walls of the ballroom.

The fresh air rushes through my curls and the train of my dress as we run through the familiar grounds of the estate. I still hear Rostair yelling after us, and more guards burst through the passage doors to protect their Lord while Alcor leads me away from the continued tumult. I see glimpses of blue-clothed warriors swinging their knives with lethal precision, providing us with enough time to leave the estate. I see Helzaf, screeching in anger at Rostair's bleeding wounds and barking profanities at a female warrior who stays close to them both, watching them with intense concentration, hands held in front of her. I see the Keepers that watch in wonder, witnessing a breach in their security, in their lives as they know them. I see Asha joining the fight, the bottom of her golden dress ripped to reveal her strong legs lined with sharp stars of steel. She presses her back to Gallen's, protecting him as the guards press in closer. Soon, their figures are too far to distinguish as I look back. The yelling fades too, replaced by the calming chirps of nighttime insects and the soft crunching of our shoes against the grass and roots and soil.

I hear Alcor pant, "We just need to make it to the edge of the estate. We will be safe there."

There are thousands of questions that run through my mind yet the only one that matters is, "Will they be safe?"

He rasps a "yes" as we continue to navigate through the woods that surround Endoneth in the pitch-black. Alcor appears unfazed by the lack of light, finding a clear path through to the edge of Rostair's land. I follow surprisingly well, staying close to my savior as we maintain an impressive pace. I suppose there were few reasons to run during my stay at the estate, yet it appears a natural talent. Just as my legs begin to burn from effort, I see small dots of light ahead. Alcor runs faster as he sees the lights grow before us.

More figures emerge in the moonlight, dressed in the same uniform as the others: navy-blue tunic, black leather tights, and heavy brown boots. A bright-eyed, sprightly woman meets us immediately as we slow to a halt in front of a group of maybe a dozen Star Realm warriors.

They all look to Alcor expectantly before the first woman speaks, "Quickly, we must join the others." She offers a leather canister to Alcor and nods to a few other warriors, communicating instructions as she hastily turns and walks away. Alcor sips from the cup before handing it to me. "Drink up." He smiles as he runs after the woman.

"Zeffra, prepare the remaining warriors in case we need to stage a second rescue."

The woman, Zeffra, turns around yet continues to move backwards through a clearing in the woods. "Of course, Your Highness. We have collected food to sustain us for at least another day or so. It is packed and prepared for a swift retreat." She tosses her silky auburn hair over her shoulder, her deep brown skin as shimmering as the stars that sparkle above us, and offers a hand to Alcor, a genuine show of love and support. The relief in her twinkling green eyes tells more about their relationship than words could. The slight glistening of tears lining her lids betray her concern at the potential of loss, of death. He sees the same gleam in her eyes and catches her hand, pressing it to his lips. The moment is swift, intimate. I find myself turning away, giving them space as they enjoy each other's company, the reassurance of one more night together, alive.

Despite my attempts to minimize my presence, Zeffra looks over Alcor's shoulder and says, "I am so glad to see you, Sol. Truly." The words bring a brief smile to the King's serious face. He looks to the stars, his eyes moving from one blinking light to the next, calculating in his mind.

"Gallen, Ranor, Elthen, and Asha." He takes an account of those left behind. "If they do not return in a half hour, we will circle back."

The command is decisive. And so we wait.

We move a bit beyond the clearing, to where the warriors set up a small camp in the shade of nearby trees. When we arrive at the group of five tents, small lean-tos with thin fabrics laid across wooden frames, Alcor leads me to the tallest of the group, pulling a blanket to cover the warm soil and gesturing for me to sit.

"I notice your silence, Sol. What did they do in that place?" He bites his tongue as the words spill out, and I can tell he wants to be gentler with me.

"We must be close, you and me." Alcor winces as if the observation physically pains him, and I lean to touch a hand to his arm. He sits on the blanket and places his head in his hands, a frustrated sigh filling the space.

"We are." A breath escapes him as he contemplates a way to ease me into this new name. This new place and people. "We are your family here. The Night Flyers. A group of highly trained and efficient warriors. There are more of us at the border, fighting this war as we speak. I chose a few for this quest to retrieve you. And you, you are our strategist. Our eyes and ears. You and Gallen and Asha, you three are our best."

We sit in a brief silence, the information building synapses in my brain that attempt to connect the old memories together.

"Tell me about Gallen." My voice quivers as I think of one of the only memories I have from my past.

Alcor eases his body, his smile far more comfortable than before. "He is loyal, strong, and honest. You brought him to us from his home in the Ocean Realm. He's been one of our most valuable warriors ever since. Yet, honestly, you knew him far better than I." The suggestion brings a hot blush to my cheeks, and I pull my cool hands to fight the reaction.

At the response, he peers more interestingly at the scar on my cheek. "This was not here before... when you left." His hurt is undeniable.

"You have always been brave, Sol. Always known the next step, anticipated a foe's final steps. This time... I suppose the outcome was not what we all expected." Alcor scratches his forearm as he speaks, constantly considering how much information is too much for me.

"No shit." I flash him a playful smile. "I may not remember much, but I can deduce that 'willing prisoner' was not on the list of potentially successful results." He laughs heartily, the booming of his low voice pushing against the fabrics along the tent. I like this, the sitting and talking, unworried and unbothered.

The bliss lasts only a few seconds, but it is all we need. To laugh away the tears and the struggle, to focus on the good rather than becoming overwhelmed by the horrible.

I move nearer to him. "I have been trying to remember. Daily. Truly. There were a few moments of... of clarity. Where a thought, a memory, a voice would come to mind." I gasp, thinking of the pages upon pages of words tucked away in the drawers of my writing desk, of the poem and the knife hidden from plain view.

Alcor's face looks at mine, seeking an explanation for my sudden outburst. "I left notes in my chambers. The room he gave me. They were my thoughts and vague glimpses of memories. I thought I could piece it together. Then there was the poem..."

The word changes his demeanor completely. "What poem? What did it say?" he asks, eager for an answer.

I wish with all my might that I could walk back to the mattress and retrieve it. I wish I could stash pages into the leather satchel and tow it away from that place. I search for memories of the words, words that I recited over and over in my room when I felt most alone.

I recite the poem, word for word, leaving spaces for the few gaps that remain. With each stanza, Alcor breathes more deeply, tears bursting from his cool eyes, like spheres of ice.

"You remembered," he whispers. He suddenly stands to his feet, running out of the tent for a few minutes before returning with a quill and muddy page in hand. He sits on the blanket, a bit closer to me this time. "I am afraid these are the supplies we have, but they will suffice." With this, he writes frantically, using his leg as a makeshift table. After a few minutes, he presents the sheet to me with a giddy smile on his face that warms my heart.

I read the poem, the words flowing effortlessly, the gaps filled with words that bring the work to life:

*A starry night, away from war,*
*Where we the children lay before;*
*These four words, to one so far,*
*Hold close to heart while never near;*
*Remember, Sol, your purpose be,*
*For realms and people you are the key;*
*With bated breath I always hold,*
*'Till you return, our brave and bold,*
*For the good of all should ne'er be sold.*

"You know this?" I hold the paper between us for emphasis.

"Of course," he replies. "I wrote it."

When Alcor initially led me through the woods, there remained a seed of doubt that this twist of fate was incorrect, that I imagined the look in Rostair's eyes as he said my new name, that he was not my captor and that Alcor was still my enemy.

However, as Alcor reveals this piece of information, the poet to my source of comfort all these months, it solidifies my allegiance. "I wrote this work for someone I love, someone who ventured on a journey to another realm. A friend, a warrior in her own right." He says the words carefully as if holding back so as to not overwhelm me with all truths at once.

Sitting with him here, his freshly scribed poem in my hands, it feels like a memory that we already experienced in a time before. He takes my hand, again so careful, likely afraid any sudden movement will frighten me and force me further away from him. "I wrote this poem for my sister." He presses my hand slightly and looks at me with the warmest affection.

The words take a moment to settle, to fully take hold of my mind and finally provide me with the clarity I have desired for so long. The seed of doubt rears its selfish head once more. This is all too convenient, too sudden, too unbelievable. And, if I am not to trust Rostair or Mairette or Asha, who can I truly believe?

"What are you implying, sir?" My voice sounds foreign to me, struck with grief and terror.

I see Alcor's reaction to my suspicious tone, his eyes piercing like beautiful daggers, seeking to speak to the depths of my soul. "I wrote this poem for you, Sol. My only kin. Please, please say you recall." Desperation laces his voice as he chokes on the words. He sees the turmoil as I sit motionless, my brain attempting to process all that has happened and what he implies.

An idea seems to spark in his mind, the thought stirring him to move, looking for a particular item as he falters through the dimly lit tent. He smiles broadly when he sees the satchel, a leather bag so similar to the one I left behind. Lifting the flap, he reaches in. "Perhaps this will spark a memory."

I wish I could tell him that pleas are useless. That I have attempted to learn for months. Before I can, he raises a knife from the bag, a knife I recognize instantly.

"How did you retrieve this?" I sit back, amazed.

In his hands is the same knife that was left in my chambers, the same knife that at this very moment hides in a leather bag in the drawer of a wooden piece of furniture. He extends the dagger toward me. Lying flat on his palm I see the familiar black marble, the sharp steel blade.

"They exist in pairs," he says excitedly, noticing the effect it has on me as I reach my hand to touch its hilt. "You kept one blade and told me to return its match to you when the time came. It appears it has."

Any doubt evaporates.

It must be real. This tent, this man, this king.

And I, his family, sent to the Ice Realm as what? To what end?

While the world around me continues to spin, my mind refusing to focus on an object long enough to keep the motion at bay, each new piece of information spawns more questions. Despite these unanswered queries, for the first time I can remember, I understand something about me that is real: I am Sol, sister to a King.

Zeffra pushes through the layers of fabric that serve as the entrance to the tent. "Alcor, do you have a moment? There is news from the front."

My brother's eyes remain tied to mine as he answers, "Of course." He pulls a small stack of folded clothes from the edge of the tent and sets them near my knees. "For you, when you are ready. We will wait for our remaining warriors for as long as we can, but we cannot wait for much longer."

He squeezes my hand one last time, seemingly torn between staying with me and doing his duty, and rises to join Zeffra and the others outside. I hear their muffled voices fade as they walk away and look at the clothes sitting by my side.

Article by article, I hold each piece out in front of me, gently placing them on the blankets before me. I pull at the heavy fabric of my gown, now appearing garish in our present circumstances. My naked body waits for a moment, enjoying the cool feel of the spring night, before I pull the uniform of the Night Flyers over my head. I run my fingers over the red moth. I look at the crumpled gown lying in the dirt and spot the figure of the moth peeking through the folds of flashy fabric. My heart aches as I think back to my pull to such symbols: the moth, the primrose. As if a part of me realized the entire time who I was, where I came from. I pull the black leathers onto my legs, the pants almost tailor-made for me. They hug my curves and rump as closely as possible without being too tight. Before I move outside to meet the others, I see the glint of the knife, left by Alcor for me to keep. One of a pair, he said. I grasp the hilt in my hand, the same feeling of anticipation, the same spark of power and authority flowing through me just as they did when I held its match in my room. I sheath it in my right boot, a compartment sewn in the side to hold a blade just its size.

I breathe deeply, embracing all that I have just learned and all that I am, before I move the fabric tent aside and step into the night.

"We need to formulate a plan."

The tense words ring from Zeffra's mouth as the group of men and women gather at the edge of the clearing. Alcor concentrates on the stars, reading them like a map or guide. The twenty-seven-minute mark he noted before passed ten minutes ago with no word from the four other warriors left behind in Endoneth. They each stand at the ready, a ragtag group of warriors from vast corners of the Nine Realms. All serious-faced, loyal servants. None but Zeffra have presented their own opinion on the matter at hand, though many whisper to one another, nodding and plotting, considering a number of tactical options.

Alcor turns to one, a lanky, middle-aged man with sharp teeth and pale eyes, and says, "Luminor, what say you?" The eyes of each warrior look to Luminor as he uses a knife to pick his teeth.

His gruff voice is softer than I initially assumed, with a strong accent that stresses every 'S' as he speaks. "Sire. The night will last only a few hours yet. Shall we send separate groups, some entering from the ballroom at the side while others enter from the roof? Or perhaps another group distracts from the front hall?"

The king considers this, his broad hand tugging at his chin. Another warrior voices a new concern: "Yet, how are we to leave? When we find our friends, how shall we return here?"

Murmurs of affirmation sweep through the camp as every warrior considers this truth. There must be a way to leave the estate safely, a way to avoid the paths that are no doubt now crawling with Endoneth guards, figures I have never seen before today. This notion causes multiple others to chime in, creating numerous conversations simultaneously thinking about the best plan of action.

I silently raise my hand, the warriors continuing to debate amongst themselves which scheme is safest, which would guarantee the most success. Zeffra notices my hand and loudly clears her throat to gain the group's attention. The silence is stark as all eyes turn now to me.

"I may have a plan, if you are willing to hear it."

Alcor's eyes shine with both pride and fear. "We cannot lose you again, Sol." His concern touches me, yet I know what must be done.

"I have lived amongst Endoneth's people for months. I know the halls. I know the resources and the various paths. I firmly feel the best option is for me to join you."

As soon as the words fall from my mouth, Alcor shakes his head profusely. "Sol. This is no time. The last time you struck out on your own, you were captured."

"No time for arrogance." Zeffra huffs and eyes me carefully. "The King may tread lightly, but there is no time to dance around your feelings."

"Zeff," Alcor grumbles at the woman.

"She must know, Alcor! It was you that went into that wilderness on your own after we *explicitly agreed* to wait and ambush Rostair's estate together. You dismissed us. Dismissed *your brother*. Your *King*. You allowed your arrogance to overtake you and it nearly got you killed! May still get Night Flyers murdered, and for what? Your pride?!"

Zeffra was screaming now, the frustration as blatant on her face as my red scar.

"Enough, Zeffra." Alcor stomps his lumbering feet toward her, yet Zeffra maintains eye contact with me.

The faded memory of the ice storm shocks my system, a position I suppose I created for myself. And due to my disobedience to the King. I nod, honestly seeing Alcor's perspective. "I realize this may appear rash. However, I do think this is the best path. Just… listen to my thoughts. I will never have to be alone; we should move in groups, as Luminor said."

Over the next few minutes, I outline my plan, which I conjured up in my mind as easily as anything else. Rather than discounting my idea, the group appears contemplative, nodding as they think through the details.

Alcor looks to the stars once more. "Gods, why are you so good at this, Sol?" The tone of his voice is frustrated, yet he barely hides the smile that fills his face. "Do as she says: three groups, no hesitations. Any questions."

The Night Flyers each nod, some wearing looks of concentration, preparing their minds and bodies for the task ahead, while others look excited, jumping up and down eagerly. Alcor looks directly into my eyes, his voice low, and says, "Are you certain of this, Sol? I realize there is much you still do not know, still do not recall. I do not want to lose you, not again."

I touch my hand to his arm. "Dear brother. Never worry about that."

The path back to the estate fills me with a sense of anger. This fantastic world I once knew is filled with evil, with lies and hatred. I do not want to consider the complicity of those who saw me every day. Of those who watched me struggle with my sense of self. Of those who lurked nearby as I attempted to reconstruct my memories. Of those who allowed me to develop feelings for a man who holds such malice toward my home and my people.

Rostair has revealed his true colors, but what of Mairette? What of Piré or Junsen?

What of Gazil? The thought of him threatens to break me, to force me into the deepest sort of depression where there is no escape. After the past few hours, his final night with me in the archives takes on a completely new light. He wanted to *save* me. He cared for me, like a friend, like a sister. And, like an ignorant fool, I believed he wanted to have me intimately, to abuse my trust. I hate myself for ever crying over his betrayal, when, all along, he wanted to take me far away from Endoneth, to save me from the embarrassment of the primroses and Rostair's wrath.

Even with this knowledge, there is still so much unknown. Why did no one warn me of the truth? If I am such an important figure, how could no one have recognized me, especially those who visited from outside the realm? What of Asha, a person who seemingly fights on our side?

These questions remain unanswered as we run toward the estate.

The warriors divide into three smaller sections to enact my plan: Zeffra leading ten, Luminor leading another eight, while I join Alcor and two others toward the main house. Another two remain with the tents in case the warriors return or the plan sours. The plan will not fail— of that, I am convinced.

Alcor quietly stays close by as we swiftly weave through the woods between trees and vines. The other two Flyers, Kelmin and Arwelia, run on each side of us, focused on their respective sides while Alcor and I keep our eyes ahead, looking back every so often in case a guard attacks from behind.

Despite everything that has happened that night, surprisingly we do not come across any guards. I move toward a window that had been shattered earlier that night and carefully peer into the ballroom, which looks seemingly empty save the decorations still scattered throughout the space. Alcor nudges my arm with his elbow, his fists clenching two knives with yellow hilts. He extends one toward the left before walking carefully to the right. I follow his instruction, stepping to the left of the stage, attempting to limit the noise as my boots crunch pebbles of glass and loose stems of greenery. The other two warriors move around the outside of the estate, checking the periphery. A door opens at the far edge of the ballroom, and footsteps following shortly after along with the sweeping of brooms and sloshing of mops.

My body is frozen, yet my heart beats incredibly fast, my chest the only part of me moving up and down. I risk peering over a line of bushes, desperate to see the source of the noise. A number of Gold Wing Keepers hold brooms and brushes in hand, cleaning the mess after the event. Another group files into the hall, bringing large buckets, and begins gathering old plants and flowers. They do not notice us, too busy with their tasks. After a few minutes, my heart rate slows to a more comfortable pulse, my mind less flustered and more observant.

I hear the Keepers speak in spurts about the night, using a sort of code to discuss their opinions. "Horrible situation, absolutely frightful. The Lord himself did us a service, to be certain. The Red are bolder than I once thought, and I hope, I hope the rose found a way."

The Keepers become bolder, speaking louder and louder as more workers enter and share their thoughts, feelings, hopes. "Would it not be better if we follow the leader in the South?"

"How many Keepers do you know who feel the same?"

"I hope she made it out of this place. Pretending had become almost too much to bear."

Their words give me a bit of hope that the artists who developed paintings in the Red Wing were vast in number and willing to help. Their presence reminds me of the tasks at hand: Find Piré, find the warriors, and leave.

When Alcor asked who I would recommend to lend their knowledge of the estate, Piré seemed the perfect choice to trust with telling us the location of the prisoners. Before tonight, I would have claimed Mairette as a confident source; however, with her position in the household she must have known far more than she led on. I continue forward, pushing aside the continued feeling of betrayal and sadness, one I wish I could leave behind, back in the shadows of the woods or the warmth of the tented camp.

Despite my fervent desires, the emotions remain deeply ingrained in me, flowing through my legs as I continue further into the ballroom, tiptoeing inch by inch until I meet Alcor and the others at the hall's entrance. He looks to me to lead, and I venture forth into the Gold Hall. The tiles that once entranced me with their intricate designs now mock me as we make our way toward the Red Wing.

When we reach the edge of the Red Hall, where the golden tiles turn to blood beneath our feet, I begin to relax. We venture deeper into the dim hallway, the pages of decorated papers strewn across the walls, and it is only when the light of the Gold Wing is muted, replaced by the slight glow of the lanterns lining the hall, that I whisper to my companion, "We should be able to speak more freely here. Only Keepers enter this wing."

He nods as we continue down the well-trodden tiles, looking intently at the various drawings as we pace forward, toward the end of the hall and the open space below. "How many Keepers trust in our cause?" His fingers trace one of the posters as we pass, the crescent moon shedding yellow light upon a gloomy land of ice— symbols calling attention to the secret supporters of his ascendancy.

"I cannot know for certain, but there are at least a few. Maybe more than a few. Piré would know more than I." He nods again and looks forward, toward the spiral staircase.

When we grow closer, the sound of voices meets us— shouting and debating and confusion. The noise leads us down the stairs until we are standing in the front central hall, which is in a state of panic. Keepers crowd the main room, most yelling across each other while a precious few attempt to enforce a sense of diplomacy. It is difficult to ascertain the source of the confusion, as the voices all muddle together, making clarity impossible.

The commotion allows us to slip in undetected, and we move to the side to witness the chaos from a safe distance and potentially remain masked in shadows. The scene is especially jarring for me. Even in their most vulnerable moments, I have never seen Keepers so vocal in their discontent, concern, and outspoken disagreement. Throngs of Keepers fall into camps, some voicing support for Alcor and the team of rebels, while others defend the traditions held so dearly by Rostair, their Lord and authority. Heated side discussions peel outward beyond the central focus of this ongoing outpouring of emotion. Such individual squabbles threaten to overwhelm the space with their yells of discontent, the tension so tangible in the air it threatens to suffocate me as I stand a mere observer.

I scan the room, searching for Piré's petite frame amongst the crowd of shifting people. I am unsure of where I would hope to find her, yet my heart flutters as I see her boldly posed on the side of the royalist, shaking her pale fist in the face of an elderly woman, spit flying from her mouth as she screams her protestations. My smile dims subtly as I realize the difficulty of retrieving her from the center of this struggle. If those who are less gracious to our cause see us in this space, we risk being caught.

As I weigh the positives and negatives of reaching Piré, her hands waving in frustration, I see a cloaked figure approach her from behind. His shoulders are broad and gait lumbering. The figure places a careful hand on her shoulder and ushers her toward the edges of the crowd, away from her opponent who immediately starts another argument. The hooded stranger grips Piré authoritatively, the brown of the cloak masking any form of identifiable clothing. The figure barrels through the crowd, using one arm to hustle through the crowd while the other drags Piré behind. I see Alcor's smirk emerge beneath the brown felt and move to the stairwell with reinvigorated purpose.

Piré does little to hide the smile radiating on her face. When we arrive in the Red Hall, Alcor begins detailing our dilemma. "Young one, we must find our companions, those who intended to free Sol. We understand many Keepers hold such knowledge. We would need a guide, someone to navigate the passages…"

Her eyes grow wide as our purpose becomes clear. "Please, Piré." I attempt to convince her myself. "We would be indebted to you. If you fear consequences from Lord Rostair for helping us, you could follow our journey to another realm?"

My heart aches for this young girl, so willing to pursue justice while certainly aware of the cost. Alcor nods his agreement. "You would have safe passage. If not to the Star Realm, then to any other you desire."

She clearly considers this proposition, placing a pale hand on her cheek as she thinks through her options. What remains unspoken is no doubt clear to Piré: If she assists us, helps us escape Endoneth, there is likely no life left here for her. What we ask is not merely this one favor, this one source of information. It could mean the end of her time in Rostair's employ or, potentially, her time in the Ice Realm. She looks at the pictures lining the hall, clearly a source of imagination and introspection for her, as she considers her next move.

She turns to us. "Of course. However, we must be wary. There are many guards who haunt these halls; their heavy feet usually foretell their approach." She pauses before a look of determination comes across her face and she says with strength and fortitude, "For King and Sol."

The phrase, so confident in her use, in the natural way it falls from her lips, lifts my spirit, sends it soaring above the house, the realm, into a place of peace and joy and confidence.

My only response is in kind: "For King and Sol."

The passages that Keepers use to navigate Endoneth's wings are confusing, dim, and cavernous. The air in each hall is musty, and the walls are made of a cheap plaster that barely covers the old and chipped bricks. The floor reminds me of the Keepers' Red Wing basement: well-trodden dirt, void of the colorful tiles that mark every other space. Piré's footsteps kick up small clouds of dirt as the five of us wind through various passageways that cross periodically, forcing her to turn left and right with intense speed. While the movements appear nonsensical, and the path leads up and down several sets of stairs before swirling in rapid zagging patterns. Without Piré to guide us, the passages would have been impossible to manage. As we walk briskly to follow the delicate steps, I try to imagine a visual of these paths, a map of the crossing passages and sudden stairwells and how such an image would stun even the most expert adventurer.

After a journey of what felt like hours but was likely minutes, Piré stops and turns abruptly. "Here. I have yet to see a guard. They must be marching the wings rather than their usual posts." She shifts from one foot to the other, looking left and right as if to catch a glimpse of one hiding in the shadows.

The sudden appearance of the guards did strike me as odd during Alcor's first rescue, a presence that went unnoticed during my many months in Endoneth. The shock of seeing those guards, with stark white blazers bejeweled by golden buttons down the center of their chests, did little to quell my already unsettled mind.

Piré continues, "If we haven't seen them down here, they are likely swarming out there. Be careful." She emphasizes this point, gesturing her head toward a small door carved into the plaster walls.

Alcor moves ahead, placing his head on the door before pressing it slightly open. He nods to us, and a beam of light from the hall of the mysterious wing highlights the blue in his eyes as he watches for guards or guests, both an obstacle to our final purpose. It takes only seconds before he calls us to join him in walking through the door and into the brightly lit hall.

I look instinctively toward the tiles below, seeing twirling, orange designs. Looking from side to side, I reorient myself. The Orange Wing, near the studies.

Alcor again looks to Piré to lead us, and as she steps forth into the hall, we hear footsteps from a nearby corridor. Quickly, I rush toward the end of the hall, seeking a cove to duck into or a closet in which to hide. Before I find something suitable, Piré pulls the edge of my navy sleeve, ushering me into another hidden door. Hot air fills the secret passage as we each breathe in heaves into the space, my heart beating nearly out of my chest at the newfound fear of Endoneth and its inhabitants.

Before today, the isolation was painful; now it is dangerous. Each guest is now a potential threat to my personhood and people. The stakes are much higher than they were when reputation is all that separated me from those who frequented social events or knew the names of each attendant.

When the footsteps of the passerby echo into the distance, we follow the same pattern as before, inching our way into the hall before Piré points us toward a wayward study at the end of the longest orange hallway, guarded by two soldiers clad in white. Alcor presses a finger to his lips before slipping into the hall. Before I can register the movement, both guards crumple to the ground, blood staining their pristine uniforms. Alcor scans the hall before waving us toward the door.

In my time at the house, I may have visited this door once, perhaps twice. Gazil and I favored the larger libraries and studies where the most guests stayed and the most gossip could be overheard. The tiny door leading to this particular study is unassuming, painted a pale orange that suits its place in the wing. The golden knob is also painted with a faded orange color that peels at the base, a clearly older and forgotten relic of a different time in the realm. Alcor discreetly presses an ear to the wooden door, attempting to understand the landscape of the room before barging in. His expression of assurance, of relief, precedes his confident push into the space, immediately followed by the sound of sighs of relief.

Gallen is the first to jump toward us before being violently pulled backward. His hands are secured to a wooden chair, and his blue face is dotted with dark purple hues of bruises. The chair itself, like the three others beside it, is nailed to the floor. The tiles crack in appalling and uneven segments beneath the prisoners. I see Asha, flashes of pain sweeping over her features, look desperately toward the now open doorway. The climate of the space is plagued with evidence of torture and suffering. Blood splatters the floor and our companions. The sight itself falls so distinctly contradictory to the Endoneth I experienced, with its the glorious halls of learning and light. Rather, this study has become a place of pain and incivility, capturing the very worst of what those of any realm or race can accomplish with enough malice.

Ranor and Elthen join Asha and Gallen in a loose circle, the chairs close enough for the prisoners to hear and smell one another, yet far enough away as to prevent them from feeling more tangibly each other's presence. The blood trickling down the arms, legs, and heads of Gallen's compatriots somewhat explains their silence and inaction at our appearance in this chamber. Both figures slump over the chairs, one unmoving as the other struggles to eke out crackled, labored gasps for air. Alcor's face expresses a brief twinge of horror, an acknowledgement of the terrible position of his warriors, his friends.

Yet his role as a leader takes hold as he bursts into action. "Gallen, report." He reaches for the warriors who have yet to move, checking their vitals before swearing quietly.

"The task was complete. You found freedom. After which we relinquished our own freedom, allowed the guards to take us in, assuming we could find a way to escape ourselves." Gallen's hands shake as he speaks, the shackles pressing even further into his bruised flesh. "Our intel, what we've known about this place. It was misplaced."

The words seem to cause a more visceral reaction for Alcor than the chamber, his thoughts scrambling as he further assesses the room. Feeling absolutely helpless, I stand aside with Piré, whose pale face turns sour as she holds her midsection, knees growing dangerously wobbly as the reality of the last few hours sets in.

"How much blood did they lose?" Alcor's voice is commanding yet gentle, concerned yet impatient.

It is difficult to hear Gallen's descriptions. "When they brought us to this chamber, guards dressed in black arrived to gather information." Piré's gasp underscores the difference of these men to their white-coated counterparts. "They spent their time methodically, which I suppose was fortunate for us. Rostair," he spits the name like acid, "he said he was taking care of us last. The man shows little care for life, for much of anything. The methods of information extraction... they were brutal to say the least..."

His voice peters out, the struggle to follow commands in tension with the fresh trauma of the torture. He finally turns from Alcor—who looks pensively at the shackles, quietly finding the easiest way to release the four captured allies—and meets my gaze. His eyes, their desperation, pain, and love, pull me from my complacency, urging me to help him, help them. The distance between us suddenly feels too far. I pace over the blood-stained tiles until he tilts his head to maintain eye contact, my legs only inches from his knees. Falling to the floor, I join Alcor in searching for an escape, a way to release Gallen and Asha and the others from their imprisonment. "He is returning. I am unsure when, but he will return. He swore it," Asha seethes through her teeth, the words almost choked in the center of her throat.

I turn to her, my newest friend in this horrid place. "I am sorry, Asha." It is all I know to say. Sorry for dragging her into this conflict and potentially getting her killed in the process.

She chuckles, the bruise lining her throat rippling as she cringes in pain. "Sweet Sol. I have been a part of this for far longer than you know."

The concept had not crossed my mind, yet before I could pursue the thought further, Alcor speaks above it, "Sister, there will be time for reunions after we are all free." Reunion? I pray the memory returns soon, the possibilities of my past still whirling in my mind like fog.

Rather than protest, I nod and examine to the shackles once more, the steel is tied like a knot and chained to the wooden chairs. Despite Gallen's and Asha's strength, the wood itself remains resilient to their most fervent attempts to break it. The metal seems equally impenetrable, nothing like I have seen throughout the estate but surely a creation of the Ice Realm, if none of our warriors understand its potential. Piré still stands by the door, holding her stomach and whispering unintelligibly. I feel conflicted about bringing her into the fold, forcing her to witness the evils of her own home, perhaps completely shattering her sense of belonging here, of safety.

But what sort of life is one lived in ignorance? I walk toward her, placing a light hand on her shoulder, her twirls of blonde hair shaking as she nervously looks up to me.

"Could you look for us? You may have a better understanding of such metals or restraints..." Her eyes twitch at the final word, but she slowly shifts her body forward, her feet barely leaving the ground as she trudges toward the prisoners. The tiles are sticky from the remnants of blood, so sloppily mopped up after the interrogation, and Piré certainly notices. She tilts her head upward in an attempt to ignore the realities of the room. When we're behind Gallen's chair, she inhales deeply in preparation for a closer inspection of the shackles. At first, she squints her eyes and barely glances at his hands; however, as the blue gleam of the metal comes into focus, I see her face turn thoughtfully stoic.

She extends a fair hand to the metal before thinking better of it and pulling back. "This is no mere metal." She scratches the top of her hair as she speaks. "We have ovens created with the same material. It is enchanted, imbued with magic that makes it stronger than others."

Alcor steps behind Piré, his broad shoulders towering over her petite frame, the difference made more staggering as she hunches over the metal chains. "How do you destroy such metal?" His voice booms after the gentle sweep of her fluttering words.

"It is not done," she whispers disappointedly. "The power is inherent in the home. It originates from a source known to a special few. The Lord of the home, he trusts only a few in this realm… He has much power, that is how he was able to control us all during your stay."

She looks toward me for a moment before returning to the shackles. "There are rumors… that the labor of the fairies is for far more than capital gain." Piré says the words with such conviction as if this trade is common knowledge. I think of the Fairy in the woods, its glow fading as its life withered away. Rostair appeared so caring then, so concerned. Yet perhaps he was not concerned about their lives but their productivity.

"What gain, Piré?" I ask.

It is now Alcor who gives a sympathetic look. "The Ice Realm is not as it appears, sister. If," he catches himself, "when your memories return, all will become clear."

Tears threaten to fall, but I bat them away with the back of my hand. I think through what I know of the fairies. "I may have information. Alcor, could you stay with the warriors? I will be swift!"

Alcor appears hesitant. "Take Kelmin or Arwelia to protect you."

I press back, "Time is wasting away, I am quicker alone."

"Bring Piré, then. She knows the way better than us all. Please, I do not. I cannot lose you again." The final words from his mouth are quiet, yet he remains determined.

Piré's face remains pale, her body shaking.

"I believe I will be quicker alone…" I start again.

"She will join you," he interrupts sternly before returning his attention to Gallen to hear more about their time here.

Rather than listen to his descriptions of the torture they all endured, all to rescue me from a prison I did not even know was prison, I grasp Piré's arm and walk out quickly, eager to see my old chambers—my respite from a world of whispers.

The halls are eerily quiet. Every so often a guest passes or a guard circles by. With the commotion of the attack, most guests must be in their rooms. At least that is all I can assume as we slink through the halls, finding safety in the alcoves and shadows, and at times using the Keepers' halls. I prepare myself to find a guard posted at my former chambers, yet when we finally reach my room, it is empty.

My heart confuses my mind, and calm and warmth emanate from my chest throughout my body. I should not feel so at ease, but the starlight bursting through the stained glass urges me to sit in the velvet red chair and rest. It is sickeningly sweet how conditioned my body has become, how the smell of the bed linens reminds me of late mornings and heart-to-heart discussions with Mairette, how the writing desk is filled to the brim with my thoughts, fears, hopes, desires. It is utterly unfair. Only this morning I was considering my life here, what I could be to the Ice Realm and its people, to Rostair.

Yet, that dream is a lie, just like the feeling of calm and the desire for Rostair's coaxing voice or Mairette's freshly brewed tea. It was a lie that they all knew, that they all hid.

I briskly walk toward the chest of drawers on the edge of the chambers while Piré remains near the door. I snatch the satchel from its place before gathering anything in sight that I may want. Despite the disgust at myself, I cannot help but want these memories. I grab a collection of notes from the writing desk, the poem from beneath the mattress, and, most importantly, the book of fairies I began regarding so long ago. I consider taking the entire history tome, but the practicality of lugging such a weight appears foolish. Instead, I quickly search for the pages with annotations, rip them out, and stuff them in my satchel.

"You are fortunate that I convinced the guards to leave this place." A voice emerges from the shadows of the far corner.

My heartbeat increases, blood pounding in my ears.

As she moves from her hiding place near the mirror, a wide cape draped over her face, I immediately recognize Mairette's frame. I have to restrain myself as my body instinctively surges to hug her, to cry on her shoulder and sense her motherly touch bringing me back to normal.

But that was the Mairette I once knew. The Mairette from this morning.

I look for Piré. She remains by the door, seated on the ground like a small child. Mairette either did not notice her or does not care.

"What do you want?" The words spit from my lips in a voice unlike my own.

She feels the difference, too, a slight look of shock evident even in the shadow of the hood. "I have come to explain—"

I barely allow her to choke out the words before interrupting, "There is nothing I want from you." I move to leave, wanting to leave this life, this dream, behind and her with it. "There are people who need me. I thought before you could understand such a concept, yet I'm starting to believe perhaps it is all merely for yourself."

She whimpers and I feel a sort of satisfying pleasure in hitting my mark. "Centrea, he is powerful. Too powerful. He threatens us all. We live under constant vigilance in Endoneth." Her eyes move from side to side as if searching for him, underscoring the truth of her words. "But for many of us there is nowhere else to turn." She stumbles uncharacteristically over her words. "He has control of my family. You know this. You must understand."

Rage burns through my veins, coursing its way through me like venom. "There is nothing you can say to atone." The words are much louder than is wise, but nothing in this world matters in this moment, selfish as that may be. "You deceived me, gained my trust, and set me upon a pedestal to be torn apart by the wolves. Wicked. Wicked is all I can think to describe your actions, your position. And all the while, as I struggled to understand myself and who I am, where I came from. All the while you knew. And that is the cruelest of all, Mairette. You allowed me, for months, to parade around the estate like a clueless child. Did the guests here, with their whispers and stares, did they know who I was? Who I *am*?"

She scoffs at my words. "Do not place yourself in such high regard. Many never pieced the information together. As the enchantments fade, your memory should return, and you shall realize that my position here was not as devious as you describe." Her words are more matter-of-fact, less pleading.

Then they sink in. "What 'enchantments,' Mairette?"

Her eyes look slightly sympathetic while, her lips quivering, she admits, "There is a reason only I served your tea."

My stomach drops as she continues, walking closer to me as I step backward.

"I watched it all." Her words are laced with sorrow as she continues walking, almost as if sorry for what she must do. What she has already done. "I watched as you fawned over the Lord and, to your credit, I think he does feel something for you. Perhaps a hiccup in his overall plan. But nonetheless, he would never allow his personal lusts to cloud his ultimate goal." Her voice grows louder with each syllable. "If I bring you to him now, he will reward me greatly, don't you see?" The pleading in her eyes turns to desperation. "I would never worry again. My family, all of them cared for. And all for one, little, princess..." I fall to the floor as she approaches, rearing her hand back, ready to strike.

Before she can, a thud echoes through the room, and she falls to the ground. To my surprise, Piré's small figure fills the void where Mairette once stood, the history tome held high above her head, eyes wild with rage and fear and confusion.

"I am... I am so sorry, Miss. I just could not watch her. I..." she continues, her high, mousey voice ringing in my ears.

I rise to embrace her. "Thank you."

Before we leave the chambers, perhaps the final time I will ever see the place, I look at Mairette's slackened body on the floor, the shadow of her hood gone and her face as gracious as the first day we met. Her chest rises and falls in even movements, even with the awkward position in which she landed on the floor.

"We should go." My voice feels stronger, filled with purpose.

The walk back to the prison room is filled with similar twists and turns—hiding in alcoves and the Keeper's passages. When we return, Kelmin and Arwelia are guarding the door, and a few additional guards lie dead on the floor. Inside, Asha sits unconscious while Gallen discusses maneuvers with Alcor.

"What did you retrieve?" He stands and takes a few steps toward me.

"This, it is just a theory." My confidence wavers a bit as I reach for the book of fictitious tales of the fairy monarch. "I feel that the story is meaningful." I rustle through the pages before I find the source of my curiosity, the story of the Monarch and their Warrior:

One morning, the two leading fairies, their lights blazing together like two beacons of hope in the wooded darkness, came under attack, arrows flying through the air. Melara swoops to protect their warrior, a selfless act fit for a monarch. Yet, despite their greatest attempts, both figures fall victim to fate, being captured by rulers of realms beyond their own. Their horde suffered, grieving the loss of two prominent and revered members. The woods were never the same.

It is believed the light of both Melara and Caliam still glow, bringing light and power to the thieves who cage them. The purple and blue lights cast a burning reminder that they remain unwilling servants to an unforgiving master.

"Does this mean anything to you? Anyone?" The three figures stare at me, motionless, the only sound coming from Asha who flows in and out of consciousness. Gallen looks toward the ground, deep in thought, and Alcor begins pacing the blood-stained tiles. Piré holds her chin in her hands, tapping a delicate finger along her jaw as she considers the importance of the story.

I see her eyes dazzle as she realizes the significance of the passage. "I may know where they are held."

Alcor glances toward her, confusion and frustration filling his features. "This is a story, correct? Shall we take it as fact? We are wasting time!" His voice trembles with annoyance, and I empathize with his plight. We have managed to waste nearly an hour since arriving at Endoneth and, while we have Gallen and Asha, we have no way to free them and still must make the perilous journey out. There is also the notion of Rostair's imminent return to his prisoners, a notion that fills me with dread.

But, while the story may be fiction, it is all we have. "What are you thinking, Piré?"

She smiles at me, turning her shoulder away from Alcor's judgment and toward the book still laying open in my hand. "The colors of the two leaders," she begins. "I have cleaned the Gold Wing since I could hold a broom." I wince at the thought of one so young tethered to a life of servitude. "The lanterns in the ballroom. Have you ever wondered how that space is enchanted? Where the power comes from?" An image of the ballroom rolls through my mind, the two massive lanterns floating in the corners as the room itself appears open to the elements.

I gasp, "The purple and blue."

Piré nods in agreement. "The purple and blue."

It takes only a few moments to update Alcor on our theory.

The lanterns? This entire time?

Perhaps this is just the whims of two women, eager to find a solution to a seemingly unbelievable problem. But… the lanterns. They do glow magnificently, one purple and one blue. And where else would the estate gain such immense power?

We conjure a plan: Piré, Kelmin, and Arwelia will stay near the study-turned-prison to keep a watchful eye on our prisoners while Alcor and I venture to the ballroom. While the plan requires us to explore the Keepers' tunnels alone, we thought it best to have her find and alert us should Rostair return. We promise to return within the hour, a hollow promise but one that forces a sense of urgency for the two of us as we begin walking toward the Gold Wing. I hope for a bit of discussion between my brother and me, however the walk remains silent as he concentrates on the many twists and turns in the tunnels. The occasion is quite somber, so perhaps the quiet is for the best. There is still so much I wish to know. The swirls of memories, faded and blurred, are beginning to unravel in my mind. It is difficult to tell what I know based on memory or what I have learned since Alcor's arrival.

However, as we wind down a set of dirt stairs, I begin to sense a feeling of normalcy with this man, someone I am sure I care for but cannot place. But each step seems eerily familiar, the smell of the earth, the darkness of the tunnels, the rush of adrenaline as we push forward. Even the sound of Alcor's labored breathing and frustrated sighs appear familiar in my mind. Mairette was right, if I can trust her, the memories are returning, slowly, even if still muffled.

The run through the tunnels earlier was certainly quicker than our current journey. When we finally reach a door that leads to golden tiles, we are both spent, laboring for full breaths and leaning on the edges of the doorframe. I look forward, seeing the arched entry into the ballroom before glancing to scan the hall for unwanted attention. A few stray guests are gathered in front of a wall of artwork while Keepers filter in and out of the ballroom carrying various topiaries and statues. I see two guards stationed outside of the ballroom who were not there before, perhaps looking for an intruder or maybe to keep guests away as Keepers attempt to return the space back to its normal appearance. We duck back into the tunnel to regroup.

"We need a distraction for the guards," Alcor says contemplatively. "Is there another doorway we can access or something we can use to cause a scene?" I think over his words, mapping out what I know of the Gold Wing in my mind and sorting out our options.

"There may be something I can do," I offer. "Just be sure to run when you get your chance."

Alcor nods, a hint of caution in his movement. Nonetheless, he allows me to slip out of the tunnel and lurk in the shadows of the night through the hall until I reach the art installation I need. The glass lining the walls of the hallway reminds me of the beauty I once saw in every inch of this house. A beauty that is now soured in my mind, only a fraction of what I once knew. I collect myself and pick up one of the pieces from its place on a pedestal. Before I make any sudden movements, I look behind me, seeing a quick escape to my right, enough space for me to creep in the shadows.

*I am brave. I am bold.*

I hold the glass statue over my head and throw.

# Twenty-Three

The sound of shattering glass is louder than I imagined it would be. It is as if the entire hallway caved in on itself. Glass from above cascades into the tiles below, dragging the pieces on the walls, on shelves and pedestals, down with it and piercing the silence of the Gold Wing and bringing with it the frantic attention of the two guards posted near the ballroom. From the shadows I see them appearing, glancing hesitantly into the hall where glass continues to break, a domino effect that lasts far longer than I could have predicted. Much to my benefit, I think to myself as I slip past the guards, who are wide-eyed and mesmerized by the beautiful destruction before them. Despite my size, I'm quick on my feet, reaching the arch of the ballroom just as Alcor crosses the threshold. We both scurry to the corner of the room, avoiding the eyes of the many Keepers still working within. The distraction also helps us avoid their curiosity as they ignore us completely, intent on seeing the remaining shards of glass in the famed hall.

"Imaginative." He winks, clearly impressed.

I shrug and look intently toward the other end of the room. There they shine, now seemingly brighter than I have ever seen them. Piré was certainly correct in her memory. The lanterns burn in pastel purple and blue, respectively, beckoning us toward the now-shattered window.

"We must reach the lanterns." I search the space for any useful tool, anything to raise us from the floors.

Alcor pulls me forward, seemingly reading my thoughts. "We will find something useful on our way there."

With that, he charges toward the broken window, keeping to the side walls. The room appears to be shrinking with each passing hour, smaller than it was when we returned for Gallen and the rest. It takes seconds to make it to the center of the space, where only a few flowers and decorative pieces are left strewn across the floor. The tiles, gleaming in a dazzling golden hue, glimmer as they shift into smaller squares. Alcor stops every few feet to search for something to reach the lanterns. Surely the Keepers use ladders or platforms to reach the ceiling. Yet with each brief pause, my hopes for a simple solution dwindle. When I place my hand on the corner column, we are left with nothing immediately helpful.

"We may need something unique to reach so high."

I follow Alcor's eyes to the top of each column where the large lanterns burn brightly in the corners of the room. My eyes fall back to the ballroom. Keepers filter back in from the hall and walk briskly toward their work. The platform and primroses remain as we left them save the glass and blood covering the scene. It is difficult to look at a place of such embarrassment, where I felt such joy one moment to be ripped into reality the next.

"Look there." My brother's voice refocuses my attention as he points toward a pile of rope near the edge of the stage. Without waiting for a response, he crouches low and skips toward the rope, keeping his head alert as Keepers continue sweeping and carrying plants out. His navy tunic skims the floor as he moves seamlessly to the platform, clutching the coveted rope in his hands before twisting toward me, grimacing.

My heart drops a bit as he makes his way back to the corner. "It will not be long enough," he huffs. "There must be another way."

I consider our options, again sweeping my eyes over the remaining tools at our disposal. For a second, I think of risking our progress to seek help from the Keepers, all looking weary after a long day. However, not all in this estate are supporters of Alcor's realm, *our* realm. I look again above us, the lantern appearing so very high, just out of reach.

"The plants could assist us?" I suggest, thinking about how long we have been away from Piré and hoping Rostair has not returned.

"Mmm." Alcor considers this, reaching for a series of flowers. "If a vine were here, perhaps that would suffice. I fear these stems will not hold our weight."

He's right. I fiddle with the hem of my tunic, the fabric distracting me from the circumstances before us. Despite the minutes ticking away, Alcor remains calm and collected, clearly thinking through each potential option. Throughout the night, I have witnessed firsthand his leadership and have been quite impressed. He's decisive yet considerate. Our current predicament is indicative of such, and it becomes all the clearer to me how people look to him to lead. As his brow furrows in concentration, I could imagine a crown gracing his head.

"Do you think we have time to return to the Red Wing? There may be more tools there to use?" He turns to me, genuinely seeking my expertise. The trust is daunting yet reassuring. He believes my words are worth hearing, my opinion worth considering.

Unfortunately, my opinion is not a positive one. "It would be a risk, especially considering the close call with the guards. It is possible they come to this room searching for the culprit of the glass hallway..."

I clench the bottom of the shirt in my hands, the long pieces of cotton easing the stress a bit as I twist them in my hands. Then, an idea. I hold out the edges of the tunic with both hands, the long flap of fabric creating a useful amount of extra material. With a swift movement, I rip the bottom of my shirt from one side to the other, creating a strong strip of fabric. Alcor's eyes widen and he immediately begins ripping his own shirt as I continue adding to the pile of rope on the floor in front of us. Once the front of my tunic is in tatters, I begin working on the back flap, creating more and more strings of material.

When that portion of the shirt is also spent, I fall to my knees and add the fabric pieces to the end of the rope, praying the length is enough to reach the lantern, and that the rope itself will hold.

In Alcor's hands, the makeshift rope appears frail. "We may not be able to use it as a climbing rope, but it should reach the lantern."

He makes a thoughtful point. I feel for the pocket in my boot, pulling out my dagger. "Attach it to the end." I hand my precious weapon to Alcor. "It should be strong enough to break the glass, do you agree?"

Tying the knife to the rope, he nods. "The metal is strong enough to penetrate almost any material."

I tuck the piece of information for another day, adding it to the list of questions I must ask when we are safe again. He steps forward, squinting upward and taking aim. The knife glints as it spins through the air. Alcor creates tight circles, building momentum before releasing the end of the rope and the dagger with it. I hold my breath as the onyx hilt sparkles and soars through the air before it hits the glass of the lantern with a satisfying crack.

"Again," I whisper, peering behind us to ensure no one hears our work. My words are unnecessary as Alcor immediately starts winding the rope and releasing again. The few Keepers still shuffling around appear unbothered. I know Piré is on our side, and maybe more Keepers want Rostair's demise—hope for Alcor's rise.

Another crack, but no break. After the third hit, the lantern shakes, beams of light bursting through the new crevices in the glass. I hear bright pings of bells, reminding me of that day once more, of the cries of the wayward fairies and their fallen friend.

Again, Alcor releases the dagger, another crack.

The sound of bells grows louder as the purple light emanates from the broken lantern, the metal hinges of which creak desperately from the strain. One more thwack from the knife, and I am certain Melara will be free. Taking a deep breath in, Alcor winds the rope in a tight circle and releases it toward the sky. The crack is much louder than the ones before, a sharp screeching sound accompanying a blinding surge of light. I cover my eyes with my hand for a moment before blinking away the dots lining my vision.

When my eyes clear, I see a purple being glowing before us, holding their hands in front of their lace dress. Their hair is braided delicately behind their back, and with eyes wide they stride toward us. They halt, quickly looking over their shoulder to the other lantern, which glows a pale blue. Their eyes, a warm, deep, comforting green, wilt as they look for their lover in the sky. Without hesitation, they spread their wings, stretching them completely, perhaps for the first time in decades. They look powerful, beautiful. In a moment, the fairy monarch is airborne, facing the second lantern in the span of a few moments. I blink once, and the fairy already has the glass pierced, using their bare might to penetrate, as if they needed a small crack to break some sort of spell that quelled their powers. Melara slips down to the floor in front of us once more, this time holding another figure in their arms, the new head resting on their shoulder.

Together the two look complete.

When the brightness fades, I crane my neck to check on the working Keepers still in the ballroom only to see their gaping mouths and wide eyes. We need to leave. I walk toward Melara and Caliam, the couple sharing a sensitive reunion, visceral and emotional. My heart breaks to interrupt this moment, but we are running out of time and every minute counts.

I reach my hand toward the monarch. I am unsure if they will understand me, but I must try. "We need your help."

The tunnels are more familiar to us as we run back to Gallen and Asha and the others. Melara and Caliam's lights help us navigate the dark halls. The two grow brighter with each step, holding onto each other as if one misstep will lead to their separation once more.

Alcor leads and I stand bring up the rear, soaking in the sweetness of the fairies' love; their connection tangible is we weave through dirt-covered paths. I wonder what their release will do to this estate, if the loss of their power will have immediate consequences. If the house itself absorbed their enchantments, it may keep a reservoir that will take a few hours or so to use up. I also wonder how many aspects of the estate and its leader the fairies empowered, and for how long. Hopefully, Rostair feels his authority fade as the two figures before me restore what is rightfully theirs.

"Is it to the right, Sol?" The question takes a moment to register as I adjust to my name. Alcor looks back for a response, slowing his pace as we approach another fork in the tunnel.

I peer past the couple, still clinging to one another with reckless affection, to determine the correct path. "Left," I call. "We are nearly there."

I feel useful having remembered our way back to the Orange Wing, and the feeling eases ever so slightly the guilt of our situation. The two Fairies nod their approval, either from confidence or knowledge, I am unsure. We continue our quickened pace toward our imprisoned compatriots, who are still hopefully safe from our menacing host.

Alcor stops suddenly, leaning against the hidden entryway and pressing his hand against the sleek metal handle. Each door pulls into the tunnels, perhaps to avoid contact with any passing guests in the main halls, which presents another obstacle to consider as we survey the space before blindly exiting. Additionally, the Fairies' light, which served us well on the journey here, is now another way of alerting attention. No longer will the shadowed alcoves provide us with a safe passage to the study.

Following my line of thought, Alcor turns to the three of us. "I shall venture out and signal when it's clear for you to follow."

Nodding, I look at the couple who seem to understand him perfectly, and they shift back to avoid casting too much light into the wing. He sucks in a breath and walks out, shifting his weight to his toes as he paces toward the other edge of the hall. A few moments pass. With each passing second, my heart rate increases, fear settling into my stomach as I strain to hear anything resembling a signal from my brother. Melara and Caliam must also sense my anxiety as they whisper in bright chirps to one another, their communication growing faster as the minutes slowly tick away.

My heart jumps into my throat as I hear yells from the other side of the wall. My companions begin shivering as they recognize Rostair stern voice along with a few others.

Helzaf's laugh is unmissable as she cackles with an ominous shriek. Without thinking, I rush through the entrance, looking left and right for Alcor and the pestilent Lord.

"How very brave." Rostair's voice makes the hairs on my neck stand on edge, his condescension morphing my fear into calescent anger.

I turn just as Alcor gasps. "Run," he says. His throat is caught between Helzaf's sharp, blue nails, each jutting out nearly five inches from her hands. Her red lips snake into a smile that is devious yet alluring.

"You should listen, trollop." Rostair emerges from the shadows behind them, his eyes glaring at me as he cackles, entertained by our attempts at escape. "You really should not have returned here, Sol. It is unheard of to find a way out of my grasp, and impossible to do so twice. You don't know this, of course." He waves a casual hand my way. "But you will. Once that poisoned tea wears off..." his voice falters as I see the glow of purple and blue cast incandescently from behind me. Rostair's face turns feral, anger spewing from his lips. "Clever wench."

I briefly glance at Alcor, who urges me onward, *Go*, he seems to say with his expression. *I will be alright. Go.* With his blessing, I turn, grab Melara and Caliam by the arms, and run.

The study is not far from the passage entrance, yet guards holding spears block the path. I contemplate our chances, thinking of the safest way through while running. However, as I reconsider our odds, I feel the tiles evaporate below me. Eyes wide, I screech in horror before I turn to Melara, whose wings flutter with might. Caliam, too, barrels with great force, flapping their iridescent wings so quickly that my hair flies in its breeze. Rather than approach the guards head-on, the fairies skirt above them, kicking their feet as we fly across the ceiling. They gently prop my body against the study door, my knees giving way to the sudden rush of flying.

Melara, their hands both warm and cool simultaneously, cups my face, offering a reassuring grin. Their touch immediately eases my worries, my stress melting away as their wide eyes bore into my own. Their face is narrow, cheeks hollow with either age or maltreatment. Their hair falls in beautiful curls on either side of their pointed ears, and the dark brown ringlets complementing their pale purple skin. They look every bit a leader.

Caliam links their fingers with my own, pulling me forcefully toward the door as Malara faces a crowd of Ice Realm guards. I pull the door closed with a loud thud, barely registering Piré's embrace as the blue of Caliam's glow flits toward the prisoners. With one touch and a small spark of light emanating from Caliam's fingertips, the metal shackles turn liquid.

Gallen messages his wrists with his hands, expressing his thanks in high-pitched bell tones. Once freed, he immediately checks on the two fallen prisoners, their bodies now cold and lifeless, before running to my side. "Alcor?" he asks, a look of panic returning to his features as Caliam releases Asha from her cuffs.

"Outside. Rostair." Before I even finish my sentence, Gallen is moving to the door, rushing out.

"Come when you can," he calls out, barely turning his head as he runs toward an intense battle between Melara and the guards.

I can see a few guards twitching on the tiles, their blood seeping into the grout as they strain for life. "Sol, we must leave while we have the chance." Asha's voice is strained, clearly exhausted yet intent on getting our group to safety. Her dark skin looks more pallid than normal, the youthful vigor of her typically gorgeous face marred by gashes and bruises.

My hatred for Rostair, for this place, will stay with me forever, just as the image of my friend's face will remain within me reminding me of a world of injustice, a world that must be stopped.

Our group forges ahead, and Piré and Asha fall behind me and Caliam as we join Melara and Gallen. Only a few guards remain upright when we reach them. Gallen urges us to instead find Alcor. Caliam refuses, seeing their lover in a burst of passionate rage, taking out decades of pent-up emotion on the guards of their prison. I grab Piré and Asha by their hands and pull them with me, running toward the far end of the Orange Wing, where I hope to find Alcor alive.

# Twenty-four

Blood drips down the side of Alcor's face as he kneels upon a small rug covering orange tiles. He looks weak; pools of sweat and blood soaking through his clothes. Rostair towers above him, one knife in each hand. Streaks of red stream along Rostair's cheeks and jaw as my brother's blood stains his face, evidence of the violence within the Ice Lord. He flips one of the knives in his hand, chuckling slightly, his grey eyes filled with sick pleasure. "I never understood the Southern obsession with these daggers." He grabs the knife at the hilt and throws it down. The sound of splitting flesh fills Rostair's study as the steel sinks into Alcor's calf.

Alcor's muffled scream brings hot tears to my eyes. "Rostair, set him free!" My voice cracks as I see the blood from Alcor's leg join the stains on the carpet.

Helzaf's laugh, cruel and snarled, erupts from behind Rostair's wooden desk, her feet propped up as if this is another day in Endoneth. I rush forward, stopping only when Rostair brings the remaining knife to Alcor's throat. "Now, I would not move another step."

I hear rushes of footsteps emerge in the doorway behind me, Gallen and the fairies having surely bested the guards just outside. I feel Asha's hand upon my arm, not so much to keep me from moving forward but rather to indicate her support in my decision either way. We only need a little more time. Fortunately, if what I know of Rostair is true, and with perhaps the image of what I once knew becoming less murky, it may be possible to buy a bit of time.

I hold my fists clenched close to my sides, my heart beating in quick spurts as my mind works rapidly, thinking through the minutiae of my plan that we set in motion at the camp. That meeting feels like a lifetime away.

"Rostair." The word is painful, my jaw clenching tightly as I speak. "Did you care at all?" I try to steady my voice, summoning tears to perfect the visual: a naive and self-centered woman who fell for his treachery and demands his affection nonetheless. Only partially untrue.

The facade catches his attention, stoking his pride and piquing his interest. "Knowledge is a powerful tool; your old friend—my traitorous uncle—would say such things often. Well, as foolish as he was, that sentiment is true enough."

He keeps the knife close to Alcor's neck yet snaps the fingers of his free hand to summon his henchman, and, like a loyal dog, Helzaf slides to his side. He hands her the knife, her smile widening with the feel of the hilt on her palm, and begins pacing around the room, eyeing our retinue with delight.

"Capturing you was easier than I anticipated. You, Lady Sol, are far more arrogant than I understood. Gazil assured me of your prowess in battle, your resilience." He pauses to scoff, shooting a look toward me. Asha squeezes my arm, fearful of my anger. But I refuse to move, no matter how many insults he throws at me. I hear the rustling of Gallen's boots and pray he follows suit.

Rostair ignores him and continues his pacing. "However, how to make one forget who they were, who they are? Now that, that was harder. I turned first to Gazil and his archivists, but even they came up short. But I knew a Keeper, one who was making her way up the ranks, who knew ancient ways. A request from one's Lord, with a bit of extra... persuasion. Well, who was she to say no?"

I think of Mairette lying on the floor of my chambers, surely coming back to consciousness soon. Although her deceit grieves me, I am beginning to understand what a person would do for those they care for.

Melara and Caliam.

Gallen, Alcor, Asha.

These are all people who risked their lives, their lands, their people for someone they loved.

And I must do my part.

"Is there a Lord in the Mountains waiting for her daughter?"

He snickers, "I told you of my love for stories. This was an act of my own genius."

I thought back to my interactions throughout my stay in Endoneth. "Why did no one else approach me? How did I remain here for five months without hearing my name from one of these guests? From the Keepers? Surely you could not *persuade* them all?" I meet his gaze, echoing his veracity, his confidence.

This seems to only fuel his pleasure. "Oh Sol, with no memories and no confidence, it is just too easy, isn't it?" He directs the question to Helzaf who giggles and gleefully nods. "I merely gave a direct order to all who entered Endoneth: Speak nothing of the fictitious King in the South, nothing of his sister. If you do, a curse will kill the one you love most."

The information resonates with me, and I turn to Melara and Caliam to weigh the truth of this assertion. Melara's eyes are grievously solemn, and Caliam's head turns to the side, anger and shame written in the furrow of their brow.

So, it is true.

I turn my glance to Asha, a face that looks more familiar now than it did this afternoon. Her hand trembles on my arm but refuses to let go. "I am... I am sorry." The whisper escapes her lips and makes my heart ache.

"This one did surprise me." Rostair waved an uninterested hand toward Asha. "The architect's daughter turned Night Flyer. It was a slip on my part to be certain. However, Zeal always tended to the details of the guests here."

"And Gazil?" I almost wish I could leave Endoneth in ignorance of the truth, though I know I would regret it.

This question gives Rostair the most disturbing satisfaction, and he twists his face into a devilish display. "He said too much." He pauses a bit, thinking the suspense will unnerve me rather than play directly into my own plans. "So, he had to be sacrificed, lose his life. It was only fair, and quite merciful if I do say so myself." Rostair brings his hands to his face, examining his nails which were decorated for the Greentime Ball and are now stained with dried blood. "Now, this one, she toed the line, of that I know. So clever, staying ever so close yet within the bounds of my commands." He walks toward Asha.

I step between them, my hand moving reflexively forward as Rostair inches closer. "Do not dare touch her; this is about us. You and me. Nobody else."

Rostair spits on my boots. "This was never about us, Southern whore." A look of embarrassment lingers on his face, too long for his own comfort as he attempts to mask it with disgust.

So, the lust, it was real.

"You are sick." I stand straighter, my face a mixture of sorrow and anger, hoping to incite action. "Lusting after your enemy, your prisoner. What kind of Lord do such actions make you?" The words are like arrows aimed at his ego, his sense of authority, of gallantry.

He sneers, "You know nothing, pet."

My words struck true. It is now I who dons a grin, maniacal and scheming. I look past Rostair, to Alcor still kneeling, his breath coming in short gasps. It must be near time now, I am sure. Only a few more minutes.

"Ahh, that was the only way to best me. Create the only scenario for success. A woman who is beholden to your will, who knows nothing of this world and her place within it. The coward's way, would you not agree, Melara?" I dare not look at the fairy monarch, keeping my eyes fixed on the demon before me. But I feel their glow swell behind me. "I am sure you did not take these powerful creatures yourself, as that would require someone and tactics far too sophisticated. However, your abuse of them, inherited or not, is your sin to bear."

Rostair's eyes shrink into small slits as he weighs the utility of my being. I imagine he's considering ending me now, despite having to face my companions after such an action. Instead, he walks back toward his desk, gripping the edge with both hands. "Again, you know nothing. There are connections, powers, plans that were set in stone long before either of us were born. You may never grow to learn, but—"

Before he can explain further, two warriors burst from outside through the wall of the study, bricks flying through the air, knocking both Helzaf and Alcor to the ground with the force. Kelmin and Arwelia run through the makeshift entrance, yielding their weapons like masters of their craft. They look tired yet alert, a sentiment shared by us all. In a flash of movement, Luminor joins us in the study with his retinue of warriors. The Night Flyers crowd Rostair, slashing at his arms and legs before forcing him to the ground. Helzaf, still stunned, shakes the soot from her golden hair and screams toward the scene. Quickly, Asha jumps toward her, grasping Alcor's knives in her hands and pinning her down on the tiled floor.

Finally freed, I reach for Alcor; his head is still bleeding and his eyes roll into the back of his head. Gallen's body appears behind me, reaching to assist in holding his King upright and shuttling him toward safety. Asha beats Helzaf with the butts of both knives, causing a shock to her body that echoes through the small study.

At the same time, both Kelmin and Arwelia grasp Rostair by each hand and tie his arms to the side of the desk, spreading his chest wide. Melara steps forward, quietly powerful in each movement. The warriors step back, leaving Rostair wide-eyed and whimpering as he attempts to break free. The monarch swirls their hand over the ropes, the strong twine transforming into a tight metal, similar to those used in his own prison.

"You are all dead. No realm will follow you." Each face turns to me, looking for both a response and a command, since Alcor is not well enough to lead.

All I can do is walk away, toward the hall and to the quickest path outside this estate.

When we arrive at the Green Wing, guests begin emerging from their chambers, perhaps hearing the commotion of combat or sleepless from a frightening night at Endoneth. Either way, the sight of bloodied bodies flooding the halls discourages too many prying eyes.

The group of Flyers is enough to fell any lingering guards, some valiantly attempting to stop our retreat while others wisely remain in the shadows.

We need to reach the sky, that much I know. And, as I thought of the map in my mind, the skylights seem the simplest solution. Kelmin begins using knives to scale the wall toward the ceiling while Melara and Caliam fly me upward. I use the hilt of my dagger to crack the glass, smacking the window a few times before the pieces of glass fall to the floor. The fairies set me upon the roof of the house, the stars twinkling as I breathe deeply in the open air, my mind the clearest it's been all night.

Our winged friends bring Alcor, Piré, and Asha up next, then Gallen and Arwelia emerge from the skylight soon after, climbing the wall on their own. From the roof, it is easy to see the edges of Endoneth, and we scope the number of guards lining the grounds.

"This place is a maze." Kelmin sits near me, sighing as he stretches out his arms, "We would have found you far quicker. You should have warned us of the winding paths. Why do so many lead to nothing?"

I stifle a laugh, remembering my early struggles to navigate the house. "Thank you for your rescue." I look to the sky. "It was aptly timed." I point ahead.

In the distance, white specks come into view, elegant wings bringing forth the final phase of our plan.

Zeffra leads the group of pegasi toward the house, her warriors truly earning the name "Night Flyers." She smiles broadly as she approaches, only wavering when she sees Alcor's body, limp and bloodied, slumped on the edge of the rooftop. Her pace quickens, her heels kicking into the horse's sides as she urges him on. When she reaches the rooftop, she is already dismounting, running to Alcor and demanding an explanation.

"First, we must find safety. We will explain everything then." The command comes naturally, almost as if my mind spoke before I had time to process what the words mean.

The group nods in agreement nonetheless, and the group of winged beasts lands on the roof. We each join a warrior on their steeds, braving the cold spring air to reach our encampment. I jump behind Luminor on a slightly grey pegasus and the warrior's body is at ease as he clicks his tongue to communicate. We are airborne in mere minutes, the cool breeze on my face like a splash of water, refreshing after a long day and even longer night. The stars provide another source of reprieve, casting lights that dazzle before us, seemingly brighter now that we all have left Endoneth. The weight of the satchel settled across my body reminds me of what I have overcome and what is left to learn.

The purple and blue glow of the fairies follows close behind, their lights even more magical in their natural environment. Their home. The steady beating of the horse's wings settles me and, as I clutch Luminor's waist with my arms, I am lulled to sleep.

# A Letter from the Front

*Sister,*

*There isn't much time...*

*If this war has taught me anything, it is that the enslavement of others is not worth protecting. The systems we are fighting for, they are not right.*

*Nothing is right.*

*A King may be what Nourels needs. What our Realm needs. What our family needs.*

*I won't leave here alive. Know that I love you.*

*I hope you remain safe. Remain in the Lord's good graces. Remain vigilant, dear Mairette.*

*For King and Sol*
*J*

# Part Four

The Star Realm camps mimic their homesteads: tents held together with twine and wood, thin and thick fabrics shading their travelers from the elements, and each person equipped with tools of astronomy so they may always find their way home.

I wake to sounds of calm: rushing water, a crackling fire, gentle voices, rustling leaves in the wind.

The sun shines through the thin fabric of the tent, and I settle deeper into the blankets lining the floor. It could have been a dream. Although, my body protests such a notion; my muscles ache from exertion and anxiety. I notice my clothes are gone, but I remain filthy, blood and dirt creating a film along my skin.

I cannot help but smile. The encounter with Rostair and the image of him tied to his desk, bonded with an impenetrable metal, is sweet enough to eat. Though, recollections of last night also remind me of Alcor, of the two fallen warriors, of Gallen and Asha. I rise quickly, looking around the small tent to find appropriate attire and to inquire about my friends and their well-being. Before I can move, the outer fabric of the tent is thrust aside, letting in a blinding beam of light along with the broad shoulders of my brother. Shrieking, I pull the blankets over my chest to shield him from my nakedness.

Alcor only laughs in response, plopping down in the corner of the room, "Well, good morning, Sol."

My heart races as I contemplate how quickly it will take to leave the Ice Realm. Visions of the map of Nourels play in my mind as I trace a way out. A way far from Endoneth.

"Should we not move out of the realm? Rostair could return any moment—"

My brother raises a hand. "I thought similarly, yet the fairies promised protection. They insist upon us taking as much time as we need to regroup. At least, this is what Gallen translated to us. He knows many languages, your man."

I settle back into my sheets, my anxiety easing slightly.

"Well, how are you feeling after a successful mission?" His smile practically glows as he speaks, and the cuts on his head and neck are covered with blue cloth while his left hand is placed in a splint.

"Would you call *that* success?" I nod my head toward his body.

He only grins in return. "You do not remember now, but we have both experienced far worse than this." He winces as he raises his left arm to show me. "Besides, what fun is a mission without a few twists and turns, eh?"

While his voice remains confident, his expression is less convincing. "I am just glad to see you in one piece." I sigh. "How are the others faring?"

He pauses before responding, "We, of course, lost two Night Flyers before our arrival. But the others remain well." His expression is somber for a long time before his mischievous grin returns. "You may want to tend to your Keeper friend. She is very concerned about her treason to the Ice Realm and is quite... overwhelmed."

I think of how Piré must feel after deciding to join our cause so quickly last night and nod. "I will speak to her, of course."

Alcor rises quickly. "Amazing. We will move out in a few days' time."

I follow his figure as it traipses toward the tent's entrance. "Where are we moving to, if I may?" I am realizing now how scary it will be, if I cannot remember where I am going or where I have been. The memories may come back over time, but how long and how many?

Alcor grins again, his ease relaxing my anxieties. "Sol, we are going home." He rips the fabric back and barrels outside.

For a few minutes, I sit and contemplate what I know of my home. Stars and lights and buildings—well, frames of buildings and fabrics. The memories are still blurred, but they're becoming more solid now, less shaky. At times, they feel like a dream or the life of another person altogether. I continue to think about these things as I dress, putting my legs into another pair of dark leathers and pulling a navy-blue tunic over my head. It pains me to put clean clothes over my stained body, but I have little choice. The sound of flowing water gives an option for at least a rudimentary bath later today.

Pulling back the thin layers of fabric, the varying gradients of blues and silvers shimmering as I move them aside, I step into the heat of a springtime day, squinting as the sun gleams overhead. The campsite is nestled in a small clearing in the woods, and beams of sunshine filter through the canopy of leaves above, highlighting the vibrantly green grass made even more pronounced by the deep brown of the surrounding tree trunks. I see the simmering river near the camp's edge, not quite a mile wide, as the melted snow of a month ago develops into a clear blue waterway. The sound of the winged horses neighing nearby joins the natural melody. Several tents are in various states of completion, the wooden frames holding up anywhere from one to twelve delicate rectangles of fine fabric. One of the tents, poised in the center of the clearing, is left open. Alcor and Zeffra are having an intense discussion while looking into a large telescope. She holds a large book bound in navy leather and points toward the pages as the two continue conversing. Surprisingly, only Luminor sits on the grass in the clearing; the other warriors are tucked away in their respective tents.

"You warriors of the Star Realm have always avoided sun. Even Night Flyers, who've adjusted to the light. Even you all remain in your tents." Luminor looks upward at a bright blue, cloudless sky. "I do love the tents, do not misunderstand. I just, I have always loved the *sun*."

I walk toward him, settling onto the ground, feeling the cool blades of grass tickle my palms. "Is that where the remaining warriors currently stay?"

He doesn't move as he answers, his eyes fixed on the sky. "I believe they are asleep. We all had quite the night. I imagine many will not leave their tents until tomorrow."

I nod, thankful for their fortitude and their willingness to retrieve me.

"It is only the King and his first that need to be awake. They will inform us of our next plan tomorrow."

I look again at Alcor in the tent, now hunched over a tactical map. I lift myself up slowly, breathing in the fresh air as I prepare to approach my brother.

"You may not recall," Luminor calls out as I begin walking, his head still poised toward the noontime sun. "Before your capture, you were Alcor's first in command. In your absence, another has risen, taking up a hefty mantle." He moves slightly to itch his neck. "Zeffra is his first. You are his sister. Both important, and both extraordinarily headstrong."

It feels strange for him to tell me about myself, giving me advice based on how I would normally behave in this circumstance. However, I welcome the insight into my former self. Perhaps these nuggets of knowledge will spark a memory. "Be gentle is all I ask. I would like to enjoy a nap, and an afternoon brawl would assuredly interrupt." He crosses his hands under his head as he lies flat on the ground, then closes his eyes and sighs deeply.

I cannot help but roll my eyes, grinning at Luminor's gentle demeanor masked sloppily by his dry humor.

As I walk into the main tent, I immediately recognize the tension filling the space. Zeffra sees my entrance and ignores it, continuing her thought. "They cannot. The warriors on the front are tired and our insights into their patterns are seemingly useless."

Alcor tinkers with a handheld astrolabe, its golden gear-like circles reflecting the sun as he turns it this way and that. I see Gallen sitting in the corner of the tent, whispering with Caliam as Alcor and Zeffra debate the best course of action.

"Unfortunately, Sol's rushed mission has not yielded a return. No offense." It sounds as if she does indeed mean offense with the jab. Gallen looks up, the pale blue of his cheeks turning a light shade of red at the comment, but stays silent.

Instead, Alcor lifts his eyes from the tool, placing it gingerly in a pocket of his leather satchel. "Zeffra, let us focus on some of the positives. We have yet to actually explore how much Sol learned in her months there. If my perception is true, she had access to sensitive information, although she did not realize this at the time. There are likely useful tidbits we may use." Alcor's confidence is sincere, chipping away at my guilt over our current position. As if hearing my appreciation, he turns to me, smiling as he continues, "What do you think, sister? Would you try to apply some of that social capital to our wartime strategy?"

While the question is genuine, Zeffra remains unconvinced. Nonetheless, she offers no refutation and merely looks at me expectantly, pulling her fingers through her tangled hair. I look at the table, at the map covered with chalk smudges and lines connecting various borders and marked circles. "We gained this map from a trusted source," Zeffra explains. "The markings are our own. Circles indicate a group of warriors while a line projects the enemy's movement." She points to the various lines and evidence of former markings.

Turning my head to the side, I concentrate on the realms and numerous circles and lines. To my surprise, there are no colors despite this being a map created by the Ice Realm. "You are certain this is from them directly? It is not a recreation?" I wring my hands into the long fabric of my tunic, attempting to mask the skittish energy that pulses through my blood. Thinking back to my time at Endoneth makes my skin crawl. The pleasant memories seem somewhat tainted now—now that my life in that house has been exposed as largely a lie.

"The source may be manipulating the information, leaving certain facts or details out it seems." Alcor's deep voice commands the tent as he grievously sighs. "Playing both sides."

Refocusing, I look at the order of the lines, trying to find anything even remotely important, familiar. Gallen slips to my side, and the smell of citrus settles my heart.

"It is perfectly understandable if you cannot place what you know now," he whispers softly, his breath barely brushing the side of my neck. His voice is reassuring and kind, giving me a much-needed boost of encouragement.

Flashes of memories begin flooding in, just pieces of much larger scenes: a dress, a hand, a dance, a kiss.

Blood rushes to my cheeks, my heart fluttering as I remember feelings, although I cannot quite place the full memories that adjoin them. Much of my past remains blurry.

I place my hands on my cheeks, clearing my throat and zoning in on the map. The lack of colors still shocks me. I hear Gazil's voice in my mind, his many rants about Ice Realm's obsession with order, structure, and color.

"There must be a piece we are missing." I plant my hands on the edge of the table before turning my head to the corner where Caliam still sits, holding their hands in their lap. "Gallen, could you ask Caliam if they know anything about the enchantments used by the Ice Realm?"

Nodding, Gallen chirps in bright bursts at the fairy, and in response, their glow flickers with great interest. Their wings twitch a bit behind them as they consider the query. The tent fills with the sound of baritone bells, the voice deeper than Melara yet quietly authoritative. I remember the tale from the book, the role Caliam served in their horde—the warrior leader. This is a figure who is accustomed to battle, a figure who also witnessed the world of Endoneth for centuries, hidden in plain sight.

They walk toward the table, and Alcor and Zeffra dip their heads in deference as the petit creature swooshes forward. Gallen pulls a small chair toward the table, allowing Caliam a place to stand as the map sits just out of their natural eyeline. Now looking above the parchment, they see what I saw: simple realm boundaries and chalk markings. As they continue to stare, however, Caliam turns their head to the side, squinting their large eyes a bit as they think. The bells sound once more, Caliam's voice explaining something to the group with growing intensity, their hands hovering above the map.

"They say the map itself may well be enchanted. They have seen some forms of spiritualism and fairy magic in Endoneth. It would not surprise them if the military utilized such talents at their disposal. Rostair is particularly obsessed with the fairies and their labor." Gallen chirps a bit in response, causing Caliam to turn their face downward, attempting to hide the concern on their face.

Alcor and Zeffra peer over their shoulder, looking again at the map with this new information. "Is there a way to access the map without the enchantment? Could Caliam remove it?"

Zeffra pulls again at the auburn hair tangled in a loose bun on the top of her head.

Gallen relays the question, and it takes seconds for an affirmative response. "They say it is possible. Unlike the shackles from Endoneth, this may take some time to decipher. They will have to examine exactly what enchantment was used and how best to reverse it."

Nodding, Alcor considers the insights from our mystical ally. "Let us leave Caliam alone in the tent and give them time to examine the map in peace." He ushers me and Gallen toward the entryway before turning to say a few more words to Zeffra.

I feel a bit happier leaving the tent than I did entering, feeling my guidance is potentially worth something in this conflict. "There is a river if you need to clean. It may be an opportune time as the others are resting." I see Gallen's wry grin as he offers backhanded advice.

"I am certain I do not smell overly horrendous!" I feign offense, grinning delightedly at this innocent verbal sparring.

He begins walking backward as we continue our banter, his golden-blonde hair like a halo over his head. "Well, I do know that there must be a reason no one wishes to share a tent with you. It could be your position, certainly." He waves his hand. "But I am sure the fresh air is worth bunking in threes. Even the young Piré insisted upon staying in the kitchen tent."

Poor Piré, likely seeking the space that feels most like home to her.

Although Gallen tries to remain serious, his voice breaks into a charming laugh, the timbre of which is like a sweet song that I once knew so well. The visions begin again. Short glimpses into my past flicker through my mind, teasing me mercilessly as I walk with someone I surely loved, or perhaps love.

"Answer me truly." I attempt to keep the lighthearted tone as I seek something more serious. "Was the tent once shared with you?"

Gallen stops in his tracks, his expression softening. "It was." He offers a hand to me before quickly pulling it away. "I do not wish to deceive you, Sol. We were something. Everything. Then..." he casts his eyes downward, "you left."

The clearing suddenly feels quite suffocating.

I become aware of our proximity to the other tents, only thin fabric stifling our voices, and to Luminor who still lies in the grass, his eyes thankfully closed. I charge toward the trees that guard our camp and encircle the several small tents in a protective layer of leaves and bark and shadows. As I walk, I sense him following, eager to explore what I know while trying to give me space for what I do not. I do not envy his position, but I know I would rather him here with me than anywhere else— however selfish that may sound.

We walk in silence for a few minutes before reaching the mouth of the river. Its crystal-clear water reflects the sun in its ripples. Gallen immediately drops his feet in the water, closing his eyes and breathing in deeply. Joining him, I run my fingers through the stream of water, the glacial cold shocking my system.

"Do you know why I left?" The question sounds senseless, but there is no way to rephrase it.

He scoffs a bit before turning his eyes to meet mine once more. His gaze is feral, lustful, wanting. Rather than submit to such feelings, he attempts an answer. "There were many times where you made a decision on your own, working out the various scenarios in your mind before choosing the best option."

I consider this for a moment before urging, "And the mission to Endoneth, this was my concept, my plan?"

He nods, deep sadness now joining the medley of emotions floating through his face. "You claimed that the best way to know a place, a people, was to get inside. To be a part of the society, of the events and gossip. I am unsure if you considered the possibility of being tricked by Rostair, but you knew the importance of information." He sighs, clearly frustrated with my actions despite the logic there. "I knew you wanted to complete this task yourself, even offering to go with a few others, Asha and Zeffra in fact. Alcor swore against such actions, urging us to wait until we learned more from this informant of his." Gallen continues, as if opening up is allowing him to process what happened while also helping me remember. "Regardless, we all thought it might not be the most useful plan. Especially considering you and Alcor together, the vision of a royal family of sorts, is essential to gaining allies. But you felt so deeply that we needed to make the plan happen before Rostair sent his armies further south. That, we were definitely unprepared for."

He shakes his head, chuckling again. "After everything—you leaving camp in the middle of the night, the snowstorm forcing us to hunker down, and the immediate attack from Rostair's warriors—you were correct in a way. We needed action, and you took it."

He places his hand between us, his smallest finger grazing mine as we sit and watch the water rush by. "I admire this about you, Sol. You act with conviction to protect those you care for. I am certain, regardless of what you've forgotten, that character has not wavered."

The moment brings a warmth to my heart. The confidence Gallen holds for who I must be whittles away at the remaining shame, the guilt, the sorrow. How I ever cared so dearly for Rostair, or rather who he pretended to be, is a devastating thought. Especially as Gallen sits near me, clearly still deeply in love and providing me the space I need to process. There is a part of me that fully embraces my part in all of this, that it was I who made the choice to leave, I who got lost in a storm, I who gave into petty lust, I who made myself a fool, and I who forced the Night Flyers to return, to fight, to die. The image of Ranor and Elthen strapped to the chairs, slumped over lifeless, lives in my mind, playing over and over.

"Do you think it was worth it in the end?" The question leaves my lips as a plea, a hope that Gallen will assist in ending my suffering, to help me grieve the choices I had forgotten I made.

His eyes take in my emotions, considering which words will lessen the pain, perhaps even remove it completely.

We both know nothing will.

"There is a saying in the Ocean Realm. My father would recite it to me in my darkest moments, when I saw no hope in our world: *The lives we live for those we love are always worth the price we pay.*"

The words, compelling in their simplicity, float in the air as we sit in silence, the water trickling before us, the sun now high in the sky, beginning its descent as the afternoon wears on.

"I did love you." I mean to ask it as a question, but it sounds more like a statement, my voice much stronger than it has been since waking.

Gallen covers my hand with his, sweeping his other thumb over the scar on my cheek. "I know you did. And I hope you realize just how much someday."

He does not attempt to hide his sadness; he merely sits with me, the water lapping up the sides of the bank, my hand in his. "Know this, Sol. Even if you never truly regain your memories, I will still love you. But do not think for a moment I will allow you to tether yourself to me if you no longer wish it. You are just as much Centrea as you are Sol."

My eyes must display my shock as he uses my Ice Realm name. "Alcor informed me."

I feel the pull of his thumb on my chin, forcing my eyes to meet his own. "You are your own person, not just the woman I knew before. You should be proud of that fact."

I realize his words are difficult for me to accept. That the persona I developed for myself should bring me pride but, if anything, I see it as evidence of my many follies, as a tool to foolishly escape my past and forget what I have done and who I have hurt. But perhaps Gallen is correct in saying there is a world where I can be both.

As I contemplate this, Gallen pats my hand before standing up. "I will leave you to wash. Do not rush to return. I was honest when I told you the rest of the camp will remain there for a while yet."

I nod my appreciation as he turns. And when his figure evaporates in a layer of trees, I begin removing the Night Flyer uniform before dipping my toes into the freezing water. It is doubtful I will last more than five minutes in this temperature, yet I dunk my head under, the cold numbing my body like snow.

I feel both in control and without control, a perfect metaphor for my life since Rostair found me fumbling on his estate. I shiver once before my body stills, succumbing to icy water, the numbness, the danger.

I refuse to move, allowing the cold to fill me, and briefly ignore the world.

The sun is hidden in the trees when I return to the camp, refreshed and reset. Luminor no longer lies in the grass, and the clearing is empty save the excited sounds of voices from the center tent. Alcor sees me from inside the tent and waves me over. My pace quickens, the grass crushed by my bare feet as I hold onto my leather boots. I rush to the tent, eager to see the source of the enthusiasm. When I enter the space, I see Caliam standing on the same chair as before and Gallen pacing the floor while Alcor and Zeffra exchange indiscernible words. I see Piré's small frame lingering in one of the corners, clearly interested yet slightly intimidated by the characters of great importance in front of her, particularly Alcor, whom she idolized for so long.

The fairy warrior holds their hands barely above the parchment, closing their eyes in deep concentration. The map on the table shimmers, the grey color of the realm boundaries morphing into various shades of orange, yellow, and green.

Gallen rushes to hold my arm squealing, "You see, Sol? You were correct! The colors, they spell out the enemy's plan!"

Alcor's eyes widen as the colors continue to shift, attempting to piece together the importance of each color as they fade in and out. "Does Caliam have an idea of what the colors represent?"

Zeffra sets her palms on the other side of the table, to the side of Caliam who still silently works to break whatever enchantment holds the map hostage. Gallen conveys the question in bouncy whistles, moving his hands in emphasis. Without moving, Caliam responds solemnly.

"They are unsure of the direct purpose, yet they can sense the colors correlate with movement. Also," his hands clench open and closed, "they say the map is recent, no more than a week old based on the strength of the enchantment." Placing a hand on Caliam's small shoulder, Alcor signals a reprieve, offering his deepest thanks to the magical being and insisting they rest before attempting to decode the map again.

Caliam takes a deep breath before fluttering their wings slightly and landing on the carpet covering the grass floor. I realize, much to my delight, my feet are still sinking into the earth, which is bare and cool in the spring air. As the sun lowers in the sky, the wind picks up and the fabric of the tents shutter in the breeze. I step outside, away from Gallen, Alcor, and Zeffra who begin feverishly discussing the implications of this discovery.

Piré follows close behind. "Would you enjoy something to eat, Miss?"

I smile broadly, hoping to quell any fears that may plague my friend. "Of course! I hear you have become well-acquainted with the kitchen tent."

She blushes slightly as we enter the space together. The tent is filled with three long tables that sit low to the ground, surrounded by pillows. Along the walls, additional cabinets and tables hold provisions: food, drinks, and utensils. Before I can register the options, Piré has assembled a plate of bread and cheese accompanied by glasses of clear, cool water.

"Tell me, how are you?" The words should be so simple, yet I know they hold so much more than simple inquiry.

She knows as well, swallowing a large bite of bread before answering, "It is strange. I have lived in Endoneth my entire life, wishing to leave, to serve a leader who is honorable and good." She looks at her hands which sit folded neatly in her lap. "However, now I cannot help but think I am being quite selfish to leave. To abandon the people who remain there, having to endure Rostair's wrath..."

Hearing her voice his name is jarring, yet comforting, a sign that sweet Piré is growing accustomed to a life away from servitude and expectation after only one night.

I reach my hand to touch hers. "You need not feel such ways. You were in a position of servitude to one who cared nothing for you. Who cares little for anyone, it would seem. You belong here, Piré. And know that if you ever feel unwanted, you may seek me out. You will always be my friend." I smile at her, the young and innocent being that I brought into this mess. However, I believe with everything in me that this is where she is meant to be. "If you wish, you may share my tent tonight. I understand this may remind you of home, but I also understand how lonely it can be in a new place with completely new people."

Her face lights up at this offer. "Oh yes, Centrea. That would be wonderful."

I nod, plopping a small sphere of cheese into my mouth. "Wonderful."

After a few hours of talking with Piré, having found a jar of wine to help us relax and talk frankly about our experiences, I stretch my arms above my head as I walk out of the kitchen tent. Piré heads for our tent to rest as I walk further into the clearing. The grass looks so inviting as I breathe in the fresh air, my chest still a bit sore from the actions of last night. Dipping low, I find myself lying flat on the ground, channeling Luminor's relaxed disposition. It is not long after I close my eyes that I sense another person lying nearby.

"Another close call for us, my friend." Asha's voice sounds sore, yet I can tell the day of rest did some good.

"Tell me about that life, Asha." I try to picture us together before. Like with Gallen, the memories are becoming a bit clearer, still just barely unattainable, but the feelings are far more honest than they were.

Lying in the grass, eyes closed, mind steady, I do not doubt my care for Asha, our closeness. "We have known each other a long while," she begins. "Met as youths, learned from similar masters about similar skills in battle." This sounds vaguely familiar, like a dream. "My favorite quest was to the Ocean Realm. Their fabrics are filled with glimmering threads and pearl beads. The land is marked by sandy beaches and sunshine. A beautiful place where we found ourselves in heaps of trouble." I hear the smile in her voice as she reminisces.

Envy strikes me with little notice, and I am suddenly desperate to know more of myself, who I was, and what sort of "trouble" I would get into with a friend in a faraway realm.

"Tell me more," I encourage.

Asha sighs. "There were so many happy moments. Helping people with no other options. Meeting disparate groups, you meeting Gallen. A love for the ages." She pauses, her tone shifting even before she begins again. "But there are many things you are fortunate to forget. People we have maimed, killed, abandoned." She tenses in the grass, and I hear her nails dig into the soil beneath us. "I wish I could forget those moments. Moments where our expertise was used to cause harm, even if it was for the greater good."

I allow a few moments before prying one last time. "And what were we, Asha?"

I have a sense of what I once did, but I must know for certain. Asha seems to understand, her shoulder brushing mine as she shifts near me. "We are the Final Warriors. Those who are called upon to conduct the most gruesome acts, tackle the most complicated situations, or break into the most guarded places." The wind picks up once more, the leaves rustling together like a natural melody. "We were at once the best and the worst of humanity. We saved and destroyed. But, this work, our work, it is necessary." I consider these words, Asha's transparency and willingness to admit our faults while defending our profession.

"Why are you not still working alongside these warriors?"

Without hesitation she replies, "What do you think we are doing here?"

Asha's voice seems to quiet the leaves, and the grass feels a bit rougher beneath my palms. "You needed to return to the Star Realm to join your brother. He knew that with his claim to forming a kingdom—uniting realms together under leaders that will decide the justices of the world and punish the evils—he would need you as a figure of support." Gallen mentioned something similar near the river. "The people, they adore you. You are Sol, a figure of strength, a person who will free people. Realms."

I think about the banners. The paintings. The flyers. Piré's words.

"It is important that you are seen supporting the King and his reign. Even if you do not fight." She assures me, "Your reputation has already defined you as a formidable figure, someone the people will follow." Asha leans closer to me, understanding the weight of these words, this conversation. "I know it is much to process. But it is true. For the success of the South, for us all, you are the key."

Asha and I talk through the night. She tells me of her home and her father's pride in her role in the Final Warrior guild. I talk to her about my hesitations and fears, but also the rare excitement at relearning myself and my relationship with each of the people in my old life—my old friends who are now new. When I settle back into my tent, the fabric feels like home, the blankets covering the grass like a sanctuary and the dim light of the springtime moon like a beacon of hope. Piré lies peacefully on one side of the pile of blankets, seemingly dreaming as small snores escape her lips.

I look to the corner of the tent where my brown satchel sits. When I retrieve it, the leather smooth beneath my fingertips, I find myself hesitating. Despite my reservations, I flip it open as I sit cross-legged on the floor and rifle through the clumsily stashed papers, the notes and drawings and poetry from a time of great, ignorant joy. I reread page after page of notes, attempting to piece together who the figures were from my dreams and my nightmares. I smirk when I see the words about Gallen, the warmth I remembered certainly holding true, perhaps a testament to how strong our bond was before the poison set in. The words about the "mysterious figure" hidden by shadows yet clothed in strength I see now relate to Alcor, the Kingly figure of my horrified nights. Near these descriptions, I included depictions of the artwork in the Red Wing, attempting to understand how deeply supportive some Keepers were to the cause of the Southern Realm. Just behind these pages is the painting of Alcor, draped in kingly majesty, a symbol of hope and promise. It is these words, the realities of good people fighting for righteous things, that help me drift off to sleep.

The morning arrives too soon; the blankets provide a warm and comfortable place to dream. Unlike the day before, when I walk out this morning, I hear a group of voices in a number of tents, their fabric entrances pulled to the side and tied to welcome anyone who wishes to join.

Asha's laugh sings through the clearing, a beautiful noise in the midst of the grief that many Night Flyers still reckon with after the murder of their two friends. My brother and Gallen discuss the warmth of the sun as I see Zeffra attempt to weave a wide-brimmed hat to block out the brightness. To the right of the central tent, pings of bright voices gently coo at one another as Melara and Caliam sit together, looking deeply into one another's eyes as they stay close to the trees. Both appear stronger than before, their lights brightly sparkling in the shadows of the branches above them, their wings sprawled wide, as if not wanting to take the space for granted. I had not looked closely at their wings before, but in the early morning light the two pairs are breathtaking, so different yet both intricate in their coloring and patterns. Melara's wings, a shade of pale purple mixed with streaks of light pink and blue, look like woven lace, the edges curved in large, scalloped swoops. In contrast, Caliam's wings are more jagged at the edges, coming to sharp peaks at the top and bottom. Their color is more muted—a delightful blue that fades into a dark green. As the couple shares a bit of shade at the edge of the wood, the world seems to pause, feeling their appreciation of this freedom.

"Freedom after captivity. There is no other feeling quite like it, the relief mingled with pain—pain at the knowledge that others may never experience the same fate—indescribable, really." Luminor's statement interrupts my moment of innocent spying.

"Do you know of it, Luminor?" I hope the answer is no, yet my gut senses the opposite.

Rather than validate my assumptions, he turns the statement away from his own life. "These leaders must know much of this grief, watching helplessly as their people are forced into a similar situation... and with their own magic. The cruelty of the Ice Realm knows no bounds." The information filters into my mind. Luminor seems to see my reaction as he faces me. "We may discuss it in painstaking detail later, if you wish. I cannot imagine the frustration of forgetting all of this." He raises his hands to emphasize his point. "I will say this though: Enjoy this blissful unknowing while it allows you the freedom to enjoy your days with less grief. We all wish for such a gift at times, for what that is worth."

I look again at the two fairies sitting in the grass. "I am sure they would."

I make a mental note to find Luminor later tonight while I turn toward the central tent. "Have you eaten yet?"

Luminor leads me to the kitchen tent where Asha and the other Night Flyers sit on shallow pillows around one of the tables. The group is smiling as they consume a mixture of bread and fruit, taking in the happiness of friendship and company.

I join them merrily, reaching for a nectarine as the conversation continues around me. "We all remember your last journey to the Ice Realm, Asha," chirps a young woman at the end.

"Yes, and I am sure half the females of that estate remember vividly as well." An elderly man cackles, clutching his stomach.

Asha rolls her eyes. "It is no fault of mine that my mere presence breeds lust." She sips a mug of tea as her eyes dart to the young warrior.

A brief blush stains my cheeks before I take a bite of the fruit, hoping the conversation distracts the others from my reactions. To my dismay, it does not.

The elderly man, Ott, directs his next statement to me. "I do think I will like this new Sol. So bashful."

Asha places a reassuring hand on my arm. "Ott enjoys nagging us young folk."

He shakes his head, forcing his black curls, stuck in place with some sort of gel, to move ever so slightly. "No no, I do mean what I say. Perhaps erasing one's past allows them to see more clearly what is important, what is at stake." The pointed statement appears affirming rather than facetious. "I appreciate a leader who is both experienced and not. Someone who knows to fight but also understands loss—and knows more clearly what it is to lose what they have once known."

The young warrior at the end of the table scoffs loudly. "There will never be a way to justify what was lost. No way to get them back." Without warning, she darts from the tent, small sobs growing quieter as she runs into the clearing.

"Do not mind the child; ones so young have experienced little of loss." Ott dismisses the interruption with little pity as he sips a cup of coffee.

"Ranor was special to Malinar," Asha whispers to me.

My heart sinks at the news. "I would hate me too," I admit to the table as I take another bite of fruit, the sweetness now turning sour in my mouth.

"Would you like some tea? I make the most delectable blend. Or, like old Ott, you can drink coffee. It is far more bitter than tea but keeps one alert for longer." Asha stands and walks toward a long, thin table filled with various jars of herbs, teas, and dried fruits. Several cups are stacked by a few kettles. "We need to warm a bit more water but that is no trouble, truly."

I shake my head softly. "Maybe tomorrow." I smile. I have yet to tell the others of Mairette and the source of my memory loss, but I am sure all will be revealed in time.

I turn back to Ott who has begun cheering up some of the other young Flyers as they echo sentiments of loss and grief. "I will say, I may appear bashful upon first glance, but I do love a salacious story." This draws the eyes of all around the table. "In fact, one of my closest friends would often regale me with the most dramatic sagas. I often consider recording these tales for posterity. I am certain others would enjoy them just as much as I."

Ott places his arm flat on the table and leans forward. "Please, do tell. These young ones tend to be so noble, never sharing details of their escapades."

The warrior nearest Ott rolls his eyes as Asha giggles.

I smile wryly. "Oh, I do not mind sharing all of the gory details." With that, it is Ott who giggles gleefully as I begin the first story that comes to mind. "This is considered the most embarrassing slights a man has ever felt." As I describe the woman wearing her scarlet dress to the evening ball, I think of Gazil's voice as we talked in the study, a warm cup of tea in my hands and a stemmed glass of wine in his. I remember his smile, the flick of his wrists as he described parties in the Green Realm. I try to channel his spirit in my own recitation, attempting to paint the picture like he did, telling a story like a song where the characters are friends and the stakes immeasurably high. "When she ventured down the steps of the stairway she made her decision public. Rather than choose her suitor, the man known to be part of her retinue and likely her partner, she nods her head to the other man, his brother."

The group of Night Flyers at the table gasp, the entertainment written on their faces and all I can think is how happy Gazil would be to know his memories live on.

The morning goes by swiftly, followed by an afternoon of regrouping. Several Night Flyers practice sparring and throwing their knives, using trees as makeshift targets. Alcor walks through the clearing a few times to check in on every warrior individually, making sure all are recovering in both mind and body. He pays particular attention to the young woman from breakfast, her tears flowing freely throughout the day. Others in the camp echo her grief. Some require solitude, and others go on frequent runs through the woods or bathe in the river water. Nature offers a number of options for healing.

Zeffra trains alongside the others, taking a few hours in the middle of the day to discuss tactics with Caliam, Alcor, and Galen above the shimmering map. I had not considered my role as a leader here, but after Ott voiced his opinion, I have started noticing a sense of deference from the other warriors. It appears that the few people who treat me as an equal are those who also hold positions of authority—Luminor, Zeffra, Gallen.

I rationalize that it was merely because of my kinship with Alcor, but now I am beginning to fully comprehend my expertise. Asha did explain our past, our training as warriors. It must be that training that qualifies me for a role of military importance. But is that who I am now?

The sun sets unceremoniously, and the Star Realm warriors welcome the cool air like fish being dunked back into a fresh pool of water. They stare eagerly at the stars, looking for the various configurations and positing both fictitious and realistic reasons for the positions of the great balls of fire in the sky. While the Flyers contemplate the meaning of the constellations for their personal amusement, Alcor peers through a golden telescope. He looks every inch a professional. A small circular table sits just to his side where a page filled with notes rests atop a stack of large, leather-bound books.

Walking toward the stunning piece of astronomical equipment, I hear him mumbling as he works. Only a few words are discernible: "South… hmm, arrow… ahh smart, smart… continuing there…" I reconsider approaching as he concentrates on a particular group of twinkling lights to the west, but, just as I turn to leave, Alcor pulls his eye from the telescope and calls me over, reaching for a quill to jot down an observation in his notes.

"Sol, please come forth! I am almost finished here." He puts his eye back in position to peer toward the sky once more. I walk slowly forward, the grass pleasantly snapping under my boots.

The night air is warm, but a cool breeze brings wafts of chills through my plaited hair. "What do you see in the stars, brother?"

The night is beautiful, no clouds to block our view from thousands of stars, hundreds of constellations, all visible to the naked eye. I am certain with the proper tools, one could see so much more.

"The stars reveal our past, present, and future. If you understand the language of the stars, see what they intend to say, then, and only then, can you accurately understand their power." He continues to look intently through the telescope, breathing in slowly as he surveys the skies. "You and I were trained to understand such things, to see and feel when stars are brightest, when they are conveying something of note. Our mother taught us this." He steps away from the tool for a moment, looking at me with curious sadness. "I suppose you do not remember her."

I falter, my weight shifting awkwardly from one foot to the other as I attempt so painfully to recall anything of our childhood. Only blurred faces and muted words. I shake my head in defeat before I feel the tug of Alcor's arms around me, sweeping me into a crushing hug. "My dearest sister. I will not rest until you know who you are."

It is curious, as I stand with my brother on a starry night in the clearing of an Ice Realm wood, I have only known myself as this, someone desperate to know herself. It has been almost a year since I awoke in my gilded bedchamber, and I have attempted many ways to remember all that came before, yet only one helped me see Gallen, to feel his warmth.

"Have you heard of caverns filled with pools of magic?" His grip eases as he pushes me away just enough to glimpse my expression of genuine curiosity. "While in captivity, if you can call it such, we..." I cringe a bit recalling the experience. "I tried many times to restore my memories. Yet, there was only one solution that produced results." In the flurry of the past few days, I had almost forgotten the magic of the pools and the gleam of the glowing caverns. Perhaps I wanted to block out any memory of intimacy with Rostair, the snake who preyed on my naivety, who played with me as if he cared nothing of honor, who used me to harm his truest enemy, Alcor.

"There are caverns that are settled deep in the forests of the Ice Realm, in the mountains that line the border between estates. Rostair took me there once, perhaps unaware of the magic the pool held. He mentioned the lore of the cavern yet took me regardless. Maybe he wanted to continue his game, play the savior while hiding his true face."

Alcor looks at the ground just past my shoulder, considering my proposition. "And he said these were magic? How do you know the pools worked?"

I lift my shoulders. "It was the only time I could remember Gallen's name."

That seems to be sufficient for Alcor who begins pacing around his telescope, thinking deeply about this new piece of information.

"I apologize for not bringing this forth sooner. It is possible that Melara and Caliam know of this place?" I suggest. His pacing quickens.

"It is no fault of yours, Sol!" He looks briefly at me as a sign of reassurance. "There is merely much to accomplish and very few resources dedicated to completing them."

My heart drops slightly. "I completely understand." I feel foolish for my initial emotional grief. This is the group who altered the course of their war to plan my rescue. The warriors who used months to plan this rescue while simultaneously working to end a war and further gain support for an unprecedented reign.

Selfishly, though, I wish I could use our captured flying horses to find the pools myself. "All in time," Alcor adds, noticing the tears brimming my eyes. "As I said. I will not rest until you are restored to full health."

I smile at his compassion and chide myself for being so self-serving. But how wonderful would it feel to look at the stars and speak their language, to look at the stars and remember my mother.

When I leave Alcor, seeking respite from the emotional conversation, I stumble quite literally across Luminor who again lies in the grass as he watches the night sky. "Ouch," he says as I kick his crossed feet.

I respond quickly, "My deepest apologies! I did not see you lying there. What are you observing exactly?"

He rolls his pale eyes, and the long lashes that line his lids flutter sarcastically. "Night Flyers always look at the stars. I try to see what makes them so enamored." He barely moves as I sit by his side.

"Are you always this dramatic?"

Luminor laughs, a soft and gravelly sound. "Of course, Sol. I find it assists in relieving tension, especially in war."

Nodding, I hug my leather leggings to my chest, reaching for the ties on the brown uniform boots.

He sighs deeply. "You left a horrible people. I am certain there are good individuals, but the people condone terrible acts. In my mind, such things make them complicit."

I think through this statement, the faces of multiple guests at Endoneth playing through my mind. "What are these acts?"

At this question, he becomes solemn, considering his words far more carefully than he has before. "The two fairy leaders you helped recover from enslavement, they only represent two of many. Hundreds, perhaps thousands over the years. For all that Rostair is, he did not begin such practices, yet he insists upon utilizing them for his own gain."

The words of Alcor's poem blink into my mind: *For the good of all should ne'er be sold.*

Luminor continues, "The woodland fairies of the Ice Realm have lived as enslaved beings since the first Lord of Endoneth gained control of the surrounding natural landscapes in the North. If this were not enough, Rostair expanded his abuse. Any being he deems lesser is used for his benefit."

The birds, the winged horses, the fairies... they all provide something to Rostair, to the Northern Realms.

"But what could they gain? Fairies provide their labor, but to what end?" My question seems to still time, the air stagnant as Luminor takes his time to answer.

"What do all corrupt leaders want?"

"Power." The answer is simple enough as I send it through the night air.

Luminor nods in response. "The fairies provide labor to be sold to other estates who purchase their loyalty. Their natural resources and their magic, that is also of use to him—creating weapons, putting on airs of esteem and wealth, controlling those to conform to his will."

I think about the three fairies in the woods. Rostair appeared upset. But was it an emotion of sadness and grief or annoyance and anger?

"We now know he continues to use the winged horses, breeding them to make them faster, stronger. But I hear he also uses the most basic creatures for his benefit, to spy, to threaten, to kill."

The truth gently rolls over me: Each time he brought me on one of our "adventures," he was parading his power before my eyes, all without me fully comprehending the circumstances, the use of the birds, the fairies, the horses.

"I cannot imagine how he used you in his disgusting thirst for power..." Luminor does not ask for affirmation nor specific explanations of my time in Endoneth, yet his tense silence reveals what assumptions must run in his mind. However, he does nothing to press for information, allowing me to sit and contemplate his words.

I look at the lights above us, the stars swirling in organized groups, collecting into galaxies, some close, some too far to comprehend.

"I also lived with my life in the hands of another." Turning my head to Luminor, I see his eyes still focused on the stars as he speaks of his experience. "Before I found refuge in the Star Realm, my parents sold me to the Desert, where many are thrown into a world that is demanding and cruel." He pauses for a moment, recentering. "It is not an uncommon practice in the Desert Realm. And I am certain my father and mother needed the money to survive; that is what I told myself. That sort of environment hardens a person. When I was younger especially, there would be older enslaved who led me along like a fool, treating me like a young prince of the sand just to gain my favors for their own. It began with food, then labor rotations, even my clothing. I thought for years these were my family, that I sacrificed for them because they would surely do the same for me. It was not so…"

My eyes still stare at Luminor's face which remains unfazed as he bears his heart to me.

"I mean to say, I understand not fully understanding the extent of one's torture, until you realize what you were unaware of, what was right in front of you yet not yours."

The comparison of his life of enslavement and my months of luxury are comical in my mind. This man suffered in the Desert while I was manipulated in paradise. But while he experienced grief and pain on another level, I appreciate this connection.

"I am truly sorry you endured such a life, Luminor." I do not know what else I could say to sufficiently convey my reaction. Perhaps this was sufficient, as he merely closes his eyes, his hands behind his head, and breathes deeply.

"I know, Sol. I am sorry too. But such experiences build a strong person. We are both strong, I think."

I smile at the concept. "I would be honored to be counted among someone as strong as you."

He huffs and rolls his eyes, which, I have learned, is his natural demeanor. "Get some sleep. I believe we are heading home in the morning."

I lightly touch the fabric tent as I brush the entrance flap aside and step into the dim, warm space. Piré is sitting on a small pillow, *A Fairy Dream* in her hands. She raises her eyes from the book when I step inside.

"This world is one I learned about as a child. The world of the woods. Of magic and beauty. I am not sure how many Keepers know of the truth behind the tales, the ways our leaders have abused these poor creatures. Used their magic against them." A tear falls onto the open page as she wipes her nose with the edge of her tunic. "There are more of us in the Red Wing, monarchist supporters. You saw the paintings, the posters, the art. Your brother and you are an inspiration to many." Her bright eyes beam at me, offering me unjust praise.

I walk toward the blankets strewn about the floor and sit delicately on the soft fabric. "Piré, what do you want in life?"

The question takes her aback and her face scrunches into curious concentration. "Well..." She shuts the book and sets it on her lap as she considers my question. "I am unsure. I have never been given such options before. The life of a Keeper is set the day they are born. Of course, you may work up into a better position, a Lead Keeper, a Head Keeper. But you live and die a servant. It is the way of things. No person has ever asked me what I would actually enjoy doing with my life."

I nod solemnly, a lump forming in my throat as I think about sweet, young, promising Piré and all the other Keepers like her.

"I think," she begins quietly, "I think I would like to bake. To create food that brings a smile to those I love. I would like to create and to dream and perhaps to love."

Smiling at her I say, "That sounds marvelous, my friend."

She continues, invigorated by the feeling of choice, of wanting something other than just freedom, of planning for a brand-new future. "I would also like to offer the same choice to those I left behind. Help them escape if they wish. I know I would not be able to do this alone, but I would like to help." This request falls in line with what I am learning about Piré, someone who is willing to set out on her own, but will always think of those she cares for, those who need help like she did.

I grin. "I believe that will be attainable. And there is no one more qualified to help in this cause." Piré blushes as she nervously combs through her blonde hair with her hands.

She changes the topic. "Are you prepared to see your home?"

I have been wondering this very thing since Alcor mentioned returning yesterday morning. "I am ready to see what I can remember, and ready to make some new memories."

Her smile dazzles in response. "That sounds quite marvelous too."

We wake before the sun the next morning. Zeffra nudges our exhausted bodies until we stand to assist in closing up the camp. The matter of packing tents, materials, and personal items is complex, and each Night Flyer conducts a very particular task so that the packing moves quickly and smoothly.

Zeffra points to our tent. "You both break down the frame and fold the fabrics. On top, be sure to place the blanket and pillows. We will tell you how to tie it all together once you have it arranged, understand?"

Her tone is clipped, as if anxious to hear our answer so she may attend to another warrior. It reminds me of Mairette during the week of the Greentime Ball, always consumed by the next task to be completed. While she may not seem to like me, I do respect Zeffra for her assertiveness and drive.

Piré stretches her arms above her head as she yawns. "Alright, Centrea, let us get on with this."

The rest of the camp moves with the same sleepy speed, warriors gathering their things and tying the fabrics neatly to the tent frames. When Piré and I have completed the task, another warrior shows us how to fold the frame so each sturdy post is held together like one large staff. Then, he takes the strips of fabric and folds our clothes, blankets, and belongings inside before deftly tying it to the end of the pole.

The pegasi still remain in the camp, neighing happily as the Flyers outfit them for travel. In a matter of hours, the entire camp is enclosed in various fabric bags tied to long poles made of the tent frames. The clearing looks untouched, as if our camp was never truly there only moments ago.

Alcor, sweat dripping down his face as he approaches, looks over the clearing with a satisfied smirk as he walks toward me. "They will be happy to see you safely home, Sol. The people love you."

This sparks a bit of joy in me, to be wanted by a people, a place.

Then, a sour thought dawns on me: Is that a reason for the rescue?

The thought is wicked, a painful and horrid notion. But I cannot help but consider this. Instead of voicing my doubts I ask, "How long is the journey home?"

He looks out to see his warriors preparing for the first day of walking. "It will take six weeks, if the weather cooperates."

In a little over one month, I will become quite close to this group I see.

"You know, Sol. I have considered your place with us. When you left, you were the authority over our entire army. All of our warriors turned to you for their orders. However, I have noticed a shift in you these past few days." His blue eyes point toward me. "At Endoneth, you were just as fierce, as intelligent, as quick as ever. But, the love of tactic, of thinking steps ahead of your enemy and working up an army. Well, do you think that is still what you would want?" The question is thoughtful, no malice or judgment. Simple. Again, I see why so many look to him to lead realms. "Of course, you need not choose now. There are plenty of days ahead to consider what you want, and you can always rethink, if you would like to return to your post later that is—"

"I think I would like to write," I interrupt him gently, thinking out loud.

His eyes are bright with curiosity. "Write? Attempting to take my place as the poet of the family, are we?" He laughs heartily as I shake my head.

"Does the Star Realm have a Keeper of Records?" My hands clutch the edges of the navy tunic as I wait.

"I believe that is a Northern practice…" Alcor begins, scratching his chin in contemplation. "However, it would be a wise position to implement. Especially with a growing kingdom."

I nod emphatically. "Something I learned during my time there… both the past and the future are intertwined, and one cannot live independent of the other. And the stories of your people, your warriors, these realms, and their customs. These are all important, all worthy of recording."

A genuine smile softens his features as he brushes a loose tangle of hair from my face. "Sol: Star Realm's Keeper of Records. We may have to scrounge up materials but… you begin tonight!"

I laugh a bit. "Tonight?"

Alcor walks away and waves his hand to draw me toward the rest of the retinue. "You may begin writing about the heroic Night Flyers and their handsome and wise and poetic leader!"

He leaves me standing in front of the clearing, smiling like a young child as I think of all the things I will do, all the people I will meet, all the stories I will tell.

# The First Record

There was once a woman of the Star Realm who sought knowledge in both the unusual and the mundane, the unique and the everyday. She stood at an average height, with hips that jutted out and a chest to match. Her hair was thick and brown and her eyes blue as ice. She was once a warrior, trained by the most accomplished master in the Nine Realms. However, she was captured, kept in an estate in the Ice Realm and forced to forget her life, her past. When the future King Alcor rescued her with his Night Flyer warriors, she realized the deceit of her captor. Rather than return to a life of war, of pain and death, she chose a different path. One of writing and travel, of love and lies, and of retelling the stories most important to the realm, the future kingdom, and its people.

Now she writes, each day remembering something new, yet the memories are still blurry. Her first grand adventure sought to remedy this, to venture back to the Ice Realm, not for revenge but to visit a place of magic. Possibly the only place that could assist in finding herself again, at least the only place she was sure would work. So, her first adventure, the first of these records, began in the Star Realm with a forgetful royal, her Ocean Realm companion, and a winged horse.

Emilee NK Robbins

# Acknowledgments

This book is the culmination of time, love, and a lot (and I mean A LOT) of support.

Thanks to my family. To Cason, the best partner a dreamer could ask for. To Alison and Pam, the moms that guide me with loving and gentle hearts. To Ashley and Sarah and Abby and Morgan, the family that I chose and was lucky enough to choose me back. To my little sister and brother. To all the friends that read these words in its extraordinarily rough form. To Brighton, my ray of sunshine.

Thanks to my support system. To Lysle. To my academic mentor, Linda, who indulged my extracurricular fictional endeavors. To my editor, Molly, and the fantastic collaborative experience of writing this first novel.

I want to thank the characters that brought themselves to life. It's been a fun ride and I'm excited for the stories to come.